I0721563

Petals for Vicious Secrets

Martha Monteval

Petals for Vicious Secrets

Paperback ISBN 978-1-915193-96-4
Hardcover ISBN 978-1-915193-97-1
eBook ISBN 978-1-915193-98-8

Cover Design and Interior Page by Moonpress | *www.moonpress.co*
Editing by The Fiction Fix
Interior Design and Map Design by Martha Monteval

Visit my website at www.marthamonteval.com

About the book

This book contains subject matter that might be triggering for some,
including violence and death, torture, emotional abuse,
reference to abandonment and slavery.
This book also contains considerable profanity and sexually explicit
scenes.

Frenya Archipelago

Verdania

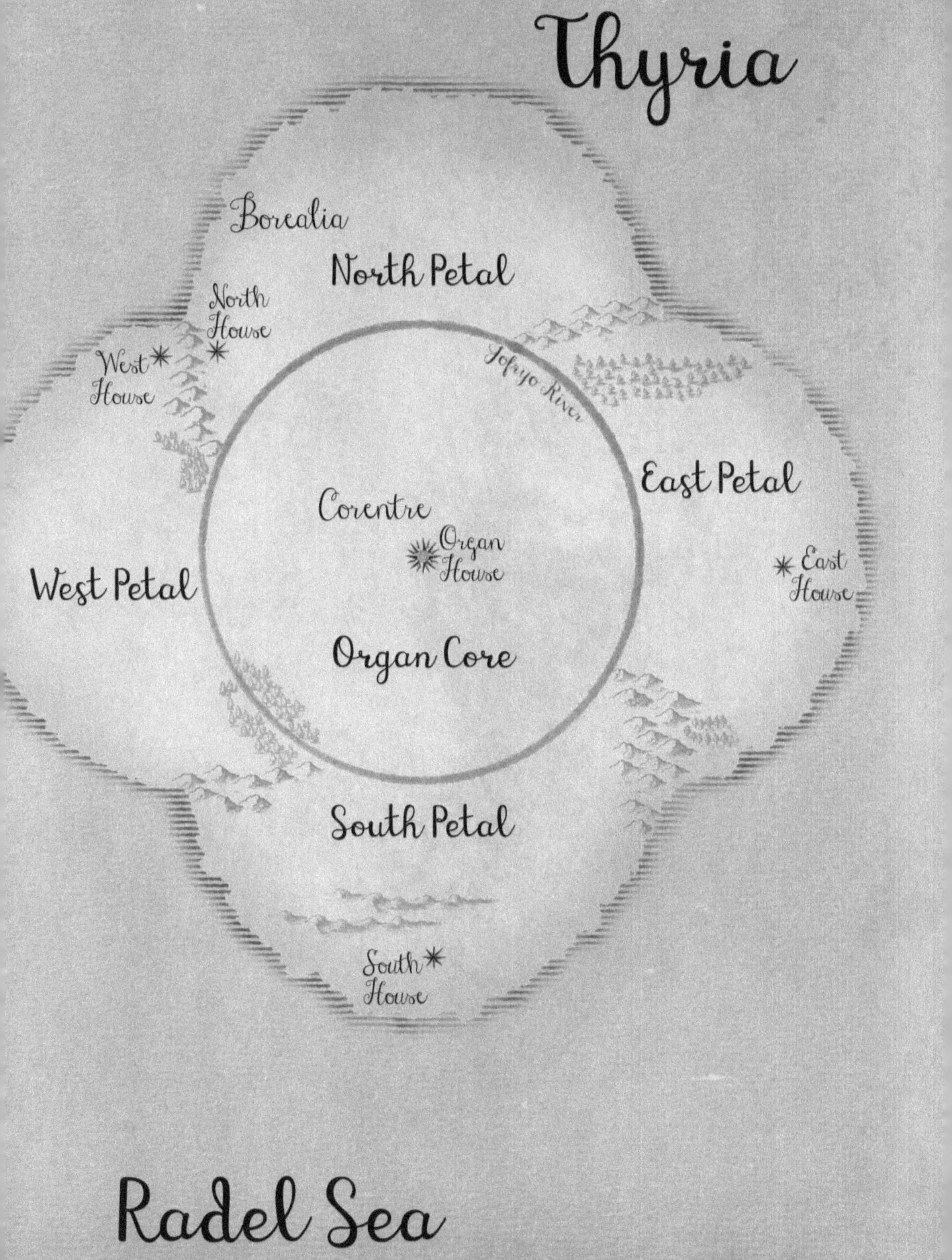

Thyria
Borealia
North Petal
North House
West House
Johryo River
East Petal
Corentre
Organ House
West Petal
East House
Organ Core
South Petal
South House
Radel Sea

To the beings who were lied to
and believed those lies with their whole heart.
To the beings who survived those lies
by being resilient as fuck.

1

The best approach to Trading Day was to kill for survival—hence why beings with a peaceful mindset never made it out alive.

The dark-haired young woman was patiently waiting for the sandglass to turn to the exact spot facing the big arena, where she had been countless times over the past six years. The only difference today was that her mother wasn't at her side. She had suffered severe injuries in the previous Trading and right now, she was clinging to life by some Cardinals-blessed miracle that surely would not last much longer.

It was a defiance on its own that none of them had ever been injured in their over twenty-four years of Trading. Her mother had always been the one who got everything they needed in Verdania. Every single Trading. Every single week. For eighteen years she had always gone alone, returned to the treehouse alone—until her daughter convinced her she could handle herself. It had only taken three years of convincing and fifteen years of learning to fight.

The rivalry between the villagers had been increasing over the years. There were more of them than ever, and fewer useful items were being provided by the Trading Table. The Rulers either grew tired of supplying long-term food, construction materials, and warm clothes, or they were deluded enough to think that giving cakes and flower vases to an island full of starved people was relevant or funny. Only one day per week could they get items other than what Verdania itself provided.

Her mother had been sweating and weak in bed since two men had paired up and stabbed her. All to steal a blanket she had gathered in her pack—if there was such a thing as stealing when it came to Trading Day. The mentality was more suit-yourself-or-kill-yourself than anything remotely similar to caring about property and ownership.

The dark-haired young woman shook her head silently. She didn't mind that her blanket had thinned over the years and that there wasn't more than a foot without a hole. No blanket could be worth her mother's life. She had made sure the two men understood that very clearly before their last breaths.

So, here she was. Her first ever Trading Day by herself. She could only hope that the Rulers had been kind enough to leave some sort of medicine at the Table. Her plan B was to get as much food as possible and try to help her mother recover.

At the heart of the expansive arena, a lengthy table was set up, offering enough space for thirty people to dine together, except there were no chairs, just a huge white cloth on top of it. Standing in a circle around the Table was a good mix of strangers: a handful of young skinny children, probably orphans like most children in Verdania, young men and women, faces focused, some older people, with tired faces and aching bodies, and a few random people who looked like they had no idea what they were getting into.

Even when she had first gone to the Trading, she hadn't been in the latter group. She had been thoroughly briefed and prepared. Her mother was not perfect by any means, but she was a fighter, and that was exactly what the Trading was about.

"The Trading is not about the oh-so-generous Rulers providing for us to survive for a week. The Trading is a game of goals and intention, a chance for them to see if we have lost the will to live yet."

Except the Trading had evolved over the years to become a survival fight, and the Rulers didn't seem to care whether they lived or died. They were Trading with their lives. If anything, the Rulers were helping by providing weapons on the Trading Table regularly.

The sand in the time-counter showed two minutes until past meridiem. Two minutes to until the sun would shine from the middle of the sky. Two minutes to focus. The plan was simple, and so was the advice.

No distractions. No pity for others. No looking at the fallen ones. If they were dead, she could grab some extra items from them, but that would take time, and she did not have time to waste. If there was indeed any medicine at the Trading Table, she would not be the only one looking for it. Not in Verdania, where people died every day from all sorts of sicknesses.

One minute left. The experienced traders started jumping, some lifting their legs up to their waist, some stretching their arms and necks, some adjusting belts with different weapons hung from them. She knew some faces from other Trading Days, but it was useless to pay much attention. People didn't live until they were old in this place, and death was only a knife away. Emotional attachments and socialization were a waste of energy.

With no warning, the cloth on top of the Trading Table disappeared, revealing everything underneath. The Trading had started. People around her started running.

It took her a half a second to take a deep breath and start her sprint to the Table. She was running, feeling her fast heartbeat, hearing her deep breaths. The floor was smooth, her steps steady, her body fast. She could see people around her slowing down, unable to keep the sprinting pace for much longer, but she could. She had been practicing for years. Even with hunger as a well-known companion, she trained her muscles. Her legs could sprint for a while longer.

She counted three young women, six young men, and an older man still running. Eleven people who would fight for the best of whatever the Table brought for them today.

She was now fast approaching the Table, and things on top became clear. There was a vast pile of clothes on her side. At the other end of the Table were plates and bowls full of what seemed to be warm food by the looks of the steam raising to the sky and the delicious smell coming from them. Her stomach grumbled, and her eyes couldn't stop looking. In the middle of the table, there was a vast area filled with a variety of small things. She couldn't tell what the items were from her distance. Four other people went straight to the middle area, running from the opposite side of the Table.

She had to hold the Table to stop from smashing against it. She grabbed her empty cloth bag from her back and started looking for things that could be medicine. The other traders were fast. She usually was much faster identifying items, packing them, and running away to safety. If she only knew what a medicine looked like in the world of Rulers.

If they are fast, I need to be faster. But where on Terrha was the medicine? She saw an array of knives, but the belts on her thighs and waist needed no more. There were small devices full of buttons and numbers, things that looked like they could make noise, stacks of paper and pens, candles, boxes made of strings, sparkly long things she guessed were jewels, wood pieces of all sorts and shapes, and so many other things that her head ached trying to pay attention. Then, next to the very middle of the Table, sat six small vials full of colorful liquid: two blue ones, two green ones, two red ones, all in a neat white little tray.

For all she knew, the liquids could be fruit juice or poison. She could not risk another week of her mother being sick without a medicine. She knew she might not make it to the following Trading.

A pale young woman in front of her stood still. Her hair was like snow, and her eyes like the bluest sky. Her pale hand was stretched towards the vials, looking at them with the same worried look she likely had. *There is no time for this. No time for distractions. Grab all the vials and run.*

The blue eyes of the young woman looked between her and the vials, which were closer to her. She could probably grab them and make a run for it, but the blue-eyed stranger swiftly picked one vial of each color and placed them in her bag, then looked at her and slightly nodded as in a silent agreement, leaving one vial of each color for her. For her mother.

If the Rulers were going to be useful for once and one vial did, in fact, contain medicine. How they would figure that out was a thought for later. Now all she had to do was pack the vials and run. From the initial eleven, only a red-haired young man picking weapons in the middle area and the young woman now on the food end of the table remained with her.

Without another look back, she started sprinting to the forest on her left. With all the other, slower villagers now approaching the Table, it wasn't that easy. The young woman felt angry stares on her, towards her bag, and she could see the reflection of blades coming out as two young women pivoted and started running towards her instead of the Table. She sprinted faster and faster. There was no doubt she could outrun them. She had to.

The red-haired young man from the first eleven was ahead of her, running towards the forest as well. She couldn't hide if there were other people around. It wouldn't be safe. She moved towards the south part of the forest.

Panting, her own heartbeat sounding in her ears as loud as drums, she stood behind a tree for a couple of breaths. Enough to acknowledge her surroundings, briefly inspect the area and assess potential risks. There were tall trees with thick bases around her in a dense, vast forest, and she couldn't see the end. She could only see the arena behind her and hear some sort of water further into the woods. There was no sight of the two young women who had chased her from the Table, but even from the woods, she could hear screams. *No distractions. No pity. Focus.*

The dark-haired woman found a tall tree separated from the others and started climbing it. She wouldn't risk staying in a tree that others could reach from nearby branches. The final choice was a thicker branch a safe distance from the ground. She just had to wait until everything fell silent again, until the screams and steps ceased, and when no one remained, she would go home.

Her sweat dried on her skin, and she could feel thirst and hunger building up. She could wait. She was probably thirty minutes away from her treehouse, from her mother. The last thing she had to eat was an apple that morning. They always kept the best ones for Trading Day.

From her spot at the top of the tree, she saw some people carefully walking through the woods. None saw her. She wore brown clothes that hid her well, all part of the elaborate plan her mother had successfully completed for years. Their bodies were similar: slightly muscled, not too tall, not too thin. That made it easier to share the few clothes they had. The main difference, though, was the hair. Mother had short, light brown hair, and she had almost-black hair, long to the end of her back, usually plaited in two braids on the sides while running or training.

It had probably only been an hour since the Trading had started, and the silence grew louder around her. Occasional branches snapping in the woods revealed people walking around them. She thought she could wait a bit more before heading home, but then, she heard the scream.

It was a female scream, loud enough to know it was nearby, and with enough pure rage and pain in it to know someone had been badly hurt.

I am safe here. No distractions. No pity for others.

Another high-pitched scream made the branches and leaves shake, closer this time. From her branch, the dark-haired woman saw a man dragging a hurt female through the woods, a white-haired young woman with her hands tied in front of her.

She recognized the dark clothes of the woman who had ceded the vials to her. By tying a piece of cloth around her mouth, the man silenced her screams. The woman kept kicking her legs, even though one leg had a cut big enough to be visible from her spot at the top of the tree.

There was a knot in her stomach as she felt the panic in the kicks of the young woman increase. A young woman who could be the same age as her. Who would die at the hands of this man if nobody helped her.

No pity for others. This is the Trading. We all know what we come for. We all know what can happen.

She knew how to fight. Her mother had taught her how to defend herself since childhood. "You can only trust yourself; always be prepared to strike and save your life," she always repeated.

"Don't bother with the kicks, Nina. You know how this is going to end. You've seen it coming for weeks," said the man, who made a bored hand gesture while looking at the sharp dagger in his hand.

The white-haired woman stopped kicking and looked at him in the eyes. There was rage in that stare. From the top of the branch, the dark-eyed woman could sense the hatred that flowed between them.

"It is very easy. You just need to tell me where you are hiding your little brother, and I'll let you go," he continued. She very much doubted that was going to be the case. He added, "Or, if you choose not to help, I will kill you, and when I find Raoul, I will kill him too."

Her feet moved quietly on the branch, but the blue eyes met her dark brown ones for less than a second. She could see the defeat in them, the impotence, that she was assuming this was her end. And her brother's end too, apparently.

She assessed the situation. It was only this man and the tied woman underneath her tree. She could easily take over one man and then help her get out of here. It was just him. She could do it. It wasn't risking too much. A voice in her head told her this was exactly what her mother always told her to stay away from: trouble not directly related to her. But this woman, this Nina, had helped her. Without her, there would be no vials in her bag. Thanks to those vials, she maybe had a chance to help her mother live through next week.

Without thinking about it again, she unsheathed two of her daggers, so long and sharp that they almost looked like spears. She grabbed one in each hand and carefully moved through the branches to position herself on top of the pair as he continued talking in the same bored voice.

"I don't have many places to be today, which works out well, as I can enjoy your death. We'll take it slow. There is no rush. So, where shall we start? Shall I break the bones of your arms, or shall we have a different type of fun?" he asked while stretching his wrists, looking at her with a satisfied smile. Nina had stopped moving, her breath steady and charged with fear. The only noise coming from her was the blood dripping from her leg, making a small puddle.

He took one step, and a dagger neatly stuck his foot to the ground. His scream was short and acute, his eyes moving desperately to see who threw the metal weapon.

The dark-haired woman jumped to the ground, landing quietly within arm's reach of the man, and spiked the spear through his throat with a neat strike. He could only open his eyes wide while he choked on his blood and fell face-up on the ground, his stuck foot bending in an awkward position.

Nina's blue eyes were wide, looking at her in a combination of awe, relief, and horror. Did she think she was going to hurt her?

"I will not harm you," she said. "If you want, I can untie you and try to fix your leg so you can get out of here." Nina nodded, a tear appearing in the corner of her eye.

She removed the cloth from Nina's mouth and undid the tie that held her hands together.

"Why?" was all Nina said, relieved tears now silently flowing down her cheeks.

"You were generous before," she said while tearing a long piece of her shirt. She started wrapping it around the cut on Nina's leg like a bandage.

"I need to go, but I can help you get somewhere safe first." They were too visible sitting there on the ground, and the blood would start attracting animals soon enough.

"Thank you. He would have killed me. The last time, I barely escaped," she said. Her white hair was so bright, it was impossible to camouflage in the woods. "What's your name?"

She hesitated. Giving out one's name was like giving one's hand, and hadn't she just done that?

She swallowed and opted for the truth. "My name is Hope."

2

Lenna

After a long day, all Lenna could think about was the tremendous waste of time her political education had been so far. Surely there had to be more interesting things in Terrha to worry about than the topics her father forced Leo Pharlin, her mentor, to cover. She was fed up with going over the geography of Thyria, the names of every single living and dead member of the Houses, the lines of succession from the very beginning, and House disagreements that had happened so many years ago, no one she knew was even alive.

"All of this is important to understand how our society works, Lenna," Leo said the third time she rolled her eyes in the last session.

"No way. Really?"

"Really. And if you could concentrate a bit more and pay attention, maybe you would see how all these people you say you don't care about shaped your world today."

"I'm paying more attention than I should. I cannot seriously understand why knowing that Carl-whatever went to bed with Johanna-whatever over two centuries ago has any relevance."

"It is relevant because she was a nobody, and Carl Heinf was a House Ruler. They went against the Thyrian Laws, and that ended in both being discarded and the East House having no heir, as Carl did not have any successors. So, the Thyrian magical system was unstable until the Organ Mandor decided who to assign as the East Ruler."

"And as the daughter of a Ruler and his extremely lucky successor, I must make sure to have some kids sooner rather than later for the sake of the whole of Thyria. Fantastic. I'm thrilled knowing they cannot fix their beloved island without the help of a twenty-four-year-old's uterus. Lesson learned. Can we finish this now?" She did not enjoy speaking rudely to Leo, who only taught her the Curriculum, as per her father's instructions, but this topic made her blood boil.

"There is no rush. Your father will live for many more years, but it's good to understand how the magic dynamics work. I think it's better if we continue the lesson another day."

"I can't wait." Lenna quickly packed her blank notepad and quilts into her bag, stood up, and went to the door, doing her very best to calm herself enough so as not to slam it.

The rage had been with her until supper, and her dear sister Ayla asking questions of their dear father about the dear politics of their dear House didn't help her mood. Why was Ayla always so interested to know every single detail? Her twin was always so annoyingly pleasant to her father and mother, it was unnerving.

"And then Clement explained how bravely our ancestors fought for our House, and it made me realize how lucky we are to have Mother and you to defend us," Ayla said with awe as she looked at their parents.

Of course she did.

Lenna did her best to concentrate on her plate and finish quickly so she could leave before starting an argument. The best way to avoid an argument these days was to keep her mouth shut.

"It's our honor to do so, Ayla. The North is an important part of Thyria, and we are proud to represent it," Mother said. "After the Fifth Ceremony when you turn twenty-five next week, you'll understand."

"Understand ruling over slaves while pretending they're not?" Lenna asked sharply. The rage from the session with Leo apparently made her temper even shorter than usual. She usually could keep quiet for longer while they talked about "sensitive topics", as her parents liked to call them.

"Not again, Lenna." Father put his fork down, staring at her.

"You know they are not slaves, Lenna. They serve us because they want to, because they are grateful," her mother said.

Lenna snorted, also putting down her fork. "Like hell they are. They are slaves because they know if they don't obey your stupid laws, they will be discarded."

"Enough, Lenna," Father insisted. "Leave. Now."

"My fucking pleasure." Lenna grinned with a fake bow.

She was at the door when she heard her father mutter, "So much for the heir of this House."

That had been a summary of her day: two rows for the price of one. That was more than average, and even the floating sparks in her room didn't seem to be enough to make her feel less like shit.

It had not been the best day, and her not sleeping wouldn't make things easier for her the following one.

She decided she would apologize to Leo as soon as she saw him in the afternoon for their daily lesson. Leo was kind and patient with her and did not deserve to be the person she blamed for how shitty things were in this place. As Lenna closed her hand, the golden sparks stopped, and she closed her eyes. Hopefully, it wouldn't be too long before she fell asleep.

Theon had no mercy.

In case the dark areas under her eyes were not proof that she hadn't slept one-bit last night, she told him.

"Could we have an easy session today, Theon?" Lenna yawned.

"You didn't say the magic word," the muscled, brown-haired man said with an honest grin.

"Please." She rolled her eyes with a small smile.

"Please what?" Theon went on. Lenna tried to never complain about the tough trainings they did, and he was clearly enjoying this too much.

"Clever Theon I admire so much: since you are so kind and generous, could we have an easy session today, *please*?" Lenna gave her best attempt at an innocent smile.

"No," Theon laughed while throwing her two metal balls attached to a metal chain.

"Oh, come on!" Lenna grabbed them in the air.

"What a better opportunity to practice overcoming your body's needs? Sleep is overestimated, you know. People don't need to sleep as much as they think." Theon grabbed another set of steel balls and moved around the training area until he was in front of her.

"Says the man who takes a two-hour nap every single afternoon while I'm bored to death in my be-a-good-heir classes," Lenna replied.

Theon laughed loudly in a sorry-not-sorry gesture, lifting his shoulders, and he started the motions with the steel balls she had to repeat. Training with Theon was almost her favorite part of her day.

He started training with her a few months ago, after asking her parents for years to learn how to defend herself in battle. They kept telling her that no such things were needed in Thyria, since all they had to do was rule and make sure no disturbances happened, and even if they did have an issue, panoms had magic to fix them. The only way their parents finally accepted the training with an experienced warrior was by telling them that if one day, the magic became unstable because one House had no Ruler or a panomquake destroyed the land, then she would be exposed. She knew she hit the nail when Mother and Father looked at each other, trying not to look worried. And then, Mother turned to her and said, "Fair enough. We'll find you someone suitable, and we'll clear your schedule in the mornings to allow training sessions."

This suitable someone happened to be a very good-looking young man with more muscles than shyness, and enough of a sense of humor to take her out of her misery each morning.

A suitable someone who suddenly increased the speed of movements to make her focus, to keep her pace, as if he could see she was thinking about everything other than the two heavy steel balls they twisted around them.

When she started training, she found it hard to finish the lessons as her body ached, even in places she didn't know could be sore. She also found herself distracted sometimes by the muscles of Theon's arms, chest, legs, and every other Cardinal-blessed part of his body. She'd gotten used to all of it now, and even the hardest sessions didn't end with her moving like a worm around the North House like she used to. Warrior-muscles wise, she usually tried not to look too much at them, as he would take any opportunity to thoroughly enjoy even the smallest admiration.

"You are somewhere else today, Lenna. Is everything okay?" Theon asked, leaving the steel balls on the floor and starting to practice kicks.

"Next week, I'll be twenty-five, and the Rulers will make their grand bullshit ceremony in Corentre so we can learn about useful powers for once. I'll have to do it with Ayla, so I am very much not looking forward to it."

"I am not meant to know about these things, Lenna," Theon said quietly between steady breaths as he kicked sideways.

"And you very well know I couldn't care less. You are my friend. I will tell you things, end of story." Lenna was fed up with all the laws, the rules, the same old secrets that followed her since birth, all because she was the daughter of a damn Ruler. She trusted Theon. She couldn't say that for many people.

"Do you think being with Ayla for longer periods of time will make you explode?" Theon said, unsuccessfully trying to hide a smile.

"I guess we'll find out soon," Lenna said, lifting her eyebrows as she kicked.

3

Hope

With Nina barely able to walk with the deep cut on the bottom half of right leg, it took them a while to reach her safety area. The place Nina lived with her brother Raoul looked as rudimentary as Hope's home, but it was in a hidden cave instead of at the top of a tree. It was unexpectedly bright, with a handful of cavities in the stone walls allowing the sunny rays through.

A young man with white hair was next to one wall, laying on what looked like a mattress made of leaves and clothes. He did not open his eyes or move when Nina and Hope approached him. From a few steps away, Hope could not even see if he was breathing. Nina got closer to him with a worried look.

"Raoul," she whispered, shaking him. "Raoul, I'm back." The young man moved a few fingers and grunted softly.

"What happened to him?" Hope asked. She wasn't expecting much of an answer, considering how people usually minded their own business.

Nina's look was worried. "I am not sure. I think they attacked him."

"They?"

Nina kept silent, as if she was hesitant to share any more information.

"I'm sorry. I hope one vial has something to help him," Hope said honestly. She didn't know why she cared about this stranger. "Is he your brother?"

"Yes," Nina said shortly, signalling the end of that conversation. "Have you used medicines before?" she asked, looking at Hope.

"My mother always kept one vial with her when I was little, just in case I got injured. The best way to check a liquid is safe is to put a drop on something alive and wait for the reaction," Hope explained, heading towards the entrance of the cave and finding her three vials in her bag.

Nina followed her slowly, careful with her injured leg, her own three vials in her hand. Hope walked until she found a small patch of grass with poppies nearby. She helped Nina sit on the ground, and she sat in front of her as Hope opened the green vial and put a drop on the pod at the center of the poppy's petals. The poppy vanished.

Hope moved her hand to where the poppy was just a few seconds ago. It had not become invisible. It simply had disappeared, leaving no trace.

"What is the green liquid?" Nina asked, frowning.

"Whatever it is, it doesn't look like something we'd want to give to your brother or my mother unless we want them gone for good or Fifth knows where."

"Is your mother hurt?" Nina's blue eyes were full of concern.

"She was attacked during the Trading last week, but she'll survive." Hope was convinced of it. She would have it in no other way.

Nina lifted one corner of her mouth in a smile.

"I'm sure she will. Which one shall we try now?" Nina was holding the blue and red vials in each hand.

"You pick. The colors and their properties change every time," Hope said, admiring the redness of the surrounding poppies, brighter than the blood soaking Nina's cloth around her leg.

Nina opened the red vial and carefully let a drop fall between the red petals of the poppy. For a moment, nothing happened. Then, the petals shrunk, and the poppy died in front of them.

"Oh." Nina sighed.

Hope wondered if the red liquid would work that easily with people or animals. It would be a quick way to get rid of enemies or predators.

Hope opened her blue vial and was about to try it on another poppy when they heard a man scream. She stood up in one move, her body alert, looking for any signs of peril nearby.

Nina's already pale face had gone paler. "Raoul."

Hope started running towards the cave at the same time she grabbed her daggers. She didn't want to leave Nina behind, but her leg wouldn't let her sprint to the cave.

When Hope reached the entrance, she moved, listening for any noise that could help her guess what was happening inside, but she couldn't hear anything at all. A quick look inside told her there was no wild animal there, at least not a big one, because the deadliest ones were the smallest. The sunny rays through the cave's natural cavities illuminated a completely empty space.

There was nobody there, not even Raoul.

Nina arrived inside the cave, and the way she stood without limping made her think maybe she had indeed found out if the blue vial was a medicine and taken some herself.

"How did they—" Nina started in a voice filled with the same horror her blue eyes showed. She started walking towards the corner where her brother had been a few minutes before.

"Who are they?" Hope was not worried about animals of any sort, but she did not like the pure fear in the eyes of this young woman. She took cautious, silent steps and followed Nina inside. If this was some trap, she would fall right into it. There were warning bells sounding in her head, and her intuition was telling her to get out of there. Only the silent goose-bumps on her back seemed to tell her to get closer and continue forward.

"Why did they..." Nina continued, talking to herself in the same quiet voice, as if she hadn't heard Hope.

"What is this about, Nina? Who the Fifth are they?"

Nina reached the mattress where his brother had been, and after looking at the wall, she fell to her knees and started weeping. Hope laid a hand on her shoulder, trying to give her some sort of reassurance. She wasn't sure why she felt the need to comfort someone who she'd known for a handful of hours. She bent her knees to get closer to the spot Nina had her eyes fixed on while tears ran down her cheeks.

Only then did Hope see the carving that had appeared on the stone in black ink: the four-petal shape of Thyria that no one ever wanted to encounter.

"We have to run," was all she said before grabbing Nina's arm and pulling her out of there.

4

Lenna

Lenna was on her way to Leo's class in the East Wing of the North House, smiling while remembering how she and Theon teased each other. Theon was to her what most people would consider a friend, except as a member of a House, she could not have friends outside the Elite, and a trainer was nowhere near that. Quite the opposite, actually: they were merely considered education servants.

"What could make my angry-with-the-world sister smile?" asked Ayla, appearing from behind a door.

People always said they were not similar enough to be considered pure twins. They were both standard height for the North, Ayla more straight-built than her, and Lenna was quite proud of her wildly appreciated curves. The fire-red tone of their hair was identical, but the waves of Lenna's were as uncontrollable as her character, completely different from the sleek curtain of Ayla's. And then, there were their eyes: Ayla's green ones, which were narrowing right now, looking at Lenna's golden ones.

"What do you want, my pain-in-the-ass sister?" asked Lenna with a forced smile, not stopping her steps.

"I wouldn't be so rude if I were you," Ayla said, walking next to her, her steps echoing in the empty corridor.

Lenna rolled her eyes. "You might trick Mother and Father into believing you are a pleasant being, but you can quit your bloody act with me. I might vomit."

"I came to share some interesting news with you," Ayla went on as they twisted left and entered an enormous room full of instruments.

Lenna halted and moved to face her. "Enlighten me."

Lenna couldn't tell if her sister was playing with her, or if she did indeed have important news. Ayla played her House Ruler's noble daughter role so well, including keeping abreast of *gossip*. "Information and secrets are the keys to power," Father loved repeating every time he had a chance.

"I am very generous in sharing secrets with you, you know? I could keep them to myself." Ayla moved to a chair in the room and elegantly sat, crossing her legs and her arms, looking at Lenna defiantly with a half-smile. "My information has a price."

Lenna chuckled. "You don't even know what generosity is, but I wasn't expecting anything different."

"Oh, and you do?" Ayla's smile disappeared. "Because you care about all the poor little people who suffer so much in this world? Let me tell you something: caring about them doesn't change their unlucky fate or their meaningless lives. They are here to serve us, and if you could, for once, use your small brain to understand that, you would do all of us a favor."

"There's my very polite sister." Lenna winked. Ayla's jaw trembled with rage, but Lenna couldn't care less. She loved making Ayla show her true personality behind the gentle façade. "I'm late for class. What's the price of your information?"

"Oh, so you do want to know. The cost was going to be three of your nightgowns, but now, it's going to cost you much more than that," Ayla said, touching the tips of the fingers of both hands together. "I want you to be one hour late to the Fifth Ceremony next week."

Shock went through her body. The Fifth Ceremony was the most important event in the life of any House member. It was one of the few occasions the five Rulers of Thyria came together under one roof, and it was for a very important reason: to unleash the powers of the person who had turned twenty-five. After the powers were unleashed, the person would become panom.

"You are out of your mind." Lenna had heard enough. She started walking towards the other side of the music hall, heading towards the door. What was wrong with her sister? Did Ayla seriously think, even for a minute, that Lenna would consider being late to her damned Fifth Ceremony, or did she just say that to piss her off?

Ayla stood behind her, opening her hand and turning it sideways. The door in front of Lenna closed with a click.

"Are you sure you want to play this game?" Lenna asked, turning to Ayla and lifting her own hand mid-air. "Do I need to remind you what happened last time?"

"You will hear what I need to tell you." Something like pain shone in Ayla's green eyes—if her sister could feel something like that.

Lenna couldn't take her eyes off Ayla's. Ayla was many things, but she did not use her magic often, especially not out of anger. She didn't need to.

Ayla had all the words in her brilliant little mind to manipulate people with no need to use any powers. Not that they had much more than sparks, ink, and a couple more tricks under their sleeves until their Fifth Ceremony.

Ayla swallowed. "Raoul was moured to the West House this morning."

"What?" Lenna said sharply, her expression dropping as if she had been punched in the gut.

"Your friend Raoul is at the West House."

Lenna couldn't think clearly. "You are lying." She had to be.

"My sources swore it on the Fifth." Ayla's face was serious, no trace of irony or rage in her expression.

"He was discarded. He can't be at the West House," she said in a low voice, pain in her chest, tears building behind her eyes. She made her hands into fists so hard, her nails stuck to her skin. She would not cry in front of her sister.

It made little sense. It couldn't be possible. If this was a lie, she swore to herself she would make Ayla pay—*for good*.

Lenna stood still for a few seconds before heading towards an open window. They were on the first floor of the North House. It wasn't a big jump to the ground, and the servants' kitchens were close enough to sneak into the garden passages without being noticed.

"Where are you going?" Ayla asked.

"Where do you think I am going?" Lenna looked at her sister with a very honest, worried face.

"I'm coming with you."

Before jumping out of the window, Lenna opened her hands as she twisted them, and golden sparks flew towards a door. She didn't know if it would work, but it was worth trying.

5

Hope

H ope looked around her, inhaling deeply, trying to calm herself. From her safe spot at the top of the tree, she could see all of Verdania. When her mother built their home in that tree twenty-four years ago, it was one of the reasons why she chose it: seeing the lands that extended around them in all directions until the Radel Sea gave them a sense of control.

In a place where control was an illusion, having a sense of it was as good as it could get.

Of course, her mother could have lived with most villagers in the small towns distributed around Verdania, but Mother did not like being surrounded by so many people. She said there was no way to differentiate a common villager from an undercover member of the Roix, the military organization that acted on behalf of the Rulers.

Nobody dared talking about the Roix, because if roixers found out, or if another villager reported you, you would be in deep trouble. Still, the Roix was present in every small town, in the Trading itself, around Verdania, and even in some parts of the woods. They made sure no one stepped out of line or voiced their opinions too much.

Villagers could live but could not become inconvenient.

From the wooden platform, Hope could feel calm coming to her. Her definition of peace was being surrounded by nature, hearing the rustling sounds of the leaves and the chirping noises of birds and small animals looking for food. This was exactly what she needed to unwind from the events of the past couple of days and digest everything that had happened.

"Hi there, little buddy." Hope smiled as a red-feathered bird landed at the end of the platform. "I forgot to bring you food today. My apologies."

The bird looked at her, moving its head to the side. Funny how Hope had seen this little one since she had memory and still hadn't picked a name for her long-term visitor. *Fireball* seemed far too aggressive for such a beautiful thing, even though it perfectly matched the red tone of its wings with golden specks at the ends. She did not know how long this species usually lived, but it had definitely exceeded any expectations she had.

Hope undid her two identical plaits and left her dark, long hair loose. She couldn't remember when she cut it last. It had probably been years, considering the tips reached the end of her back. Time passed by fast in this place. Days became nights before one could realize. When they were not picking fruits from the woods or tending to their vegetable patch, they were hunting or training how to defend themselves. When they were not cooking, they were fixing furniture for their treehouse. The days became weeks, and what truly made them acknowledge time was Trading Day. No week in the entire year was exempt from that.

"Is it okay if I join you?" Nina asked, her head appearing on the ladder that led to the platform. A ruffle of wings, and Hope knew her feathered friend was gone before she could even turn.

Hope felt tension shooting to her shoulders. She still had not gotten used to seeing Nina in places that Mother and she never shared before, places that were sacred to them and kept them safe from the Roix, from the Rulers, from the dangers of the woods and Verdania.

"Sure." She moved to one side to leave space.

Nina reached the top of the ladder and looked around, whistling in admiration. "This is beautiful."

Hope smiled. It wasn't just beautiful; it was marvelous.

Nina remained standing for a few minutes, going in circles to admire the views from that special spot in Verdania. Hope started plaiting her right braid while thinking maybe it was nice to talk to someone other than Mother, the animals in the woods, or herself. The treehouse was a safe but lonely place to live.

"I'm glad your mother is feeling fine now," Nina said while sitting, the wood cracking a little to adjust.

"Me too. I couldn't imagine her being sick or..." Hope swallowed, not finishing her sentence. She had not allowed herself to think about what could have happened if the vial of blue medicine hadn't worked. She should have probably kept some of the healing liquid for another occasion, just like Nina did when she took a few drops and healed her leg but saved some to fix Raoul.

Raoul. Hope still couldn't wrap her mind around what happened to him in that cave the other day.

After seeing the Thyrian Rulers' symbol carved on the wall of the cave, all Hope's inner alarms had gone off. She had pulled Nina's arm until Nina seemed to come back to reality and started running next to her, not merely being dragged by Hope. They only stopped running when they reached the treehouse and climbed to enter.

"I didn't know people lived in treehouses in Verdania," Nina said. "But I can perfectly understand why."

"I knew some villagers live in caves, but I had never been to one until the other day," Hope said, making a knot at the end of her long plait and braiding the other one.

"We only moved there recently," Nina said. Hope gave a curious look, inviting Nina to tell her more if she wished. Nina sighed, her blue eyes following a black bird flying across the sky. "My brother lived in one house in Cralia until I found him a month ago. I thought he was dead for years, but someone heard rumors he was here, and I came looking for him." Nina looked at Hope's dark eyes.

"Why did you think he was dead?" Hope asked quietly, finishing her second plait and putting her hands on top of her legs.

"He was discarded from Thyria two years ago." Nina's worry was almost palpable.

"Oh." Hope knew most people arrived at Verdania after being discarded from Thyria—sometimes because they committed a crime, sometimes by a specific order from the Rulers themselves, and sometimes, there was no explanation at all. Hope's mother told her once that they both arrived at Verdania after being discarded shortly after Hope's birth. Mother didn't enjoy talking about it and usually went silent for hours after any conversation related to Thyria.

"Raoul told me he never found out why," Nina explained, as if knowing what Hope was thinking. "When I heard he might be alive, I figured it was worth the risk, and I got myself discarded, hoping to be sent here."

"You were discarded on purpose?" Hope said, lifting her brows. Hope couldn't imagine anyone would want to be dumped at Verdania for the rest of their lives.

Nina nodded. "I didn't know another way to get to him," she said. "But I was scared people would start talking about us, as we look so alike, and with the Roix so close, I didn't want them to realize I had been discarded on purpose to reunite with him. It felt like cheating the Rulers."

Nina and Raoul looked very similar indeed. They both had white wavy hair, very pale skin, and they were stunning. Hope hadn't seen Raoul's eyes, as he had them closed when she briefly saw him in the cave, but if they were anywhere near as beautiful as his sister's... She guessed villagers would have talked about them even if they were not seen together.

"You are very brave," Hope said.

"It was useless. The Fifth only knows what they have done to him now." Nina exhaled deeply, trying to hold her tears back.

The symbol carved into the cave next to where Raoul vanished couldn't be a sign of anything good. Hope felt a weird feeling down her spine thinking about it. The four-petal mark was the emblem of the Rulers, but why would a Ruler come to Verdania, to a cave, and take a young man?

"We'll find him, Nina," Hope said with determination.

6

Lenna

By the time Lenna and her sister were close enough to see the West House, the reddish moon had made an early appearance in the still-darkening sky. Lenna wondered what was happening at that very moment at the North House.

If their parents knew of their absence, they would have instructed the roixers to start a search. If that was the case, they would have to be extra careful. Patrols would likely look for them all around the five areas of Thyria, including the West Petal, where Lenna and Ayla were now waiting behind the entrance of a market.

Lenna had grabbed two hooded capes from a non-frequented cupboard next to the kitchens of the North House before sneaking out through the passages into the gardens. Ayla had not seemed surprised. Whether her sister knew of Lenna's frequent visits to Borealia, the capital city of the

North Petal, or she thought Lenna was a weirdo who had clothes hidden around the House just in case, Lenna didn't give a shit.

Years had passed since Lenna's last visit to the West House.

Thyria had the same shape as the panom mark that all the Rulers and panom members of their families bore on their skin: four equal-shaped petals around a middle round area. The North, East, West, and South Houses and their respective cities were in the petals, while the middle part was home to the Organ Core. In the Organ House lived the Organ Mandor, to whom all the cardinal Houses and their Rulers answered. Lenna was not looking forward to seeing the Organ Mandor and his family for her Fifth Ceremony and pretend to admire and respect their tedious grandeur.

Other things had to happen first. The most important thing was to determine if Raoul was alive and safe, starting with discovering how the Fifth he had ended up back in the West House.

Lenna still couldn't get her mind around it. Raoul had been discarded a couple of years ago. Anyone discarded disappeared from Thyria, never to return. Nobody knew where they went or what happened to them. While she was the heir of the North House and the daughter of one of the frightening and well-respected Rulers, it had been useless when she begged and cried to her father to bring Raoul back two years ago.

Lenna could still see the disgust on her father's face, the sadness radiating from her mother as she tried to cuddle her, the incredulous look in her sister's eyes while Lenna had screamed the place down. She had screamed and shouted, kicked and sobbed for hours until she had passed out. She remembered how she woke up in her bed the following day with the clearest mind and swore to herself to make them pay. She would make them pay for discarding her childhood friend.

"What now?" Ayla asked, looking at Lenna from under her hood.

"We wait until the market closes, and then we enter the West House through the corridors underneath," Lenna said without thinking twice. Ayla blinked in silence.

Lenna was familiar with the place like her own hands. She had visited Raoul in the West Petal many times after his family had left the North House to serve the West House, and he had taught her all the secret paths.

The market closed, and they were off.

Many dark, subterranean corridors, heavy metal doors, complex locks, and forty minutes later, they stood sweaty and dusty in front of a grey marble door that led to one of many long-term sheds. Lenna was not sure where to go from there.

The West House, even though not as big as the North House, was so big that it would take them hours to check every single room, not to mention the risk of being caught. Two hooded people might not be relevant in the middle of the busy city of the West, but they would definitely be spotted inside the Ruler's House. What Lenna was going to do when they found Raoul, she was not sure either.

"Here." Ayla got her makeup bag from a pocket and gave it to Lenna.

"I knew you were not the cleverest but, this? Seriously?"

Ayla's expression hardened as she took a step towards Lenna, closing the small distance between them.

"Let me get things clear, Lenna. I want to know why my sources told me before our parents told us, if they even know this. Why is Raoul here and how did that happen? I'm going to get in as much trouble as you for disappearing without a word, so if we can try to work as a team for once in our lives, instead of being at each other's throats, we might get our answers sooner and get home before everything is too fucked up. Now, put this on your face." Ayla handed Lenna the makeup powder and a brush.

"I don't need makeup," said Lenna, not believing her sister could think that was a priority in the moment.

Ayla snorted quietly. Lenna lifted her eyebrows.

"This is not makeup, you idiot." Ayla put some of the tanned-colored powder on the brush and lifted it to her face. She made a stroke with it, and her face features changed, becoming someone Lenna had never seen before. Ayla's green eyes had turned brown, her soft features gone to leave space for a defined jaw. "You are not the only one with funny items." Ayla's grin told Lenna she was enjoying this too way much.

"You could have used it hours ago!"

"It is very expensive and hard to get. I try not to use it unless I must."

Lenna applied the makeup to her face and felt a tickling sensation. She could bet everything she had that this powder was as illegal as fuck, and there was no way their parents knew about it and let her sister keep it, which meant they didn't know about it. *Cheeky little Ayla,* she thought. Lenna wondered if Ayla had any other items that would put her in knee-deep shit if anyone found out.

Ayla got a small, black hairbrush from the makeup bag and gently combed her straight, long red hair. With each touch, Ayla's hair became blond and wavy. She looked so different, Lenna found it hard to remember it was her sister.

When Lenna brushed her shoulder-long red hair, it turned black and curly. A part of her wished she had a mirror close by to see how it looked on her. As if reading her thoughts, Ayla passed Lenna a small mirror from the same bag.

"That's quite the bag." She looked at herself in the mirror, and where, usually, there were big, honey-colored eyes, now, two sunken blue eyes looked at her in surprise. "This is as far as Raoul ever took me, but we'll figure it out."

7

Hope

Acouple of plain chairs sat around an oval-shaped, oak-tree wooden base that did the job as a table in the main room of the treehouse. They had a metal fire pit on one corner, rudimentary but lifesaving on the cold winter nights, next to one of the three windows that covered the walls. The windows were open and big enough to act as doors when they climbed home.

"Are you sure this is a good idea?" Hope lifted an eyebrow. She couldn't see where her mother was going to sleep in this room that was cramped with many items they had gathered throughout the years in Verdania.

They had a considerably large number of books, many pans, pots and cooking utensils, a large stash of weapons mainly comprised of knives and daggers, various racks and tools they regularly used for growing their own food, many hunting devices, from fishing nets to big animal traps, and a whole lot of other stuff.

In the other room, they usually slept on two homemade floor mattresses.

"I don't mind sleeping in this room, Aurora," said Nina. Since the day she arrived at the treehouse with Hope, Nina had been sleeping on one side of the room, beside the table.

Aurora looked at Nina with a smile. "I prefer you two to use the bedroom. If it's not cold, I usually go to the roof most nights anyway."

At night, the rooftop was... magical. The sky almost felt alive with thousands of twinkling stars that seemed to talk to each other. The red tinge of the moonlight over the dark trees of the island was breathtaking.

"Mother, would you come with me to fetch some water please?" Hope asked, grabbing the big pitchers from the top of a shelf. Aurora looked at her with disguised relief.

"Sure, give me a minute."

Aurora put her boots on and packed different things in the loose bag that hung from her shoulder. Nina grabbed a ragged blanket and the book she started reading the day before and went to the bedroom she would now share with Hope.

Hope climbed down the tree, smiling at the birds and squirrels on nearby branches. After all their years in the woods, the animals were used to their presence. When Hope reached the floor, she stretched while taking deep breaths. She could feel the tension of the past few days building up on her shoulders and neck.

They started walking quietly towards the river. Hope always enjoyed walking in the woods—the crunch of the leaves and branches under their feet, the distant animal noises, the sound of the leaves moving to the gentle wind made her heart feel whole.

"How are you feeling?" Hope asked while stopping to pick some ripe apples.

Aurora sighed, as if looking for words. "I'm not sure."

Hope waited in silence, giving the much-needed time her mother required any time she was about to talk about anything that mattered.

"I don't understand why the Rulers were in Verdania looking for that boy. It worries me they might come back for Nina, and you would be in danger too, since we're helping her," Aurora said, stepping over two big roots that shaped the path. "But, on the other hand..."

"On the other hand?" Hope asked when her mother didn't finish the sentence.

Aurora swallowed and looked at Hope's big, dark eyes, a reflection of her own. "On the other hand, I think I shouldn't have allowed us to become so... distant from the world."

Hope knew what she meant. Other than the people they rarely saw in the woods or on their occasional visits to Cralia and the other towns, they barely interacted with any other human beings. Ever.

She looked down as a ray of sunshine came through the tree branches and illuminated the long scar that crossed her mother's neck.

"I think many changes have been long overdue," Aurora sighed, bending to pick some berries from spiky bushes at the edge of their path. "Nina seems like she has lost so much, and I doubt she will betray us. Besides, it's nice to have her around. Life might be too short to spend it alone. What do you think?"

Hope couldn't help but smile.

"If we don't risk, we might not get."

They finally reached the river and, after filling their pitchers and washing themselves, they sat at the edge of the riverside with their feet in the cool water. Hope made a ball with her jacket and used it as a cushion as she laid down to look at the blue sky, her hands behind her head.

"Do you think we can help Nina find Raoul?"

Aurora stayed quiet for a while. "I know for a fact we can," her mother finally said. Hope looked at her, lifting an eyebrow with a questioning look. "What I am not sure about is if we want to."

"What do you mean *for a fact*?"

Aurora hesitated, as if wanting to pick the right words. "I never lied to you, not in my whole life, but I might have not told you some things. Being injured... It made me reconsider my approach." Aurora put both hands on her knees and looked at Hope. "I didn't think you were ready, but I can see now how wrong I was."

Hope sat down and stared at the water. "I feel ready for anything, Mother," Hope said without judging her. It might have been a bold statement, but she had truly felt ready and capable of anything life threw at her for months, perhaps even years.

"I know, my brave girl." Pride beamed in those dark eyes.

"So, tell me: how are you so sure we can find Raoul?" Hope asked, throwing a small pebble into the water.

"Because if the Thyrian mark was on the wall, it means the Rulers have been here, and that means the Roix is involved. I know how the Roix works because before being discarded to Verdania over twenty years ago, in Thyria, I was their captain," Aurora said.

Hope felt cold sweat roll down her spine.

Fuck the Fifth. She hadn't been ready for this.

8

Lenna

As Lenna pushed the white marble door directly into the West House gardens and saw what was waiting for them inside, she gasped.

It had been too many years since she last saw the magnificent blue lake surrounding the white castle. The reddish moonlight illuminated the multiple turrets and towers, and the reflection of the moon on the calm water felt pure. It was almost too beautiful to be true.

Ayla stepped out of the corridor a step behind her. "Oh," Ayla said, holding her breath, her brown eyes wide, trying to absorb all the surrounding beauty.

From the edge of the lake until the exterior walls that separated the West House from the rest of the West Petal, there were gardens with summerhouses and small sheds like the one they stood by. It was difficult to think how such a place existed so close to the market, where people of the city were begging for food to feed their children. This was a fortress made of water and moonlight.

Lenna considered their options: ruining their futures by trespassing on the grounds of another House, or return home before it was too late and figure out another way to find Raoul.

"I had a feeling you would come for him, Lenna," a cold male voice said next to them. "I admit, I was not expecting the other one."

Lenna turned to face the man so fast, she felt her neck crack. Where darkness and shadows had been a few seconds ago, there was a man leaning casually against the wall of the fake shed they had just come out of. He was in his early thirties, with blue eyes and long dark hair falling past his shoulders, one arm replaced by a metallic mechanical one. He was staring at the castle beneath the lake in front of them, as if he could not be bothered to pay attention to the twin sisters.

"Ciaran." Lenna smiled. "How the fuck did you know it was us?" She knew she should probably be ashamed, but she was more amused that Ciaran hadn't changed one bit in the past two years.

"No one else would be stupid enough to come here," Ciaran said, now looking at the full moon. Lenna had always thought Ciaran was handsome in a very serious and devastatingly unique way.

"You could stop playing the clever one and give me a hug. It has been two years." Lenna put her hands on her waist.

Ciaran slightly lifted a corner of his mouth, the closest he usually got to a smile. "I would if you didn't look like a stranger."

Ayla started opening her pocket to get her bag, but Ciaran lifted a hand. Lenna felt like a blanket lifted from her face and hair, and she touched her hair to confirm what she knew: the fake black curls were gone, and her red waves were back in their usual place.

Ciaran took a few steps towards Lenna and gave her a tight, short hug. "You have less than a week until you become panoms. It would be a good idea to avoid getting into serious trouble before then."

Lenna looked at him. Ciaran had always been like a big brother to her, and she hadn't realized how much she had missed him until now. Since the West and North Houses had distanced themselves two years ago, there had been no social events like there used to be. Ciaran, like Lenna, was the heir of his House, and unlike her, a very experienced panom.

"And what is this about?" Ciaran said to Lenna, pointing at Ayla.

Ayla's face was the definition of indignation. "Excuse me," she said, as if expecting an apology.

Ciaran completely ignored Ayla and continued looking at Lenna, as if waiting for her to reply. "My dear sister is so snoopy, she couldn't resist me finding something out before she does. She must think she is the best spymaster of Thyria or something," Lenna said, feeling the angry stare of her sister.

"So," Lenna continued, now serious, "is Raoul truly here?"

Ciaran turned his face towards the lake again, holding his palms together. "He is," he said, his voice troubled.

"And where is he?" Ayla said sharply with a demanding tone.

Ciaran looked at Ayla from top to bottom with visible disgust on his face. Lenna didn't blame him. Ayla had fucked up any possibility of having a cordial relationship with him a few years ago. With no other acknowledgement that he had heard Ayla, Ciaran turned his face to Lenna. If the matter wasn't so serious, Lenna would probably enjoy the rage emanating from her sister, who was clenching her fists at her sides.

"Raoul appeared at the entrance of our castle this morning," he told Lenna. "We're not sure how or why."

"I thought mouring is outlawed on the grounds of any House," Lenna said, lifting her eyebrows. Some experienced panoms, including all the Rulers, had mastered the ability to move themselves and other people through space using their magic.

"Unless you are a panom and a resident of the House you are mouring in or out of. Otherwise, the epitellia wards are likely to hurt or kill you," Ciaran said. "My father and I received the news about Raoul's appearance together, and no one else meets the two criteria for mouring here."

Removing the epitellia wards was like leaving the doors open to a normal house, hanging the keys on the door, and putting a big note saying, "Thieves, please do not steal while nobody is in." Lenna doubted Cobrian Castel, the Ruler of the West House and Ciaran's father, had taken such a risk.

Ciaran nodded, as if reading Lenna's mind. "I know," he said. "I don't understand it either, but thank the Fifth nothing happened."

"Have you seen him? Is he okay?" Lenna asked.

"I haven't. The healers told me he's in a room in one of the towers, but—" Ciaran hesitated.

"But what, Ciaran?" Lenna prompted impatiently.

"The two healers I spoke to said Raoul is not *wholly* here." Lenna felt the blood in her veins go cold, but Ciaran continued. "They said he looks like he is asleep, but they cannot wake him. They said it is as if his mind is somewhere else."

"Where the fuck is *somewhere else*?" Lenna spat, devastation and anger growing inside her. If someone had done this to Raoul, she would make them pay, if it was the last thing she did.

"The healers are trying different ways to bring his mind back, and they said my father ordered some researchers to be permanently assigned to the Learning Commons until further notice."

Lenna felt her knees tremble, a hurtful knot in her chest. She leaned against the wall and let her legs drop her to the grassy ground, where she crossed them and stared at the silhouette of the white castle.

"It's still early, Lenna. He hasn't even been here for a day," Ciaran said, looking at her with empathy and sadness in equal amounts.

Lenna said nothing as a rumble of thoughts crossed her mind at a hurried speed. She needed to know why they had found Raoul and why anyone wanted him back in Thyria. Why they had overrode the sentence that got him discarded two years ago. She couldn't think of any other case when someone had returned to Thyria after being discarded. She didn't even think the laws allowed such a thing, and she doubted the other Rulers, including her father, were remotely aware that Raoul was here. And why would Cobrian Castel, one of the powerful five Rulers of Thyria, have gone through all this trouble of researchers and healers for Raoul, the son of two discarded ex-servants? None of it made any fucking sense.

She didn't dare contemplate what would happen to her friend if his mind didn't return from "somewhere else", whatever the fuck that meant. Lenna sank her fingers into the grass, feeling the soil under her nails and the wet freshness of the thin leaves touching the palms of her hands.

After a while, Lenna turned her face from the mesmerizing waters that surrounded the small island in front of them and looked at Ciaran.

"I'm glad Raoul is here," she said.

She truly was. Even if she couldn't reach or see him yet, it was better knowing he was here than the Fifth knew where.

Ciaran nodded in silence. Next to a tree, Ayla was standing with her arms crossed, staring at them with rage in her eyes, her jaw tight.

"What?" Lenna snapped.

Ayla's fingers were tense against her arms. "I don't believe him." She tilted her face towards Ciaran.

Ciaran snorted, not even bothering to look at Ayla.

"*You* don't believe *him*?" Lenna asked her, as she stood.

"That's exactly what I said," Ayla replied with a superior smile. "I don't believe any Ruler would move a finger for that boy, least of all bring him to his own House and use their personnel to help such a *nobody*."

She should have expected that her haughty, self-important sister would consider her sister's friend a nobody. Anyone who did not belong to the Elite was not enough for superior-ass Ayla.

"She's not worth your rage, Lenna," Ciaran said calmly. Lenna looked at him and realized her body had been on alert. She had unconsciously adapted the same position she used to fight when training with Theon.

Theon wouldn't let Ayla get under his skin. Theon would fucking laugh at her face. Lenna knew he would because he had done so when Ayla had the bad idea of trying to undermine him. Lenna, with bitter anger still roaring in her veins, looked at Ciaran and thanked him in silence.

"I'm so over you two." Ayla stomped towards the white marble door that had taken them into the grounds of the West and disappeared behind it. Lenna would be impressed if her sister remembered the way back to the market. It had taken Lenna many times accompanying Raoul to the door until she could remember the complicated paths and turns she had to take.

Ciaran was trying to contain a smile. "She's going to get lost down there."

"I know. What a moron of a sister, seriously," Lenna said, shaking her head.

"Well, at least she's not the heir to your House. Imagine having her as your Ruler for the rest of your life," Ciaran said, stretching his arm on top of his head.

Lenna chuckled. That would be absolutely unbearable. Lenna was fully aware of how much her narcissistic sister found it unfair that Lenna was the heir to the North House instead of her. Ayla considered herself much more prepared and aligned with "the House's vision" than her twin sister.

Lenna wasted little of her life thinking about her future life as the heir. She didn't give a shit most of the time. But to think Ayla was the alternative... *Cardinals, yes, I'd rather be a Ruler.*

"I can moure you to the North Petal, if you'd like," Ciaran said. "As close to your House as I can get. It's almost ante meridiem."

"Wait, what? You can moure?" Lenna shouted. She took Ciaran's grin as an affirmation. He should grin more frequently, she thought. She patted him on the mechanical arm with too much excitement, and she almost felt the bones of her hand complain.

"We have a lot to catch up on," he said, still smiling.

"It's been so nice seeing you," she said, returning the smile. "My parents are probably freaking out and mobilizing the roixers by now, unless a message I sent got delivered in time."

"How did you send it?" Ciaran asked, curiosity sparkling in his eyes.

There were three main ways to send a message in Thyria. Members of the Houses did not use messengers because of the high chances of a leak. Owlings were effective, reliable, and fast, but the creatures were extremely rare. And the third way was...

"Magic," she said. Even though they had magic in their blood, they officially could not use it until they had their Fifth Ceremony, when their full potential would be unlocked. Their parents had threatened them when they were little, saying if they used magic before they became panoms, they would lose the petals of their panom mark. But many flying vases, rogue pieces of furniture running around the house, and pets turned into decoration later, their parents stopped and just pretended they didn't know.

"I think I would have been disappointed if Lenna Brachyan had learned no magic before her Fifth," Ciaran said. "Who has been teaching you?"

"Nobody. I stole a couple of books, and I have been practicing here and there on my own."

They heard a dripping noise coming from the corridor behind the marble door next to them, and they both turned to face it. Ciaran lifted both hands in front of him, ready to use them, and Lenna took up a fighting stance.

Ayla appeared, slogging through the door archway, fully soaked with some sort of sticky liquid that smelled like rotten eggs. Her usually perfect long hair was a mess. Reading her face was a challenge.

Lenna looked at Ciaran, lifting her eyebrows and biting her bottom lip, trying to contain a laugh out of some undeserved pity for her sister. Lenna sent a silent thanks to the five Cardinals for their payback.

"I thought you knew about our neighbour," Ciaran said casually. "I hope he was not too rude to you."

Ayla walked towards Lenna. "Let's go home. Now."

"Ciaran is mouring us," Lenna said with a false apologetic look.

Ayla took a deep breath with her eyes closed, probably trying to find the latest bit of her patience. "Moure us now," she ordered.

Ciaran looked at Lenna, lifting his eyebrows. "Do you want me to moure your sister too? She's very dirty."

Lenna laughed, knowing Ciaran was enjoying this as much as she was. "I think it's better if we both get home at the same time. Otherwise, I'll be in even more trouble," Lenna said.

Ciaran closed his hand, and the stickiness of Ayla's clothes and skin disappeared. Ayla clenched her jaw and said nothing.

"You're welcome," Ciaran said, getting closer to the sisters. As he touched the back of their necks, the three of them vanished into the night.

9

Hope

The red-tinged moonlight was so bright and clear, they didn't need any candles or torches to illuminate the treehouse. The thick trees provided cover from unwanted visitors. If someone didn't know their home was there, they wouldn't have spotted it.

If her mother hadn't been on the roof platform, Hope would have probably gone there a few hours ago. It was her favorite place to think, to plan, to decide, and to listen to herself. And what her mother told her a few hours ago...

Hope knew little about Aurora's life before she was discarded to Verdania. She had imagined her mother had worked in different jobs to have so many diverse survival skills, but this? Not in a million years could she have imagined her mother was the Roix Reigner, the highest authority in the Roix.

Hope couldn't wrap her head around it. The shock had been such that she couldn't even ask her mother anything on the way back to their house from the river. She wasn't sure where to even start.

There were so many things Hope wanted to know, so many answers she had wished for for a long time. She could still remember when she was barely four or five years old and she asked mother why it was just the two of them in the world. Mother would get sad and stay quiet for a long while. Sometimes for a few hours. Sometimes for a few days.

As Hope grew older, she learned which things were triggers for her mother to distance herself from the outside world and get lost in her inner one.

It was painful to remember the sadness and frustration on her mother's face when Hope, a few years ago, gathered her courage and asked her if she had a father. Mother didn't speak for two whole days after that.

Nina made a small noise and turned in bed. Hope admired the whiteness of her long wavy hair, which seemed to shine to a pink tone with the red rays of moonlight entering the room.

Hope didn't know if this was going to last for much longer, but for now, maybe it wasn't just her mother and her in the world.

When Hope woke the next morning, the bright sun shamelessly inundated the empty bedroom. She closed her eyes tight against the bright light and stretched her limbs while yawning. Someone chuckled next door.

It took Hope more than she would have liked to get herself out of bed, finding a pair of socks and splashing some water on her face from the small pitcher near the window. When she opened the door, she saw Nina sitting at the oval table of the main room.

"Morning, Nina," Hope said, walking towards the fruit bowls on the counter and grabbing an apple and a handful of berries.

Nina looked at her from top to toe and grinned. "Good morning."

Hope's mother appeared at the treehouse doorway, and Hope gulped her berries down.

Aurora was forty-something, and Verdania's nature seemed made for her. Whenever they visited the towns near the coast, she and Hope were often mistaken for sisters. Both had the same almost-black eyes. Their bodies were fit and muscled from all the hours they spent together, practicing with their stash of weapons and hunting animals. They were taller than average. The main physical difference between them was the long scar that crossed her mother's neck and the two plaits Hope wore versus her mother's shorter hair.

Hope hadn't known her mother without that scar. She could remember asking about it on different occasions, but she never explained how she got it.

"I used to hate it, but I learned to embrace it. It's part of my history, of my life. It's part of who I am," was the most she said about it. And it had been enough for Hope to learn to love the small scars she had collected here and there during those years in the woods.

She knew her mother well, but what Hope had never seen was the metal box she carried under her armpit. Mother walked towards the table where Nina and Hope sat, sat it down, and shook the top part of the box with her hand to get some soil and dust off it.

The box was plain and grey, which was not unusual. The maximum decorations they had were flowers they picked in the woods, and some carvings they had done on a few pieces of rudimentary furniture over the years: a small snail on the corner of a shelf, a butterfly at the top of the doorway, a dandelion-looking flower next to the window, and a few others.

Mother stared at the box long enough for Nina and Hope to look at each other with questioning looks, wondering if they should say something or if it was wiser to wait. Hope's impatience was increasing by the second, and she had to bite her lip to give mother time to gather her words.

"I figured the Roix quarters would be a good starting point to where your brother is," Aurora said without taking her eyes off the box.

"What's in the box, Mother?" she asked. Her patience had given up.

After opening the complex metal lock, Mother opened the lid, revealing the contents. At the bottom of the box, there were a few dozen papers, and Hope recognized her mother's handwriting. Sitting on top, was a small gold locket with a chain, a pair of old-looking, tiny wool socks that would only fit a baby, and...

Nina gasped and pointed at the last item in the box, then looked at Hope's mother, lifting her other hand to cover her mouth in shock. "What is a compassom doing here?"

Hope looked more carefully at the said compassom. The palm-big, transparent square looked like some sort of glass with thin red lines on the sides, as if framing the central part. There had to be something else there to cause such a reaction from Nina.

"It was mine," her mother said, her gaze fixed on the compassom. Whether because it brought her many memories or because she was consciously avoiding Nina's gaze, Hope was not sure.

Nina's white brows flinched at the reply, and she started hyperventilating. "But..."

"Is this something from when you worked at the Roix?" Hope asked her mother without hesitating. Nina gasped.

As far as Hope knew, only the Rulers and the roixers would cause such a frightened reaction in someone. Hope saw no reason not to share with Nina what her mother confessed to her the day before.

Nina was sleeping in their house, eating at their table, and if she wanted them dead, she would have probably killed them already.

Aurora looked at Hope's dark eyes, assessing her question and the silent statement that Nina was to be trusted, and gave the smallest nod.

"I worked in the Roix in Thyria before we were discarded here twenty-four years ago," Mother explained, looking through the window as if remembering it. Nina's eyes widened to where Hope could see the whole blue iris surrounded by white. "It's not something I am proud of. I... I was obeying orders from the Rulers, but the blood landed on my hands, not theirs." Mother swallowed. "I did many things I will never forgive myself for."

Nina couldn't keep her scared blue eyes off Aurora's. She cautiously put her hands on her lap. "Even if you... worked at the Roix, why did you *own* a compassom?"

"I should have specified that I was the Roix Reigner," Mother said, an apologetic plea in her semi-black eyes. "My compassom was broken on my last mission as a Reigner."

"Fucking Cardinals," Nina muttered and put her elbows on the table while covering her eyes with both hands.

"What's this compassom thing?" Hope asked. A small part of her was glad her mother was explaining more things. *Important* things. But she couldn't help but be pissed at the fact that she had just explained more things to Nina than to her in her whole damned life.

"It's a device the Rulers of the five Houses of Thyria and the Reigner of the Roix use to... detect panoms," her mother said, as if fighting against herself to say the last two words out loud.

"Detect *what*?" Hope asked more sharply than she wanted.

"Cardinals spare us." Nina lifted her head from her hands to give a come-on type glance to Hope's mother, as if she couldn't believe she hadn't told Hope.

Aurora gave a sharp look to Nina, her mouth in a thin line.

"Panoms have special abilities. Magical abilities. All the Rulers are panoms and their blood lines have the potential to become one," Mother said. Well, maybe that would explain why the Rulers were so feared and respected.

"Panoms have the four-petal mark magically inked on their skin during the Fifth Ceremony, but... the symbol is present on the skin of a potential panom since birth. It's not visible, but it's there. The compassom allows us to see it."

Hope felt a list of questions piling up in her mind, but before she could decide which one to shoot first, her mother continued, now leaning. "Compassoms shouldn't exist. There are secrets that are best kept that way."

Aurora got the papers out of the box. They looked a bit discolored, but the black ink was readable. Hope was handed a bunch of them. Some of them looked like drafts of maps. She continued eyeing the pages, and she realized she was reading lists of roixers' names, ranks, physical features such as scars and permanent inks, average age, and...

"Which House *owns* them? Seriously?"

Mother sighed and nodded, taking a deep breath. "When we become part of the Roix, we resign from our own will and family. We technically become property of the Houses, even though we are only allowed to answer to the Ruler of said House, the Roix Reigner, and the Organ Mandor."

Hope remembered the political terms from the lessons her mother had taught her over the years, only mother had clearly "forgotten" to mention that said Rulers were damned magical panoms. Hope tried to avoid clenching her teeth at the exasperating thought.

The Organ Mandor was the Ruler of the Organ House, in the circular area in the middle of the four-petal shape of Thyria. All the other Houses were connected to the Organ, and even though the cardinal Rulers, from the North, South, East, and West Houses, had the power to mandate within their own territories, they ultimately had to answer to the Organ Mandor.

Hope's mind was spinning in circles. "If you had to resign from your own family, how did you have me?"

Mother closed her eyes. Her face was unreadable, even for Hope. She simply said, "We will have this conversation another time, Hope."

Hope realized Nina was sitting there, even though her stillness and silence had almost made her forget her presence.

Hope had been waiting for answers for years. *Years*. She had asked for them, only to get silence or a straight no as an answer. Repeatedly. This time, Hope did not even bother to hide her desperation.

Mother seemed to know exactly what she was thinking. "Soon, Hope. I promise."

Hope said nothing and pretended to read the lists of names she had in front of her as if she cared about them, silently trying to avoid the tears building in her eyes. *Soon*. She had heard that dreaded word so many times, she had lost count.

But she had made a promise. At least she had that. Her mother never broke a promise. This promise was not specific enough to mean much, though. "Soon" could be a day, a week, or a year, for all she knew. Hope breathed in and out, trying to get her frustration off her chest.

Nina moved on her chair opposite Hope and drastically shifted her position to face Aurora, who had gone back to sit on top of the shelf in front of the window. Hope appreciated the small privacy of not having anyone directly facing her as she wiped the corner of her eyes.

"So the plan is to enter the Roix quarters?" Nina said in an incredulous voice, as if she couldn't believe what she was saying. "I can think of another hundred ways I'd prefer to die." Hope agreed, her tears drying as fast as a lightning.

Aurora chuckled, as if realizing how stupid it sounded. "The Roix must know what happened in the cave, especially because there was the panom symbol carved on the wall. At least the higher ranks must know."

Her mother turned her back to Nina and grabbed a leaf from the nearby tree peeking through the window, bending it in multiple folds while she paced the room. "We can't enter the quarters and leave them without a fight," Mother said as if that was a possibility.

Against the Roix. *For Cardinals' sake.* Hope didn't know whether to laugh or cry again.

"Each roixer has twenty-four hours off duty every week. It's one thing I got to introduce as the Reigner. They are on a rotation pattern, so there are the same numbers off at any one time. Usually, one out of seven is off. Before I left the Roix, there were thirty-five roixers assigned to Verdania, meaning five would be off."

Hope flinched at the awful thought. Did Roix workers only have twenty-four hours every seven days to themselves?

"What do they do with their free time?" Nina asked, her brows showing her concern.

"In Thyria, most do everything and anything not allowed when they are on duty. I used to stay in reading or go to the woods at the borders of the Core. Most pay for sex or company," mother said.

Considering these people were, apparently willingly, separated from their families, it made sense that they would seek any sort of emotional connection they could. Since meeting Nina, Hope had experienced first-hand how nice it was to talk to someone, to feel understood and have a laugh.

"If we could find out where they go, I could try to get close to them," Nina said, her silver hair covering the side of her face.

Hope opened her eyes. "You don't have to do that, Nina. There are other ways. There have to be." But her mother had fallen silent, studying Nina. "Mother, she doesn't have to do that," Hope said a bit too loudly.

"She doesn't have to do anything she doesn't want to do. But she is stunning, and her features are unusual enough to make anyone pay attention. So unique, in fact, that they would recognize her resemblance to Raoul immediately, if he looks like you said," Mother said, almost muttering, as if she was talking to herself. "Unless she approached a brand new roixer, or someone in the lower ranks."

"I will do it if it gets me closer to finding Raoul," Nina said, making Hope silently curse all the Cardinals. Nina continued, confident but serious, "I won't do anything I don't want to do. I have played with men before."

Hope tried to hide the deep shock she had after Nina's statement. She couldn't imagine the sweet, vulnerable Nina playing with anyone, especially not in that way Hope had only ever read about.

Aurora considered Nina's words before saying, "It's worth a try." Hope couldn't believe the pair she had in front of her and realized she was annoyed about the shit plan. She wanted to protect Nina from harm, like she had done the first time she saw her being dragged in the woods.

"I suggest we head to Cralia after the next Trading Day. Hope and I will stay nearby, and we will come for you if you shout for help, Nina," her mother said, casually grabbing a dagger from one of the weapon shelves and a whetstone to sharpen it. Hope was glad she was not the only person in the room who cared about Nina.

"Oh, it shouldn't get to that point," Nina said, with a small, appreciative smile to Aurora for her offer of protection. "I was planning on taking the little red vial I got in the Trading, just in case."

Hope laughed with nervous relief. She could perfectly remember how the beautiful poppy had died in front of them within seconds of a drop of the red liquid touching it. That would be a quick solution. And if, for whatever reason, Nina couldn't use that, Hope would make sure to hang the balls of whoever touched her without permission from the roof of the Roix quarters.

10

Lenna

Despite the bright light behind her eyelids, Lenna refused to open her eyes. She hadn't had a good night's sleep in the Fifth knew how long. Just five more minutes.

"After the trouble I went through yesterday, you could make an effort and move your ass," an amused, masculine voice said.

"Fucking Cardinals, Theon," she mumbled, her voice almost too sleepy to be understood. Lenna recognized his voice and tried to open her eyes against the monstrous force trying to keep them shut.

"Morning to you too, sleepyhead," he said, walking towards a table where she kept everything she didn't know where to put or couldn't be bothered to find a place for. Theon sat on her chair, put his feet on the table and his hands behind his head while admiring her bedroom.

Lenna rolled her eyes and turned to the other side of the bed, pulling the blanket that was a mess on her feet up to her neck. "What are you doing here?" she asked. She was fully aware that the floor-to-ceiling glass doors to her balcony were open wide.

It was no mystery in the North House that Lenna had visitors every so often when she fancied some nocturnal entertainment, one of the *many* reasons her dearly concerned father was not happy with her. He was not concerned about Lenna, but about what the North people would say if they knew the heir to the House enjoyed sex with strangers, very non-panom and non-Elite strangers, on a quite regular basis without being dutifully married and bearing babies for the line.

Still, Theon had never visited her in her bedroom before. Why would he? They only had their daily training sessions together and went out in Borealia, the principal city surrounding the North House in their petal, with Elite friends a few times. The so-called Elite "friends" were more a pain in the ass than anything close to actual friends, even if they had known each other from birth. They were more friendships born out of elitism than anything real.

Lenna always thought most of them had nothing else to do with their lives than flatter her father's ass, and then they would hand in an embarrassing amount of money to her already annoyingly rich family and make it worse. Didn't they have anything better to spend it on? *Starting with not letting kids starve to death on the streets.*

Theon was not a member of the Elite—he was "just" her trainer and therefore a mere servant. The fucked up social standards in Thyria were something that would never not unnerve her. Not that those standards and rules had stopped Lenna from inviting him out with them.

Her politically correct sister had given Theon so many disapproving looks and not-so-subtle comments that first night that Lenna and Ayla ended up in a big fight when they got home. Lenna didn't know if Ayla had finally understood that Lenna would do what she wanted, or if Ayla thought she was a lost case, but she hadn't been so intense toward Theon after that. Thanks to *him*, Lenna actually had fun and laughed on those occasions.

"I figured that, with all your secret business yesterday, you wouldn't have known they cancelled our training session today," Theon said, looking through the balcony to the beautiful view of the city.

Lenna frowned and said, "House, what's my plan for today?"

A paper appeared on top of her chest, and she picked it up to read it.

10:00 Fifth Ceremony Dress Fitting

01:00 Lunch with guest

03:00 Curriculum Lesson with Leo Pharlin

She covered her eyes with one hand in desperation.

"What is it so important that made them cancel training?" Theon asked.

Even if her parents had agreed to the sessions, Father usually found any excuse to cancel training, which meant adding something stupid to her agenda. Lenna knew her father was fully aware of how much she enjoyed her sessions, and she had definitely seen a correlation between pissing-Father-off and training-session-cancelled over the months.

Theon had laughed when Lenna told him one day that their session had been cancelled because of "Teaspoons Selection". Coincidentally, it had been the day after Lenna spent the night with a blond visitor and had forgotten to shut the doors of the balcony. She guessed the not-so-musical sounds that had come from her room had pissed Father off more than usual.

Lenna propped herself on the bed by her elbows. "The damn Fifth Ceremony dress fitting."

"Serious fancy panom stuff then." Theon looked at her, lifting his eyebrows up and down.

She had no clue what she'd have to do during the fitting. Everything about the Fifth she had ever asked Leo during her sessions was about the powers themselves, the bit of the Ceremony she found useful.

"I just hope they don't want me to wear something ridiculous," Lenna said, sitting on the edge of her bed. She wouldn't accept being dressed like a puppet. She sighed and tried to remember everything that had happened the day before. It seemed like it had been ages ago. "What did you do yesterday, by the way? I was expecting a full Roix campaign here."

Theon put a hand on his chest and opened his mouth, pretending to be offended. "I thought you had more faith in me, Lenna." He smiled with his full lips closed. "After you almost gave me a fucking heart attack with your sparkly floaty or whatever-that-was message, I would expect more confidence from you."

Lenna grinned. "I can't believe it worked. It was the first time I sent someone ink."

"Seriously? Well, it did work, and other than scaring the shit out of me, it was interesting to see," Theon said, returning the grin.

Lenna had always enjoyed practising and experimenting with her magic. She had written golden notes on the wall of her room, but never had she tried to send ink to a person or to a place not within reach of her sight. Apparently yesterday, she had achieved both.

As if Theon had read the curiosity in her honey eyes, he said, "I felt a tickle in my forearm, and I saw tons of small sparkly stars going *into* my skin, bending together and making shapes. After a moment, it turned into a message in shiny golden ink. It disappeared as soon as I read it."

Lenna could remember the message she sent in desperation.

Leo is waiting for me. Ayla and I must do something and won't be back soon. Please cover for us. L

"I asked the housekeepers to take me to Leo, and I told him there was a last-minute Elite meeting in the city," Theon explained.

Lenna smiled. She wasn't entirely convinced that Leo bought the excuse, but she was thankful to him for not having raised any concerns to her parents. Otherwise, they would have been knee-deep in trouble.

She appreciated Theon not asking what she and Ayla had done to need such a last-minute cover. Despite knowing she shouldn't, Lenna felt the need to inform him about the entire Raoul situation. She knew it would make her feel better about the knot in her chest.

Lenna took a deep breath. Having the Fifth Ceremony in two days didn't help, but on the other side, maybe when she finally learned how to use her panom powers beyond the very basic stuff she had figured out until now, she would have more resources to help her friend. The knot in her chest tightened.

"Thank you for yesterday. I owe you one," she said, straightening her wavy red hair with her fingers. She realized Theon was looking at her with attention, trying to decipher her suddenly serious expression. "I need to tell you something, but I can't be late to the dress fitting. As grateful as I am for yesterday, I would appreciate some privacy."

Theon stood up. "Sure. I will enjoy my day off in peace, but expect that tomorrow's session will make up for today's. I'll make you sweat." He winked, headed towards the balcony, and jumped without looking back at her. Lenna exhaled while heading towards the ensuite bathroom, already dreading what he would come up with—as if it was her choice to do the damned dress thing.

She let the water run in the huge circular bath while she looked at herself in the mirror. Her fire-colored hair didn't look as bad as she had expected, and her tan face looked almost acceptable, considering how stupidly tired she felt. The orange satin top and the matching pajama shorts she was wearing, though, looked impeccable.

Theon had seen her in multiple revealing dresses on their nights out, and he'd never seemed interested in her.

He always had a long number of young, attractive beings staring at him, from his brown hair to his enchanting smile. Theon wasn't easily impressed by a pleasant look or a seductive smile.

She couldn't get the sight of Theon leaning on her bedpost off her mind, though, and soon, the room felt warm, and not just because the hot water was almost filling the bath. She sent some sparks to deliver an ink to Theon.

Incoming announcement for brave warriors who have heart attacks when they see sparkly messages.

Lenna grinned, thinking he would be cursing right now. She sent the second part of the ink away.

Don't get used to entering my bedroom without having your ass kicked.

Lenna was writing in her book of Cause in the middle of the quiet library at the North House, writing her thoughts and notes as she had done for years.

Suddenly, the quiet library was quiet no longer when her father, Jasper Brachyan, stormed in with Ayla and someone else in tow.

"It was a much-needed discarding if they had been repeatedly stealing food. Shame the roixers didn't catch them earlier. Here you are," said her father. Lenna didn't lift her eyes from the sentence she was finishing, whatever they wanted from her was not more important than not losing her trend of thought. "We have visitors, Lenna. I'm going to ensure lunch is ready. If you can kindly introduce them, Ayla?"

"Give me a minute." Lenna continued writing as her father left.

A low chuckle came from the third person, and Lenna lifted her gaze from the book of Cause, shutting its cover with a bang that hopefully stated what she felt about being interrupted in the peace of a library.

The man looking at her with a side smile was the most handsome man she had ever seen. His amused silver eyes pierced into her, in contrast with his black hair and his smooth skin. He was dressed in dark, neat leathers that marked his torso and arms but also made him someone to be respected, maybe even feared.

"What's so funny?" Lenna asked, standing up from her chair and sitting on the corner of the table she had been using.

"I am trying to figure out which one of you was moaning so loudly the last time I spent a night here," the man said, the corner of his lips still upward.

Ayla shook her head, covering her green eyes with a hand as she said, "Cardinals guide us. Lenna, this is Jake Coralt, heir of the Organ House and son of the Organ Mandor. Jake, as you know, this is Lenna, my twin sister and heir of the North House."

"The moans were mine. Thanks for your concern," Lenna winked at him, completely ignoring her sister. "Staying in the guest house in the gardens, I take it. Discarding duty brought you here?"

Ayla answered for him, "He kindly discarded a family of seven last week for sleeping in the streets of Borealia, disrupting the flow, then today, two teenagers who had been caught stealing. Jake has been very generous and offered for us to join him next time, after our Fifth Ceremony."

Lenna was going to be sick. "And you will gladly join him, will you not, sister?"

"Won't *you* be joining me?" Jake asked Lenna before Ayla could reply.

"I wouldn't join you over my dead body. You and your discarding duty can fuck off."

Jake Coralt lifted his chin just a tiny bit, surveying Lenna from top to bottom. His eyes darkened, as if he was mentally listing all the ways he could have her at his mercy. He was definitely used to being feared and obeyed.

"Not in your wildest dreams," Lenna said.

"It is precisely in the wildest ones that we would have the best time." He smirked.

"Shame I don't fuck entitled pricks," she shot back—especially not ones used to getting everything and everyone they wanted.

"But you do fuck many others. I wonder if you'd benefit from another cock in the room. Just in case."

Ayla almost choked. "May I remind you that profound intimacy between heirs of the Houses risks a panomquake. It would cause so much disturbance. I'm sure it's not worth your hormones."

Jake's dropped his stare to every profound bit of Lenna, a silent side smile on his lips, as if he'd love to take the risk of shaking the entire island just to taste her.

Lenna smiled. "She's not the heir. Feel free to offer your cock to her anytime."

"It isn't her I want. You will come begging, sweet fire, and I'll be waiting for you." His voice was a whisper, and Lenna's core unavoidably tightened.

11

Hope

From her spot in the wide circle of beings that surrounded the Trading Table, Hope looked to Nina on her right, who half smiled. A smile on her pretty face might have meant pure innocence to a stranger, but Hope knew exactly where Nina's daggers were hidden in her boots.

Hope looked to her left and saw her mother staring at the sandglass. If looks could kill, that sandglass would have already exploded. Her mother's curled lip was a promise of death.

The sandglass was suspended in air right above the Trading Table, dropping grains of sand, marking the remaining minutes until past meridiem. Every trader had by now assumed the raw reality: the Trading was not about getting a full stomach or finding useful devices that would make their lives easier. No, the Trading had become a trading for their lives, a weekly civil war with just one rule: do not approach the table until the cloth drops.

Hope repositioned her belt with four daggers on her waist. She readjusted the two swords on her back, tight to her body and as comfortable as they had always been. They were not her preferred weapon by any means—too big, too bulky, but a clear sign to anyone who dared to even think about becoming a nuisance.

No distractions. Find clothes for Nina's mission with the Roix. Find more red vials. Grab some food to satisfy their already used-to-starving stomachs.

No pity. Not after anyone who came to the Trading knew what could happen. Not after the attempt on Nina's life. Not after her mother almost bleed out two weeks ago. It wouldn't happen again, because she would kill them first.

Focus. In and out. Their job would be done. They would go home. They would be safe.

The sandglass marked less than five minutes left until meridiem, when the sun would be above them in a straight line. Less than five minutes to analyze the unusually flat shape under the massive cloth hanging on top of the long Trading Table.

The previous week, Hope had only seen one big mountain shaped lump under the cloth, which turned out to be a big pile of clothes.

Four minutes left. From her distance, Hope could only see a flat-line covering the length of the table.

Three minutes left. The Table was annoyingly symmetrical. In a place full of nature like Verdania, such perfect bilateral symmetry was not unseen, but it was unusual. She had seen flowers in full bloom that seemed to challenge perfection.

Two minutes. The Trading was not remotely close to perfection. Hope looked around the wide circle of people; more than a hundred had come.

Everyone was waiting for the last grain of sand to fall and the cloth to drop before making the run. Before being exposed to the fights and kills that would take place.

One minute. Nina was doing small jumps next to her, a final attempt at warming up her body. Hope felt her mother move to prepare to sprint; Hope half kneeled her back leg to do the same.

The last grain of sand fell, and the cloth was pulled.

"What the…" Hope breathed in, unable to move as she took in an empty table—an empty table with two tall poles on each side, in front of dozens of people waiting to get what they needed.

Aurora was running, already a good few meters ahead, Nina a few steps behind her, but close enough that they were likely to reach the Table at the same time.

"Hope, run!" her mother shouted over her shoulder with an angry voice, as if she couldn't believe Hope remained still. "Right. Fucking. Now."

Hope, taken aback, wasted no time running as fast as she possibly could. She had to be faster than usual to catch her mother and Nina, as they had a few seconds' advantage.

Hope wasn't sure if it was wise to run to an empty table, but everyone else was running to it. Had the Rulers decided to stop pretending they were generous by giving Verdania's villagers weekly provisions? She trusted her mother, and if she was running, so would Hope.

A tall, blond man in his twenties was going to reach the Table first. He was merely a few meters away, right across the middle of the Table in front of Hope, Nina and Aurora. Then, Hope watched his face slam against an invisible wall.

"What the fuck?!" Hope heard the blond man shouting at the sandglass, as if it was alive and would respond to him.

The other faster runners had slowed their pace. Some people behind them had completely stopped, not daring to step closer. Hope would not be surprised if some people had turned around altogether and gone home. This had to be a damn joke.

Her mother's hands turned upward, palms vertical against the invisible wall preventing them from reaching the Trading Table. The expensive wooden surface shone under the sun, completely empty, save for the two long wooden poles at the ends.

"What is happening?" Hope asked quietly, looking from one side to the other. The blond man managed to stand and was right in front of Nina, on the other side of the Table, an enormous bruise beginning to form across his face.

"Hope, stay here. Nina, move to the pole on your side. Discreetly. Now." Her mother's voice was quiet but firm, with no hesitation. It was the voice of a captain, of someone used to command people.

Before Hope could ask what they were meant to do, Nina was walking to the right end of the Table and her mother towards the left.

The sandglass above made a metallic clicking noise and started turning sideways. Suddenly, a voice resounded around the Trading arena, as if it was coming from the sandglass, from the sky, and from the ground at the same time. It was a voice old and new, male and female, sharp and soft.

"Esteemed guests of the Trading Table. With great aspirations to restore the harmonious communion of Verdania, we take immense pleasure in offering you the fulfilment of your most profound necessity. It is imperative that you partake in this gift in private. With the warmest of regards, The Ruling Body."

Hope felt her blood freezing in her veins. Right at the same moment, a thick depth of green grass covered the table, and dozens of unique roses popped up, the middle covered by a short white rose with no leaves and massive thorns.

"Are they taking the fucking piss?" said the blond man in front of her, his eyebrows raised and his jaw tense.

Hope said nothing, but she couldn't agree more. Had the Rulers seriously swapped the Trading for... *a full-on flower festival?* Everyone else remained still and quiet, as if waiting for the voice to say something else.

The blond man slowly stretched an arm in front of him and tried to reach the Table. Without warning, he managed to do so, the invisible wall gone.

Hope looked at the roses in front of her, and then she saw it: her name elegantly written in dark green ink on a petal of a beautiful, blood-red rose.

Hope Nevada

Traders around Hope showed recognition on their faces as they read their names on the petals or stems of their respective flowers. Some villagers grabbed theirs and started moving across the crowd to leave. The crowd was pressing around the Table, everyone eager to find their bloom.

A teenager on the other side of the Table looked at his rose and frowned. He went to remove a petal of the flower, and he vanished at the same moment the petal left the rose—completely gone, flower with him, as if he never had stood there. A young woman who had stood next to him screamed, wide-eyed with fear.

It is imperative that you partake in this gift in private, the voice had said. Hope felt anger rising inside her.

The teenager was gone. *Gone*, all because he hadn't listened to the Rulers' cardinally stupid conditions.

Hope carefully placed her rose inside her cloth bag. She was expecting its petals to bend or even break as soon as she did, but the rose looked as perfect as it had on the table. Suspiciously perfect. Which reminded her of...

Hope looked at one side of the Table, spying a head full of white hair moving between the people, and felt a small bit of relief at locating Nina in the crowd.

They reached the treehouse in silence, but Hope didn't place her dagger in her belt until the three of them were inside. She'd noticed the tension in her mother's shoulders and neck all the way through the woods too.

Nina sighed, sitting on a chair, her bag on the oval table. "What the Fifth was that Trading about?"

Aurora walked towards the table and opened her bag, taking her yellow rose out. "I have two theories, and I don't know which one I like less."

"And they are?" Hope asked as she took out her own rose. It didn't look like any rose she had ever seen. It looked much sturdier, perfect and special, as if the flower had its own characteristics.

"One is that the Rulers are extremely bored in Thyria, which would mean trouble," Aurora said. "They are sick and evil, and if they want entertainment... that will not end well for us."

"And the other theory?" Hope asked impatiently.

"The other," Aurora swallowed and continued in a quieter voice, "is that a Ruler wants to communicate with someone here."

Hope didn't understand why the Rulers would want to say something to someone discarded. Why would they go through all the fuss of making a Trading like today's to do it?

As if reading the impatience in Hope's eyes, her mother headed towards the bedroom and said, "Let me check mine out first."

In case it's poisoned or she vanishes.

Aurora closed the curtain between both rooms, and silence followed.

For a moment, Hope feared she vanished exactly as that teenager had, the Fifth knew where. But a second later, her mother appeared, her nostrils flared, tearful eyes and a pale face. She sat down in the free chair, clenching her fists.

"Everything okay?" she asked.

Aurora nodded, looking at a spot on the oval table. She slowly opened one of her fists and revealed a small piece of paper, a handwritten note with dark green ink. Hope picked it up swiftly and read it.

It's time.

Time for what?

"I'll go next," said Nina.

Instead of silence this time, Hope heard a surprised gasp. Nina ran back, holding a square of rusted paper. She laid it flat on top of the oval table. It was a map of Thyria, the four petals marking the delimitations of each House, the central circle uniting them all.

Nina put a finger on top of a spot marking the West Petal, tears pouring out of her eyes. And then Hope saw it: right in the middle of the West House, next to a small cross, was an even smaller name handwritten in dark green ink.

Raoul.

"No way, no way, no way!" Hope said, lifting her hands to her mouth as she felt tears building behind her own eyes.

"There is someone trying to help you, Nina," Hope cried as she hugged Nina, the tears from those ocean-colored eyes wetting Hope's shoulders.

Aurora was not smiling as she looked at them, a silent tear flowing down her cheek. "There is hope. There is always hope," she said with a broken voice.

It took them a couple of minutes to let go of their tight embrace, and as soon as they did, Hope grabbed her red rose and entered the bedroom, shutting the curtain behind her.

She looked at the petals and started pulling them one by one, her hands cold with nerves and expectation. She pulled the last petal, and the stem and the core vanished, leaving a solid object in its place.

A compassom.

12

Lenna

Lenna was as eager to win the next round of hand-to-hand combat against Theon as she had ever been, but right now, she was miserably spread on the floor, Theon standing on top of her with a sideways *I-told-you* smile and an eyebrow raised.

Indeed, Lenna should have expected Theon to send her to the mat by quickly sweeping his foot under her leg.

"Don't even start, you evil being," said Lenna, accepting the extended hand Theon offered.

She had lost sight of his legs for just a moment. He said that any proper warrior, or at least the ones that liked to remain alive, must be able to see things outside of their direct line of sight. Peripheral-vision-whatever.

"Let's go again, Lenna. Actually..." he said. Oh, no. Lenna knew too well what the spark in his eyes meant.

"Since this is the last training session before you become a mystic power badass panom. We won't finish until you send me to the floor."

That was his brilliant idea? She had never won a combat against him, not once in two years.

Lenna crossed her arms. "Do you want me to be late to the Fifth Ceremony tomorrow or what?"

Theon laughed. "Come on, you're not that bad. I taught you some good stuff. Anyway, less moaning, more fighting." Theon closed his fists in front of him and placed a foot in front of the other while bending his legs.

Lenna took her fighting stance and breathed in deeply, preparing herself to attack or defend, whatever she needed to do to finish this as quickly as possible.

She didn't know where to start. She moved in circles around him, fists tight and ready to go. She took a fast step forward to—

Fuck. A kick from Theon straight to her guts sent her a few steps backwards, and it took her a few seconds to catch her breath. Well, this was going to be difficult.

An hour later, Lenna was sweaty, her entire body screaming at her. She needed any strength she could find to push herself and stand up. How was she meant to beat him in this condition?

"Any tips to win a fight when I feel like crawling all the way to my bed?" Lenna said, looking to the high ceiling.

"I didn't know you were a crawler," Theon said, lifting his eyebrows with a sideways smile. Lenna couldn't resist her chuckle. "Tip for when you are tired beyond tired? Do not think. Let your body take over your mind. Your body knows the movements, but your mind is not letting go. Empty your mind and… let go of yourself."

She would be happier to let go of herself in his muscled arms and around his powerful neck and shoulders than have another fight. She closed her eyes. Cardinals give her patience. And focus.

Theon and Lenna adopted the fighting position once again. It was just them in the room. She was ready to let go of her mind. Knowing Theon, she trusted him not to inflict more harm on her than she could bear. As he shouted "Fight!", Lenna stopped thinking.

Lenna felt her body move by itself, as if she was watching someone else fighting, someone else blocking strikes, someone else counterattacking.

Theon gripped her wrist and tried to send her to the floor by twisting upwards, making her whole body move with it, but she twisted her way out of it. As she took one step backwards, she lifted her front leg and kicked him in the jaw.

Theon opened his eyes wide, a rough redness already appearing in his jaw. Lenna was equally surprised that she had actually touched him before he had time to block it, but that was not enough. She was going to finish this nonsense, never-ending fighting. She allowed herself half a second to let go of her mind and—it was too late.

Theon stood behind her, his chest against her back. He held her hands together behind her with one, too-fucking-strong hand, the other across her chest. He was so damn close, she could feel his warm, steady breathing in her right ear.

It was like time had slowed down. Lenna felt strands of his unexpectedly soft hair over her shoulders, and she was suddenly very aware of how comfortable his muscled chest was against her back, how warm it felt, exactly how many inches taller than her he was as his cheek rested against her wavy red hair. He was unusually still, as if he was also taking in this moment, breathing it in, absorbing it as much as he could.

Being careful to not move any other muscle on her body, Lenna lifted her right foot in the air, bending her knee in front of her. Gathering all the strength she hoped she had, she sent her heel down on Theon's foot at the same time as she moved her face to the right and bit down.

"Fuck!" Theon shouted, letting go of her hands as he moved.

Lenna used both hands to hold one of Theon's, and with a quick sweeping movement of her leg under his hurt foot, she sent him to the mat.

"About fucking time." Lenna was grinning in triumph.

Theon chuckled. "I knew you could beat me. I just wasn't expecting a dog-bite/elephant-stomp from a future panom, but still." Theon offered a hand to Lenna. "A beat is a beat."

Lenna stared at his hand, her grin still on her face. "Am I meant to shake this? Is this your official loser declaration?"

Theon laughed. "Oh, enjoy this as much as you want. You caught me off-guard. It's not likely to happen again."

Lenna was perfectly aware of how off-guard he'd been. She could still feel the warmth of his body behind hers, his breath on her ear.

She stood up, stretching her arms to release the tension from all the fighting. It had been draining, and she *definitely* wanted to get away from whatever *this* was.

Lenna started removing her makeup, patting creamed cotton pads around her cheeks. Her reflection was wearing bright yellow pajama shorts and a top, and a difficult-to-ignore, worried frown.

The last day of her not-yet-panom life had gone too fast. Even the tense dinner had gone fast, maybe because her sister and parents had been unusually quiet, as if they too had been thinking that their lives were about to change.

She was both excited and nervous. Lenna had been waiting for this moment since she could remember. She couldn't even count the times her mother had told Lenna that the Fifth Ceremony would mark a before and after in her life, that having unrestricted access to magic was dangerous and beautiful, how important it was to use it properly.

Lenna looked at her hand, seeing her reflection lifting it too, and opened it slowly, releasing golden sparks, allowing them to float around the wide marble bathroom connected to her bedroom. Over the years, she had somehow gotten attached to them, to their silent but bright and playful company.

Still, even the well-known sparks were not enough to avoid the guilt punch in her guts at remembering how she had tried to avoid thinking about Raoul. She had been postponing it after the Fifth Ceremony, and the days had gone too damn fast to even squeeze a moment to figure out what to do with her friend. His body being in the West House, and his mind Cardinals knew where. She felt the need to explain all of it to Theon. He tended to be matter-of-fact but positive, so maybe he wouldn't think the situation was royally fucked up.

Lenna peeked at the small silver clock on the wall of her bedroom. Almost ten o'clock. The sky was dark, and she had to be up by eight to get to the Organ House in time for past meridiem, when the Fifth Ceremony would start.

Theon would probably be partying in Borealia, as they didn't have a training session tomorrow, or maybe even enjoying some feminine company at his house. Lenna would have preferred her nostrils not to flare at the thought. It wouldn't be a good idea to contact him. In fact, it would be selfish.

They were friends. He was a disgustingly sexy friend, sure, but nothing had ever happened. Maybe it had been him not talking to her as if she was superior just because she was a panom-to-be, North House heir.

Theon wasn't like that. He had given her a hard time the first few months of training, laughing at her any time she complained, which was often. He had not seemed impressed when a maid entered the middle of a session with a towel to dry her sweat and give her a cold refreshment. Lenna could perfectly remember his are-you-fucking-kidding-me face. It had been the first and last time because the embarrassment Lenna had felt had reached a new limit at being treated like a fucking damsel in distress in front of the non-Elite trained warrior that was teaching her.

That was exactly why Ayla had three maids assigned to her. She loved being pampered and having help to get dressed and bathed and whatever the fuck they did together. Lenna had one maid assigned to her, because her parents refused to *leave her without service*. She sometimes was curious about what Irina, her middle-aged maid, did with her life, because Lenna's orders had only been to leave her alone, thank you very much.

He'll kill me for this but... fuck it, Lenna thought as she moved her hand in small circles to gather the exploring sparks. She sent the sparks with a message to Theon:

Can you come to my bedroom?
I want to tell you something.

She hadn't seen what the sparkly messages looked like when they appeared on his skin, but she hoped they weren't too bright or too obvious in case he had *some* company.

She suddenly realized her message had been way too serious, and she was probably overthinking it, but she sent some more golden sparks his way:

It's not because I want to rub
it in that you lost today. Oops.

And that was it. Inks sent. Silence.

"House, lights off," she said out loud, and the bright lights on her ceiling dimmed immediately.

Lenna made new sparks float around her as she laid on her bed, on top of her bronze duvet with floral details. She knew she could get in trouble if the Rulers found out that she had been using her magic before becoming a panom, but she trusted Ciaran to not get her in trouble, not when he could already have done so when he found them on the West House grounds.

Lenna didn't even know if her message would travel as far as the West House, but it was worth a try. She knew all the emotions and thoughts would not let her sleep much tonight otherwise. She sent the sparks, thinking about Ciaran and hoping he would know the message was from her.

Everything OK?

Less than a minute later, her forearm tickled, and she sat up with a halt as dark ink appeared on her skin:

No news. See you tomorrow.

As soon as she finished reading it, it was gone.

Lenna laid down again and stared at a picture of dawn falling over the Radel Sea on her wall. No news was not always good news, clearly. She could have hoped for many other answers to her hopeful question, but Ciaran was not the most expressive. At least he had replied. Still... *See you tomorrow?*

Her parents had never gone into much detail about the Fifth Ceremony, never actually said much, other than the five Rulers would be there and only panoms were allowed. Lenna had always assumed it meant her mother would be present, but if Ciaran was going to be there, there was a high chance panoms of every House would as well, and she knew of another silver-eyed panom who was likely to make an appearance.

13

Lenna

Lenna opened her eyes and miraculously resisted a scream when she saw Theon sitting on her chair, his arms crossed and head leaning on the wall. She had left the balcony door open on purpose, even though a part of her had felt stupid doing so. Cardinals, how long had he been sleeping in that chair? It was still pitch dark outside.

"Theon," she whispered from under the duvet. He didn't even move. "Theon," she insisted, a bit louder, with no success.

Lenna stood, ruffling her hair and regretting the open door as she felt the cool air on her exposed legs. She walked towards the chair and kneeled in front of him; she didn't want him to sleep in a chair for the rest of the night, especially not when he had come because she had asked him to.

Lenna slowly put a hand on his thigh, feeling the texture of his dark jeans, hoping to wake him up without a scare. Theon opened his green eyes, moving no other part of his body as he stared at her.

"Hi," she whispered with a smile. She looked at the clock on her wall and...damn, she had finally fallen asleep after ante meridiem, and it was two fucking thirty. She couldn't go to the Fifth Ceremony with two hours of sleep. "I need to sleep; we can talk in a few hours."

Theon looked at her and nodded in silence. He adjusted his body on the chair to get comfortable.

"You can come to the bed if you want," said Lenna, fully aware of how it sounded. "It's big enough," she added. *It's big enough that we won't touch each other.*

Theon cleared his throat. "Are you sure?" His voice was low and cautious.

Lenna stood up and went straight to her spot under the duvet on one side of the four-poster bed that could easily accommodate three people. "Unless you prefer to not be able to move your neck for the next couple of days," she said, and tugged herself. The temperature under her silk duvet was so much nicer. "Night."

Theon didn't move from the chair for a couple of minutes. Two minutes that felt like two hours. He then took slow steps towards the other side of the bed and—Was that him removing his shirt? Cardinals' fuck.

She felt his weight as he laid down on the other side of the mattress and she felt some relief at him not going under the duvet. *Thank each and every single Cardinal,* because she didn't trust herself to keep her hands to herself and it was too damn late. She took a deep breath and closed her eyes, hoping a kind Cardinal would send sleep her way so she wouldn't collapse in the middle of her damned Fifth Ceremony.

Light came through the windows and the glass balcony doors when Lenna woke up to an interesting smile on Theon's relaxed face. His head leaned on his hand with a propped elbow, and he only wore his dark trousers. It was a great morning view, but maybe too motivating.

"I must admit," Theon started with a sideways smile, "that after your request, I was not expecting such a... snoring welcome."

"Asshole. I didn't think you would come, you know."

He used a hand to comb his brown hair, a more unconscious movement than an actual attempt at straightening his rebel strands. "I had my doubts, believe me," he said. He put a hand in his pocket, and the movement marked every single muscle on his arm and his abdominal wall of steel. "But then I remembered..." Theon took out a small box from his pocket and gave it to her with a smile. "Happy birthday, Lenna".

Lenna couldn't find any words as her stomach tightened, and she sat down on the bed, crossing her legs on top of the duvet as she picked up the small white box. With all the fuss about the Ceremony, she hadn't even remembered that today, she turned twenty-five. Twenty-five was a sacred number in Thyria, marking the first quarter of a century and its closeness to the Cardinals. That Theon had remembered filled her heart with something very similar to joy.

She undid the elegant lace that held the box together and gasped at the precious golden blade with a rose carved on its side. It looked like it was made centuries ago.

"This blade gives strength to souls who crave it," Theon said.

Lenna managed to take her eyes off the beautiful piece and looked at him. It didn't look like something you'd find in Thyria.

"Where is it from?" Her voice almost broke from all the emotions.

"It's from Beyond," he said, confirming her suspicions.

Lenna admired it once more. Even if a part of her was dying to know how he had obtained such a thing, there would be many opportunities to talk. As there would be opportunities to talk about all the Raoul situation. Everything seemed less relevant right now. As if the world was on hold for them. For this.

"Thank you, Theon. It's beautiful."

Theon looked at her and put a piece of her red hair behind her ear. "My pleasure." His voice was low, his eyes intense. The skin on her back felt tight.

She stopped his hand in the air and put it on top of her thigh. It felt warm and familiar, as if it belonged there.

A part of her wanted to get her lips on his, to explore *all* of him with absolutely no rush. Another part of her hesitated that whatever that would mean would change their relationship forever. She wasn't sure she was ready to even consider losing a true friendship over some...high temperature closeness? Whatever this was. Theon squeezed his hand on her thigh, and Lenna felt the nerves in different parts of her go crazy at the touch.

How long had they been staring at each other? Someone knocked on her door, and it felt like she had been slapped. Theon quickly removed his hand from her thigh and stood, looking for his shirt. It was only after the second, more insistent knock that Lenna realized she hadn't replied.

"Yes?" she shouted, not bothering to keep the annoyance from her voice.

"Miss Lenna, we should start getting you ready for your special day," Irina begged. Lenna couldn't blame her, though. She had always refused her help to get dressed, but today's attire was too complex to put on without help.

Theon was heading to the balcony, picking his black jacket up from the table on his way and hanging it over his shoulder. He smiled at the recognition of Irina's voice and whispered, "Is that your towel lady?" he smirked. "Need someone to get your clothes off?" His wink and that sideways smile made Lenna's inside twist.

"I can very much do that myself," Lenna chuckled as she stood, still holding the golden blade in her fist. She took some steps to cut the distance between them and added with a hand on her hip, "unless you'd be up to help?"

Theon's eyes darkened, and his chin moved slightly upwards, considering the challenge. "It would be about time," he chuckled, taking a step closer, "to finally have some fun." His voice was low and damn all the Cardinals if it didn't make many parts in Lenna tighten. He lifted a finger to her ear, and slowly, *very* slowly, he moved it down her shoulder, making her yellow strap drop as he moved.

"Miss Lenna?" Irina insisted with another knock. Theon's finger stopped on her skin, and Lenna closed her eyes. It had to be very damn late for Irina to be insisting like that. She didn't want to look at the clock on her wall. She didn't even want to open her eyes and see exactly what she was about to be missing out on.

Lenna felt Theon's soft hair brushing her cheek as he inclined his head and placed his lips on her collarbone. Her knees wanted to give in. Her hands wanted to rip his clothes off. "I'll see you soon," he said in a low, soft voice. Lenna opened her eyes in time to see him leaving through the big balcony and jumping.

Another insistent knock was followed by a pleading, "Miss Lenna, *please.*"

Lenna took a deep breath. She'd need more than one to get her to cool the fuck down. That squeeze on her thigh. That warm kiss on her collarbone. For Cardinals' sake, how was she meant to concentrate on anything else?

She walked towards the door, and she found an almost teary Irina holding a full rack of attire and accessories and hairstyling and Fifth knew what else.

Irina exhaled deeply. "Thank you, Miss Lenna. We must hurry."

14

Lenna

Lenna looked through the window of the waholt at the houses they were passing at a vertiginous speed. She couldn't help but acknowledge the advancements that made the floating vehicle incredibly comfortable. Even at such speed, she could not even feel a tremor or a noise.

Her chest felt small as she observed the buildings where people lived in the suburbs of the North Petal, each second farther from the North House grounds and its closest city: Borealia. As they approached the Organ Core, the circle-shaped territory in the middle of Thyria that held the Organ House in in the middle of the capital, Corentre, the scarcity of trees or nature because of lack of space between the cramped half-broken buildings made Lenna feel breathless. That people lived like this when her father's gardens and any of the Elite's rich-ass manors could accommodate hundreds of citizens... It just wasn't right. Maybe when it would be Lenna's turn to rule, she could change something.

"I can't stand it," Ayla sighed from the opposite side of the wagon, shutting her curtain with a sharp movement. "Can anyone please remind me why people choose to live in these abhorrent, disgusting places again?" she asked in a bored tone, examining her manicured nails.

From the comfortable sofas around the delicate table, their father cleared his throat, a warning to Lenna to keep her mouth shut. They had heard her thoughts too many times.

Lenna snorted. "They live like this because their Ruler allows it," she said, looking at her father with a hateful smile. "This father of ours, I mean. The one sitting on a couch that costs more than a dozen of those barracks."

Father interlaced his hands on his lap and looked at Lenna. Him not saying anything for a few seconds made her brace herself for a storm. "We're not having this conversation today."

"Surprise, surprise," Lenna drawled, serving herself a glass of scented water from the drinks cabinet. "Is this when you give us the talk about playing happy family while we're in the Organ House? Because you can spare us the lecture."

Lenna could feel her mother's stare, her lips curled downward, her brows furrowed. Ayla was still standing tall next to the window with the curtains shut, expectant and eager to see how Father was most likely going to tell Lenna off. Even with her expression, she looked stunning.

The pearl dresses the sisters wore for their Fifth Ceremony were truly astonishing. Thousands if not millions of small transparent beaded pearls covered their bodies from the neck collar to the high heeled transparent shoes. The long sleeves ended in a diamond ring around their middle finger. When Lenna had first seen it, she had thought it would be both uncomfortable and extremely revealing. They were revealing because the minuscule pearls adjusted to every single curve of their bodies, but it wasn't exactly see-through thanks to the reflection on each round pearl. Somehow, her dress was extremely comfortable. It felt like a second skin.

Her father cleared his throat again, and Lenna was about to ask him if he wanted a fucking mint when he finally spoke. "It would be convenient to be seen as a cohesive family." Here was the talk, then. "Today will change your lives and those of everyone in Thyria. The focus will be on you."

Ayla lifted her chin a bit more, if it was even possible. Lenna was more excited about what would come after the Ceremony: becoming familiar with her magic and how to use it than the Ceremony itself. She had never been to a Fifth Ceremony before and no one had answered her questions during the past few weeks about what actually happened in there, so it was difficult to have any realistic expectations.

The waholt finally stopped, right in the poorest suburb at the edge of the North Petal, in front of the bridge that crossed the Jofryo River to the Organ Core. Tents made of branches and homemade bricks stood against each other, and skinny, barefooted children paused their ball game to stare.

Waholts were only used by the Elite or the Rulers around Thyria, and even though some families liked to use them frequently, especially amongst the Elite, they were unusual enough to make a bunch of kids stare at them. Technically, they were staring at the technological pomposity of the metallic floating vehicle, not at the people inside, since the windows were one-way only.

The driver's voice resounded through the speaker. "Waholt N462 requesting permission to enter the Organ Core at 10:47 ante meridiem on Sunday Fifth of May. Five passengers on board, all alive and in good condition." Lenna cringed at the need to specify their living condition. The driver continued, "Passenger Jasper Brachyan, blood panom, Ruler of the North House of Thyria. Passenger Veronica Brachyan, acquired panom, wife of the North House Ruler. Passenger Lenna Brachyan, human and panom-to-be, first daughter of the North House Ruler and heir of the North House. Passenger Ayla Brachyan, human and panom-to-be, second daughter of the North House Ruler. Passenger Anton Gerdan, human, driver of the waholt, speaking."

The silence that followed was tense. Lenna knew what the tight lips of her sister meant. How much Ayla hated to have been born second, by mere minutes, and therefore the second everything. Second daughter, second in line, second on the list. Maybe one day she'd grow out of it, but for now it stung her sister like a bunch of thorns thrown at her face.

Lenna was not happy with what she had just heard: her mother, her sister and herself had been described in relation to her father. Wife *of*, daughters *of*, as if they were no one by themselves, as if they were not worth a title, were it not because they were the relatives of the male figure of the North Ruler. As if they somehow belonged to him. She would have wanted to see how the South House members would have been described, as the Ruler was a woman. Would her life partner be described as "husband of the Ruler of the South House"?

The intercom broadcasted a female voice granting permission.

They started crossing the border after a glimpse of the kids waving goodbye while jumping and laughing, ready to resume their ball game on the street.

Ayla opened the curtain next to her with excitement in her face as they entered the Organ Core, like a child the first time they see a rainbow in the sky.

Ayla exhaled deeply, savouring their surroundings. "This is much better", she said with a grin as the waholt drove across the Organ city, Corentre, slowly.

Elegant buildings lined the clean, long streets that lead to the Organ House in the very center. Most were white, their entrances showing wide wooden or metal doors decorated with beautifully carved details of flora from Thyria.

The gardens and fountains in front of some buildings were impressive. It would take a handful of gardeners on a regular basis to keep them so beautiful. Floral trees in full bloom bordered the sides of the streets, and the gentle wind seemed to play along, occasionally sending red, orange and pink petals flying like a warm-colored rain under a sunny sky. Lenna couldn't help but wonder if this beautiful weather was the fruit of some panom influence. Regardless, it was probably one of the most beautiful views she had ever seen.

The citizens, most Elite members who were very well dressed, walked smoothly, in no rush, as if life could wait for them.

"I want to live here," said Ayla with a dreamy sigh.

"Well, you are going to live here for a while," their mother muttered, also looking through the window.

"What?!" A hopeful Ayla and an incredulous Lenna looked at their mother.

Father cleared his throat. Again. "We are not saying anything, Veronica." His voice was firm.

"What the fuck do you mean, *you are not saying anything*?" Lenna spat. "Ayla is going to be living here, and you are not saying anything?"

"We are *not* saying—" her father started.

"You too, Lenna," her mother cut.

Lenna didn't know whether to laugh or shout at them. Was this some sort of pre-Fifth novice joke? It couldn't be true. "Very fucking funny," she said.

"Don't talk to your mother like that," father told her.

"Or what? At least she is not keeping important information regarding our own damned lives from us. Who do you think you are?" Lenna knew she had gone too far, and she didn't care. The rage in her veins wanted to explode.

Her father stood up and paced towards her, the fingers of his hands meeting at the tips. "I am your father, and I am your Ruler. I rule over the citizens of the North, and as far as I am aware, you are a citizen of the North. Thus, I rule over your life." His voice was cold and calculated. "It would be good if you could stop acting like an annoying teenager for once, respect your parents, and while you're at it, shut your foul mouth at least on the day of your Fifth Ceremony, for Cardinals' sake." He had stopped two steps away from her.

Lenna's jaw clenched as she tried to get her shit together to avoid saying something stupid to the person in front of her. The person who she was supposed to *respect*.

What had he ever done to earn the respect? Other than wait on his ass for his father to die and then expect everyone in the North to obey him? Because he had been the son of a Ruler. The successor of the House. Was this what would happen to her when he died? When she became the North House Ruler? Because she sure as fuck didn't want this.

Ayla pointed to something in front of the waholt. "Is that the Organ House?" her voice was way smoother than usual. A drop of relief filled Lenna when her father stopped staring at her and walked towards the window Ayla was looking through.

Even from their distance, the House's splendour was jaw-dropping. The walls of the multiple towers were encrusted with precious stones, and the bright sun above them made the Organ House look alive. The House somehow reminded Lenna of the dresses she and Ayla were wearing: a castle made of jewels. Above the small towers and turrets, a massive glass dome crowned the Cardinals' Temple.

"All panoms, please be welcomed to the Fifth Ceremony," a friendly, neutral voice said across the air as they entered the ante chamber assigned to the North House.

A translucid glass door leading to the temple's door opened wide, an invitation to enter the brightly illuminated chamber beneath. Her father, as the House Ruler, led the way, and her mother shortly followed, giving a kind shoulder squeeze to Lenna and Ayla. Lenna appreciated the silent gesture. The door closed in front of the twins. They were not panoms. Not yet.

"This is it," said Ayla, shaking her hands as if she was trying to get rid of the tension in her body. The knot in Lenna's throat didn't let her say anything.

Maybe it was the birth connection that united twin souls what made them stand side by side in front of the double glass door. Maybe it was that silent bond that made them hold their hands together in the most important moment of their lives. They were waiting for whatever was about to happen and they were not alone. They had never been alone.

"Lenna Brachyan and Ayla Brachyan of the North House," the same voice started as the crystal door in front of them opened, "welcome to your Fifth Ceremony."

The sisters walked inside the massive chamber illuminated by sunlight radiating down through the dome at the top. Right underneath the dome, the floor was covered in dozens of interlaced translucent lines to create a circle. The panoms of the Houses of Thyria stood around the outer part of the circle. She didn't stop to pay attention to their faces. The lines on the floor filled with blueish liquid in front of Lenna and Ayla, inviting them to follow its trail to the centre of the temple.

As soon as Lenna and Ayla arrived at the middle, the panoms readjusted their positions so the circle they formed had no gaps around them. Unsure of what to do next, they faced each other.

Their vibrant red hairs were beautifully arranged and loose on top of the multi-pearl dresses that embraced their bodies. Lenna wondered if her own golden eyes would look as bright as Ayla's green eyes.

Post meridiem came, and the clouds vanished with it, leaving the sun casting its full powerful light in a straight line across the dome, right to where they were standing. Lenna held her breath as she felt the light penetrate every pearl that sat against her skin. She saw Ayla looking down at her in surprise, as if she was feeling the same warmth.

Their father was the first to move. He, as the North House Ruler, lifted his hands in front of him, both palms facing his daughters in the middle of the circle. "May the light enfold your strength," he said, and Lenna felt a powerful vibration flowing from his hands to their bodies, as if he was transferring a bit of him into them. She didn't take her eyes from Ayla's.

On the opposite side of the circle, Gabrielle Heliba placed her hands in front of her. "May the darkness accept your weakness." The South House Ruler's soft voice was heard across the chamber. Lenna felt another shot of power through her. The beads of her dress pulsed even more, as if they were also absorbing the powerful waves.

Ciaran's father, Cobrian Castel from the West House, spoke next. "May the world cherish your minds," the Ruler said, his hands sending invisible vibrations to the twins.

The East House Ruler put her hands up. "May the Cardinals guide your souls," Freya Baccate, the Ruler of the East House said, and Lenna felt her body trembling with power.

The Organ Mandor, Rhei Coralt, lifted his hands in front of him, both palms facing the sisters. Time seemed to slow down as he said, "May the Fifth unleash your magic." His voice was firm, full of authoritative power only a ruler of a nation had.

Lenna felt her own skin radiating with warm golden light. The same color her golden sparks had always been. The same color Theon said the ink of her messages on his skin had been. The same color her amber eyes sometimes were. She was glowing with sunshine.

She saw Ayla in front of her, shining with silver light. She was like the stars on a dark night. She was a silver lullaby. She was glowing moonlight.

The five Rulers moved their hands in unison, their palms now facing the dome above them. Their voices merged as they spoke.

"May the light enfold your strengths. May the darkness accept your weaknesses. May the world cherish your minds. May the Cardinals guide your souls."

The Rulers looked up as a beautiful red bird flew across the crystal of the dome towards the sisters: a cardinal. If Lenna hadn't been so focused, she might have had a heart attack.

"May the Fifth unleash your magic," they said as the cardinal reached the sisters and flew in quick, tight circles around them, lifting them in the air as it did.

Lenna knew it had happened. She could feel the fresh surge of power through her veins, through her heart, through her soul. It felt like a giant fireball, as if the other panoms had been merging their powers, blending them into one, welcoming them into the world with the help of a cardinal.

She could see it in Ayla's eyes too. She felt the mark permanently inked between her breasts: the four-petal panom and Thyrian mark.

Lenna and Ayla were not human anymore. They were golden and silver light. They were panoms.

15

Lenna

Lenna stared across the room to the Rulers sitting in a corner of the luxurious salon of the Organ House. Despite the fact that they had been talking for over thirty long minutes, some of them appeared to be struggling to keep their voices down and their emotions under control. Maybe some fun was about to start.

"Why are you so serious, golden girl?" said a masculine voice next to her. Lenna didn't have to look to know it was the Organ Mandor's son, Jake Coralt. The one who had kindly offered her to go discarding and his cock in the same conversation.

"It's my face to keep arrogant smartasses away," she said with a lip-tight smile, not bothering to look at the handsomeness that appeared to be in his mid-thirties. She took a long sip of her sparkling orange drink.

He laughed. "You amuse me."

Lenna took a deep breath. Surely her birthday and the day of her Fifth Ceremony was not the best day to make a scene, even to her low threshold standards. Plus, she was just not in the mood. She just wanted to learn about her magic and explore how to use it. Oh, and see Theon and finish whatever it was that they didn't finish that morning. Yes. She definitely also wanted that.

As the Rulers didn't seem to be about to start an entertaining argument, and since this man next to her didn't seem to plan to move somewhere else soon, Lenna put her glass down and walked outside, through one of the many corridors. Maybe she could find a peaceful spot outside to wait until they could go back to the waholt.

She was not even halfway down the marble corridor when she heard quick steps behind her.

"Not so fast, molten honey," Jake said.

Lenna stopped dead where she was. "Never call me that again," she said, her fingers curling, her jaw clenching.

He reached where she was standing and stepped in front of her, blocking her way. "I like how tense you get, sweetheart. I'm sure we could find a way to release all that tension."

"Kicking you in these balls that are obstructing my way would release some of my tension." She stared at him. "I'm more than happy to try."

"So fiery, Brachyan," Jake chuckled, a corner of his lips twisting upward. "Your dress suits you, by the way. It leaves nothing to my imagination."

Lenna was fully aware of every single curve the dress wrapped as tightly as a second skin. From her full breasts to her well-rounded hips, including her slightly narrower waist. She took a deep breath and stepped next to Jake to continue walking through the corridor. "Dream away," she said.

"We could do many things together", he said, looking at her from above, stepping in front of her again. "So many things."

Lenna knew her patience's end was just inches away. "Keep your efforts of an impressive superior man act for someone who might appreciate it," she spat. "My sister would enjoy listening to you."

Lenna felt a small part of herself flinching at her comment. The moment with Ayla before the Fifth Ceremony had been beautiful, yes, and the connection she felt while becoming a panom next to her had meant something special, but that didn't change how her sister was. It didn't change how much Ayla would love to be with someone of a status like Jake's. It didn't get any better than being the heir of the Organ House and therefore the future supreme Ruler of Thyria. Ayla would be thrilled with that.

Jake smiled, his silver eyes shining with amusement, stepping even closer to her. "I told you: where would the fun be in that?"

She would not back down. "I see. So women have to be fun to entertain your asshole majesty? So old-fashioned, Jake."

"You know exactly what I mean. Don't twist my words," he said, lifting his hand to her clenched jaw.

"Don't you fucking touch me," she said firmly, grabbing his wrist with her hand, stopping it in the air.

"Or what, sweet fire?" he said, letting out a breath that made Lenna realize how disgustingly close he was to her face.

"Or your balls will end up nailed to the wall." She twisted his hand around in a swift movement that made him let go.

"You don't learn, Jake," Ciaran's low voice said with a serious face. She hadn't heard Ciaran approach them, and by Jake's halt, it looked like he hadn't either. Ciaran nodded to Lenna. "I see you have this asshole under control."

Lenna shook her hands as if that would be any help to get rid of the anger in her body at the entitlement of the man. "He's a waste of space," she muttered between her teeth.

Jake didn't take long to stand tall and have his know-it-all look back on his face. "We were only talking about having some fun, Ciaran. Care to join us? I'd love to play with the North House hot heir and the West House cold heir at the same time." He winked with a smile that didn't meet his eyes.

Ciaran blatantly ignored him, silently inviting Lenna to walk with him towards a side corridor. She went to follow him, but her body slammed against an invisible wall between her and Ciaran. Lenna turned to see Jake holding an open hand in front of him.

"Hold on a second, Brachyan," Jake said, stepping closer to her. But he slammed against another invisible wall, raised by Ciaran.

"*You don't learn*, Jake," Ciaran repeated in a grave, menacing voice that sounded like a final warning.

Lenna put her hands on her hips and angled her head with a bitter smile. She wanted to shout at Jake what the fuck he thought he was doing, but she calmly said, "Your audacity has no limits, does it?" Without taking her eyes off Jake, she added, "Get your wall off, Ciaran. Let's hear what this prick has to say."

Jake stepped closer, wall now gone, and angled his head, meeting her stare. "He doesn't know you don't want a superior man protecting you, does he? Maybe he doesn't see what I see in you. Maybe he doesn't feel your power as I do. You will get to know me very well, Brachyan. You and all your golden sunshine."

"Oh, I don't think so. I don't waste a second of my life with entitled assholes."

Jake chuckled, biting his lip with true amusement. "Sorry to disappoint, but as your personal Panom Guidor, you are going to see me every single day for the next few months. We'll have lots of fun."

16

Hope

Hope was holding the compassom with both hands. A compassom here in Verdania. A compassom *in* the rose assigned to *her*.

She needed answers. She needed them *now*, and by the looks of it, whoever sent her that gift thought the same.

"Let's do this." Her mother sat next to her in front of the small pond of water lilies and lotus flowers.

Hope looked at her, lifting an eyebrow. She refrained from saying *About time* to avoid changing the apparent predisposition to talk. A very unusual, yet finally forced by the circumstances, predisposition. "I'm all ears."

Aurora scratched her neck, as if looking for the right words. She shook her head. "You are going to be mad at me."

"Can you please get to the point for once?" Hope didn't want to be rude, but she was not having another *I will tell you more another day*. No way. She'd had plenty of that all her life.

"Okay. What do you want to know?" Aurora's face was solemn yet determined.

Hope left the compassom on the floor next to her. So, this was finally happening. She braced herself as she asked, "Who is my father?"

"Cutting to the chase," Aurora sighed. "Your father is a very influential person in Thyria." Not as direct as Hope would like, but for her first actual answer in twenty-four years, she was going to take is as a good sign.

"How did you meet?" Hope's throat felt so tight.

"I was the commander of the Roix, as you already know, so I had to answer to the high rankings regularly. I was in touch with him for years." Aurora was looking at the pond with a painful frown as if remembering this hurt her deeply.

"But if you were the Roix Reigner, who were your high rankings? The Reigner is the top ranking of the Roix, isn't it?"

"Yes. I meant I had to answer to the Rulers."

Hope swallowed. "You got close with *a Ruler*?"

"Yes," Aurora said, letting go of a long exhale.

Fucking Fifth. That meant—

"So I am the bastard daughter of a Ruler?"

Aurora nodded in silence, now looking at her.

"Is that why they discarded you?"

"Yes and no. When I told your father I was pregnant, he said it changed nothing. He loved me, he said." Aurora chuckled with deep sadness. "I thought we would carry on in our secret love bubble as we had always done. I was stupid." She shook her head slowly, her top lip curling upward. "So fucking stupid."

"What happened?" Hope asked, a knot in her chest at her mother's pain.

"Someone came after you were born. I thought they were going to take you from me, and I was ready to kill them, but they said they had orders from the Organ House to scan you."

"To *scan* me?" Hope held her breath.

"With a compassom," Aurora clarified, her voice almost audible. "You have the panom mark, Hope. On the back of your neck."

Hope felt the floor was unstable and thanked the Fifth for already being sat down. Was it her ears buzzing or had the woods gone silent? She looked at the compassom with wide eyes, realizing exactly what anyone would see if they placed the device at the back of her neck.

"They discarded us because I was proof," Hope concluded with a knot in her guts.

"You were the evidence of a Ruler's infidelity, yes. And you were a risk for the magical system. Any panom-to-be is a liability for the system."

Was that what she was, then? A panom-to-be? Hope wasn't sure she knew what to do with that information.

"How did the Organ House find out about you? About me?" Her voice was almost a whisper.

"Because your father is its Ruler. His name is Rhei Coralt. He's the Organ Mandor of Thyria."

Hope was plaiting Nina's shoulder-long hair without paying much attention. Her hands moved subconsciously, the movements as familiar as walking.

Nina almost choked on her apple when Hope explained the conversation with Aurora. "I can't believe you are a panom-to-be and the daughter of the Organ Mandor," Nina said, shaking her head, her ocean eyes so wide, Hope could see white all around them.

"I can't believe she knew and didn't tell me," Hope sighed, finishing the simple yet beautiful braid.

"I know," Nina stayed still while Hope caressed the loose strands of her white hair.

Hope had expected whatever her mother kept from her to be something big. Maybe not *this* big, but something hurtful enough that Aurora avoided the subject and shut her emotions during years.

"I understand she didn't want to explain about my father and what happened between them, but she also forgot to tell me I am a panom-to-be? Not to mention I didn't even know what a panom was until you mentioned it the other day, for Fifth's sake." Betrayed, that's exactly how she felt.

Nina turned around to face her. "I know exactly what you feel."

Hope looked at her warily. Her friend's face showed empathy and understanding. Deep understanding.

As if reading the silent questions in Hope's mind, Nina clarified, "My parents never told me what they were really working on at the North and West Houses. I never got the chance to ask them before they disappeared."

"Are they here?" Hope's brows raised.

Nina shook her head. "My brother didn't find them in Verdania, and I had no better luck. My best guess is that they are dead." Nina sighed, as if she didn't know which option was worse.

"Cardinals. I'm sorry," Hope said.

"I wonder if it is related to why Raoul ended up discarded here, you know?" Nina wiped the corner of her eye, looking at the reddish sky above them. "Have you tried the compassom?"

Hope took out the transparent square from her pocket. "No, I haven't." Not that she could see the back of her neck even if she tried.

"Do you want me to try?" Nina asked with raised eyebrows that did not hide her excitement.

Since her mother had already told her, it made little difference to have Nina check.

"All yours." Hope handed the compassom to Nina without a second thought. Right before any possible regret set in.

Nina's warm hands gently moved Hope's dark hair from her back to one of her shoulders, leaving the back of her neck exposed.

"I am so nervous. I hope it doesn't explode or something," Nina chuckled nervously.

"As long as we don't explode with it," Hope laughed.

Nina exhaled. "Here we go."

Hope felt the cold glass against the skin on her neck, so damn cold it almost burned. Nina gasped.

"What is it?" Hope urged.

Nina scratched her forehead while still holding the compassom to Hope's skin with her other hand. "Is it meant to be red?"

"*You* ask *me*?" Hope's nervous laugh felt like a knot in her throat. "Is it the same four-petal mark we saw on the cave?"

"Yes, it is definitely the panom mark. The same shape as Thyria. But it is red. Like... very red. Does it hurt?"

Hope hesitated. "A bit. It burns like icy fire. Why?"

"Because it reminds me of arterial blood."

17

Lenna

"Welcome to your private chambers, Miss Brachyan," a middle-aged Organ servant said as she opened the door.

"Just Lenna," she said as she entered the—"Excuse me, what did you say this is?"

"Your private chambers, Miss Lenna. If they are not to your liking, I am sure we can find another unit that better suits your needs."

Lenna looked at her "private chambers" again and found it hard to believe the frown on the servant's face was honest. How could anyone not find this to "their liking"? Even if the Organ House was notoriously known for being the richest and most luxurious of all Thyria, Lenna hadn't imagined this is how they treated their temporary guests.

"This will do," she said. She could have sworn she heard the servant's relief behind her. "Sorry, what is your name?"

"Clara, Miss Lenna. It's my pleasure to assist you in any way you may need," the lady with exotic features followed Lenna inside.

Lenna looked around and snorted. Of course, it was a four-petal shaped apartment. The circular living room they were standing in could easily accommodate twenty or thirty people on all the couches and main table. It connected to two enormous bedrooms with ensuite. There was also a kitchen that smelled like warm bread and fresh fruit, and a strange, empty room with glass panel walls.

"What is this room for?"

"It's a live room. It can be adapted as you wish. You can ask the House or select whatever options you want on the deliseen," Clara said, pointing to the rectangular panel attached to the wall.

"That's some fancy shit," Lenna chuckled, touching the deliseen and waiting for it to recognize her pupils before showing her a list of popular options. Art room, music room, library, live concert... Maybe she wouldn't bore to death these months she needed to stay in the Organ House until she had mastered her panom powers.

Months with that man as Panom Guidor. For Fifth's sake, how could the most exciting moment of her life suddenly feel so dreadful? She had been so focused on becoming a panom and gaining access to her real vault of magic that she had given little thought about what was actually going to happen right after. Her new powers... They had settled in her veins, in her blood. She could feel a subtle yet constant pressure inside her, in tension and waiting patiently at the same time. Ready for Lenna to access, if she only knew how.

"I will leave you now, miss Lenna. If you require any assistance, please ask the deliseen or the House and I'll be here shortly. A special dinner to welcome our guests will served at eight past meridiem in the Core Salon,"

Clara's courtesy was an elegant half bow. Lenna didn't want to put her off too much after just meeting her, but she definitely planned to ask her to stop all the bowing, reverential stuff next time.

She headed towards the biggest sofa in the central room as soon as Clara shut the door, spreading herself in a very non-heir-appropriate way. It was so comfortable it almost improved her pissed-off mood.

Her father's order to "appreciate the effort of the Coralt family to provide the best panom education available" was nowhere near happening anytime soon. Lenna had told her father to fuck off when she heard the truth from his own mouth: Jake Coralt was indeed going to be her Panom Guidor. Ayla and she were going to spend *months* in Corentre. Fan-fuck-ing-tastic.

Lenna wasn't sure if she was more annoyed that her Guidor had to be precisely *that* one, or that she was going to be stuck in an unknown city for the Cardinals knew how long.

Yet, here she was. In another house. In another city. By herself on the evening of her birthday. The prospect of having dinner with Cardinals-knew-who was not motivating. She sent some ink to Ciaran as she got changed into a sleeveless black jumpsuit.

I need fresh air.

Shortly after, dark ink appeared on Lenna's forearm, tickling where the words read:

I can moure us from the Dawn Gate.
See you there.

The deliseen had proved useful, showing Lenna a map of the House and indicating the shortcut least likely to encounter people at this time of the day. When she arrived, Ciaran was sitting on the edge of the high stone fence that bordered the Organ House separating it from the rest of Corentre.

"You didn't want a birthday family dinner?" Ciaran greeted her.

Lenna chuckled. "I've seen enough assholes today to last a lifetime, thank you very much." That included her father, Ayla, Jake and Rhei as a bare minimum. "Do you know any cool places in this city?"

Ciaran's mechanical arm moved as his metallic hand smoothed his long hair. "Is that what you want to do?"

Lenna hesitated. She quite fancied fucking Theon, but asking Ciaran to moure her to his house was definitely overstepping. "You know what? I don't even know what I fucking want right now, but if I stay in this massive House another second, I'm going to end up climbing the walls."

"Let's get out of here." Ciaran jumped off the fence and put his hand on the back of her neck as they vanished into the night.

The loud music filled her ears at the same time as the bright lights made Lenna close her eyes. "Cardinals, where are we?" She smelled the cinnamon and salt in the surrounding air.

"Sweetgum Beech." Ciaran put a hand below her elbow to move through the crowd gathered around the source of the music. "It's worth opening your eyes."

Lenna frowned as her pupils adapted to the yellow, orange, and red lights around them. They were dim, but there were so many. Thousands of sparkling bulbs, all twinkling from the tall trees around the dozens of live fountains underneath. Even from their distance, Lenna saw where the music was coming from. In the middle of the square, there was a huge double fountain that spewed water at the music's rhythm. At its very center, a soaked band was playing enthusiastically, living their best lives.

There was definitely something more than human-made involved in such a spectacular show. Whether that meant panom hands probably created them or had some after-construction magical input, she did not know. The waves did not affect the strong and heart-filling sound and splashes around the instruments or the singer, but it amplified, so even people on the far ends of the Beech danced to it. Worth opening her eyes, indeed.

The people around them were grooving to the catchy music, ignoring Ciaran and Lenna as they walked closer to the main fountain. "This is insane," Lenna laughed as her soul and her head bobbed to the beat.

"Wait for it," Ciaran pointed to the blue-haired woman singing her way towards the guitarist on the other side of the fountain platform. The waves were now shaped like parabola curves as high as some trees. As the singer got ready to sing the chorus back-to-back with the guitarist, the water of the fountain started lighting up in a marvel of colors.

After hours of dancing, Lenna felt thirsty as the Fifth when the band wished them all a naughty night and disappeared inside the fountain. "That was so fun," she grabbed a bottle of myster from a crystal stand, the vendor not even looking at them when she left two valers on the counter.

"I knew you would like it," Ciaran winked, a corner of his lips tugging up.

Lenna elbowed him in the ribs. "Ever so clever." Even without the music, this place was magical. "You come here often?"

"Sort of. Some good friends live around here." The disbelief in Lenna's lifted eyebrows must have been obvious as Ciaran added, "Not everyone in the Elite is a piece of shit. There are some exceptions."

Lenna put a hand on her hip as she took a long sip from the bubbly myster. "I didn't take you for one of those Only-Elite-Friends-Allowed bullshitters."

Ciaran exhaled through his nose, not even a full chuckle as his blue eyes kept Lenna still. "I'd feel insulted if you thought so." He opened his biological hand with a distracted movement, sparkles playing on top of the palm. They were the same tone as the ink that had appeared on Lenna's arm before. "I was going to pay them a visit tonight. Want to meet them?"

"Shouldn't you be telling me to go to bed as it's already ante meridiem and I have my first panom instruction in a few hours?" Lenna lifted an eyebrow, the side of her mouth tilting up with it.

Ciaran crossed his arms, a challenging stare in his eyes. "I'm not your daddy. Do whatever the fuck you want."

"I'm always up to meet non-idiotic people." She winked with a wide grin. Especially if she was going to be stuck in this city for Cardinals knew how many months. She'd have to tell Theon about it, figure out how to help Raoul from here, try not to kill the arrogant piece of shit she would have as Panom Guidor and ignore her sister as much as she could. Maybe the myster helped her move those worries to a temporary drawer in her mind. There would be time to think about them—not tonight. Tonight, it was her birthday, and she was finally a panom.

The moonlit rooftop by the Jofryo river was something else.

"What the fuck is this?" Lenna asked, following Ciaran to a corner of the wide terrace. Shining, flickering bulb lights hung in the air as they walked through the benches and hammocks.

"It's an interesting mix of people in an interesting place."

"Very useful, Ciaran," Lenna said as they reached a group of people laughing.

"Look who dared to come say hi to the plebe." A beautiful woman with brown curls winked at Ciaran as she stood up, grinning widely while she hugged a stiff-as-hell Ciaran. He was always stiff as hell when it came to direct contact, though. Lenna knew it first-hand.

"Hello to you too, Sasha," Ciaran said with a friendly half-smile. Ciaran's repertoire of smiles with strangers was not vast. It pretty much could be simplified as his I'm-going-to-kill-you tuck of lips and his I'm-letting-you-live-for-now generous approach. His look now was neither of those, so definitely in the safe zone.

"Thanks for bringing fresh meat, Ciaran. I was getting tired of this bunch." The tanned woman tilted her head towards the group behind her. She turned to Lenna, still smiling. "Hi, I'm Sasha."

Lenna's eyebrow shot up at the sass and simultaneous friendliness of the woman in front of her, and she greeted her with a nod. A stunning blond man with immaculate features stood next to Sasha and put his arm around her shoulder—an arm that had more ink than many books.

"Brendon here," he said, his fingers caressing the top of Sasha's naked arm without paying much attention. "To whom do we owe the pleasure?" he asked Lenna, not taking his dark green eyes from hers.

"Lenna," she muttered, not too sure it had been a good idea to meet people at that precise moment. The day had been intense enough as it had been, and maybe she should have avoided this social awkwardness. Yes. It now seemed completely unnecessary.

"You mean Lenna as in Lenna-who-just-joined-the-panomy-club?" Sasha's eyes widened, and she stepped forward, examining her like she was a creature of another world.

"Oh, for Cardinals' sake, Sasha, keep your obsessions to yourself and give her a break, will you?" a young man snarked. He sat in front of them with a full glass of a purple drink. "She's a Scientist Reg in the Orster," he said, lifting his shoulders, as if that was justification enough. "And my sister." Lenna chuckled, her best attempt at oppressing a laugh at the resignation in his voice. "I'm Carson. I think you are at a disadvantage in this group of savages, since we all know who you are, and you clearly don't have a clue about us. I am the Gracier Officer at the Interpetal Bullef. Brendon works for the Invisible Grand." The blond man with green eyes did a mock bow, bending his upper body with a hand gesture as Carson continued, "And this lady next to me is the daughter of the Roix Reigner."

"*This lady* has a name," the black-haired woman with a perfect bob interrupted him. "Indianna. Don't judge me for being the daughter of such a bitch. I'm the first one who wants to kick her ass. I'm a healer at the Beftac Centre for Injured Beings, even though *this lot*," she tilted her head towards the others, "always seem to forget that bit."

"We would never forget that you fix all the people your mother orders her inferiors to hurt," Sasha walked towards Indianna and sat next to her on the soft, massive couch, putting a reassuring hand on Indianna's knee.

"Anyway, we're the good guys." Brendon winked, sitting back on one of the velvety couches and taking a sip of his transparent, thick drink.

Lenna spoke, not looking at anyone in particular, half asking Ciaran and half asking the four others in front of her. "I take it you are all Elite because you earned your value in society rather than paid for it?" That was highly unusual.

"She learns fast." Sasha grinned.

So, here were a top scientist of the labs better guarded by the Organ House, a communication consultant that helped ensure a respectful harmony between the petals and the Rulers and the Houses, an agent at the most secretive organization of Thyria, and a healer at the center the sickest people went who also happened to be related to the damned Roix Reigner. Damn all the Cardinals one by one if that wasn't an "interesting mix of people". And, of course, the panom heirs of the West and North Houses had just joined the party.

"These brains of ours were noticeable enough to shine during our education, and here we are," Brendon opened his arms in front of him, towards his friends. "Some of us still shine," he winked with a sideways smile.

"Some of us have a colossal head," Indianna retorted without taking her eyes from Lenna. Her stare felt like a ray penetrating her mind.

Some inner instinct told Lenna that the Organ Mandor, her own father back at the North House, and many other high-ranking commands would not be happy that such an alliance existed between these well-connected and influential people.

They didn't look like allies, though. How they moved and talked to each other... There was no apparent pretence-bullshit going on here, unlike what Lenna had very often seen in Elite gatherings. Or if there was, they hid it well. They seemed comfortable, including Ciaran, which was a very positive indicator, considering how take-no-shit he was. There was that unique familiarity that long-term friends have in the environment. That and—

"Why do I feel there is something missing here?" she asked Ciaran, lowering her voice, ignoring the fact that the others, who now were interchanging stares while smiling or grinning, could hear her.

Ciaran bit his bottom lip, his metal ring shining against his teeth. "I may or may not have donated some of my magic to them."

18

Hope

The news about Hope being a panom-to-be would have been way more exciting if she had known what to do with that information. Nina had told her that panoms used their hands to channel their magic, but no matter how many movements and complicated twirls or combinations she tried, the only thing Hope got closer to was stupidity.

"I'm done." Hope sat down, opening and closing her fists to stretch the fingers that had been submersed in an intense twisting activity and now hurt and were stiff as the Fifth. "That's as far as my imagination can go thinking about strange and not-strange things to do with my hands."

"Fair enough." Nina walked behind her in the grass patch and started giving a massage to Hope's shoulders.

Hope moaned, closing her eyes as she tilted her head upwards, "Oh Five Cardinals, you are good." Nina didn't reply as she continued with those

Cardinals-blessed relieving strokes on her shoulders and upper arms, but Hope could have sworn she was softly smiling.

By the time Nina took her hands off her body, Hope felt a deep improvement on her muscles and upper joints that had not been privy to many massages over the years of hard life in the woods of Verdania.

"Are you okay?" Two lines appeared between Nina's brows.

She gave Nina her best comforting smile. "I'm all good, thank you. I was thinking about what we are going to do next."

Nina started arranging some flowers she had picked before. "I've been thinking about that too, you know. Whoever sent us the messages and things maybe doesn't send anything else, or the Fifth knows if they get in touch again. Since the magic doesn't seem easy to learn..."

Hope appreciated Nina not saying it looked like all her attempts were a total waste of everyone's time and she better quit sooner rather than later. Nina continued, "I was going to suggest we might as well go to Cralia and carry on with the plan, see if we can find out anything else."

Oh yes, *that* plan, the one Hope had tried her best to forget. The one that involved Nina seducing a roixer—hopefully one who knew important stuff but didn't know enough to cause them trouble. That absolutely grand plan.

Hope took a deep breath and exhaled through her nose, her eyes fixed on the beautiful daisies and poppies Nina was knotting together in a small bouquet. It wasn't like they were doing anything useful by waiting in the treehouse, and magic-wise, she was definitely stuck.

"We definitely need to do something, especially now that we know where Raoul is," Hope finally said.

Nina shook her head. "I can't believe Raoul is in the West House, and that you just found out your father is... Well, wherever the Organ Mandor is. The Organ House in Corentre, I guess?"

"The books always mention that's where he resides. Everyone is in Thyria and here we are, arranging bouquets." Hope chuckled.

Nina's soft laugh was a beautiful melody in Hope's ears. "It's almost like Thyria is calling us."

"Someone is definitely calling us. Let's see if we can figure out a way to get there without getting killed."

The brownish plant-based dye on Nina's hair suited her almost as much as her usual snow-white tone, and it was going to have to be enough to avoid any recognition amongst the Roix. Considering she had not been in Verdania for long, the chances of avoiding identification were higher, or at least that's what Hope kept telling herself.

Hope and Aurora had weapons strapped to them from head to toe, mainly daggers and blades sheathed securely around their thighs and waists. Nina was armed with a red jumpsuit that exposed the pale skin on her back and under her ribs, with interlaced red straps that revealed every curve of her body. .

Walking in circles around her to double check, Hope confirmed the small pocket where Nina kept her red vial was unnoticeable. She hadn't realized a very skilled tailor was probably more likely to save her friend's life with her work than Hope or Aurora would be if they didn't get to Nina in time.

After debating whether to say something or not for longer than Hope wanted to admit, she let the words leave her mouth. "You don't have to do this, mother."

"Excuse me?"

"You don't have to do this," she repeated. "Trying to come to a place you hated, to a being that hurt you and abandoned you. You shouldn't risk your life for answers you don't need."

"I don't need the answers, but I need *you*, Hope." Aurora swallowed. "If you want to go to Thyria, I will go with you. If you want to sail the seas, I will go with you. If you want to fly the skies, I will go with you. I will not abandon you. Under any circumstances. Ever."

Hope found herself smiling despite the sudden blurry sight caused by unexpected tears and emotion that knotted her love in her throat. "Thank you. This means everything."

Aurora smiled back at her and turned to Nina. "Ready?" Aurora whispered in the small side alley that led to the plaza crowned by the Roix quarters.

Nina nodded, her eyes fixed on a door in front of which different young people now gathered, some casually waiting, some chatting and smiling, all of them dressed way too nice to be common Verdania villagers. Some clothes and jewels they bore had most definitely been gifted by the roixers unless they had gotten them from the Trading Table. Wasn't it about survival, at the end of the day? These people were very much alive, so whatever they had used to survive had clearly proved useful.

Hope squeezed Nina's hand and kissed her friend's cheek, her skin soft against her lips. Nina squeezed it back and looked at Hope. Before Hope could tell her it was not too late to reconsider using her beauty and intelligence for this purpose, or more so, through *these means*, the double metal door opened.

The artificial light from inside brightly illuminated the villagers. The laughter, hugs, and jokes were loud enough to scare any wandering animals, and Nina inhaled sharply as she prepared herself.

"I wouldn't go there if I were you." A male voice coming from the dark end of the alley startled Hope, the daggers ready in her hands before she could fully acknowledge the threat. She took a small step in front of Nina, shielding her. A shiny reflection revealed Aurora's daggers were already out. From the *beings* standing in their hiding spot, Hope corrected herself, as another shadow appeared next to the man's one.

The ricochet in the square was distracting and noisy. If Aurora and Hope killed the new arrivals, probably no one would notice. As if her mother had read her mind, she whispered "*Vitam,*" the first part of their long-term killing cooperation agreement.

Hope clenched her fists on the hilts of her daggers, an unconscious movement as natural as breathing, as she formed the second and last word of the mother-and-daughter pact "*Tra—*"

"Don't you fucking dare, Aurora," said a different voice from behind Nina. Hope adjusted her position, leaving her friend on her own against the wall. Still, she held her daggers at the ready, each to one side of the alley.

Where were these people coming from? There were no windows here, part of why they had chosen this alley, and the ends leading to the busy and loud square and the very empty street on the other end were too far. Hope did not risk a single glance up as there were three of them here, but could perfectly picture the building around them being tall. If they had jumped from there without letting them notice... *Fuck, they were good.*

The brief shock at such realization and the unforgettable fact that the man knew her mother's name. If anything, that could have been a better reason to slice them down to the ground, and no matter how good they were in the shadows or roof-jumping stuff, Hope very much doubted three of them could win against her mother and her. Still, she had not finished the second word of the agreement, the one that would give the get-go in any situation that potentially risked their lives, as they had practiced endless times.

Vitam tradere. A blood-bound effort to start killing to keep living.

Aurora sneered, "Give me a reason, Marcus".

"Only one? Can't pick, you know. For starters, we could have killed you any time in the last fifteen minutes. Aridian also told your pretty lady to not waste her time or life because we already tried what she was about to do. Our very skilled Aida was brutally fucked and killed at the hands of one of the brutes who used to work for you."

Hope's chest tightened as she inhaled sharply, taking a small step backwards so her shoulder plates touched Nina, needing to remind herself that she was warm and alive and safe behind her. For now, at least.

"Why would we trust you?" was all her mother muttered, not lowering her blade.

"Because I can take you to Thyria. Well, *your daughter* can take us to Thyria, technically speaking," Marcus explained in a matter-of-fact way. "We need her help."

"Why would I help you? I don't even know who you are, and your people don't look like a very friendly bunch." Hope's voice sounded more confident than she expected it to be.

Marcus chuckled before saying, "Courtrades, weapons down."

Hope could have sworn she heard movement not only in the alley and the roofs leading to the alley, but also in the buildings surrounding them. Cardinals, how many people were here?

He took a step closer to them, but Hope didn't relax her fighting stance. His short beard was perfectly cut, his dark eyes matching his dark hair.

"I am Marcus Olannet, courtrade from Orizane, and you are going to help me—help *us*—or otherwise, you will not get to Thyria."

As if the Cardinals would allow it to be that easy. "What makes you think I would want to go there?" Hope asked.

"Well, you were about to send the young lady you are protecting on a mission to be raped or killed by a roixer, so it doesn't take a genius to figure out you want something from them. I can't think of anything more important to risk a life for than information. Plus, considering your mother was discarded from Thyria many years ago, she probably wants some revenge. If you have any idea of the reason you two were discarded in the first place and what is on your skin, young lady, you would also want to go there and rip some throats off."

The knot in Hope's throat that kept her mouth shut was not just shock about meeting someone who apparently had known her mother long ago. It was also doubt. How could this man know about her mark? Was it common knowledge in Thyria, Orizane, or Cardinals knew where he had found out? Did anybody else know? A distant thought questioned if he would know what to do with her mark, magic, or powers, because she clearly didn't.

Aurora swiftly sheathed her dagger and spoke before Hope could reply. "Let's hear your plan, Marcus. But if you fuck us over, I will kill you. All of you."

Marcus smiled, his teeth flashing briefly under the dim light. "I expect no less from you, my dear."

By the time Marcus and Aridian had taken them to the windowless building they were now in, Hope had one thing clear: these courtrades weren't normal people.

She was convinced there had been at least a dozen of them in and around the alley, yet she didn't see a single one until they crossed the metal door. She wasn't even sure she could have spotted the building if Aridian hadn't stopped right in front of it. And the way they moved... Goosebumps rose on Hope's spine. They walked like they had a private dance with the night, as if the night was part of them.

The pale blue walls of the hall were full of beautiful patterns that resembled the waves of the ocean intersecting with each other, so different from the vast facade visible from the outside. Marcus had told them to wait there and Nina, who had been unusually quiet on their way and still looked magnificent, didn't wait to get closer to admire the artwork.

Stepping closer to her mother, Hope whispered, "Remind me who are these people again?"

"I thought the Rulers killed the last of them years ago. I don't know why they're here. But if courtrades want to go to Thyria, they are looking for trouble."

Except Hope, Nina, and Aurora *also* wanted to go to Thyria, and they didn't even know where to start. Sure, finding Raoul was one reason to go there, but Hope also wanted to look for her father. What next, she wasn't so sure about. Have a few words with him? Tell him what a piece of shit he was for discarding her mother to a semi-survival island with a newborn baby who happened to be his daughter? Ripping some throats off didn't seem such a bad idea after all. It was more than well-deserved, especially as Hope remembered all those years when her mother lived in silence with constant blurry eyes.

As for her mother, Hope had little doubt that she was solely here to protect her and not leave her alone in a search for answers that she had kept hidden for years.

She needed to figure out what to do with her mark. If it had been such a liability for her father that it had been the sole reason for getting them out of Thyria…Was he scared of it? Of her? Because if that was the case, she had even a better reason to figure things out. Hope's thoughts stopped wandering with Nina's gasp.

"What the actual Cardinals." Nina's finger was touching one of the thin lines on the wall. A line, Hope realized with surprise, that was moving slowly, separating from a bigger one and curving and stretching to connect to another one to its left.

Aridian, who stood quietly in a corner of the room, casually said with a tone that left little room for discussion, "It's a living map. Keep your hands to yourself, or someone will end up where they shouldn't."

A door to the right opened, and Marcus led them down a narrow corridor to a circular room with a long metal table. As soon as Marcus tapped the surface, forms and silhouettes appeared on it. Forms and silhouettes, Hope realized, that represented—

"The Frenya Archipelago," Nina whispered, confirming Hope's thoughts.

The waves of the false sea on top of the table were moving in unison, and different islands scattered around the dark blue depth broke the water's surface. Thyria was in the middle, with a four-petal shape Hope knew was secretly on her skin too. It was the biggest island by far. Verdania, with its uneven shape full of mountains and hills, was about a quarter of Thyria. There were some islands scattered around the waters Hope was pretty sure she hadn't seen on maps before.

"We're here." Marcus stopped walking and pointed to the mass that represented Verdania. "And we want to go there." He inclined his neck, his gaze fixed on Thyria. "I have over twenty people I need to take with me."

Aurora inhaled deeply next to Hope. "So many people? It'll be harder to stay hidden, if not impossible."

Marcus smiled with closed lips. "It's not up for debate. I need every single one of them. Besides, nobody is going to *see* us."

Over twenty people. Hope was not sure if she was more surprised by said number or his sheer determination, as if he actually had a workable plan to take them there and live to tell the tale.

Hope lifted her eyes from the islands and found his eyes staring at her. "That's where you come in." His voice left little space to argue. "We need you to avoid being *felt*, to fuel our method of transportation."

So confident, he was. So damn confident. Hope looked at Aurora, wondering if she was despising this man who wanted to boss them around to fulfill his own agenda as much as she did. Did he seriously think she was a mere asset to be used? Did he realize what a horrendous idea that was? Aurora didn't need to nod; Hope read it in her eyes.

"Do you know I am not a panom?" she said, her voice almost broken. It felt awkward on her lips, in her mind, to acknowledge her connection to something that the most powerful people in Thyria bore as an armor, something that still was foreign to her and yet was inked on her.

Marcus's eye half-twitched. "You are as close as we could find. The four-petal marks recognize each other. You have one, and that is better than none. That should work for us."

For *us*. The uncomfortable, almost unnoticeable sidestep Nina took next to Hope told her she had also noticed it. Marcus might as well have asked Hope if she could slice the mark from her neck and hand it to him, since it was clearly the only part of her that interested him. Still, Hope couldn't resist the question that followed.

"If you don't have a mark, what do you have?" Her lips thinned as her jaw clenched. It hadn't been the best worded question, but she didn't know how to phrase what she felt around them, about how they moved and interacted with the darkness.

Marcus' chuckle didn't reach his hard-as-steel stare. "I didn't say I don't have a mark. Courtrade business is no one else's business. But unlike you, I don't have the four petals on me."

Aurora's fist closed in a way Hope read as *my daughter's business shouldn't be courtrade business either.*

The scar on her mother's neck, a constant reminder of the cruel past, was enough for Hope to say, "What do you need me to do?"

19

Lenna

A pillow on top of Lenna's ears made it easier to ignore the music the deliseen had started playing in an unsuccessful attempt to wake her up. She was almost succeeding when knocks hit the door of her chambers.

Lenna almost screamed when she felt the tickling sensation on her forearm as silver ink appeared. With a tremendous effort to half-open one eye, she read:

If you dare be late to your first panom lesson, I swear I'm going to be even more ashamed of being your sister.

Lenna let out a growl and shouted across the room to make sure it reached the door, "Look who has learned a new way to make my existence miserable."

"I'm not joking. How dare you be so irresponsible," Ayla shouted through the door. Oh, she was pissed. Ayla was very well pissed and Lenna stood up with a silent laugh and a big grin.

Lenna yawned as loudly as she could and immediately heard a stomp and some more angry door-banging. "I swear if I'm late because I've been chasing you..." Almost boring how easy it was to piss Ayla off.

Lenna dragged on some tight leather leggings and a translucent shirt that left little space to imagination. She opened the door just as Ayla was about to start another banging frenzy.

"About. Time," Ayla scoffed, her lips in a line as she took Lenna's hand and pulled her towards the other side of the corridor. Why did she even care so much about Lenna being late anyway?

Lenna had no clue where they were going. She hadn't bothered to find out where she was going to spend so many hours with Jake fucking Coralt learning the only thing she cared about.

Why the Fifth damned her so the most exciting thing of her life had ended up being something she dreaded, she was not sure. Surely she had to have pissed the Cardinals badly enough for her panom instruction to be taught by entitled prick number one. Cardinals guide her.

Jake's stare almost pinned Lenna on the spot when they entered the massive bronze doors of the Coronary Atrium. She did not balk from those silver eyes and stared right back at him.

Next to him, Gabrielle Heliba was waiting for Ayla with a friendly smile. Lenna remembered the South Ruler from a couple of visits when she was younger.

"Morning, girls." Gabrielle's voice was soft, layered with the patience that only expertise could give.

"Morning," the twins said.

Lenna smiled at Gabrielle, remembering how kind she had always been with her when she was little. She had been a panom for Cardinals knew how many years, so she surely knew an awful lot. "Can we not swap Panom Guidors?"

Ayla's superior smile was another punch in the gut. She surely was enjoying seeing Lenna beg for something she had.

"You're mine, Brachyan," was all Jake said.

Lenna snorted. "I'm not into any of the male possession bullshit, and I'm very much not yours." The corner of his lips twisted upwards as Lenna added, turning towards Gabrielle, "I just don't think it's fair that Ayla gets the actual powerful, wise panom Ruler as a teacher, and I just get the wannabe."

Jake didn't even flinch, didn't even take a step; only his hands moved as Lenna felt the air leaving her lungs. He whispered into her head, *Let me prove you wrong, sweet fire*. Her legs moved against her will towards one of the closed doors in the marble hall.

A couple of seconds later, Lenna found herself breathing fast, the air given back to her. *Fuck*. It had all happened so fast, she barely had time to tell him to fuck off before he taped another door a few times, opened it, and led her inside with an "After you."

"You're disgusting," Lenna spat. "Genuinely. If you think choking me and forcing me to move is going to convince me, you couldn't be more wrong."

Jake ignored her, walking towards four stands on the other side of the room. The high ceilings were covered in something that looked like galaxies. Whether they were realistic paintings, pictures, or something else, Lenna couldn't tell.

Lenna continued, a few steps behind him, "I get you just want to piss me off by proving a point about how dominating and powerful or whatever you think you are, but I am so tired of all that shit already and we haven't even started."

Jake didn't reply, not even looking at her as he stopped in front of the first stand. They were four crystal orbs, one next to the other.

Lenna stepped between him and the orb. "Can you even be bothered to answer?" From this close distance, her voice was way louder than she intended to, but fuck him and fuck his silence, too.

For a moment, Lenna questioned how much she'd be willing to give up for the chance to kill him. Then he said, "Answer what, exactly?" She could have sworn he was biting his bottom lip, as if trying to avoid laughing in her face.

"Are you taking the fucking piss?" she spat, baring her teeth.

Jake's eyes had dark speckles in the middle of the silver, and that he towered over Lenna didn't intimidate her one bit.

"That is the first question I hear from your pretty, foul mouth," his eyes flickered, and Lenna was convinced that was freaking amusement shining on them. He continued, "You just ranted about what a scumbag I am and how sorry you feel for yourself. Now, if you're done, I can actually start showing you how your magic works, unless you'd rather be a martyr for a bit longer."

Lenna inhaled sharply through her nose. She wanted to strangle him. "Go on then. The sooner we start, the sooner this will be over."

"Fantastic," he smiled, and damn him if he wasn't a gorgeous prick when he smiled.

Jake raised his hands, and with a couple of moves, the stands disappeared, and the four crystal orbs floated around them, making a square, Jake and Lenna were in the middle of it.

He faced Lenna again. "Five Cardinals, five Houses, five parts of the panom."

He opened his hands, and a representation of Thyria appeared on the marble floor underneath them. Lenna and Jake standing where Corentre was on the map, each orb floating over one petal.

"Thousands of years ago, each Cardinal ruled a unit of the panom. Each of them had a unique type of magic. The North Cardinal could Give. The South Cardinal could Take. The West Cardinal could Heal. The East Cardinal could Harm."

"And what about the center of the panom? The circle in the middle?" Lenna asked.

He opened his hand, and the Core shone under their feet.

"The Core Cardinal was the key to keeping the balance, harmony be-tween the opposite magics so the land would not collapse. She was the one who intertwined the sources of power so each panom could use them, not just the one that belonged to each House."

Lenna's eyebrows raised. "So I can do these four magics?"

Jake nodded, chuckling at her impatience, "You will be able to when you learn to control them." As he closed his fists, the map underneath them disappeared.

"Now tell me which magic is this." Jake closed his hand, and the crystal orb in front of them was cut in half, the top vanishing.

He made it look so easy. And the movements of his hands, the way the muscles in his inked arms flexed, was slightly distracting.

"Surely not Healing. Where is it?" Lenna couldn't see it anywhere in the room.

"I Took its half," Jake said. "Whenever you Take, a part of your magic is uneven. Quite similar to how a weighing scale would move towards one side when given too much weight." He walked towards another orb, putting the hand on top. "To reestablish your inner balance and find harmony again, you must Give." Jake opened his fist, and a silver rose appeared in the center of the orb. Beautiful.

"I see. So Taking and Giving are opposites on the harmony scale, and so are Hurting and Healing?" Lenna got closer to smell the silver rose through the opening of the orb.

"Indeed, except Hurting and Healing need way more expertise to dominate."

So the magic of the North and South petals had their own balance, and so did the magics of the East and West.

Jake approached the third orb. He opened his hands, and the orb became a massive snake slithering towards him. Lenna resisted the incredibly powerful urge to move the fuck away from the beast precisely at the time that

Jake lifted his hand and, with two fingers, traced a line across the snake's body. The head was cut, now rolling over the floor.

"This is Harming."

Lenna swallowed. "Would you mind letting me know the next time you are going to bring a dangerous beast to a room I'm in? Please and fucking thank you?"

Jake didn't look at her as he walked towards the fourth orb, again opening his hand. "Now."

Lenna inhaled deeply, getting ready for the worst, when the orb became a small, brown puppy. His rear paw was bleeding, and he was sprawled on the floor, whimpering.

Jake kneeled next to him and hovered his hand over the injured leg, tracing a circle filled with navy sparkles. *His* color. It looked as if part of a navy galaxy had penetrated the circle, and was irradiating towards the leg. "And this is Healing."

Shortly after, the puppy barked, his tail wagging as he attempted to climb Jake in a succession of failed attempts.

"You're welcome," Jake laughed as he stroked the spot between the puppy's ears. "Try to avoid picking a fight with a snake next time." He moved his hand, and the puppy was gone. Jake stood up and found Lenna's wide eyes, as if she had seen something as unexpected as the snake.

Clearing her throat, Lenna asked, "What happens if the scale is forced too much to one side?"

"If a panom uses too much of one magic without using its opposite, the magical core of the panom is at risk. The least that can happen is that they lose consciousness. The worst that can happen is death." Jake moved a finger horizontally across his neck. "Hence why the *general* advice is that it's better to not force your inner harmony."

"And your *personal* advice differs from that?" Lenna raised her eyebrows.

Lenna could have sworn Jake's stare was penetrating her own damn inner harmony, his eyes piercing her with intent. He interlaced his fingers in front of his chest.

"My personal advice is to challenge yourself, to push your own boundaries. Only you can find your limit, how much is too much on your personal scale, how far you can go. What is the depth of your core and how to stay alive even when your harmony is uneven. If you never discover that, you will just be a mediocre panom, like so many others."

Lenna swallowed, keeping that advice safe to analyse later. "It seems wrong, though. There are five Houses, five Cardinals, five parts of the panom, but only *four* magics?"

Jake walked calmly towards her, eyeing her from bottom to top. Lenna became a bit too conscious of her completely translucent top as he slid his eyes over her chest until he met her eyes.

"There is no record of anyone alive with the Fifth Power. It's mainly a myth at this point, but it existed. It was both a curse and blessing to those who gained it." His voice was deep, as if this topic was relevant to him.

Lenna almost felt bad at the number of times she had cursed the Fifth and every single one of the Cardinals.

"What about the... sparks?" she asked, lifting her open palm, facing upwards as she made some golden sparks appear on top, dancing with each other.

Jake nodded. "There are some fun perks that come with our gifts. Sparks and inking are the most common ones. They have the color of the panom's inner core, and no two colors are ever the same."

Jake walked towards the center of the room as he opened his fists again, and a line of orbs appeared in a neat row in front of him.

"Now, let's see what you can do," he said. Lenna's chest tightened, probably due to the fact that it was her first time attempting this and at the pure challenge in his eyes.

20

Hope

After days working together, Hope knew two things: Marcus had been preparing the escape to Thyria for more years than she had been alive, and there were so many things from his plan that could go wrong that she had almost lost track. Maybe that was a Cardinals' blessing, for the sake of her bravery not faltering when they departed.

Hope was still not used to being inside the vessels, and she felt somehow relieved to not be the only one. The circular tunnels filled with air in the middle of the ocean felt so unnatural. They *were* unnatural, Marcus had told them, since the Cardinals had created them when Thyria was formed.

Nina's steps next to her were as cautious and silent as her own. Stepping over a thin membrane that protected them from falling into the vast depth of the ocean underneath them was breathtaking. No matter how many times Hope had walked the vessels underneath the courtrades' quarters, she still did not trust that the membrane of the tunnel, transparent with just a smear of turquoise shine, would not vanish, leaving them to drown.

"I still can't believe that this is safe for anyone to walk in, let alone for vehicles," Nina said, pushing a strand of her silk-white hair behind her ear. It had only taken a couple of days for the natural brown dye to completely fade and her natural white to shine again.

Hope silently nodded, kneeling for the tenth time that day, poking her finger at the surface that separated them from the waters below and from every single creature that lived in them.

"As if cellholts are small and light," Hope's voice was hoarse. She hadn't been talking much and the air down here... It was rough. A normality in the vessels, apparently, that no one else seemed too concerned about.

Nina exhaled sharply. Hope stood up and stroked her hand. A silent reminder that she also wished they had a better alternative.

A few minutes later, they had returned to the blind spot that connected the quarters to the vessels, the blind spot they all relied upon for this plan to work.

The vessel in this area was so narrow that any roixers or Thyrian officials traveling in a cellholt wouldn't notice anything unusual, not unless they stopped their transport despite not having an official station nearby and looked to the roof of the vessel. Only there they would notice that the blueish membrane was perforated, the end of a rope hanging in the middle of a vertical hole that could fit one person and a half.

Hope interlaced her hands so Nina could grab the rope they had tucked in safely after they landed. A couple of attempts later, she pulled the rope down.

"After you." Hope smiled. The amount of strength Nina's legs had had to gather in these past days since they had been working with the courtrades was immense. Hope knew very well how much the legs of her friend had hurt, the pins and needles that made her moan every time she turned in her sleep in the bunk bed below hers.

But there was not much choice, not when it took two people to walk in the vessels and be able to return. Especially not when, after climbing the rope until they were out of the vessel and out of sight from any passing cellholts, they had to climb a metallic ladder drilled into the wall of the tunnel for long minutes. Until they reached the interior of a room in the building where the courtrades lived.

Hope climbed the last step with a final push, jumping into the control room where someone always was on duty, ensuring that the building stayed safe and unnoticed by unwanted beings. Nina was panting, sitting on the floor with her hands on her head, her elbows on her bent knees.

Hope sat on a table, removing some of her sheathed knives and daggers from her belt, carefully placing them next to each other. She did not remove all of them, obviously, as danger could become present anytime, anywhere. Just enough to sit comfortably with no unnecessary spiking.

When Nina opened her mouth but said nothing, Hope asked, "Are you okay over there?"

Nina nodded slowly and then changed her mind and shook her head vigorously. With her hands still covering her forehead, she gasped, "Water."

Hope chuckled, grabbing a glass from a cabinet and filling it with cool water.

Marcus was pressing some buttons on the screens that showed the live feed monitoring the blind spot.

"We had outer-vessel cameras twice, but the sea creatures ended up eating them pretty quickly." He scratched his chin distractedly. "Definitely not worth the effort and risk to put them up again if they only last a couple of days. Still, it gave...interesting views."

How the courtrades had put cameras on the outside of the membrane of the vessels would have been interesting for sure.

Marcus pointed towards the glass wall next to the screens, the one showing the living map of the wider vessels' net. "The way the vessels connect to each other is by merging membranes, so when we want to redirect some cargo to another destination, all we have to do is push it away, physically redirect a vessel to connect to another one."

Aurora nodded, her index finger on her chin. "And if someone or something is in the vessel you move?"

"They would feel the vessel shake, sort of like a magical wave, sort of a panomquake, except on a very small scale and only for a short time. I bet most times, they think it's some sort of malfunction or a sea creature hitting it." Marcus scratched his dark hair.

Aridian chuckled from another spot in front of the screens. "And thank Llunal for that."

Nina's breathing had finally eased a bit, so Hope offered her a hand to stand.

Feeling the familiar sensation of her stomach rumbling, Hope asked, "So the plan is to get into a cellholt from the tunnel you have down there, and then someone will push vessel after vessel, over and over, until we reach Thyria? What if we reach a dead end?"

"That, my friend," Marcus' dark eyes shone, "is the key to this game. The vessels always reconnect. Their nature makes them crave the connection to another one nearby. Their net exists to ensure the flow of the magic above them. There are no loose ends. Ever. And as for who will push the vessels: it will be me. Each cellholt has a living map that can be unlocked with panom blood. Your blood, in this case."

Hope frowned without meaning to. Having to go into a system of never-ending underwater magical-fueled tunnels was everything but promising.

Nina's blue eyes were wide, and her eyebrows raised as she slowly shook her head. Two firm believers in this plan, they were.

Marcus stood up, clapping his hands, "Lunchtime, everybody. Shall we?" Without looking backwards, he walked towards the dining room a few rooms down the corridor.

Courtrades of different ages and profiles occupied multiple long metal tables in orderly rows, all of them wearing black, the color these shadow-dancers seemed most comfortable in, all of them interacting like a big family.

The shock at how non-silent these meals were, how everyone seemed cheerful about being part of the group, made Hope stop dead the first time she had entered the dining room. She hadn't even considered that this would be the normality for some people. She hadn't even realized it was an option.

She missed the peace of her meals in the treehouse, or by the lake, or in the woods. This was just...too loud. Too overwhelming. It was almost impossible to avoid thinking way too much about her own life. About all the what-ifs. About what a mess of a life she had ended up living, how many times her soul had broken, and how many more it would be shattered again.

Bowl of hot soup and fresh piece of bread in hand, Hope and Nina found spots in the middle of the unfamiliar social chaos.

Nina wiped her mouth with one of the cloth napkins distributed across the tables. Black napkins with white spirals and half circumferences sewn into them. "You will regret not eating this when we are en route and eating cold tinned meat and peas for Cardinals know how long." Nina's top lip curled in disgust at the thought.

Knowing how much truth those words bore, Hope forced herself to taste the soup. It wasn't an easy feat, considering the knot in her stomach had only grown exponentially since they had entered the courtrades' quarters a few days ago.

A mix of emotions, that ever-increasing knot was. The strongest being the feeling that something in her was missing, but she couldn't identify what. Overall, it was a big damned cocktail of emotions that threatened to implode sooner or later.

21

Lenna

Lenna wanted to throw the fucking orb across the room.

The reason she was resisting the urge to smash the damned sphere was because she knew precisely which smug smile of satisfaction Jake would have if he realized she was so fucking pissed.

"Maybe it's not me, you know?" she said, her voice sharp as she put her hands on her hips. "The one who is useless at this."

She half regretted her words immediately, because how very mature of her to pass the ball of whose fault it was that she was so damn slow at learning to control her magic. But she needed to vent. They had been at this for days, for so many hours every day. It was fucking draining.

Jake snorted. "Of course it's not you, sweetheart. Controlling your magic is everyone else's responsibility but yours," he smiled.

"Fuck off," she spat. She was so done with this shit.

Except—no. Damn every single Cardinal, one by one, but if there was anything she actually wanted, it was to control her powers, to learn how to use them, to make a change and feel powerful enough to do so.

"I tried, okay? But clearly, this orb business is not working for me." Lenna waved her hands across the room, at all the orbs floating or spread on the floor, most of them with golden sparks inside them. It was all she had done until now: Give them useless sparks in their very useless center.

Jake walked towards her as he said, "The original power of your House and the North Cardinal was Giving. It is expected that you will be more prone to gaining control of this power."

He put a hand under her chin, slowly lifting it until her golden eyes met his silver ones. He was so close, she could smell his leather and ginger scent. Lenna had the impulse to push his fingers away from her skin, but his whisper stopped her. "You are harsh on yourself, and that, sweet fire, will take you very far."

Before Lenna could assess what that whisper had done to her core and how very close to a fire she was getting, he stepped away. "But I agree. It is time to try... alternative methods." He combed a hand through his dark hair, the muscles of his forearm tensing.

"I know you are so generous that you can't resist all this Giving, but it is time you start Taking. Starting with something you care about." A movement of his hands, and he was suddenly holding a candle, the other hand holding her book of Cause over the flame. The same book of Cause she had written in during her life, where she kept record of her feelings and thoughts.

"Don't you fucking dare." Lenna's eyes were wide, her voice a gasp. She didn't know how he had brought her damned book of Cause from her bedroom in the North House to here, in Corentre.

"Focus all your rage on your goal," Jake ordered. "Your goal is to Take this away from me. Nothing else matters right now. Gather your power in its source: your panom mark. Visualize how you would pull the South petal from your skin and close your hands, as if you are actually pulling it, and *Take* this from me before I burn it to ashes."

Oh, she was going to burn *him* to ashes if he so much as inched the vivid flame toward the book that had accompanied her all these years. She was going to—

"Focus," Jake insisted, and Lenna tried. "Focus on the South petal of your panom mark, and fucking Take this away from me, or I swear I will—"

Book and candle flew across the room, violently slamming against the farthest wall and dropping to the floor as the flame spread on the wooden floor and onto the corners of the cover.

"Fuck. Fuck, fuck, fuck, fuck," Lenna shouted as she ran towards it, but Jake got there first, mouring.

"Give it water. Now," Jake ordered.

Lenna looked at the corners of her book on fire, frowning, raging tears already lining her eyes and oppressing feelings in her chest. It was a pulse between frustration and panic, raw, hateful panic.

"Focus on the North petal of your mark. Think about Giving water and open your hands. Now," he urged, "or it will be too late."

Her breathing cutting as she tried to fight her sobs, she focused on Giving the damned water to stop this tedious fire.

A water curtain fell from the ceiling, soaking them, book, flame, and all the orbs included.

"So aggressive, Brachyan," Jake murmured approvingly.

Lenna kneeled on the floor, breaking the damned candle in half and throwing the pieces at him. "You have no clue about how aggressive I can be." She bared her teeth. "Not a fucking clue."

Jake stared at her, his soaked clothes clinging to every single muscle of his body. "I like a challenge." He smiled, a silent invitation.

She picked the soaked book up from the floor. It was ruined. Fucking *ruined*, and she was going to kill him.

"Don't look so devastated. Your powers can always be used to your advantage, and as long as you know which petal you are pulling from and you focus on it, you can make your magic work. Think about how to fix it and do it. And maybe also stop this shower while you're at it."

He made it sound so easy, and it made her feel so stupid. She hadn't tried to Heal yet, but technically, only living beings could be Healed, so that was not an option. Giving and Taking would have to do.

Lenna focused on Taking the water as she closed her fist sharply. The water curtain stopped falling from the ceiling, and the book became dry.

Half-sighing with relief but also dreading to see if the ink was now splattered and illegible, Lenna opened it, only to find the pages blank, not a single word in the entire book. For a moment, she wondered if she had Taken the words from it by mistake. For a moment, she thought she had royally fucked up.

"I only paid attention to the cover when you were writing in it at the North House library, so that was as far as my replica went." Jake crossed his arms.

"Your *what*?" she shouted.

"The actual book is safe wherever you left it. I figured you would benefit from some motivation." His clothes were dripping on the floor. "And I was right. You Took and Gave in different ways. This is the most progress you have made since we started. By far."

Lenna looked at him, rage burning in her chest. He was so convinced that he had done the right thing, that he had done her a favor. He was not even considering apologizing for almost giving her a heart attack at the thought of losing one of the most precious items she possessed.

His eyes pinned her stare on the spot and she became very aware of her peaked nipples under the soaked cold shirt. She didn't fucking care. She was so angry she didn't even know if she could talk.

"You are powerful, Lenna." Her first name on his lips felt unfamiliar, the respect in his voice too. "More than you think."

"Shame that this is me fucking done with you, Jake Coralt." Lenna pushed the blank, useless book against his chest. She could have sworn his eyes flickered in amusement as she stormed out of the Coronary Atrium, biting her lips as in a failed attempt at trying to keep her tears in. She was so, so done with him.

22

Hope

The day had come. It was time, and Hope couldn't help but feel like it was the beginning of the end. The end to all the lies and half-truths. The end to a life accepting her fate as a discarded being and not doing anything about it. The end to an isolated life in the woods. The end to questions that had marked her mind, and she had learned to live with.

She was both excited and scared about this new beginning. The beginning of her search for truth. The beginning of Cardinals knew what else her life would bring for her. Maybe even the beginning of her life as a panom, if she figured out what to do about that useless mark.

In the control room that lead to the vertical tunnel connecting to the vessels, Marcus and Aridian were waiting for the arrival of the largest cellholt.

"And here it comes." Marcus inclined his head towards the approaching dark dot on the living map of the wall.

Aridian pointed at it, signaling to Nina, Aurora, and Hope which of the multiple moving dots Marcus meant. As if they hadn't been staring at this massive map for weeks and were not perfectly aware of where they stood and precisely which cellholt they had to intercept.

"Careful with that finger," snapped Marcus. "If you move a vessel by accident, we will have to wait another five bloody weeks for this big one to pass underneath. I will have plenty of time to cut your balls slowly during that time."

"Savage." Aridian flinched but quickly put both hands in his pockets.

Hope looked around the crowded room. Some courtrades were rearranging the weapons on their belts, mainly an assortment of knives and daggers, but also the one most loved by them: a dark metal semicircle that appeared sharp on both ends. Hope still hadn't figured out how did their hands not bleed to death when handling these weapons. Every courtrade had their own "crois" as they called it, and looked after them as if they were part of their own body.

Hope adjusted her own belts full of daggers. The ones at the waist and under her breast. The ones on each thigh. The ones in each boot, tucked in nicely.

These learned, unconscious movements comforted her. They felt as natural as breathing. As natural as being always alert, aware of any danger nearby, always ready to strike.

Hope would probably never return to Verdania. She was not sure if she would even be alive after confronting her father. But at this point, Hope didn't care. If he took her down, she would be ready to take him down with her, even if it was the last thing she did in this damned place of a world.

Leaving this island was leaving her past behind, leaving behind the biggest part of herself. Ironically, leaving it was probably even more risky than living in this place where only killers survived.

"Everyone steady now," Marcus' voice sounded across the room, everyone focusing on him and shutting up. Hope saw the cellholt almost at the intersection where Marcus would push the vessel on the living map, redirecting it to the one under the quarters. "Jessica, ready to sound the bell in thirty seconds."

A middle-aged woman with short, dark hair, Marcus' third in command was kneeling next to the opening of the tunnel, a black bell on her hand as she looked at Marcus, awaiting his order.

Hope knew the ladder inside the tunnel was full of courtrades ready to pass the supplies they needed for the five-week journey as soon as they obtained the control of the cellholt. In order to do so, four of the most experienced and lethal courtrades were waiting for the bell to sound before jumping into the vessel.

"Fifteen seconds," Marcus said, his index finger closing in on the intersection of blue lines as the dark dot approached it.

They had practiced most part of the process a few times these past days. How to move supplies down the tunnel passing them from one person to another, the precise order in which they would descend, if the bell was heard from down the tunnel. They had practiced all kinds of things. Except the most important part: intercepting a large cellholt full of roixers, stopping it in the middle of a vessel before the roixers raised the alarm, entering the cellholt and killing said roixers.

"Three, two, one. Bell!" Marcus shouted as he pushed the vessel towards the one right underneath the courtrades' quarters.

The silence and tension in the tunnel and the control room gave Hope goosebumps. She felt the usual adrenaline rush before a kill, except this time, it wasn't her turn. There were courtrades down there, risking their lives.

The feed of three different cameras on the screens in front of Marcus showed the spot where four courtrades were now standing in a line in front of a fast-approaching cellholt, the loud noise of the vehicle emanating from the tunnel. As one, the courtrades held their hands up.

Shadows filled the vessel, only thick darkness visible on the feeds of the cameras. A thundering noise came from the tunnel, the only sign that the cellholt had stopped.

"Here it is." Marcus touched a button on the control panel, the feeds now showing warmth: the five bodies of the roixers moving quickly, grabbing their weapons, one of them running towards the alarm.

Hope did not even hear a sound from the courtrades. She only knew six more were now jumping on top of the cellholt because that had been the plan. A breaking sound came through, followed by the whispered confirmation by Marcus' whispered, "We're in."

The five bodies of the roixers stopped dead on the feed, as if the screens had frozen. The courtrades were not anywhere on the screens, Hope realized, cold sweat down her spine.

A second later, the roixers fell to the floor, their bodies slowly vanishing from the screens as the warmth left them. "And they're out."

Excited shouts and claps came from the vessel. The courtrades in the tunnel were banging the metal ladder as if they were applauding, the people in the control room hugging each other or clapping their hands.

"You lot stop banging the fucking ladder before it falls down!" Marcus shouted down the tunnel, a nervous grin on his face. "Someone tell the assholes in the cellholt to take those shadows away. We have work to do!"

Pressing a button again, Marcus stared at the screens as a cellholt without a roof was visible again, ten courtrades inside the cellholt, smiling and showing the middle finger to the camera. One of them shouted, "You're welcome, boss!"

Hope could have sworn that silver lined Marcus' eyes as he tilted his head back, roaring with laughter.

As if reading Hope's mind, Aurora asked, looking around, "Are you sure this is the biggest cellholt they have?"

"It is." Marcus looked at her as if she had insulted him. "So be thankful." He continued analyzing the small living map in the front cabin, where the drivers sat.

Aurora spun around in a full circle, as if trying to find some hidden part of the cellholt she had missed. She shook her head in desperation as she got closer to the corner where Hope and Nina were sitting on food crates, silently whispering, "This place is going to start smelling soon."

Hope chuckled and quickly turned that into a fake cough. The last thing she wanted was to piss Marcus off when they had to be stuck in a small space with no exit for five weeks. She lowered her voice. "I bet it will smell in a week."

Nina was looking through the crystal wall on the side of the cellholt, already in motion as they were moving through the vessels. The sea was dark and clear, nearby fishes and other sea creatures a blur at their speed. She shook her head as she said, "No way, I give it two days. There are more than twenty of us in here."

"Twenty-five passengers. I can't believe he has actually taken all these people with him. It just makes things way more complicated." Aurora tapped the scar on her neck distractedly.

Hope nodded, biting her bottom lip. They still did not know why Marcus needed twenty-one courtrades in Thyria on top of him or why he was so desperate to get there that he had planned this for over two decades. But he hadn't asked for details of their mission to get there, so they hadn't asked him either. Hope preferred it this way.

Nina crossed her arms over the tight, black leathered clothes the courtrades had given to all of them. The ones they had been using since they got to Cralia and ended up in their quarters. "Not only because of the space, but also the food and water all of us are going to consume in such a long time."

Because right now, five weeks seemed like a very long time. Precisely that was what five courtrades were arranging at the other end of the cellholt: the daily rations of tinned food and water pouches assigned to each of them. The walls were full of shelves, probably used to transport stock and supplies across the islands, so that was helpful.

Along a whole side of the cellholt, another group was piling blankets on top of crates. Some were carefully drilling on the glass walls and ceiling, hanging hammocks. They would sleep in set timed shifts, never more than eight people at a time, so they would be ready should any incident occur.

On the other side of the cellholt there were three small cabins: a washroom, a lavatory, and a changing room. All the privacy they would get here.

Hope was not worried about the lack of privacy or not having even her own sleeping space. She was already missing the fresh air, though. All the previous days in the quarters of the courtrades, she had missed it too, not daring to go outside should any roixers see them. She missed the sound of the wind while she stared at the movement of the leaves on the trees, the sound the squirrels made when they climbed and jumped, the wings of the birds flapping.

All she had taken with her from home were her weapons. Everything that had ever mattered to be safe. All that would ever matter, Hope thought as she closed her eyes and let her body feel the engine of the cellholt taking them across the Radel Sea.

23

Lenna

I t had been a couple of weeks since Lenna had told Jake to fuck off, a couple of weeks without panom lessons and feeling like shit at the thought of not being able to progress further than Giving and Taking at a basic level. The morning after he had pretended to burn her book of Cause, she was still in bed when he sent her an ink.

Are you not coming today?

One post meridiem when she was hanging out with Ciaran, Sasha, Indianna, Brendon and Carson at the apartment the last two shared:

I know it was a low move, but it worked.
You can't deny it.

Last night while she was removing her makeup:

*Being officially pissed off for the rest of your life
won't make you a better panom.*

His perseverance was almost admirable, but his assholeness was something else. Lenna had decided she would only accept a full, explicit, whole-hearted apology. She deserved it. In the meantime, maybe she was enjoying seeing him chase her at different times during his very busy days and nights.

Finishing arranging her red hair into a small bun, Lenna grabbed the smutty book she had to return to Sasha. She had devoured it in one sitting until very late hours last night. Nothing was as motivating as some indecent, dirty reading when her own sex life had been reduced to pretty much zero since her arrival to Corentre. Something she was determined to change as soon as fucking possible, thank you very much.

She closed the door to her private chambers and started walking down the corridor towards the Dawn Gate, her steps echoing across the marble thanks to her high heels. She heard Ayla bossing someone around before she saw her.

"Of course, you can wash my clothes properly, because I don't exactly know what they think they do here but they are *destroying* my silks." Ayla's high-pitched voice was a confirmation of her very well practiced I-am-a-Brachyan-and-you-obey-me. Rolling her eyes, Lenna almost felt sorry for whoever was receiving her sister's orders. She was about to take a different corridor to the Dawn Gate just to avoid her beloved twin when Ayla turned a corner with somebody else.

"What is she doing here?" Lenna asked, pointing at the lady wearing the dark brown uniform of the North House.

"Good post meridiem to you too, my dear sister." Ayla's chin lifted, as if she had realized she had caught Lenna by surprise. "I'm guessing you are not going to the Atrium. Poor you, missing out on all the fun in learning the four powers."

Lenna tried to ignore the invisible punch in the gut. Cardinals knew how much Gabrielle had taught Ayla so far if she was already referring to the four powers. She had barely managed two and didn't even know when she would learn any further at this pace. There was not even a pace, actually. Just a pause, because she was too damn proud to go back to Jake without his apology, even if he had shown no intent to apologize at all.

But Lenna was definitely not giving her sister any reason to mock her. Plus, she truly wanted to know, so she repeated, "What is Lidia doing here?"

"Well, Lidia has proved her value all these years as my personal assistant back home, and the servants of this House clearly don't meet my standards. I requested for her to be brought here, and they obliged."

Lenna didn't even know where to start, if it was even worth starting. Lenna had sought Clara's help twice since their arrival at the Organ House and she had always proved both efficient and resourceful, but she knew perfectly well that Ayla's definition of "personal assistant" was closer to "personal slave".

It was a miracle that the North House still employed Lidia and she hadn't quit or pretended she was very sick during her time assigned to Ayla.

But if Ayla had permission to bring a member of their service to the Organ House...

"Who allowed her to come here?" Lenna asked almost breathlessly, a spark of excitement in her chest.

Ayla shook her head slowly, narrowing her eyes. "The Organ Mandor, *obviously*."

Lenna turned on her heels, heading towards another part of the House, golden sparks on her hand as she sent ink to Sasha:

The hall in front of the Organ Mandor's office was bright, illuminated by the flashing sun. Four roixers dressed in cardinal red stood guard by the double wooden doors.

"I need to speak to the Organ Mandor," Lenna said, her voice decisive.

"He's busy. Do you have an invitation?" one of the roixers on her left asked, stepping forward.

"Not a formal one, but I am a guest in this House." She lifted her chin in that bossy way she had seen Ayla do countless times. "I am the heir of the North House," she added. Surely, that had to count.

"We know who you are, Lenna Brachyan," the roixer said as he stepped back in line. A silent dismissal.

Lenna put her hands on her hips, frustration already evident on her face. The wooden doors opened in front of her, and Jake stepped out, closing them behind him. He halted in front of her, slightly lifting his eyebrows.

"I'm starting to think this is your favorite posture," he said as he made a signal to the roixers. "You will excuse us for a moment."

He swallowed after they'd left, as if hesitating. "What is it you want from my father?"

"His permission to bring one of my staff from the North House," Lenna said. She was not in the mood to talk to him. Not at all and not yet, but if he could help her with this, talking to him maybe was worth it.

"Permission granted," he said, walking past her and brushing her arm with his. "I wouldn't bother him for small things like this, by the way. He was not happy with your sister pretending to be a distinguished person because she needs someone to wipe her Very Important Ass." And with that, he was gone.

Lenna almost choked at the thought of Lidia wiping her sister's V.I.A. and her face lit up with a grin. That had been way easier than she had expected, and damn her if she wasn't excited to bring Theon to the Organ House.

Lenna was convinced that the long distance between the Organ and North Houses would make sending her ink to Theon a stupid option, but luckily, and unlike her, Ciaran knew a great deal of how her own magic worked.

"Don't overthink it." His blue eyes were fixed on the cards in his non-metallic hand. "The possibility that it reaches him is way bigger than not."

Sasha raised her finger in the air with worry on her face, making everyone on the terrace look at her. "So sorry, lovelies," she said as she put her dice on top of the card face up on the table, making Ciaran and Brendon immediately be creative with their swearing. "You can go cry in that corner."

She winked at a laughing Lenna and did a small dance, shaking her shoulders and full breasts that had the potential to stop some hearts and resuscitate some cocks. Elsewhere, that would be, because the two men in front of her were desperately finding some valers in their pockets to pay her fifth-in-a-row win, and they didn't seem very content with it.

"Another round?" Sasha laughed, grinning and gathering the cards and dies spread on the table and the coins she had won. Lenna had been watching a few times as they played CoreCode and was still not sure she understood all the rules, only that it always involved a huge amount of teasing and swearing.

Ciaran and Brendon looked at each other as if having some silent debate about which one of them should tell her they were done with the unfairness of life.

Sasha started shaking the dies, lifting her brows. "Aren't you tough, tough men? Already cowered by a poor young lady that only wants to have some fun?"

Lenna snorted. "Where is that poor young lady? The only lady I see here is a badass bitch."

"Only because badass bitches recognize each other." Sasha blew her a kiss and turned to the boys again. "So?"

"I'm not sure my hurt male ego can take it anymore tonight," Brendon said.

"Or my empty pockets. You are going to ruin us." Ciaran stood up, stretching his arms over his head. "And Lenna—for Cardinals' sake, just send him the damned ink."

All Lenna wanted was for her message to Theon to come across as an invitation to the Organ House, but without giving him an actual choice. After a while, she sent her ink:

Want to come live in fancy ass Corentre?
If you don't, you'll be missing out on:
drinking the best myster of Thyria, living
in the poshest place you could ever
imagine, meeting my new cool non-stupid-
for-a-change Elite gang, and the best sex
of your life.

Followed by:

The waholt will pick you up tomorrow at
eight ante meridiem.

Lenna grinned, imagining Theon swearing at the short notice and how early he had to get up. But he would come. Of that, she had no doubt, and she couldn't wait.

24

Hope

The shaking of the cellholt woke Hope for the third time that night.

The squeaky noise of the door to the restroom had been the first reason. One would have expected these official vehicles to have some regular servicing and some oil onboard, but they didn't. The cracks on the glass panel at the back of the cellholt and the splinters a courtrade got using a side table were additional proof.

The second time, a sleeping courtrade had kicked her, his feet too close to her head despite her knees being bent in a failed attempt at squeezing into the small space within her blanket by the wall of the cellholt.

If Hope had ever found her learned reflexes to be unhelpful and absolutely excessive, it had been these past two weeks, since their departure. Being very aware of her surroundings and unconsciously looking out for minimal noises that posed a danger to life, even when she was asleep, was only giving her constant headaches because of her self-inflicted sleep deprivation.

She wished her body learned to acknowledge the shaking of the cellholt as part of the norm, especially when it happened often. Usually when Marcus pushed them from vessel to vessel, or when a burst of panom power hit the vessel they were in. Which also happened very regularly, as the outbursts of panom magic stabilizing the lands above had been the main purpose of the creation of the vessels.

Marcus had pre-warned Hope that the key to this plan working was her blood. Every five days, the cellholts needed panom blood to fuel them for another five days. His hypothesis was that her blood wouldn't last five whole days because she hadn't had her Fifth Ceremony and, technically, she wasn't a full panom yet. His calculations, apparently with a healthy margin of error, concluded her blood was needed every three days to ensure the cellholt had enough energy to function, and so far, it had worked. The aching scab on her palm was not healing fast enough by the time she had to cut it open again. It had been a conscious choice to reopen the same spot to bleed, rather than have multiple injuries that could impair her further.

Now and then, the living map at the front of the cellholt showed they were approaching a blood station, and Marcus would push some vessels around to avoid it. The blood stations were heavily monitored by roixers, where cellholts stopped to replenish power and supplies when needed, so they wanted to stay *far* away from them. Especially when their cellholt had no roof after the courtrades had blown it out to infiltrate it, and there wasn't a single roixer inside. The closest to a roixer were the red uniforms they had kept from the bodies they killed under Verdania, in case they needed them.

Hope tried to go back to sleep, covering her eyes with the back of her hand.

Light penetrated through her eyelids, interrupting her dreams of pines, shadows, and night. Not blood-fuelled light like the one the orbs of the cellholt produced, but... Hope slightly opened her eyes as she stood, looking to where the roof of the cellholt should have been.

There it was: sunlight coming through the water above the vessel.

Aridian yawned on the blanket a couple of spaces from her, shouting at Marcus and earning a few grunts from courtrades who were still asleep. "What's our depth, Captain?"

"Minimum level," Marcus replied from the other side. "25 feet. Get your lazy ass over here if you want to admire the most sunshine you will see for a while."

For that was the Radel Sea's surface on top of them, and those dark masses blocking the light intermittently looked like—

"What are those platforms for?" Hope asked Marcus when she reached him.

"That, you can ask your father when you see him," he said, lowering his voice. Hope was silently grateful for him not shouting out her bloodline through the roofs. Or *lack of* roofs.

Another unanswered question to add to the list, then. The least of her priorities. She was about to leave them to go look for Nina when Marcus added, "My guess is they are experiment sites, but Llunal shade me if I wanted to know what they do over there."

Aurora was looking at the floor, swallowing as she frowned. Hope knew that expression too well. "You know what it's about, don't you?"

Aurora hesitated, not taking her eyes from the floor. "As the Roix Reigner, I was asked a handful of times to...verify the brute force needed against certain creatures." It was a visible struggle to talk about that past, as if a part of her mind had done a willing effort to forget it.

Aridian halted, turning to her. "Who wanted to verify that?"

Aurora lifted her gaze to Hope. "Both petitions came from roixers out of Thyria."

Hope could read the palpable worry on her mother's face, a hint of fear there. "The brute force needed against *what* creatures, Mother?"

"Sea creatures," Aurora whispered, as if realizing the big fuckup omitting this bit of information had been.

"Llunal shade us all," Aridian said, tracing a semicircle on his chest as he closed his eyes.

And maybe Llunal, the faceless god of shadows and darkness, was indeed listening, because a moving, appallingly enormous shadow surrounded the whole vessel they were traveling in, spiraling around it as if it wanted to squish them.

"You fucking son of a bitch with some dark sense of humor!" Marcus shouted.

Echoing his thoughts, Aridian spat, "Bastards, these gods are. Fucking bastards." Hope knew it was not something personal, but the use of that word somehow hurt.

The creature around them was closing in, black scales now surrounding them. In Hope's fists, she held her longest and sharpest blades. Not that they would help much if the thing snapped the vessel in half, leaving them to drown.

"No one do anything stupid," Marcus' voice resonated in the still-moving cellholt.

Hope found Nina's white hair in the middle of the group of courtrades. Their eyes met, and Nina nodded, walking towards the front cabin to join them. Marcus was quickly zooming in and out the living map, his quick and precise movements not faltering.

Aurora said firmly, "The orbs of the cellholt are giving our location away."

Marcus extended his arms, darkness spreading from him into each light source. "Not anymore."

Hope heard Nina's gasp next to her and put a hand on her arm. The only visible thing were the blue lines representing the never-ending vessels on the living map, interconnecting as always.

Hope asked, "Can the vessels break?"

"Not by creatures, as far as I know. The only times vessels have been known to rupture were because of panomquakes from above, or outbursts of panom forces within the vessels," Marcus said. "There has been less frequency of cellholts in these vessels, and with good reason." Hope could have sworn he was looking at Aurora intently, but it was so hard to see anything. "But the vessels are intact and the flow does not break at any point. I think it will leave us alone sooner or later."

Aridian snorted. "So the scary beast just is here because it likes to sunbathe, and we are its chasing toy for the day."

25

Lenna

L enna spent the morning playing with the deliseen and the House, after consciously ignoring another ink from Jake:

Another day, another lost opportunity due to someone's impressive pride.

It made her smirk, knowing he was waiting for her. Even though she knew she was pushing it now and she had to tread carefully or it would end up snapping in her face. He had been way more patient than she had expected him to. She'd give him that. There was a fine line to piss him off enough to compensate his big fuck up with the book of Cause, but not too much that he refused to teach her any more magic.

Her dreams these past few days had included his whispers, his leathery scent and the challenge in his silver eyes.

You are stronger than you think, sweet fire.

Maybe his muscles had also been in those dreams, and a certain offer he had made a while ago. Her core tightened at the thought.

It sure as fuck didn't help that Lenna hadn't had sex with anyone since her arrival at Corentre. She didn't feel like bringing a stranger to her private chambers, not when it would lead to more questions than it was worth it, plus she was sure that the Organ Mandor would kick her out if he found out Lenna was using his House as a fuck palace. Her own father already considered her a disgrace because she didn't give a shit in the North House, but doing that in the Organ House...he would probably skin her alive.

Lenna had found her pleasure in taking matters into her own hands, and with the occasional help of tools supplied by a surprisingly very dirty-minded House.

By the time she sat down in the new golden couches in her live room, she was happy with the current state of her chambers, and well pleased at the interior decoration options from the deliseen and the House. Good taste indeed.

If her ink had reached Theon, as Ciaran reassured her it would, he would probably already be on his way to Corentre. Lenna had changed nothing in his bedroom, leaving it for him to sort or arrange, but the rest of her chambers...

She had converted the middle core room into the library she had always dreamed about. The circular wall fully filled by bookshelves with more books than she would ever read, sparkling lights across the shelves, uniting them on a grading scale of distinct tones of warm lights. Even with her extended lifespan thanks to being a panom, she doubted she could read all of them, but Cardinals, she'd try. Especially the ones she had requested title by title, an excited scream and jumping every time the House obliged, not seeming to care that even the titles would make most beings blush.

Lenna was well past the giving-a-shit stage of her life, and right now, she wanted to welcome Theon and fuck him like there was no tomorrow. Please, and thank you.

Maybe it was the ecstasy of her friend coming, the surreal excitement at having found a way to have as many books as she would ever need, or that she actually wanted to continue learning and discovering the limits of her powers. Maybe her anger had just faded with the days, but she walked towards the Coronary Atrium at last.

Lenna entered the room they had used those previous days. The Orb Room, she had named it. Alternatively, it could have been The Shower Room, but that sounded less mysterious.

Ayla and Gabrielle were back-to-back in the middle of the room, an array of silver and violet animals flying in circles around them. The animals, Lenna realized with both jealousy and awe, made of sparks. She started at the doorway, stunned by the beautiful dance in front of her: silver cats chasing violet butterflies, violet deer calmly pacing while silver rabbits jumped around their legs. Both panoms had their arms extended in front of them, opening their hands with grace as new animals came forth. The smile on Ayla's face, the peace and happiness in her relaxed features as silver animals continued pouring from her hands... She looked like an entirely different person.

"Isn't it beautiful?" Jake's voice caressed her ear from behind.

Lenna nodded, unsure about her ability to talk, unable to move her eyes from the view in front of them. It was…magical. There was no other word to describe it.

Her eyes ached as she swallowed. She had been blessed by the Cardinals, and what had she done? Wasted her time in nonsense arguments. Wasted *precious* time she could have used to improve, to get better. Time she would never get back.

Jake's warm hand touched her elbow, inviting her to follow as he said, "We need to talk, Brachyan." The skin of her arm reacted to his touch, and she wasn't sure if in fear or something else.

Lenna walked next to him, and he didn't break contact at any time. If that hadn't been the case, she wouldn't have known how to get to the pitch-black room they were now standing in, the door silently closing behind them, leaving them in utter darkness.

She inhaled deeply. "We need to talk, I get it, but does it need to be so… creepy?"

Jake chuckled, as he finally let go of her elbow, leaving the skin there so cold. Lenna felt a movement and knew he was standing close, completely ignoring her personal space. If she could see at all, she would be probably staring at his neck in front of her.

"Darkness can help find a focus," he said. A handful of navy sparks flew from his fingers and found their way into the corners of what seemed to be a horrendously big room. "Better?" he asked. The minor sources of dark blue light were enough for Lenna to see the reflection of his silver eyes above her, so she nodded.

"Do you have any idea why I asked to be your Panom Guidor?" Jake asked, his voice lowering.

Lenna put a finger to her lips, pretending to think carefully. "To piss me off? Because I refused you? To prove a point?"

Jake shook his head in silence. "I chose you, Lenna Brachyan, because you have the fearless heart of those who change worlds. I chose you because I can see who you are behind your walls. I chose you because even if you have accepted that everyone who should love you has given up on you, I know you are worth fighting for. I chose you because I know you can be as powerful as I am, if not even more. And I chose you, sweet fire, because you are absolutely insufferable, and I can't get you out of my mind."

Lenna's lips curled up, her eyebrow raised. "I have an official *I-can't-stand-this-bitch* fan club. You might need to wait in line, though."

"Did you even listen to what I just said?" She could have sworn he was frowning in the dark.

"My hearing is fine, thank you. But until I get a full apology, we are not even. So please repeat after me: *"I am so very sorry for the other day."*

"For Cardinal's fucking sake, Brachyan, you're still not over your little tantrum?" he said, lifting a hand to his black hair. When she didn't respond, he repeated, his voice exasperated, "I am sort of sorry for the other day."

Lenna grinned, knowing she had won. *"and I will never, ever use any of Lenna's belongings against her."*

Lenna felt Jake grinning as he said, "and I will never, ever use any of your belongings against you. Unless you explicitly ask me for help to use one of the many filthy toys you have in your chambers."

Lenna's jaw dropped, and his index finger immediately moved from her top lip to her bottom, and then to her jaw, lifting it. "Close your mouth like a good girl. May I remind you that you are living in my House, sweet fire? And I don't like secrets."

Lenna took one step backwards, hands on her hips. "You creepy bastard. That is not fair, and you know it. That fucking House of yours is as dirty-minded as you are."

"As *we* are," he corrected with a side smile. "It only provides what its resident needs." Then, he was gone as he moured, and she felt his warm body behind hers, so close, she could feel the muscles through the clothes against her skin. She held her breath as he whispered against her neck, "And whenever you need more," she felt his tongue sliding against her neck, "you know you can come beg."

The fucking heir of the Organ House moured away, leaving Lenna's back extremely cold and her core not cold at all. He stood a few steps from her, hands in front of him, his palms faced up, small galaxies of navy sparks floating from them. "Show me your golden sparks, sweet fire, and let's light this up."

Cardinals guide her, she was fucked.

26

Hope

I t had been over twenty hours of the creature circling the vessels relent-lessly. The sea beast hadn't lingered to feed, and it seemed extremely content to continue around them.

Though the courtrades didn't seem to mind the darkness, but Hope was fed up with not being able to see what she was eating, what or who she was stepping on, and if she had any weapons pointed at her neck.

She didn't trust the courtrades at all. Unlike Nina, who knew every-one's names and kept talking with them and helping whenever she could, Hope preferred to mind her own business. Her own business being her assortment of weapons that had never been so polished, planning the next steps of her journey which differed from Marcus' plans, and right now, the long-lasting darkness no one seemed too concerned about and, in case they hadn't realized, was not keeping the sea beast away.

An exasperated exhale told her she was not the only one done with darkness.

"I agree," Hope said, earning a chuckle from Nina.

"I just can't believe they don't even care." Hope felt Nina shake her head next to her. "Do you reckon they can see in the dark?"

They sat on top of some crates around the front of the cellholt, where they had the faint light of the living map.

"It's not that we can *see*," Aridian clarified from nearby. "More like we perceive what the shadows know. Seeing without actually seeing."

"Don't forget their whispers," Marcus added.

"Of course, the whispers of shadows. How ordinary of us to have forgotten about them, Nina." Hope rolled her eyes.

"Whispers of night, we call them. Which, by the way," Marcus' voice moved, as if he was now facing Aridian, "should have reached the courtrades in Thyria a few days ago. We must not alter our course, or we won't get there on time."

"They make us normal beings not blessed by any god or goddess look abhorrently ordinary," Nina told Hope, but as if she remembered her friend was indeed blessed by the Cardinals and their magic, Nina added, "Extremely boring being is not applicable to you either."

Hope tried to elbow her, hitting Nina with her first attempt. "Not that it matters much, and not that there is anything wrong with being ordinary."

"When will you decide to stop downplaying the fact that you have the potential of becoming the most potent panom in this world, Hope Nevada?" Marcus said, and maybe it was his shadows, or maybe his message, but her skin tensed uncontrollably.

Hope struggled to talk past the uncomfortable knot in her throat. "That is a lie," she managed to say.

"Aren't you the daughter of the Organ Mandor?" Marcus asked. Hope could swear her mother's eyes closed at the truth spoken so brashly. "Won't you become the first female blood panom in the Organ bloodline in centuries?"

"What do you mean?" Hope asked shakily.

Nina explained for him when he paused. "The five Cardinals are goddesses and firm believers in female blood ruling over male. The female panoms of any bloodline will always be the most powerful and the truthful heirs to their Houses. So male panoms have killed females of their own Houses for centuries, because many will never accept female blood ruling over them."

The silence that followed didn't help Hope's feel less on edge, and it surely helped her world feel like tilting upside down, vessel and beast included.

"Shame that I am not interested," she simply said. She knew that her mother's eyes showed an immense relief, even if she still could not see them.

"The shadows have whispered, Hope Nevada," Marcus insisted. "And they never lie."

Hope cleared her throat. "I am not interested. I don't want to rule anything."

Because she would not call him "my father" in front of Aurora. He wasn't her father. He wasn't her anything. Not in any way that mattered. Only the man who had sired her by mistake.

"But I am *very* interested in getting this creature out of our way so I can see something again before some of us end up hallucinating." Because not seeing anything other than wings and night in her dreams was going to end her sanity and her patience.

"The darkness has not made the beast stop chasing us," Aurora added, clearly grateful for the change in subject. She was also very eager for this pitch black nonsense to stop.

Marcus hummed in agreement. "You three might want to close your eyes," he said, and they all did precisely that as he took the shadows of the cellholt away.

"Thank you and each Cardinal for the light," Nina said, hands covering her eyes, excitement already in her voice. She couldn't wait for them to adjust until she could look around again.

"Something as ordinary as seeing. Nothing ordinary should ever be taken for granted," Hope said, already removing the cover from her eyes as she started opening them. Hope grinned at the sight of Nina's hands still covering her pale face, the white strands of her usually smooth hair quite a mess that hadn't been fixed in all those hours. Her mother, already pushing her dark eyes open despite the discomfort, just as she had done herself. Her dark, short hair shaping her face, the scar on her neck in its usual place.

Courtrades hadn't even flinched at the brightness, and they carried on doing their usual duties as they had been doing before. Rearranging the crates, sorting out food rations and water, playing games with pieces of broken glass, chatting in small groups. Still, they seemed tense, not able to stop the frequent glances at the massive scales of the sea creature surrounding them.

"Time to scare the beast away," Hope said as she walked towards the orb that kept the cellholt together. The redness at the bottom of the orb was proof her blood was still fuel for a while. But Hope didn't want a simple refuel. She wanted an outburst of power that shook the vessel enough to scare or electrocute the creature.

With one hand holding her sharpest dagger, Hope opened her other palm and held in a painful gasp as she cut through the scab, letting panom blood pour freely into the center of the orb.

27

Lenna

By the time Lenna returned to her chambers, she felt excited and ravenous in equally massive parts. It had been so damn fun Giving her golden sparks and letting them flow into the darkness, Taking Jake's navy ones while they teased each other for hours. She couldn't believe it was almost sunset by the time he told her they'd continue tomorrow, and she found herself looking forward to it. To all of it, maybe even seeing those silver eyes somewhere else than in her dreams.

After today, it was easy to forget that he discarded beings as part of his regular duties, and that he played a huge role in this broken shit of a system. By being the heir of the biggest and shittiest House of all, nonetheless. The House famously known for having no pity for lower beings, the one that commanded the roixers and the Roix Reigner herself. Which was, Lenna reminded herself with disgust, the one that ordered innocents to be killed left, right and center.

She almost felt guilty at having put her hate aside for a few hours. How could she even consider having fun as an option when it was with someone who ruined lives and families, who despised human beings, on a weekly basis? She *almost* felt guilty.

Lenna opened the door that led to the circular library of her chambers and heard the voice of the House talking to somebody. "Enjoyable as it is flirting with you, Lord Chloid, I'm afraid I can't take a physical form to fulfill your wishes."

Lenna laughed out loud. "What the fuck are you asking the House, you dirty asshole?"

Theon peaked from his bedroom with a grin...*shirtless*. "Nothing a true woman would refuse," he said, lifting his eyebrows.

Lenna walked towards him, shaking her head vigorously but unable to stop smiling. "And *Lord* Chloid? Seriously!?" She gave him a tight hug, feeling every muscle against her cheek and breasts. "I've missed you. Have you missed me?"

"Have I missed you? Mmm." Theon took a step back, intently avoiding her eyes. "House, have I missed this red-haired trouble?"

"A true man would know the answer to that," the voice of the House resonated. Theon's brown eyes widened as his jaw dropped.

"You've offended her, you prick. Say sorry," Lenna shouted, hands on her hips.

"Sorry, Walls," a wide-eyed Theon said dubiously, then got closer to Lenna's ear and said quietly, "But she isn't a true woman, is she? Even though by how personally she took it, she might actually be."

The House said nothing. Lenna sat down on his massive bed.

Theon sat next to her, his knee brushing the arm she was leaning on. "So you were so busy, you couldn't welcome me to... what is this? Your new house? My new house?"

Lenna shot to her feet, extending her arms at her sides and spinning around as she said, "Dearest Theon, welcome to *our* new shared chambers."

"Shared, as in... Shared, shared?"

"Well, technically it belongs to the Organ Mandor and his family." She did a conscious effort at not visualizing a precise member of said family and she added, "But these are my allocated chambers while I stay in Corentre, and as my trainer you will share them with me. So you better become friends again with the House."

His eyes narrowed. "Since when do trainers live with the people they train?"

"Since my sister lives with her own wiping-ass assistant from the North, okay? She brought her here, so I thought I could bring you too. If you wanted." Lenna's lips tightened. "But if it is too much of an inconvenience for Lord Chloid, then I'm sure we can request separate chambers."

Except she would have to ask the Organ Mandor, or more realistically Jake, for that. She wasn't entirely sure it was a good idea. Even though Jake definitely knew about the pleasure-giving belongings she had in her chambers. He had even kindly offered his *help* with them, for Cardinals' sake. Lenna threw a grim look at the walls, because he definitely wouldn't have known that, were it not for the House being his accomplice.

It was tempting, though.

So, so tempting, to see how much and how fast he could know about what happened or didn't happen in her chambers. It would serve Jake well, to realize he should leave Lenna's privacy alone.

"Come see this," Lenna took Theon's forearm, unavoidably biting her lip as she acknowledged the muscles there and the strength behind them. She led him to the deliseen. "Ask this room for whatever training supplies you need. Whatever you want."

Theon made some lengthy and specific requests and made some impressed sounds as the deliseen obliged again and again. By the time he decided it was enough, the room had the most varied arrangement of weapons Lenna had ever seen, an awful lot of intimidating machines and devices she did not know how to use, ceiling-to-floor windows that showed the starry night outside, and some intense music beating on the background.

Theon sized Lenna up, looking at her bare arms. "You haven't trained at all, have you?"

Theon laughed as Lenna's nostrils flared. "I'm going to beat the shit out of you."

"I'm sure you will, and hopefully, in more ways than you think," Lenna said calmly as she winked. Theon's eyebrow quirked as his lips curled upward.

"Is that what the roomies situation is truly about?" Theon's voice was deadly calm. "Do they not have anyone worth it in this big city that you had to bring a true Lord from the North?"

"For all I know, the not-true Lord from the North might not be worth it either."

He took a step closer, his dark eyes pinning her down as he grabbed a bunch of her red hair firmly in his fist. "So you like it rough, then?" He let go of her hair and moved a slow finger from her neck to the mark between her breasts. "Or are you more of a softie?"

Lenna felt her nipples tighten underneath her bright-red lace bra. She put a hand on Theon's pants, feeling his length stretching against the leather. She pushed her hips against it as she licked his neck, inevitably remembering a lick on her neck that had her core tightening earlier that day. "I need it rough," she gasped. She needed it silver-fucking-eyed too, she realized.

Theon lifted her chin just enough to meet her stare as he opened the button of her pants and slid his hand down until he found her clit, circling it incessantly as he pushed Lenna against the main door of the chambers. Theon licked the soft spot behind her ear as the movements against her core became more intense. "Fuck, you are wet," he purred.

Lenna closed her eyes, feeling the wooden door against her shoulder blades, her body trembling a bit as she tried to stay standing while he moved his hand and tongue. "Fucking wet for you, Jake," she breathed.

"Are we role playing here?" He bit her neck, two fingers now finding their way to her inner walls. Lenna moaned against his brown hair, but before she could register anything, loud bangs at the door slapped her to reality.

"Open the door," a voice demanded from the other side.

Theon's eyes were wide as he removed his hand from her underwear.

Three more bangs, followed by another barked order. "Open the fucking door now."

So, Lenna did.

"Bossy, as always," Lenna smiled, enjoying the view of Jake's angular jaw tightening as he eyed them up. Those silver eyes peered at her golden ones, at the open buttons of her shirt showing her red laced bra, the button of her pants undone. At Theon's wet hand.

As if noticing Jake's stare, Theon put his still-wet fingers in his mouth and sucked them slowly, his lips curling upwards.

"Who the fuck is this?" Jake spat, eyes back on Lenna's.

She had fucking known he would be notified about anything interesting happening in her rooms. She had fucking known that he would invade her privacy again, either with perversion in mind or whatever else. What she hadn't known was that he would be so agitated at the fact that she was going to fuck another man.

"Jake Coralt, meet my personal trainer, Theon Chloid. I was just welcoming him to your House."

28

Hope

The rumbling of Nina's empty stomach made her blush. Hope smiled.

Hunger was not entirely new to her. She could remember the raw pain in her abdomen from when she was a child and Aurora hadn't been able to move and find some food for them. She remembered the empty stare in her mother's unfocused gaze. As if she had completely given up on life. On them.

Hope had cried to sleep many times those years, feeling completely abandoned and alone in the universe. It still hurt to remember how she pulled on her mother's clothes as she begged for help. Only for Aurora to look at her daughter with a completely blank face, as if she was so far away from reality that she couldn't even hear her desperate pleas.

It hadn't been until she found some nuts at the windowsill of the tree-house and almost choked, devouring them within seconds, that she had decided to venture into the woods and find anything that would ease the pain in her gut.

Hope had a clear memory engraved in her mind. In her heart. A memory a few months after she went to hunt for food for the first time. Of looking at her own hands and wrists and poking at the meat in them. The *meat*, instead of the shape of the bones, peaking through her skin.

And it might have been there and then, when she realized she didn't need anyone to survive. It might have been there and then, when she realized that waiting for other people to act was a waste of time and a risk to her own life. It might have been there and then that she realized she could do anything. She could fight the world by herself. And no one and nothing could stop her.

And even if Hope would say she was hungry now, sitting on an empty crate in the roofless cellholt that had been taking them to Thyria for over four weeks, this was a different type of hungry. It was a *I'd like some food* hungry, not a *I'm going to actually die here if I don't eat* hungry.

"Recount finished," Jessica said from the middle of the cellholt, and everyone quieted for her to continue, dread already set on many faces. "You want the bad or the worst news first?"

"Fucking Llunal," Aridian said, covering his head with his hands from where he sat next to Nina and Hope. Other courtrades echoed alternative swearings.

"On with it, Jess," Marcus ordered, frowning. "Worst first."

"Almost three quarters of the food we have left has worms." She gagged, intentionally avoiding looking at the rear of the cellholt where a pile of bags with multiple knots sat.

"How did that happen?" Marcus' voice was sharp as a knife.

Jessica turned her serene face to him, her eyes narrowing as if she was trying to figure out whether he was trying to blame her for this. "How would I fucking know, Marcus?"

"You were the one responsible for sorting out the subsistence for this mission." Marcus crossed his arms over his dark clothes. "Were you not?"

Jessica's lips were a thin line, and her eyes still narrowed, looking at Marcus. She nodded quietly, her expression becoming more angry as each second passed.

"That was a question," Marcus insisted in the middle of the silent courtrades. "Were you not the responsible for subsistence and therefore the one who should know precisely why the fuck we have fucking worms in our fucking food?"

"You can shove all your fucks and fuckings up your ass, Marcus," Jessica spat, not backing down. "That right there is your fucking problem."

Aridian said quietly next to Hope, "Here we go again." Hope didn't need to see him to know he was rolling his eyes. But only Nina and she seemed to have heard him.

Jessica continued, "You always rely on the shadows, telling you every single thing before you make any decision. Before you make all your big plans. But they don't know everything, Marcus. They don't always get it right. Life happens. Mistakes happen. You can't plan your life based on whispers of night. You sometimes have to take a risk."

Marcus inhaled sharply, his fists tightening in his still crossed arms. Hope wasn't sure if there was a hint of hurt in his eyes. He said, "My fucking problem right now is that I have twenty-five people to feed, and no food to do so."

Jessica put a strand of blond hair behind her tan ear. "As a matter of fact, you do. If you could have resisted the urge to spill your blaming shit on me, I would have already told you the bad news." She turned to face the courtrades around her, Nina, Aurora and Hope sitting amongst them.

"There are four rations of food per person, and we have four days left until we reach the vessels underneath Corentre," Jessica explained, lifting her eyebrows with intent as she added, "Be *thankful* we found out before we ate everything edible, so at least we won't be semi unconscious by then." With that, she stormed into the changing room of the cellholt, one of the very few spaces that provided any privacy in this place.

Nina did not need any reminder to think about her brother. Hope saw it in her face every single time she was staring outside the cellholt, the unavoidable frown in her pale face. It might have been the fact that Jessica had mentioned being semi-unconscious, or simply that they were four days away of finally reaching the island where her brother was.

"I can't believe we will be in Thyria so soon," Nina said. "When I was discarded, I never thought I would see it again."

Hope made space for her friend on the blanket on the floor. Nina sat next to her, looking at the blue waters behind the glass walls of the cellholt and the vessels.

"You never told me," Hope said as she finished polishing one of many blades. "How did you get yourself discarded but not killed?"

Nina half-smiled. "I was caught short, to be honest. The Organ's heir sometimes visits the Houses to discard beings, so I waited for him to pay one of his visits to the West House, and I stole something from him."

Hope's eyebrows lifted. "Stealing from the Organ House's heir?" She chuckled. "I didn't take you for a thief."

"Well, I am not a good one, and he caught me before I even started," Nina clarified.

"What did you want to steal?" Hope asked.

"The servants he brings always carry his belongings. I wanted to find a compassom, to make it harder for him to know who to discard," Nina explained. She exhaled deeply before adding, "Even though, knowing his reputation, he would have probably ended up killing the people, or discarding twice the amount of people he had doubts about instead. So maybe it was a good thing I never got my hands on one."

Hope waited for her to continue, so Nina did. "He found me poking around in the guest rooms he always used. He returned sooner than I had expected him to. I think he had forgotten something or he just knew someone was there." She shrugged. "With panoms, it's difficult to tell which things are just a coincidence."

"What did he do when he saw you?" Hope asked.

Nina swallowed. "He asked why a moon-haired sweetheart was lost in his rooms," she said, tensing. "He said something about a Cardinals' attempt at blessing his night. For a moment, I thought he was going to... force me. Into pleasing him." Nina swallowed, and Hope felt the skin on her spine tense. "But he looked at me and laughed, telling me he wasn't interested in low beings. He told me he would make me pay for treason to the Organ House. And that the payment was going to be my life."

Hope couldn't see the embarrassment in Nina's eyes now looking at the floor of the cellholt. "You are not a low being, Nina. Don't believe that for a minute."

Nina looked at her, her blue eyes as honest as the first time Hope saw them. "Ironically, it was another panom, the one who saved me from death, who convinced the Organ's heir to discard me instead."

"Why did this panom care about you?" Hope asked. She knew that if she ever ended up becoming a full panom, she would not treat the rest of the world like inferior beings.

"He is from the West House. You know, the one we lived in and my parents worked at before they were..." Nina closed her eyes, inhaling deeply. "He must have made some sort of bargain with the Organ's heir, because that panom being would accept nothing he didn't gain from."

Hope looked at Nina, stroked her arm gently. She could imagine how scared she must have been while they were bargaining with her life, how desperate she had been to even take the chance at trying to get discarded to find her brother.

"Who is the panom who saved your life?" Hope asked.

"Ciaran Castel, the heir of the West House," Nina said with a half-smile.

Hope nodded, silently registering that name as she added, "And that jackass? If he's the Organ House's heir, Rhei Coralt is also his father, and therefore, he's my half-brother."

Nina's eyes widened then narrowed, scanning Hope. "I never realized you have the same black hair and full lips as Jake Coralt."

29

Lenna

Lenna grinned at the golden feline cub rolling happily on the floor of the Coronary Atrium. There were some of her spare golden sparks floating around it, still trying to find somewhere to go in this new being she just created.

"I shouldn't be surprised about your soul animal being a big cat," Jake said next to her, a hint of a smile in his voice.

"She's not a big cat, you idiot. She's a tiny, cute lynx cub." She kneeled and extended her hand to stroke its glowering golden fur.

The golden animal twisted her mouth to Lenna's stroking hand and bit it sharply before running to the other side of the room, making Lenna do a high-pitched scream. "Tiny cute bastard, is what she is!" she shouted, her jaw dropping.

Jake laughed, tilting his head back. "That is literally the best representation an animal could have done of your soul," he said. "All nice and cute on the outside, probably also cute on the inside, but ready to rip your head off should you attempt to approach her."

Lenna Took the blood drops from her finger and Gave a tissue to her other hand so she could press it to the wound. She lifted her gaze to Jake. "Nice and cute on the outside? Is that your best description of *my outside*?"

Jake's eyes glowed. "What about attractive and sexy as fuck, with these ridiculous golden eyes that rip souls apart, and this fire hair of yours that can burn a man?"

Lenna put her now scarred-but-not-bleeding finger on her lips, thinking. "Better."

Jake continued walking until he was standing right behind her, but she didn't move. He lowered his head until he was speaking straight into the spot underneath her ear. "If you thought the show you put on at the House two weeks ago with your "trainer" would make me want you more, you were Cardinals-damned right, sweet fire." His breath on her neck was warm, and she might have arched her back a little at the sound of his voice.

"Don't think I have forgotten what you looked like during your Fifth Ceremony." He smiled and Lenna felt the muscles of his cheek moving against her skin as he did so. "You and your gold, sweet fire, have been chasing my dreams."

"Pity that I'm sharing my rooms with another man," she said. Because she would not talk about how he had been appearing in her own dreams. Too fucking often.

"Pity you haven't fucked that man yet so I can hear your moans through the walls," Jake whispered.

She had had no interchange with Theon after his very pleasant but short welcome, mainly because she had spent so many hours in the Coronary Atrium with this busybody.

"You had that pleasure when you were staying in the North House, didn't you? You have always been a creepy stalker." Lenna spun around over her feet, ending up extremely close to his gorgeous face and full lips.

"I wasn't the one moaning through the gardens," he said. He did not take a step back even though they were so close that Lenna could see dark blue dots on his silver irises.

"I need to show you something useful about your mark," he said, the corners of his lips curling upwards. Lenna nodded, giving him permission, trying to stay calm.

"Don't kick my balls, okay? They are very precious," he added, making Lenna snort.

He closed his hand in front of her chest, leaving the skin and the bottom part of her lacy white bra exposed as he Took a chunk of her shirt away.

"Golden skin, golden sparks, golden ink, golden mark," he said, placing his index finger on the top petal of her panom mark between her breasts, tracing its shape.

"Golden heart too," Lenna winked, trying not to shiver at his gentle touch. At imagining precisely where she wanted that finger to be.

His eyes shot up from the mark under her breasts to her amber eyes. His nostrils flared slightly, as if he knew or could sense the line of her thoughts. "I'm trying to concentrate here," Jake said.

"So sorry, Panom Guidor." She blinked a few times in a false apology.

"You see how your North petal becomes bright?" he asked.

Lenna looked down at her chest. "My big besties don't let me see past them, actually." She held her breasts tightly against her body with both hands, separating them just enough to see the golden panom mark underneath. "I see. What about it?" she asked casually.

Jake inhaled sharply, nostrils definitely flaring now.

"You have been Giving for a few weeks and sort of control it, so your body acknowledges the North Petal. It recognises the magic ability in you to Give, as the North Cardinal used to."

"I very much doubt I can Give anywhere like the North Cardinal could," Lenna said.

"You certainly can't," he snorted. "But you get the point. If your petal glows, your magic considers this skill mastered, and you will be able to use it at will. It might be time for you to take it a step forward, to expand the strength of your Giving."

His finger traced the bottom petal, and Lenna's chest expanded as she took a deep breath in. Again, she felt a small ticklish sensation. The South Petal also became bright, a line of golden sparks matching the one above it.

"You also control Taking."

"Thank the fucking Cardinals for that. Only Giving, and I would have collapsed by now," Lenna said.

Jake met her stare, not taking his finger off her panom mark yet. "What do you feel when you Give too much without Taking to compensate your harmony scale?"

"I feel as if I have been drinking way too much myster on an empty stomach," Lenna said, ignoring the smirk on his lips. "Dizzy, as if would lose the ability to stand straight. Tired. I see golden sparks floating on the sides of my vision too. Not my real golden sparks. They don't shine as bright."

"Interesting. Different panoms, different symptoms," he said.

"What do you feel?" Lenna asked.

"Pain."

Lenna lifted her eyebrows. She wasn't sure what type of pain he meant, but he looked down at her panom mark, clearly not interested in talking about it further.

"You have two petals under control," he continued. "I'm going to trace the West and East petals now. I want you to close your eyes and tell me which one you feel more."

Whatever the Fifth that meant. Lenna closed her eyes, feeling his finger move gently across her skin.

"Nothing?" Jake asked.

"Other than your touch? No. Nothing," she said with her eyes closed.

Jake's finger moved again, and she felt her spine tensing. "I felt something now," she said. She did not know if any panom magic had caused the feeling, or it had been her body reacting to his touch, though.

"Open your eyes," Jake said, and Lenna found him smiling at her. "You are not only a generous Giver, dominating that skill before any others, but you are also more prone to Healing than Harming. Cute on the inside, indeed, sweet fire."

The West petal had caused that sensation, then. Coincidentally, it was in the West House where healers were still working day and night to bring Raoul to consciousness, Ciaran kept reassuring her. It had been way too long, with no improvement at all. Way too long since Raoul had been brought from the discarding island.

It was well known that Healing and Harming were considerably more complex to master. Lenna tried to stay patient these weeks while learning to Give and Take, but Cardinals guide her if she would not try her damned best at mastering Healing. If she had any chance to help Raoul, to wake him up from wherever his mind was, Healing was probably the way she could do it.

Jake removed his finger from her skin, and Lenna immediately asked, "What about the inner circle of the panom flower?"

He tilted his head to the side, as if considering if she was genuinely curious or just wanted his touch on her for a while longer.

"Your arms must be getting sore from holding your *besties*," he said, a silent offer in his voice.

"Worry not. I would rather be sore than have someone with no morals holding my besties," she spat. The Fifth would damn her for being such a liar.

"So we're back to the no morals situation." Jake's eyes narrowed.

"You are one of the key players in the discarding game of this society, the game your daddy is a master at," she explained. "Don't think for a minute that I forget who I am talking to and all the shit you do. How you ruin people's lives for no reason."

Jake held her stare. "Someone needs to discard the lower beings, so the lands keep their balance. So that our islands don't sink into the seas."

Lenna made a mental note of the plural. He didn't consider his island just Thyria, if there was more than one he felt possessive about.

"I thought you were all about pushing boundaries and testing limits," Lenna replied. As far as she was concerned, there was no difference between him pushing her to make her own harmony scale uneven, and him not discarding people to make the harmonic balance of the land uneven. Her raising anger showed in her palms, pressing harder against her breasts.

Jake swallowed, an emotion Lenna couldn't identify crossing his eyes. He put his finger back on her skin, tracing the circle inside her panom mark. Lenna inhaled, her chin lifting at the touch.

"History says that the inner circle of a panom mark would brighten only for those who gained the Fifth Power," Jake explained. "As I told you, there is no record of anyone alive with it. No matter how many times I trace it on you, it will not brighten."

He opened his hand and Gave the missing part of her shirt back to Lenna. She finally changed positions and crossed her arms, her lips in a thin line.

"I love it when you are angry," Jake said, his eyes darkening. "You want a reason to hate me, to resist the need for my cock inside you. I told you once, sweet fire, and I will say it again: you will beg for it. Sooner or later, you will beg for me."

"Take a seat and get comfy," she spat, but Lenna's core tightened as her eyes narrowed.

The side of his lips curled upwards. "But if you want to hate me for having "no morals", I will tell you a little secret. You and I, Brachyan, will never be together. Heirs of the Houses can't be together, not without causing a panomquake that will break Thyria in half. So all this teasing," he grabbed her breasts, squeezing them as Lenna gasped, "is because I like to play with fire. And when you finally beg me to fuck you, sweet fire, I will refuse."

30

Hope

Aurora brought a pile of clean courtrade-black clothes to Hope and sat next to her on the crates of the cellholt. She held Hope's hand tightly in between hers. "I don't think I tell you enough times how proud I am to be your mother and how much I love you."

"I love you too, mother."

"Are you nervous for what you will find in Thyria?" Hope didn't need her to mention her father. Both of them knew that was what she wanted to find in Thyria.

"I am. Nervous, excited, curious and impatient. Thank you for coming with us. I know you said you wanted to, but you didn't have to. I appreciate not being alone in such an important moment of my life."

Aurora smiled with all the kindness and love that a heart could bear. "You didn't leave me alone when I wanted to end my life in this world. You were little, and yet you didn't leave my side. You didn't stop insisting I ate.

You looked after me when I couldn't look after either of us. You are brave, my dear Hope. You have always been."

Aridian passed by and must have overheard the last few sentences as he started and grinned at Hope. "If you're so brave, come throw some of your precious daggers against me."

It was her turn to throw daggers, and the courtrades were making too much noise. They cheered on Hope while she got ready to throw her blade across the cellholt again, aiming at the empty crates on the opposite side. She preferred this annoyingly loud excitement to the moaning rounds of how hungry everyone was and the useless conversations about what they'd love to eat.

"Difficult to guess who you'd like to win," Aridian snapped, an incredulous look on his face as he played with his next blade. "I thought us courtrades had a real family bond."

"Don't be a baby, Ari," Jessica laughed. Nina was also laughing next to her. Jessica added, "The bond is there, but this woman is wiping your ass with her blades. How much longer will it take?"

"Ready to go," shouted the courtrade who just finished piling the crates, adding some extra support from behind to avoid them crashing against the back wall of the cellholt.

Hope's last throw not only reached the middle of the cross they were aiming at, but it made all the crates fall on top of each other, which lead to Marcus shouting that they *would end up playing in the fucking sea if they broke the cellholt with this dumb game.*

But Hope knew Marcus was looking at *this dumb game* from the cabin he had barely left the four weeks it had taken them to reach Thyria. She certainly did not want to break anything, not when they were less than two days away from reaching the exit from the vessels to Corentre.

Thyria. Where Hope would finally meet the male who gave her panom blood and find the answers she needed. Where Nina would finally be closer to reuniting with her brother. Where Aurora, Hope remembered with sudden angst in her chest, would have to face the beings she led all those years ago as the Roix Reigner. But more importantly, her mother would have to face the male she had fallen in love with. The one who broke her heart, mind and soul in such small pieces that took years to put them back together. The one who discarded her and their newborn child because they were inconvenient.

Hope knew deep down that nothing was going to stop her. She was a survivor. She was still alive after over two decades of fighting against all the odds. Her determination and perseverance, her will to achieve whichever goal she set her mind to, was proof that she didn't need anybody or anything to get what she wanted.

In the cellholt, the courtrades stopped cheering, letting Hope focus as she lifted her blade next to her face. But she didn't need to focus. She already knew precisely what she was aiming for.

With the right amount of strength to rip the hypothetical veil off the truths she was chasing and break the crate but not destroy the cellholt, Hope threw her blade.

The blade hit the cross, and the crate was propelled backwards against the protective blankets. Most courtrades and Nina started clapping and shouting with excitement. *Most* courtrades, because Hope felt Marcus' quiet stare on the back of her neck, and Aridian was damning Llunal and all his shadows.

Suddenly, the cellholt shook vigorously, the same strong shaking Marcus usually warned them about when he was about to push the cellholt from their current vessel to one further apart. Except Marcus wasn't touching the living map of the cabin. He was running towards it to find out what had just happened.

Hope, Aurora, and Nina entered the cabin after Aridian and Lidia. Marcus' second and third in command stayed alert and silent, awaiting orders. Marcus' jaw clenched, his fingers touching and adjusting the multiple views on the living map in front of him.

Hope saw the fear in Nina's eyes and the calm storm brewing in her mother's dark eyes. Only experience let someone stay in control of their rawest emotions when everything around them was collapsing.

"That was not a burst of panom power," Marcus whispered. "And for the cellholt to move from vessel F35C to D19H... That is a massive jump. It can't be accidental. Which means..."

"The roixers know where we are, and that we are intruders," Aurora finished for him.

31

Lenna

There wasn't any space left on the tables at their usual spot on the rooftop where Lenna, Theon, Ciaran, and the bunch sat around.

The table in front of Lenna had an array of empty and half-empty glasses of myster, cards and dies that had escaped the deck pile, empty plates of snacks that had kept them entertained for a few hours now, and spare valers and grolls here and there that had no clear owner after so many rounds of CoreCode.

The sky was dark, the red moon and its Cardinals-lightened stars the only sources of the reddish light above them. Next to Brendon and Sasha, Theon finally stood and walked calmly towards the pretty woman on the other side of the rooftop who had been eyeing him all night.

"I saw that coming," Lenna chuckled, turning to Ciaran. "You never told me how you donated petals to this lot to make them panoms," she said, pointing at Sasha, Brendon, and Carson.

Ciaran looked at her, swiftly combing his dark hair with his metallic arm. "I only donated a petal to each of them, so they are not panoms. Not fully. They have barely enough to send ink, create some sparks, and not much more. A bit like what you could do before your Fifth Ceremony."

"*Not much more* your ass," Sasha said, the hand that wasn't holding her current myster glass on her hip.

"Don't be rude, Ciaran," Brendon nodded in agreement. "We aren't part of the super fancy panom bosses, but we can do some pretty cool stuff. The sparks are always a winner in bed."

"Until one of your lovers tells the roixers and it comes to bite your ass," Sasha spat.

Ciaran's lips curled in a half smile. "I've told him to keep quiet more times than I can remember. He can't resist showing off."

"I mean, why would someone who works at the most secretive organization in Thyria not be able to keep his own secret? It would make absolutely no sense." Sasha rolled her eyes and took a long sip.

"Leave the Invisible Grand alone. One thing has nothing to do with the other," Brendon said, frowning under his blond strands.

"The lady asked you a question, Ciaran," Carson said.

Lenna smiled, nodding. "Thank you. He isn't the best at sharing information, but he knows how to ignore."

Ciaran was looking at the other side of the rooftop, at Theon and the pretty woman now sitting on his lap as he whispered things in her ear and she chuckled. Ciaran's mouth curled in disgust.

As if sensing that it was time to step out of this conversation, Carson, Brendon, and Sasha started another round of CoreCode, giving Ciaran and Lenna some privacy.

"Your interest in donation is because you want to give *him* powers," Ciaran said, his long hair moving with the gentle breeze.

It wasn't a question, Lenna realized. It pissed her off. "Well, you donated to your friends, so I wondered why the fuck I couldn't donate to *my* friend."

Ciaran took his blue eyes off Theon and looked at Lenna. "That man is not your friend."

"Excuse me?" her eyebrows raised. "If you mean that I've wanted to fuck him since I've known him, that does not make him any less a friend of mine. And this," she pointed at the tangle of lips and tongue that Theon and the woman now were in that chair, "means nothing. We have nothing. I genuinely don't give a shit. He can fuck whoever he wants, and I can fuck whoever I want."

It was true. Lenna couldn't care less about who was in Theon's mouth, chair, or bed.

It probably wasn't as true that Lenna could fuck whoever she wanted, not until she figured out the mess she had in her head and core these days.

"I didn't mean that," Ciaran said, pausing. "I mean that Theon Chloid is not who you think he is. You would regret donating part of your magic to him for the rest of your life."

Before Lenna could tell him to fuck off because no one had asked his opinion on her personal relationships and that he could shove the donation information somewhere she had no interest in seeing, Ciaran stood up abruptly.

Half a second later, a sweaty Indianna stormed through the door to the rooftop. Carson, Brendon, and Sasha stopped their game, worry in their frowns.

"What the fuck?" Lenna asked.

Indianna reached their corner, panting. Lenna felt Ciaran lifting an invisible barrier surrounding them, as if he had Given it silence. A way to ensure those curious looks from all the other tables minded their own business.

"Catch your breath, girl." Sasha put a hand on Indianna's shoulder, her usually immaculate black bob all over the place. Lenna had almost no doubt that she had run from the other side of Corentre, where her workplace was.

"What's wrong?" asked Ciaran as he opened his hand towards her. She inhaled deeply, thanks to the presumably hyper oxygenated air he Gave her.

"Found out," Indianna managed to say, still panting. "Furious."

Lenna clenched her jaw with impatience. She knew she was not the only one who didn't understand anything. Sasha pulled Indianna down onto a couch while Ciaran opened his hand a few more times, allowing her to take some deep breaths.

Indianna's brown eyes finally focused. She lifted her head to the sky, and she almost looked like she was going to cry. Lenna was going to cry from frustration soon too if this woman didn't chill and talk.

"Sorry," Indianna said. "The Organ Mandor brought Raoul to the Beftac Center an hour ago. He ordered us to put him in the highest security medical vault and to not provide any care until he found out who had brought him back from Verdania. I came as soon as I could leave the unit."

Lenna felt the floor disappear from underneath her feet, and thanked the five Cardinals for being sat down already, immediately regretting any thankfulness and damning every single one of them. They were fucked. She looked at Ciaran and saw the concern in his frown, too.

Raoul had been in the West House, cared for by their healers all this time. Lenna knew Ciaran and his father wouldn't have informed the Organ Mandor of his body's return to Thyria—because who knew where his mind was—so this would most definitely be considered treason.

Ciaran and Cobrian Castel were going to be punished for trying to keep Raoul alive. Every single one of those healers was probably going to be killed, unless the Organ Mandor felt generous and discarded them instead. And why would he feel generous when a discarded being had returned against his orders and it had been kept from him?

Lenna felt a sting in her arm at the same time as Ciaran twitched his biological arm. Both looked at their skins simultaneously. She knew that every panom in Thyria had just received Rhei Coralt's ink, and that every panom would also have felt the pain. It was not normal ink, Lenna realized with horror. It was bleeding ink.

The Organ Mandor summons you to the Cardinals' Temple.

Lenna tried to wipe the Organ Mandor's bleeding ink from her arm, but it was not going away. She had already tried Taking it from her skin with no success.

"It will not go away until we're there," Ciaran mumbled, as if his mind was somewhere else.

Ciaran had moured all of them from the rooftop to his apartment in Corentre—all of them except Theon, who had been so busy playing with the woman that he had missed the commotion Indianna's sprint had caused. By the time Ciaran started mouring them, he was nowhere to be seen.

Ciaran put his metallic hand over his eyes as he muttered, "Something is very wrong."

"I agree," Lenna said. "We're cardinally fucked."

Ciaran only shook his head slightly, his silver fingers protecting him from the light in the room, as if he was trying to concentrate.

"I'm pretty sure if we are late to this summoning, it will be five times worse. Shall we go?" she said. Ciaran ignored her, still shaking his head. Lenna wasn't sure if he had even heard her, so she insisted, "Ciaran Castel, can you moure us to the Temple right now, please?"

He finally stood up and placed his hand on the back of her neck. Lenna couldn't identify the dark glimmer in his eyes. Her best guess would have been extreme dread or extreme worry. She would definitely agree with both.

32

Hope

Marcus walked to the doorway that opened to the rest of the cell-holt, all the courtrades standing in line.

He walked between both lines, his firm steps not faltering as he said, "We are less than forty hours from reaching the tunnel underneath Corentre. The tunnel will take us to the city above the net of vessels, where the Thyrian courtrades will be ready to assist us."

"But it looks like the roixers have somehow detected that this is a rogue cellholt and are pushing vessels around to intercept us." His voice was as sharp as the blades Hope and Aridian had been throwing minutes before. "I do not plan on dying in the middle of a Llunal-damned vessel, nor letting any of you die at their hands."

Hope saw a few courtrades nodding in silence as Marcus continued, "I want everyone armed to the teeth with every single weapon you have. I want everyone to put two food rations in your pockets, packs, or wherever you deem comfortable. I am going to set up multiple automatized vessel jumps in the living map to mislead them while we run on foot through the vessels until we reach our destination. We start running in fifteen minutes."

Marcus went back to the cabin and started making carefully thought movements on the living map, including multiple calculations that had probably taken months to figure out.

"The only way to make them believe they are chasing us is to base the future pushes of the vessels on the usual panom forces across the net," Marcus explained as Aridian and Jessica donned on every single weapon they owned. Nina and Aurora were outside the cabin, getting whatever they needed. Marcus looked at Hope and said, "I know you have all your blades and weapons on you every single time you are awake, but you need to grab your two rations of food."

"I can look after myself," Hope said.

Aridian rolled his eyes, "We know you are a super powerful woman that does not need any help ever, but take these two rations and shut up, will you?" He threw two portions at Hope's chest and she grabbed them before they hit her, pocketing them quickly.

"How much blood do you need for all these jumps you are scheduling?" Hope asked.

Marcus looked at her then at the crystal orb that stored the source of energy that her panom blood had now become. "Twice the usual amount, just to be safe," Marcus said. "In usual circumstances, it would fuel the cellholt for six days, but if I can instruct the pushes to be more intense, the cellholt might get farther, traveling faster."

So, by the time the roixers intercepted it and saw there was no one inside, they would be too far to catch them within the vessels before they made their way out. Without further explanations, Hope cut her hand and let the blood flow inside the crystal.

It was all about time. Reaching the tunnel before the roixers caught them and tried to kill them all was like going against a time-ticking panom bomb.

Marcus soon walked outside the cabin and said, "Time's up. We jump from the cellholt while it's moving. If they are monitoring the living map and they see a decrease in speed, they will know when we have abandoned it and track us from here."

"Isn't it going faster than ever?" Nina asked Hope.

Hope held Nina's hand, unable to ignore what the cold sweat on her pale skin meant. She looked at Nina, who was staring at Marcus with wide eyes and a deep frown, presumably considering if he had lost his mind.

"It is going faster so it can go farther and buy us some time," Hope explained, but Nina didn't take her eyes off Marcus. "We are jumping together, Nina. As we will climb the tunnel to Corentre. Together."

Nina swallowed, her frown still persistent. Hope continued, "Your brother might be right above us right now, and he needs you. But we need to get out of this net of vessels first. That is all we have to do. All we will do, and we will do it together."

Hope squeezed Nina's hand, and she returned the squeeze. Before Nina could reconsider, Hope pulled until they were behind Aurora in the long line of beings. The line of courtrades was facing the back of the cellholt, where crates were now piled forming steps that lead to the roofless top of the vehicle. As Marcus gave the signal, they started jumping out one after the other. Without hesitation. Without fear.

Far from fear, some courtrades seemed extremely excited to have some action after dull weeks sitting inside the same four glass walls of the cellholt. Never minding the fact that this action involved lethal military-trained roixers chasing them in an underwater net of Cardinally created vessels.

Aurora's turn to jump shortly approached, and she winked at Hope and Nina before jumping out. Hope and Nina were next, only leaving Lidia, Aridian and Marcus behind them.

They climbed the crates to the top, unable to fully stand as their heads would hit the blueish and fast-moving top of the vessel. Hope held Nina's hand tight. She was perfectly aware of how much sweaty and much colder her hand had become in the space of a couple of minutes.

"I've got you, Nina," Hope said. "Let's make this trip worth it. For your brother." She counted to three, and their feet shot into the air.

33

Lenna

T he Cardinals' Temple was full.

The Organ Mandor had presumably removed the epitellia wards of the Organ House to allow the panoms to answer to his summons.

Panoms were separated into different groups, mostly the members of each House sticking together. There had to be almost a hundred of them. Some looked spotless, as if they had been readying for an encounter with the Organ Mandor for days and they considered it an honor. Some looked rather wrecked, especially the parents of very young children who carried these in arms. A new mother was nursing her baby while she stood in the waiting crowd, the look on her face much closer to pure anger than fear.

Lenna didn't want to get anywhere near the what-have-you-done face of her sister or the already judging expression of her father, nor her mother's concerned eyes. She hadn't missed them one bit since she had moved to Corentre. Lenna nodded in silence and that was as much as a hello-long-time-no-see as she wanted to offer.

She preferred to be with Ciaran, who was next to his father and who she guessed were a multitude of cousins, uncles, and aunts. She knew that affiliating herself with the West House was not a clever choice, considering where Raoul had been found and who would be the first ones expected to give explanations.

Before she had time to search for someone in particular, the massive doors to the throne room opened, and everyone made their way inside. After the last person crossed the doorway, the doors closed with a loud bang.

Rhei Coralt moured straight onto the throne made of black feathers and bones on the altar a few steps above. His short, black hair framed silver eyes, a look of pure dominance on his face.

Lenna held her breath as Jake moured in after him and stood next to his father. His face was completely emotionless. The face of the discarder of Thyria. The face of the Heir of the Organ House, only son of the Organ Mandor.

Lenna felt her guts twisting at that sight. She didn't recognize him.

A baby cried at the back of the room and Rhei Coralt bared his teeth at the noise. He closed his hand sharply, Taking the voice of the child. Lenna hoped he had only Taken his voice and not the air of his little lungs too.

Nobody made a single noise as the Organ Mandor opened both hands, two sharp daggers appearing in them, one made of Cardinal-red crystal, one made of obsidian. The Lawful Stabs. The unbreakable ones used for centuries to inflict punishments.

Lenna held her breath, trying to ignore the shaking of the panom next to her.

Rhei Coralt looked at every soul in front of him, his somber face twisting as his stare moved from one being to the next. "Someone must explain how a discarded being returned to Thyria."

The room was silent. The only noise was his impatient tapping of the red dagger's glass against the bones on his throne.

Cobrian Castel took a step forward, his old voice rough. "The discarded being was found in the West House. As the Ruler of the House, I will endeavor to provide an explanation." A wave of panom power pushed the crowd, and he soared across the floor until he was in front of the Organ Mandor.

Ciaran walked next to where his father had been forcedly taken, and Lenna moved behind him, despite the barely recognizable alarm she read in Jake's eyes. Cobrian, despite his advanced age showing in his many wrinkles and white hair, could have perfectly walked to that same spot. Being moved there by force was just a reminder of who had the biggest power on this island.

"Explain," Rhei Coralt ordered.

Ciaran's shoulders shook slightly, his chin slightly tilting upwards.

"He was a servant of the West House before he was discarded more than two years ago. His body appeared on the doorstep of our castle a few weeks ago," Cobrian said, his voice even.

"By magic?" Rhei Coralt snorted.

"None of us certainly brought him there."

The Organ Mandor asked, "And you forgot to mention this on the occasions we have met?"

Cobrian shook his head lightly. "I didn't think it was relevant compared to the paramount matters the Organ House has to control." He bowed his head deeply with respect. Ciaran bowed his head slightly too, even though his icy stare didn't reflect the action.

The Organ Mandor tilted his head slightly. "The discarded being has been taken to Corentre. I expect you or your heir to dispose of him as soon as he is ready."

Lenna's heart couldn't beat any faster, any stronger. Cobrian paled as he asked, "Dispose of the man?"

"He is not a *man*. He is a discarded being," Rhei Coralt clarified sharply. "The healers at the Beftac Center will analyze his body for information about how he returned to Thyria. It would be helpful to examine his peculiar... psychic state. As Ruler and heir of the House, I cannot kill either of you without altering the lands we live in, hence why your punishment will come in another form." The blood in Lenna's veins froze.

"Your ancient body will not survive what you deserve, so I need to make some adjustments," the Organ Mandor told Cobrian. "You will receive five strikes from the red Lawful Stab, and your heir will receive the remaining twenty. And when he is ready, one of you will kill the discarded being."

"No!" Lenna shouted, her voice leaving her mouth before she could reconsider. The corner of her eyes registered Jake's wide ones. She stepped forward, standing next to Ciaran. "You can't kill him," she said.

"Excuse me?" The Organ Mandor's eyes were practically slits.

"You can't kill him," Lenna repeated before adding, "Please."

The Organ Mandor laughed. "In case anyone here ever dares challenge what I can or can't do, let me remind you." He stood and walked to the front of the altar.

"Despite whatever illusion of power being Rulers and heirs to the petal Houses gives you, there is only one ruler in Thyria: the Ruler of the Organ House, blessed by all the Cardinals and the Cardinal Queen herself," he said, his voice resonating off the walls. "I rule this city, this country, and this Cardinals-blessed world. Everyone answers to me. My generosity is letting you live."

"If you were so generous, you would let him live," Lenna insisted. The fear in her was so real, it was palpable. Fear for Ciaran's punishment. Fear for Raoul's life. She saw Jake closing his eyes briefly.

The Organ Mandor looked at Lenna, and Lenna felt her knees bending against her will, leaving her kneeling in front of him. "Having someone with such a mouth as the Heir of the North House is going to bring problems."

"So I have been told all my life," she spat.

Jake's voice sounded inside her head: *Shut that pretty mouth of yours for once, sweet fire.* Lenna tried her best to not jump at the sudden mental whisper. Jake's face was mainly impassible, only his eyes showed a glimpse of anger.

"I have always been devoted to integrating crucial messages from a young age, in unforgettable manners," Rhei Coralt said, and Lenna could have sworn Jake shivered, his upper lip curling. "Since your parents clearly failed at teaching you, I must ensure sure you learn discipline, Lenna Brachyan."

He closed his hand, and her upper body was exposed. Lenna didn't know if one of the few gasps from the crowd belonged to her sister or her mother. She felt Ciaran's body next to her tensing.

Despite her legs still locked in a kneel, her arms weren't locked, so she covered her exposed chest.

"You will receive five strikes with the red Lawful Stab. You will be locked in the subterranean cells until you remember your place as the heir of the North House and who will always rule over you. Until you ask for forgiveness."

"Fuck you," Lenna spat.

Rhei Coralt closed his hand, and Lenna found her voice leaving her, almost choking. She knew that if she tried to speak, only silence would come out.

"In fact, let me return your voice," he smiled as he opened his hand and the sensation on Lenna's throat disappeared. "I want to hear you screaming while you learn this lesson."

She didn't feel the Organ Mandor mouring until he was behind her. She didn't feel the Lawful Stab approaching her skin. She only felt the first deep cut from the top to the bottom of her spine as Rhei Coralt pushed it through.

The pain was unbearable. The Lawful Stab had been infused with power for centuries, and its touch was enough to leave her unconscious on the floor.

Brachyan, open your eyes. Brachyan! If you close them, he will strike harder.

Lenna tried to open her eyes at Jake's mental request, but it was so damn hard.

The pain.

It was so painful. How was she going to take four more? How was Ciaran going to survive twenty of these?

She tried to get ready for a second round, to tell herself that it was almost over, that it would finish soon. But it was nowhere near over, and she couldn't do it. She couldn't endure it again.

The glass cut her skin in a different place this time, and her scream deafened her own ears.

She heard Ciaran asking the Organ Mandor, "May I please take the remaining three strikes in her place?"

But the request was denied between vicious laughs. "She must learn. But I will add three more for you, since twenty seems to not be enough."

She needed to wake up from this painful nightmare. She needed to get out of here.

Don't give him the satisfaction of breaking you.

But he was breaking her. Lenna bit her bottom lip to rein her sobs back in. She tried to open her eyes, the salt of her tears stinging, though barely noticeable compared to what was happening on her back. She heard the blood dripping onto the floor. The clothes on her legs getting wet. The iron-infused smell.

You are much stronger than this, Brachyan. Don't let him break you. He doesn't deserve it.

But the sharp red glass sliced her open again, and she clenched her jaw as much as she could, her teeth aching at the pressure to keep her scream in. Her nostrils flared as the tears flowed freely down her face. She couldn't endure two more. She simply couldn't. Rhei Coralt was going to end her here, in front of his throne and all these panoms, just to prove he could.

She lifted her gaze and looked straight into Jake's eyes. How had he survived this when he was a child? How many times had he endured this? She saw his shoulders and arms tense, his lips in a tight line, and his eyes—his eyes were the definition of rage. His eyes were violence.

"That's enough," Jake's voice cut the air, just as his father was lifting the red Lawful Stab again, ready to strike Lenna's back for the fourth time.

The Organ Mandor's face turned towards his son. "Nobody interrupts the delivery of a punishment, boy, not even you." His face was livid. "*Especially* not you."

"She has learned the lesson. She is an heir. If you kill her, the island will collapse," Jake said, walking down the steps from the altar until he reached his father.

"She won't die from two more strikes." The Organ Mandor grabbed his son by the chin. "But you will do the last strike, boy."

The Lawful Stab hit her again. She couldn't tell if it was making a fresh cut this time or only deepening a previous one. Lenna felt very dizzy. She didn't feel her knees or her back. Her body wasn't hers anymore. She needed to lie down wherever she was going to be sent. Lie down and sleep. For days. She needed this to be over. She knew Jake was going to be punished if he refused to hit her. She only needed him to do it quickly before she collapsed.

"I will not hurt an heir," Jake snapped, removing his father's hand from his face. "I am not as fucked up as you are."

Jake's feet trembled, as if his father was trying to force him into moving but he was resisting.

"Seems like you need discipline too, boy. Again. You will take your favorite number of strikes and some time in the cells while you reflect on your behavior, your priorities, and your duties as the future Organ Mandor," Rhei Coralt said.

Jake's stare was predatory. His eyes held a promise. But Jake kneeled in front of Lenna, closing his hand to Take his own shirt, leaving his exposed back before his father could do it for him. She couldn't focus her stare, but she was damning him for refusing to hit her so he could avoid his punishments. She was starting to think that maybe dying was the best option to stop feeling this excruciating pain.

The Organ Mandor walked behind Jake and sliced his skin open. Lenna only knew because of the ripping sound it made. How he did not even react to such pain was beyond her. How could he master to not scream, when her throat was dry and rough from it?

You are stronger than you think, sweet fire, Jake said into her mind before the glass sliced her for the fifth and last time, and she lost consciousness.

34

Hope

Running had never proved more lifesaving. They were racing for life, against death. A race to get to safety and see tomorrow. A race before the roixers found them in the vessels. A race that had been going on for hours.

Hope was perfectly aware of her ability when putting her body against physical duress. She knew running for hours without a pause was nothing new to her mother, either. She had been impressed at the training of the courtrades before, so seeing them not get tired or complain was not unexpected news.

What Hope hadn't expected was that Nina could run for so long, keeping their quick pace without passing out. The sounds of her own steady breathing and footsteps as they hit the floor intertwined with Nina's next to her. But what Nina's eyes reflected... That was stronger than any physical force. It was stronger than muscles and time. It was sheer determination.

Marcus had instructed them to run as a pack, weapons at the ready, to have a better chance if roixers were waiting for them on the next vessel. Or the one after that.

It would have taken less than a second for Hope, her mother, or most of the highly skilled courtrades in front of her to unsheathe their blades. Which would be less than a second too long. So she had been running with her sharpest blades in each hand. The wound on her palm was still open from when she had last given her panom blood to fuel the cellholt. The weapon she held tightly, rubbing against the dark red bandage covering the open cut, was not the best path to healing. Not that she had the time to care about it.

Hope did not know who had made the first living map of this underwater net that stabilized the islands above, but she had already thanked the Cardinals a few times for only reflecting the cellholts and not the beings within them. Maybe it had been created by the Cardinals themselves. She had a feeling Marcus would probably know.

Marcus, who was leading at the front of the pack, increasing or decreasing speed as he deemed safe, entering new vessels as if he had memorized the living map. Marcus, who held the fate of the twenty-five of them in his hands. Who had held their future on his shoulders since they had stepped into the cellholt, leaving Verdania behind.

Verdania seemed so far. It seemed another life, one Hope was not willing to remember right now. She needed all her focus on these last few hours until they reached the tunnel they'd climb to get out of this blue-tinged labyrinth. Because they were going to make it. There was no other option.

That no one had found them yet could mean two things: their cellholt was still on its way and the roixers were still trying to intercept it, or the roixers had already found it. In the second case, it was a matter of Cardinals-blessed luck they didn't cross their path.

After entering a small vessel to their right, Marcus lifted his arm. The signal to stop.

Hope sheathed her blades on her belts. Next to her, Nina put her hands on her knees, trying to calm her breathing down. From how her legs shook, Hope knew precisely how much effort the last few miles had required.

"I can't believe I haven't fainted yet," Nina chuckled.

Hope smiled, grabbing her leather pouch of water from her pocket and opening the buckle at the top with a hiss. The cloth around her wound moved, sliding down. She inhaled sharply at the rough pain in her palm when the buckle hit the now bleeding spot.

Nina frowned, looking at Hope's hand, her blue eyes widening. "Cardinals guide us. Your hand...It looks awful." Hope didn't reply as she chugged some sips down. "How long have you been bleeding like this? This is going to be infected, Hope. It's terrible."

"I've had worse." It was true, and there was no point in talking about her hand when they had bigger issues to worry about.

"It's not too painful. I promise," Hope said with her best attempt at a reassuring smile.

"Your definition of painful differs from the rest of the Terrhan population." Nina lifted her eyebrows. "But I am seriously concerned about the risk of infection. Let me."

Hope opened her mouth to reply, but before she could tell her to not waste the precious few drops of water she had left, Nina poured a generous amount of water on a clean piece of cloth. She started cleaning it and Hope bit her lip, her nostrils flaring. Nina cleaned the rest of her hand, insisting on the parched areas until her hand was fully clean. Just a clean, deep cut with a bit of redness around it.

"Thank you very much." Nina had done an immaculate job.

Nina smiled softly, blushing a bit. Her blue eyes met Hope's almost-black ones. "I would have loved to be a healer in the West House. But I couldn't receive the proper formation because I was just... Well, a servant. I used to visit the library often though, and the books somehow eased my need to know."

The cloth bandaged around her hand was being moved by very capable hands. If Nina truly hadn't been taught, she definitely had a calling.

"We can share my water when yours runs out," Hope said, glad about Nina nodding instead of refusing.

No one had much water left. Nina prioritizing Hope's healing against her own wellbeing was... Very Nina.

If the thirst was their only thing to ration, they would probably feel lucky, but it wasn't. The food was running low, most of them with one ration left. Some courtrades were eating a quarter or a half of it right now.

And then there was the sleep. Or the lack of sleep, if semantics ever mattered in a situation like this. The maximum rest anyone had gotten was five-minutes laying on the floor of the vessels before running resumed under Marcus' orders.

The good thing about the courtrades was that they seemed in mission-mode. Looking around, Hope could see the signs of tiredness, thirst, and hunger: the dark bags under the eyes, the stretches of backs and necks, the tongues wetting lips, the stomach rumbles. Still, there hadn't been a single moan. All of it would be over soon, if the Cardinals blessed their luck.

A new noise was approaching the spot, aA noise that Hope had become familiar with during the weeks of traveling inside its glass walls.

Everyone stilled, Marcus walking to the back of the pack. He extended his arms and shadows surrounded them, thick, black shadows covering the vessel as if it simply wasn't there.

Hope felt a warm hand on her elbow and knew her mother was there. Nina was on her other side and her blades were already on her hands, ready to attack—if the approaching cellholt didn't run over them first.

The cellholt passed through the circular opening, connecting both vessels. From the cellholt, the roixers would have seen a dark circle where an opening to another blue-tinged vessel should have been, but if the roixers hadn't been looking outside at that moment... Perhaps they stood a chance.

The noise of the cellholt kept moving farther away, disappearing into nothingness with each second. Marcus took his shadows away, his eyes severe.

The risk that the roixers had seen the abnormality in the vessels was too great. They could have perfectly seen it and not raised the alarm on purpose, to keep them convinced no one knew where they were. Right at this moment, other cellholts could be heading their way to this precise vessel. They could be organizing a trap based on their current location.

It was paramount that they moved. Fast.

"You have thirty seconds to get your shit together," Marcus said, his serious voice cutting the surrounding air. "Because then we run, and we don't stop until we climb that fucking tunnel and get the fuck out of this net."

35

Lenna

Lenna woke up with a gasp. She did not know how long she had been on her chest, only that her body was freezing. She tried to lift her head to see where the Fifth she was, but a stinging pain on her back stopped her from doing so. She groaned as the memories returned to her.

The fucking Organ Mandor had put her here, in this subterranean cell. He had left her half dead. With only five strikes of the red Lawful Stab. Lenna was utterly disappointed at her reaction, at not being able to endure the strikes with a smile that would have pissed him off even more.

All she had managed was to keep from begging Rhei Coralt to stop. That had been all her self-control. But the rest? Screaming her lungs off after each hit, her vision blurring from so many tears... She had been no better than the crying baby in the throne room. She thought she was a strong woman, but this was proof that she wasn't. She was fucking weak and breakable, and she hated herself so much for it.

And because she had been such a pitiful show, Lenna knew the fucking idiot had enjoyed every single moment of it. Maybe even her own father had enjoyed it. Or her sister.

Lenna knew who hadn't enjoyed it. Her eyes stung, remembering how Ciaran had offered to bear the pain in her place. At how her friend would bear twenty-three strikes like hers. How was he even going to survive that? She moved an arm and pinched the upper part of her nose strongly, painfully, to keep those tears from falling. She wouldn't cry again.

Had Ciaran already received his punishment? Had Cobrian, his father? Had they gone somewhere safe afterwards, to recover? She doubted they would have been able to moure themselves out in such a state. But with Ciaran, it was always difficult to know what he could or couldn't do.

Silver eyes full of violence crossed her mind. She couldn't push any longer, not thinking about him, about what Jake had done, challenging his own father in front of the panom society, about what that would mean for the political stability of the Houses, for the future of the Organ House. Not that she gave a shit about any of that. They could all drown in the Radel Sea after Thyria collapsed, for all she cared.

No. That wasn't true.

Because if Thyria collapsed, she might not see the challenge in those silver eyes again. She might not hear his voice, ordering her to not give any satisfaction to his father, even if she had fucking done exactly that. Jake had told her she was stronger than this. Did he truly believe his own lie? Had he not seen what a pathetic being she was?

He had tried to protect her.

Lenna felt a deep pain in her chest, too difficult to identify if it was caused by what that might mean or because of her realizing she would have indeed benefited from protection. She, who had always refused to accept any aid, especially from a male. She, who had always believed she was an empowered, independent woman who needed no one on a sentimental level. She, who had fucked and played with every being she wanted to over the years, always avoiding any serious feelings growing and definitely any long-term commitment.

Here she fucking was, hoping with a bigger part of her soul than she would ever admit that Jake Coralt was as fine as he could be. That whatever number of strikes Jake had endured because he'd tried to stop her pain wouldn't have broken him. That, unlike her, he had managed to not give his father the satisfaction of breaking him.

The room started spinning around her, blurring. Her throat needed water. Her back needed her skin sewn together. Her pain needed immediate relief. Her mind needed rest. She needed sleep.

A loud thump crashed against the floor inside the cell. She turned her neck as much as she could, biting her lips at the pain. Amongst the dark specks and the blurriness of her vision, she could see a body, a chest barely raising with agonizingly slow breaths.

Lenna held her breath in as she tried to spin her body on the floor, containing her tears at the pain in her sliced back and her breasts against the rough stone as she pushed herself. She recognized the ink on those arms. She knew that black hair.

That stillness, though. That was new. The overwhelming copper smell of his blood was new too. If Rhei had just finished with him, Lenna guessed she hadn't been in the cell for long. She hoped she hadn't.

Lenna got as close to him as her body could without collapsing again, which was close enough to touch his bare shoulder with her stretched arm.

Her touch caused a sharp inhale, as if it had awoken something in him. The room was spinning again, so Lenna laid her face on the floor, her eyes fixed on the back of his head. Slowly, Jake turned his head towards her, his neck muscles presumably also giving up as he laid his head like hers, his eyes still closed.

He was handsome, Lenna realized. This man who had tried to protect her was handsome. As much as he was brave.

Jake opened his silver eyes sluggishly, as if his eyelids weighed a ton. Lenna wished her head would focus and the world would stop spinning so she could fixate on them. Maybe the Cardinals heard her for once.

The corner of his lips moved with effort, curling upwards. Lenna could only blink at him.

She blinked again before her eyes closed and didn't open this time. She heard his arm moving until his hand held hers. Whether his words were spoken in the cell or in her mind, she couldn't tell.

Sweet dreams, sweet fire.

36

Hope

Regardless of how many vessel changes Marcus guided them through, the sounds of the moving cellholts kept closing in. They hadn't heard any alarms, but that didn't mean the roixers weren't somehow communicating.

Even if they were now under Corentre, the abundance of cellholts around them was too much. They were hunting for them. That's what they had become, Hope thought with a mental snort: prey for the roixers. Shame her goal was the Organ Mandor and not just his roixers, because otherwise she would have been interested in finding out who was prey for who.

Marcus' memory was admirable, as was his sense of orientation. He kept guiding them towards the east in as straight a line as possible—or what Hope wanted to believe was the east. They just needed to advance a few miles more to find the tunnel above them.

A wave of panom power threw them to the ground as the vessel they were in moved and attached to another. Before they had time to stand, the other end of the vessel disconnected, and Hope saw the circular shape of the other vessel closing in.

The dark waters around the vessel net didn't enter the intra-vessel space, though. They respected its interior, and as soon as the end connected to another vessel, another burst of panom power shot through their bodies, leaving them on the floor.

"Two vessels pushed in a row," Aurora said angrily, standing up and walking towards Marcus.

"I've noticed. Thanks for stating the obvious," Marcus snapped. Aurora's lips became a thin line, but she crossed her arms and kept silent.

Marcus turned to face the twenty-four beings waiting for his master plan. Marcus always seemed to have a master plan, or resources and experience enough to make up an improvised one. Hope could have sworn his eyes showed a glimpse of doubt. Or was that fear?

"We are very close," he started, but the expressions of his audience must have been disbelieving, so he added, "We are a few vessels away."

"A few vessels away as in five vessels away or fifty vessels away?" Jessica asked, tilting her head.

"I think closer to ten, but we have a…" Marcus swallowed, as if trying to find words with more positive connotation than *big fucking problem*, "slight complication."

"You are lost," Aurora said, with the authority that her years as Roix Reigner must have given her, the voice of someone used to be listened to and not argued with.

"I'm not," Marcus said, and Aurora's eyes narrowed. The silence emanating from her was pure rage. The sight of her mother's tense body, the scar on her neck, the weapons securely tight against her tight, and most of all, the severity of her face... It was terrifying.

Marcus must have agreed, because he added, "I'm a bit disoriented, that's all. It's impossible not to be when the image of the vessel's net ingrained in my brain might not be accurate. Not anymore."

"We knew it was a living map from the beginning, and the vessels moving were one of the major risks," Hope said, crossing her arms as well. "Another major risk is the cellholts, trying to find us, so what about we postpone this blaming debate for later?"

Because those noises were getting closer again.

"And what? We run blindly until we see the damned tunnel?" Jessica spat.

"Unless you have a better idea," Marcus said. "If a cellholt appears in front of us, we use shadows."

Hope and Aurora would have to fight in the dark, and Nina would hopefully manage to not get killed between shadows, weapons, and vehicles. A brilliant plan.

Not waiting for anyone else to discuss this further, Marcus started running again.

He was changing vessels often, trying to gravitate around the same area. When a vessel led them to a louder noise, he ordered a 180-degree direction change, running back to where they had entered it. The chances of miraculously finding the tunnel while playing hide and seek with the roixers were close to none.

A cellholt ran past the end of the long vessel they were in. Marcus extended his hands, and shadows slipped from his fingertips into the bit that connected both vessels. Aridian extended his hands as well, and so did other courtrades, the shadows becoming as thick as they were black.

A physical wall now stood where the opening had been, a thick wall that would buy them a few more minutes.

A cellholt ran past the other end of their vessel, and Hope felt her heart clench like a fist. This one was close enough to identify around ten roixers wearing their usual bright red uniforms inside the vehicle. And that loud screeching sound… That was the cellholt stopping.

They were too close, too damn close to be safe. Hope didn't dare take her eyes from where the cellholt would appear any second now. She didn't need to look at Nina to see the fear emanating from her, or to know that Aurora's eyes were cold, calculating.

A few courtrades were sending their shadows towards that end of the vessel corridor. Another physical block. Another few minutes it would buy.

But that would be no help if the tunnel they were looking for was in those vessels or any others that derived from them. They were lost. And the net of vessels… It was a dangerous labyrinth.

The tunnel was the only way out of this trap. Daring to believe the shadow blocks could stand against forces from the other sides, Hope turned to Marcus. His face was pale, utterly grave.

That they were not running yet was the only real indicator that Marcus didn't know where to go. He didn't know what to do.

Hope bit her bottom lip, inhaling sharply. There had to be a way to find the tunnel. She refused to believe their fates were doomed because the roixers had found them. There had to be an alternative. There was always an alternative. But right at this moment, what she desperately needed was what she had always rejected.

She needed help.

The noise of another cellholt approaching through one of the smaller vessels was evidence. The bangs coming from the shadow blocks were evidence. The third shadow block being created by the courtrades, this time led by Jessica, to cover the connection to the smaller vessel where the noise was emanating from was evidence.

There were only three small open vessels left. They were not fully trapped, not yet, but they needed help. She needed help to save Nina and her mother. To save herself. The seconds were ticking as fast as the hits against the shadow blocks were banging, as fast as other vehicles were approaching.

She needed *help*. And she needed it *now*.

A bird with blood-red wings appeared from one of the smaller, still-open vessels. Its speed was supernatural, and its loud cry roared in Hope's blood. Her body reacted to the intense cry, to the racing wings, to what this presence could mean. But there was no time to think about any of that. There was only time to run.

Hope started running towards the bird, trying to keep the pace. She was aware of Nina and her mother following closely behind. She could also identify Marcus, Jessica, and Aridian's jagged breathing.

The red bird flew high, its wide wings almost touching the ceiling of the vessels. Its turns from vessel to vessel were sharp, determined. Every vessel it guided them to was empty. The noises of the cellholts around them were still louder than what could be deemed safe, but the bird kept guiding them through smaller vessels. Vessels where cellholts wouldn't even fit.

But Hope didn't have time to care about every member of the pack. As long as Nina and her mother were behind her, she would keep running. She would keep chasing the bird that might be their salvation.

The bird that had now turned upwards and disappeared from the vessel through a vertical tunnel in the land.

37

Hope

Before Hope reached the spot underneath the tunnel, her mother overtook her. One knee on the floor, Aurora facilitated the jump so Hope could grab the lower rail of the tunnel. A step towards salvation.

Hope knew better than to argue with her mother and trusted Nina would be right after her. Marcus would then aid Aurora, and the courtrades would follow suit.

So, Hope jumped upwards, her leg muscles tensing at the strain. Her fingertips touched the metal bar inside the caved tunnel, her palm curving around its cold shape. She pushed the rest of her body up and looked down to see her mother motioning to Nina.

Nina tried jumping twice until Hope grabbed her wrist and pulled her upwards. The noises of the cellholts were approaching once more, as if they had found them again within the net.

Her mother looked at Marcus as he lifted his arms towards her, and Hope's heartbeat halted. But shadows only whirled around Aurora, lifting her, holding her straight as they twisted around her legs and waist until Hope and Nina were rushing up the tunnel, leaving space for Aurora below.

Up they went, not looking down, not hesitating. Hope was climbing the metal ladder on the never-ending wall as fast as she could. She knew that their speed was the only thing separating the courtrades from the roixers, from the cellholts, getting closer to the spot underneath.

Because even if she was climbing, far away from the opening to the vessel with each passing second, the sounds of the cellholts were not decreasing. They were getting closer. Louder.

Somewhere below within the tunnel, Jessica shouted, "Tell that fucking idiot to climb now!"

"Marcus, climb!" Aridian echoed.

Up, up, up they went, no sign of the bird across the length of the tunnel. Yet down below, the cellholt noises were so loud. Too loud. Until they stopped. And then the screams of the physical fights started.

Hope didn't dare waste a breath looking down. She knew she wouldn't see anything other than dark shapes and a silver-haired head immediately underneath her feet.

"Fucking Llunal—climb the fuck up, Marcus!" Aridian roared, a tinge of fear in his voice.

If the roixers entered the tunnel, they would be damned. The risk was too high. Too many things could go wrong.

"I'm in! I need all your thickest shadows to form an impenetrable shadow block. Let's keep these bastards at bay. Shadows down, now!" he shouted, and Hope felt the walls of the tunnel shake, the rail she was holding shaking vigorously. If their shadows broke the rail...

But they didn't. Shortly after, the fighting from the vessels was muted. An impenetrable wall indeed.

"How many courtrades were sacrificed?" Jessica asked.

Marcus' voice was quiet, either because he was the last one down the tunnel, or because he couldn't find his strength as he said, "Six of us. Darren, Andela, Kyra, Oliver, Fiona, and Poppy. May the stars not hinder their darkness. May Llunal shade them all."

"May the stars not hinder their darkness. May Llunal shade them all," the unified voices of the remaining courtrades echoed in the tunnel. Hope shook her head, but it was not the time to mourn.

For there was a growing point of light at the end of the tunnel.

It was happening.

They were in Thyria. They had reached Corentre.

Hope stopped dead when she reached the floor level. Peeking through the opening of the tunnel, Hope examined her surroundings. Something was off. This was meant to be the courtrades' quarters. There were supposed to be Thyrian courtrades waiting for them here.

But there were only two beings in this room, and none of them bore the black clothes of the courtrades. She grabbed her best blades by the hilts and jumped out of the tunnel, throwing a blade at the shoulder of each being.

Her feet touched the floor at the same time as a massive movement shook the land. She fell to the floor, face down, her arms protecting herself from any harm as chunks of rock fell from the ceiling. The shouts coming from the tunnel meant they hadn't been so lucky, and there was probably a tangle of limbs and bodies in it.

She didn't care how strong this panomquake had been. She didn't care that it probably had been the biggest panomquake she had ever experienced. All she cared about were the two moving bodies on the floor, the smell of blood emanating from where her blades had hit exactly where she had aimed: their shoulders, to incapacitate but not kill. Not yet. She would need to extract some information from them before the killing blow.

"We mean no harm," one being said, the one at the back.

The other being was silent. He stood with the blade still stuck in his shoulder, as if he didn't feel it or wasn't bothered by it. He extended a hand in front of him, doing something with his fingers.

Hope didn't hesitate. She threw another two blades at the being, aiming for the thighs, but he dodged them. To dodge blades at that speed... She could feel his stare penetrating hers, but he was still in the dark, even if he was walking towards her.

Her next two daggers were ready to throw. As the being stepped out of the shadows, Hope met blue eyes as deep as the night sky. She held her breath for half a second, as if her heart had stopped. Maybe it had stopped, because in front of her was the most handsome man she had ever seen.

And just in case, she threw both daggers at him with all her might.

The man dodged them again, his incredibly fast movements gracious despite his very muscular body. A corner of his lips curled upwards, and something Hope couldn't identify passed through his eyes as he said, "I knew you would be worth the wait."

A knot in Hope's chest released, as if something that had been held tightly under many layers had unlocked.

Nina's white hair appeared through the opening of the tunnel. The dark-haired man looked at her friend, and Nina covered her mouth in shock, her ocean eyes as wide as Hope had ever seen them.

Hope took advantage of the man's distraction, a blade aimed at his other shoulder leaving her hand just as Nina shouted, "Hope, *stop!*"

But it was too late. The blade had hit home.

38

Lenna

Days, hours, or mere minutes had passed by the time Lenna recovered consciousness.

Something soft was against her back, something soft and warm. And the pain... it wasn't as bad. As if someone had Healed her. Lenna opened her eyes to find Jake next to her, a hand behind his head. With the state of his back, that had to be a painful position for sure. That soft thing on her back... That was a fluffy blanket.

"I wouldn't have thought your father's cells came with these sorts of amenities and silver-eyed panoms willing to Heal the prisoners," Lenna said.

"They don't," Jake said, not looking at her. Only now she saw they were in a not-big-enough four-petal-shaped cell. Shock.

She moved her shambles of a body until she was sitting, trying her best not to stretch her back, keeping her bare chest covered with the blanket.

"Why?" Lenna asked, her voice cutting at the memory of the pain inflicted by the Organ Mandor.

"Why?" Jake snorted. "Why did I bother protecting someone who doesn't want to be protected? Or why did I think you would shut your smart-ass damned mouth when I told you so?"

"Both."

"I knew you couldn't keep that mouth of yours shut, but it was worth a try. As for asking him to stop hurting you..." He sighed. "That was fucking stupid." He swallowed, as if he was resisting the urge to say something else.

"He was going to kill my friend."

"He *will* kill him. You know that already. But your fucking pride couldn't resist arguing with the Cardinals-damned Organ Mandor." He finally looked at her, his jaw clenched.

"Look, I'm sorry about him slicing you because of me," Lenna started, and Jake was shaking his head as he sat down, biting his lip. "I don't want to imagine—"

"You don't get it, do you?" he cut her off, slowly shaking his head. "I don't care about him hitting *me*. He's been hitting me all my existence. But *you*? You shouldn't have given him any reason to hurt you."

"It was only five strikes. It could have been worse," she lied. She didn't want to even imagine how twenty-three had felt on Ciaran, if he had even stayed conscious for all of them, unlike her weak body.

"Have you ever seen the Lawful Stabs used on a female?" he simply asked.

"I had never seen them used before. But I had heard of them."

"Blood of the five Cardinals was used to create the Red Lawful Stab," Jake said. "Female blood for female pain. It doesn't affect males nearly as much as females. If my father had hit you with it twenty-five times, rather than five, you would be dead right now."

Lenna exhaled softly, a part of her relieved that maybe she wasn't a pitiful coward after all. Or not as much as she had feared she was.

"How many times did he hit you?" The question left Lenna's lips before she could stop it.

Jake looked at the floor in front of him, his bare shoulders tensing and marking every muscle on his torso. He flinched.

"It doesn't matter."

Lenna put her hand on his cheek, and he lifted his eyes to meet hers again. His skin felt cool against the warmth of her fingers, and she wondered if the rest of his body was as cold. He hadn't cared to Give himself a blanket.

"How many?" she insisted.

"Fifty. Always fifty," he said, leaning into her touch.

Lenna bit her lip to resist the urging tears. There would not be more tears caused by that piece of shit of a Mandor, she had promised herself.

"I'm so sorry," was all she managed to whisper, dropping her hand.

"Don't be. Sooner or later, he will pay. I will make him pay," he said. She couldn't take her amber eyes from his silver ones, from the anger and determination in them as he added, "For hurting you."

It wasn't a hopeful wish, Lenna realized. It was a fact. A statement.

"I don't mind the pain. I only wish I could find a way to help Raoul. To save him," she swallowed. *To save you from a father like yours*, she wanted to add. "The only thing I ever wanted was to become a panom, to access my full powers. I thought they would make me whole. I was convinced they were the missing part that I had been lacking all my life. Even now, being barely capable of using two powers, I don't know what I would do if I lost them. I believed they would give me some sort of control over my life and the lives of those around me. But that was a foolish, ridiculous thought. These powers make no difference against someone like your father."

"The Cardinal powers *can* change lives, for the better and for the worse," Jake said. "But the Organ Mandor will always surpass the power and ability of any other panom. The only way to protect oneself against him is by controlling the Fifth Power, and getting it is extremely difficult, extremely dangerous."

"If I ever master the four Cardinal powers, maybe it would be worth considering," Lenna said, and a glimpse of navy sparks flickered in his eyes.

"My back would appreciate some Healing, Brachyan," Jake said, turning his destroyed back to her. She held in her shudder at the sight of what that monster had done to his son. "Hover your hand over the wounds in small circles, visualizing how the skin should look in normal conditions."

It should look very muscled, very damned muscled and terse and distracting.

Lenna extended her hand over his broken skin, tracing circles slowly over it. Jake added, "Think about the West petal of your mark as if it was medicine and you were applying it to my skin to Heal it."

So, she did. Slowly, his wounds started closing one by one, as if they were being sewn together.

Lenna felt her heart tighten in her chest. She was glad she could somehow Heal this man. This man, who had endured this torture in a failed attempt at stopping her own. One circle of her hand, another wound closed. He who had challenged the Organ Mandor of Thyria in front of all the other panoms. Another circle, another wound closed. This man, who maybe wasn't as evil as she wanted to believe he was.

A few minutes later, she placed her hand on his now scarred back. He breathed deeply at the touch. She stroked it softly, careful to not press her palm against it too hard should the wounds reopen again, should his pain return.

He turned his body around until he was facing her. "You now own three Cardinal powers, Brachyan." He lifted his hand to her face as his thumb stroked her bottom lip slowly. She opened her mouth slightly.

His hand continued stroking the skin behind her ear, down her neck. There was something very different in his eyes now, something that made her core tighten.

"You are playing a very dangerous game," Lenna said, unable to take her eyes from his full lips as he slowly bit his bottom one.

Her blood was boiling, speeding through her veins as she felt her heartbeat fastening. She wanted this so badly. She had wanted it for weeks. For months, even. But it was not just desire. There was something deeper, something meaningful, something she should truly be scared about. The need wanted to overcome the fear, even if she knew she was going to regret it.

Jake's hand continued moving down her chest, the blanket dropping to the floor as his fingers pushed it away, revealing her breasts, her peaked nipples. His eyes darkened to a gray shade as he inhaled sharply at the sight.

"I warned you. I told you I love to test the limits, to push and break established boundaries. I don't give a shit if the land collapses underneath us. All I want is to play this dangerous game with you, sweet fire. I don't mind getting burned."

Two heirs would make the land collapse, but Lenna couldn't find a part of her that gave a shit. Not as she saw the powerful length hardening against his pants. Not as he moved his other hand until both were circling her breasts. His fingers gently pinched her nipples, making her arch. She felt a slight pain in her back, but she didn't care. She needed more.

She grabbed his hands and pulled them towards the floor, to the blanket. She pushed a few dark strands of his hair away from his face as she lay above him, their exposed chests touching, their breaths melding.

His hands gripped her ass tightly, her core aching against the clothes that separated her from his very hard cock. The cock she needed to taste. The cock she needed to feel in so many places.

His silver eyes penetrated her as he said, the corner of his lips curling upwards, "You want more, sweet fire?"

Lenna licked his neck and pushed harder against his cock. She squeezed a hand between their bodies and stroked all his length through his clothes, making Jake gasp. "Didn't you say you wanted to play with fire?"

"I would love to," he said as she continued stroking his hardness. "But you need to beg first. I want you to beg me to fuck you."

"Entitled asshole," Lenna spat, removing her hand from his pants.

Jake chuckled, holding her arms with his and turning Lenna around gently, carefully dropping her onto the blanket. He spoke into her ear, making her shiver, "I'm waiting, Brachyan."

"Wait all you want," she spat. Her back arched as his head lowered and his tongue played with her nipple. His tongue was deliciously warm and wet, and she immediately wanted it somewhere else. Everywhere else. He kept circling her nipple with his tongue, his hand sliding under her underwear to where she needed him most. But the hand stayed there, waiting.

Her hands grabbed the muscles on his chest and pulled him towards her face. "I don't beg," she said as her hands admired him. Cardinals spare her if this man wasn't the hottest she had ever touched. But even for him, she wouldn't beg. There was no reason to.

As if he had read her mind, he pushed his waist against hers, that extraordinary hardness moving up and down against her clit, masturbating her across the Cardinals-damned clothes. She couldn't resist her moan.

"You don't beg, you don't get, sweet fire," he whispered, his lips so close to hers that she felt them moving with each word.

She grabbed his head with both hands and pushed his mouth into hers, tongues greeting each other in a wet dance of challenge and heat. Jake moved his cock against her core faster, deeper, and Lenna needed to get their fucking clothes out of the way.

But a panomquake shook the ground as if the world was going to end, chunks of the ceiling falling around them, on them. Jake jumped to the side to avoid dropping his weight into her body, and that sound—that was his skin ripping again, and that was blood dripping.

39

Hope

"Stop!" Nina shouted again, tears in her light blue eyes as she pushed her body out of the tunnel, Aurora ready to follow without hesitation.

The man with dark blue eyes and shoulder-length, smooth dark hair was not looking at Nina anymore. He was looking at Hope as he lifted a hand and removed one blade from his body, dropping it to the floor. He did a circular movement with his hand, and the blood stopped pouring from the insertion point.

Panom. This being was a fully powered panom. Her blades maybe weren't enough, but if she knocked him out, then he surely couldn't fix himself.

Hope didn't give him time to remove the other blade. In three leaps, Hope was behind him, climbing his back as her arms locked his neck from behind, her knees holding his arms to his sides. She didn't take his ability to breathe, though. Not yet.

This man had dodged her blades when he had been paying attention. He was extremely fast. If she had locked him like this without opposition...

The scent of his hair next to her face was overwhelming. This man was made of night and pine. She could have sworn he was inhaling her scent as well, closing his eyes as Hope asked Nina, "*Why* should I stop?"

The panom didn't reply, as if he somehow knew that no matter what he said, Hope wouldn't trust him. Instead, he removed his hand from Hope's knee lock and lifted it as if to remove her from him.

No, not her. The blade. He wanted to remove the blade from his other shoulder. As if *that* was a nuisance, not having a woman hanging from his back who had her arms wrapped around a must-have part of his body in order to breathe.

Hope didn't let her body react at the shock of seeing a shiny hand grabbing the hilt of her blade and removing it from his shoulder with ease. The same hand traced a quick circle over the wound, and the skin healed.

Hope couldn't take her eyes from it. It was a completely functional, strong, and capable hand—but it was made of metal.

Nina said, "Because this is Ciaran Castel, heir of the West House. And I worked for him."

Hope blinked, unsure if this was a trap.

Aurora, next to Nina, held her weapons in each hand. Her eyes narrowed, which was reason enough for Hope to not let go of Ciaran's neck yet, despite the frown on Nina's face. Courtrades were now filling the room, as most of them had jumped out of the tunnel. The last one was Marcus. Six courtrades less, indeed.

"This is most surely not the courtrades' quarters," Marcus said. "But if you wanted us dead, you would have started already. Who the fuck are you, where are we, and how did you find us?" His eyes were cold, assessing. His hands had shadows twirling around his fingers, as if they were ready to strike.

"As Nina kindly said," he bowed at Nina as much as Hope's arms let him, "I'm Ciaran, son of Cobrian Castel of the West House."

Hope wasn't sure if it was him knowing Nina by her first name, the respectful bow towards her friend, the genuine happiness in Nina's eyes at seeing him, or that his scent was starting to blur her thoughts, but she finally let go of his neck, jumping to the floor.

"Brendon Gallon here," said the second man, stepping into the light. He was stunning, with short blond hair and blue eyes. "We are under the Invisible Grand, and we should leave the chitchat for later unless you fancy a visit to the Organ Mandor."

Hope's eyes widened as she held her breath. Could it be this easy to confront her father at last? Adrenaline was rushing through her veins. It had been rushing through her veins for a long while now.

"No one is moving until you tell us how you found us," Marcus demanded.

It was Ciaran who spoke this time. "I heard the whispers when you left Verdania."

Marcus nodded silently, as if that made sense. "That doesn't explain how you knew we'd be here," he said.

"The Cardinals guided us here," Ciaran said, his voice tense, as if he didn't like being questioned so much.

"Metaphors are not good enough explanations," Marcus said.

"A fucking red cardinal came to me and wouldn't stop picking my already-bleeding back until I Healed myself, and then it instructed me to moure into Brendon's, then moure us both into this room. Is that *good enough*?" His patience was definitely running low.

Hope couldn't stop herself before she asked, "Why was your back bleeding?"

Ciaran looked at her, and she might have imagined the coldness of his eyes easing a bit as he said, "It's a long story."

"Did you cause the panomquake?" Marcus asked, still not taking his eyes off Ciaran.

A corner of his lips twisted upwards as he said, "That wasn't me."

"He's not a talker, you see. Don't waste your—*our* precious time. Now, can we get out of here?" Brendon urged.

"What if I *do* fancy a visit to the Organ Mandor?" Hope asked, consciously avoiding the panicked stares of her mother and Nina.

"While being starved, thirsty, sleep deprived, and with your hand hurt? A very stupid idea," Aurora snapped.

Ciaran tilted his head slightly, exposing intricate ink where his neck met his clothes. "Is that why you came to Thyria?" he asked.

"It's a *long story*." Hope smiled.

"Can you take us to the courtrades' Thyrian quarters?" Marcus asked Ciaran.

"I can moure you there two at a time," the panom said.

Marcus pushed Aridian and Jessica forward to be the first ones. "Please," he said.

Ciaran walked towards Aridian and Jessica and touched the back of their necks, the three of them disappearing from sight a moment later.

In less than a minute, Ciaran returned, and two other courtrades were ready for him. On and on, he moured them away, returning with empty hands, the caved room with fewer people every time he disappeared again.

"Are you sure he is to be trusted?" Hope asked Nina, not caring that Brendon was standing next to her, listening to every word.

"I trust Ciaran with my life," Nina confirmed.

Aurora said, "I wouldn't put my life in the hands of any panoms, least of all the hands of a future House Ruler. These beings think differently, behave differently, and live differently than the rest of us."

The disgust in her mother's voice was almost hurtful. A reminder that she didn't accept the part of Hope that was linked to these panom beings. Hope tried not to take it personally. She tried, but it still hurt.

"Most of them are a bunch of assholes, to be honest," Brendon said as a matter of fact.

Nina smiled, and then said, "I don't want to go to the courtrades' quarters."

"Neither do I," Hope said. "That's not why we came here." They had lost nothing there, and she had a feeling that the courtrades wouldn't welcome them anymore. They had worked together for a specific purpose, a purpose now fulfilled.

"Is there somewhere else, somewhere safe we can go?" Nina asked Brendon as Ciaran appeared and disappeared again. "Just until we figure out how to find... some family members?"

"If you're looking for Raoul, one of our friends has news about his whereabouts," Brendon said, and Nina lifted her eyebrows with surprise.

"The description of *completely white hair, light blue eyes, and very pale skin* is not that common, you know? Are you twins or something?"

"He's my brother," Nina said, swallowing the multiple questions she surely wanted to ask.

Ciaran reappeared, and only Marcus and a ginger-haired courtrade remained in the room with the four of them.

Marcus approached Aurora, extending his hand to shake hers as he said, "May Llunal shade your path."

"May the Cardinals guide you," Aurora replied, shaking his hand firmly.

Nina said, "Thank you for looking after us."

"You three don't need anyone looking after you," he chuckled as he kissed Nina's hand. "It's been my pleasure to meet you, Nina."

He finally turned to Hope and bowed his head slightly. She extended her healthier hand to shake his, but he turned her hand and traced a semicircle crossed with two straight lines on her palm with thin, dark shadows.

"I, Marcus Olanett, thank you, Hope Nevada, for allowing my courtrades and myself to return to Thyria using your blood. We owe you a life debt. When you seek our help, we will be there for you. I swear on Llunal, his shadows and all his stars," he said, and the symbol on her palm vanished.

Hope felt in her hand and her heart that these were not mere words. That had been a life-binding promise. She bowed her head. "It' has been my honor."

With that, Marcus and the courtrade walked to Ciaran, who had not taken his eyes from Hope's hand, and disappeared.

"Nina and Brendon, you're next," Hope said as Ciaran moured into the underground room again. Hope and her mother would be the last two, but she knew perfectly well the questions were eating her friend alive. Nina needed to go to wherever these friends were and find out more about Raoul as soon as possible.

Nina gave a brief kiss on Hope's cheek as she said, "See you in a minute."

Brendon, Ciaran, and Nina were gone, and the silence was only interrupted by Hope and Aurora's breathing.

"Now that we're here, what do you plan to do? Find him?" Aurora asked, and Hope knew exactly who she meant.

The man she had loved with all her heart. The man who had given her reasons to believe a different life was possible. The man who had given her a child. The man who had discarded this child and her mother, not caring if they lived or died. The man who had broken her mother's heart. The man who she had almost given up on life for.

Hope didn't have time to reply before Ciaran moured in front of them, extending his arms to touch their skin. Hope swallowed, unsure of what to expect. She wanted to believe this man, but if this was a trap, they would be completely at his mercy.

His dark blue eyes seemed to read the hesitation in her eyes, because he said, "Mouring is quite safe, quick."

Quite wasn't a very reassuring word, but Hope decided to not mention it as he touched the backs of their necks and the floor vanished from underneath their feet.

Lights and shadows and blurs and sounds were spinning around them in an unrecognizable chaos. The only focus of her vision were Aurora, who bit her lip in an uncomfortable flinch, and Ciaran, who started looking around with something like nervousness in his eyes.

"This is taking too long," he said, pushing his hands on their skin harder. The metal hand against Hope's skin felt smooth, slightly cool. Everything kept spinning, even faster than before, and Hope felt nausea burning its way up her throat.

"Fuck. Something is trying to redirect us," he said, closing his eyes, as if trying to concentrate more.

Their feet landed in a spacious room, and Hope would have fallen on her knees if Ciaran hadn't kept her upright with the metallic hand on her waist. Around them, there was no Nina, no Brendon, and definitely no friends. Ciaran inhaled sharply, and Hope followed his stare.

It hadn't been an external something redirecting them. It had been an external *someone*.

For the panom force emanating from this being could only belong to the Organ Mandor of Thyria.

Her father, Rhei Coralt, was staring at her.

40

Hope

The panom who sat on the throne made of bones and black feathers needed no introduction.

Short black hair, a perfectly-shaped beard, straight posture that only a Ruler of a nation could have. The shape of his silver eyes were replicas to Hope's own ones, and that look… She knew it well. It was the same as when she assessed a prey before going for the killing blow.

"For a long time, I wondered if you would ever be foolish enough to come back," he said, staring at Hope even though she knew he was talking to her mother.

Aurora didn't say anything. Hope wasn't even sure if her mother was breathing. She was so still, unmoving. Utterly paralyzed since they had appeared here.

"For a long time, I wondered if you would be as sickening as I believed you were," Hope said.

Rhei Coralt ignored her, looking at Ciaran as he said, "You are giving me loads of unnecessary trouble recently, boy. Such a passion to aid discarded beings. Maybe you would rather end up discarded yourself."

Ciaran bowed his head slightly. "I will be careful."

Hope wasn't sure if he meant he would not do it again or that he would be careful to not get caught in the future. But the Organ Mandor only said, "You *will* be careful. Your father is getting old and it would be a shame if he didn't get to live all the years the Cardinals would guide him to live."

Ciaran looked at Rhei Coralt's eyes, and Hope felt the air around him stop moving. She wasn't sure if the Organ Mandor felt it though, as he only added, "I see you have recovered nicely from your recent punishment. I will make a note to double it up next time."

As if that was a dismissal, Rhei Coralt looked at her mother again and smiled. Hope's upper lip curled. That smile was the most repulsive thing she had ever seen.

"Do discarded beings lose their voices in the woods?" he asked.

Aurora inhaled sharply, and Hope did her best to resist the urge to grab her hand. She knew the Organ Mandor would take it as a sign of weakness, and the last thing she wanted was her mother to look as destroyed on the outside as she was inside. Her mother, not opening her mouth, was not doing herself any favors.

But it hadn't been her mother who had wanted to return to Thyria. It hadn't been Aurora who had wanted to see the face of this man, to confront him and ask the questions she needed answers to. It had been Hope.

"Do you know who I am?" Hope asked.

"Of course I know who you are. You are a discarded being, like the soundless one next to you," he sneered. The power emanating from him was enough to throw someone to the floor. Hope was silently grateful that at least her mother was keeping upright.

Before Hope could reply, Rhei Coralt added, "Did you think someone with my blood could enter my nation without me realizing, girl? Because if you did, you are a fool, like your mother is for bringing you here."

"Why did you discard us?" Hope asked, ignoring the blood roaring in her veins at the constant humiliation towards her mother.

"I don't answer to discarded beings," he said, his fingers curling.

"But you must answer your daughter," Hope spat, her fists clenched at her sides.

The Organ Mandor laughed, before his face became utterly serious, his teeth exposed as his lips curled in disgust. "I damn the Cardinals every single day for letting women believe they have a say in life."

He stood up, and another wave of power hit Hope's face. They were quite far from him, and Hope did not know how she would attack him should she need to. She wondered if wounds inflicted by her blades could be healed as easily if she aimed for his heart or his brain.

"You fucker," Aurora said quietly, as if it was taking all her effort to push her words out.

"I knew the viper still kept her tongue." The Organ Mandor's lips curled upward.

"Why did you discard us instead of killing us? Does your son know I exist?" Hope insisted.

"I tire of this conversation, girl," her father said, indifference lacing his words.

"You sired me. You owe me the truth," she spat, her voice raising more than she wanted it to. She didn't want to seem like she was losing control of herself, but she was. She very much was, as this man in front of her seemed impenetrable, and she hadn't come here for nothing.

"I do not owe you anything, bastard. I don't owe you even a minute of my life," the Organ Mandor said, another wave of panom power, stronger than the previous ones, hitting her.

He flicked his hand behind his back, keeping his hands away from sight. Hope wouldn't risk it, her hands close to the hilts of the sharpest blades that could penetrate through ribs and skull at the ready.

"There was a reason you were discarded, and that is because you mean nothing. You are nothing. And so is she."

With that, a black crystal blade shot from his hand at an impossible speed. A blade as dark as a starless night sky. A blade with the presence that only weapons with their own history and name had.

A blade that went through her mother's heart before Hope could take it for her.

Aurora fell backwards, Hope unable to take her eyes off her mother's body as it fell to the stone floor. The sound echoed in her ears.

Hope kneeled next to her, gasping as she removed the black blade that had perforated her mother's heart, as she begged Ciaran, "Heal her. Heal her, please. Please, please, please."

Ciaran kneeled next to her, placing a hand over Aurora's eyelids, closing them gently, removing the awfully frightened last expression on her mother's face.

"The Black Lawful Stab allows no Healing," he whispered, pain in his voice.

Her father was a killer, just like Hope was.

What growing in Verdania had made her become: a killer, and a very well skilled at that. She had been a killer all her life, a killer fuelled by the need to live and see another day.

Hope looked at her mother's dead body with tears and pain and sorrow in her eyes.

It was too late.

Too late to go back to doing nothing about the fact that her mother had been thrown like a piece of garbage with her newborn daughter to a cruel island where only death ensured one would live. Too late to ignore the years of pain that had consumed her. Too late to not make her father pay. The being who caused her mother's soul to break into such small pieces that had taken years of tears before a half smile appeared. The being who had fucking killed her after two decades of ignoring their existence.

Too. Fucking. Late.

And as she stood up with the black dagger in her hand, Hope realized she was ready to become a killer fuelled by revenge. She was ready to make him pay. She was ready to kill her father, even if that meant killing all the truths and answers with him.

"I will fucking kill you."

The Black Lawful Stab trembled as she held its hilt tightly, as Hope threw it with all her might against the room, against her father's heart.

The blade didn't move as fast as it had moved before. No, it definitely wasn't as fast. It was actually slowing down as it approached its target. It landed slowly in the Organ Mandor's palm, his expression smug and proud.

"The Black Lawful Stab only obeys the panom blessed by my beloved Cardinal Queen: the Organ Mandor of Thyria," he smiled, and Hope's guts twisted.

Without waiting for Rhei Coralt to finish, Ciaran moved his hand, and Hope's body slammed against him. He placed his hands on both their necks, one warm with rage and one cold with death.

He moured them away before Hope could tell her father that not killing her would be the biggest regret of his wicked life.

Ciaran moured them away before the Black Lawful Stab, thrown by her father and now aimed at Hope's heart, ended her life as well.

41

Lenna

L enna was trying to force her still very heated blood to chill the fuck down after almost breaking Thyria in half because—

No, better not to remember precisely what had been pressed tightly against the apex of her legs, if she truly wanted to cool down. Shame she didn't have access to a cold shower.

They needed clothes, because she was not going to walk around with her nipples covered only by a blanket around the cell underneath the Organ House. If those strong muscles on Jake's chest were not covered, it was very hard to resist touching them again.

With a couple of hand movements, she Gave herself a black top then Gave Jake a shirt.

"I was wondering," he started as he grabbed it from her, "since my dear father will keep us here for the Fifth knows how long, if you'd like to learn the last Cardinal power?"

Lenna blinked. "I'm not Harming you," she said, twisting her mouth to the side.

"Yet you must feel the horizontal balance scale of your petal tilting towards the Healing after you worked on my back for so long. Am I right?"

Lenna nodded, lifting her eyebrows. "Still, I'm not Harming you. I'd very much rather have the balance uneven." She felt like she had been drinking myster since she had Healed him, a feeling she enjoyed often enough if it was in the right measure.

Jake frowned slightly, some confusion crossing his eyes. "So kind of you, golden heart. Let me at least tell you the theory so that if you ever need to do it, you know where to start."

Jake lifted a hand, his fingers together as he said, "When you Harm, you must visualize the desired outcome." He slashed his hand through the air. "Harming can come in many forms: a plain cut, locking limbs, internal organs damage... As with Giving, Taking, and Healing, Harming only has the limits of its wielder. Which can be many, or can be close to none."

Lenna avoided a shiver as a never-ending list of atrocious possibilities crossed her mind. How cruel must the East Cardinal have been to own this power in her soul? To think such a limitless hurting potential was in the hands of any experienced panom... "That's some scary shit."

Jake nodded in silence. Lenna asked, "Is that how you discard people? Is it a way of Harming them?"

Jake stared at her, as if he was considering answering honestly or not.

"I don't like to talk about the details of... my duties, but no, it's not Harming. Harming always involves a very unpleasant feeling, usually pain, agony, or misery. I would never Harm the babies and children I sometimes have to discard." If that was not deep relief in Lenna's chest, only the Fifth knew what it was. Jake continued, "Discarding is painless. It's more similar to mouring somebody away."

"So you do have some sort of incredibly relaxed and blurry ethical limits."

"You didn't seem too concerned about my ethical limits a few minutes ago, Brachyan." Jake lifted his eyebrow, and that slight curl of one corner of his mouth did things to her core.

"We went further than what two responsible heirs of the Houses should have ever gone. I bet you are happy with the panomquake that came out of your brief experiment," Lenna said, tilting her head. Good thing both knew they were quite far from being responsible heirs.

"I'd be much happier if we had continued."

"Shame the rocks falling on top of us didn't agree," she said. "Can you not moure out of this cell?"

"It has epitellia wards that prevent mouring unless allowed by the Organ Mandor," Jake said. "Sorry, but you're stuck with me for a while longer."

"I'm sorry too." Lenna sat down, her back against the curved wall.

"Maybe we should find out at exactly which point the land breaks in half," he said, standing up and walking towards Lenna. "If it is when I lick that wetness between your legs dry," his voice had dropped an octave, "or when I fuck you as deep as I know you want it. You know, for experimental purposes."

An experiment that had the risk of killing hundreds of thousands of people when the land truly broke in half, for Cardinals' sake.

Lenna looked up to him, past the massive bulk in his pants that was very difficult to ignore, and found Jake looking at her with the dark gray tinge in his eyes.

Before she could reply, someone appeared next to her and touched the skin on the back of her neck. Jake's own hand on the back of her captor's neck as they were moured away from the cell.

Lenna landed on her ass in the throne room and stood as soon as she could, all the heat inside her body cooling down instantly as if drowned by a gigantic iceberg. Touching her neck was the Cardinals-damned Organ Mandor, Jake removing his own hand from his neck, and next to Lenna—

Ayla was standing next to her, a confused look on her face, as if this had been an unexpected mouring summoning for her too. Ayla's green eyes kept looking up and down Lenna's back, as if she couldn't believe she had recovered so quickly.

"Change of plans," Rhei Coralt said, mouring onto his throne and facing the three of them. "Women with defiant attitudes keep proving to be a vast annoyance. Despite a variety of punishments, some women don't seem to learn. Some aren't *capable* of learning. I have a feeling, Lenna Brachyan, that you are one of them."

"What do you want?" Lenna spat.

"I want you to prove here and now that the five Stabs helped you recognize the only true Ruler in Thyria, the one you must listen to, obey, and respect." Rhei Coralt's eyes were bright. "I want you to apologize for being rude and disrespectful and to swear your complete loyalty to me. On your panom blood."

A blood swearing only death could break.

"You represent all I have ever hated about this putrid nation of yours."

Ayla gasped and Jake kept quiet, even though she felt a hint of amusement and deep fear coming from his body. She hated his motherfucker of a father so much.

"The discarding of innocent people at your mercy, under your orders," Lenna added, and her heart thundered in her chest with anger. "The roixers roaming free and killing whoever they want, whenever they want, with no consequences, with your permission to use brute power to impose *your* laws. The degradation you need to inflict upon others to place yourself above them. Because that is the only thing you truly are: an evil, wicked thing who cares about nothing and nobody other than your damned self."

Lenna's body was trembling with anger, her teeth clenching anytime she shut her mouth. "And you want me to learn *what* from your punishment? You want me to learn to behave when your fucking exemplar behavior is making us bleed? I thank you for your punishment, because it has clarified any doubt I could ever have about who the fuck you truly are and how you want to rule over us. I will never apologize to a piece of shit with powers."

Rhei Coralt clapped his hands, the sound echoing in the throne room. "Very clarifying for me too, Lenna Brachyan, to hear of your torments. As I had rightly believed, you are incapable of evolving. Some beings are narrow minded like that."

The Organ Mandor moved his silver eyes to Ayla, who was quiet as the dead, probably not even daring to breathe too loudly.

"Luckily, I have an alternative option for the heir of the North House. A much more suitable option. An option that, according to the Librarians of Time, is close enough that it shouldn't alter the flow of the magic too much."

Rhei Coralt continued, "Why complicate my life with a rebellious little panom heir playing empowered woman when the panom you shared your womb with can obey my rules? Why should a few minutes of difference at birth make any difference twenty-five years later?"

"Since I have memory, I have wished to not be the heir of my House. You'll be doing me a favor." Lenna winked.

The Organ Mandor smiled as he extended his arms, and a continuous arrow of black sparks flowed into Lenna's chest, extracting a small North Petal golden shape and sending it to Ayla's chest, who inhaled sharply and paled.

A panomquake followed, much smaller than the previous one, and the only panom who didn't move his position was the Organ Mandor, his ruling ass on his ruling throne. Ayla, Lenna, and Jake readjusted their positions.

"Happy heirloom-stealing day, sister," Lenna said. "Your wishes came true at last."

"True destiny always delivers, Lenna Brachyan," Rhei Coralt said, still smiling. Ayla said nothing, but her body shaking next to Lenna's probably meant she was holding her happy tears in.

"Destiny is a piss-taker. I only believe in the twisted minds of the Cardinals," Lenna said. She didn't feel any different now.

"Twisted indeed. Female minds, twisted indeed." Rhei Coralt nodded.

Lenna was hoping for a dismissal so she didn't have to see his wicked face for a second longer. But that horrific grin appeared on his lips again, as if he had had some sort of last-minute revelation.

"I think it's time to leave problems knotted properly. You and your twisted mind, Lenna Brachyan, are one of many problems I have no time for. Since you haven't liked the peculiarities of my punishments so far, I would like to try something I haven't used in a long, long time. Will I be *doing you a favor* if I take your panom powers away?"

Lenna's heart stopped, time seemed to stop. "You can't do that," she whispered.

"Incapable minds don't learn." Rhei Coralt grinned. "I can very much do that, girl." He extended his arms in front of him again, blackness aimed towards Lenna's chest again. She covered her panom mark with both hands, golden sparks flowing from her hands as she Gave herself a barrier.

The golden barrier of her magic was translucent, laced with navy reinforcements, allowing her to see the delighted face of Rhei Coralt as he welcomed the challenge with open arms. Lenna was busy enough concentrating on keeping the black strikes away from her chest to look at Jake, but him standing up for her against his father again did something to the rhythm of her heart.

The barrier became all navy then, golden and black sparks flying around it before the navy sparks sucked up the black ones, making them disappear.

The barrier was gone.

Lenna stopped, feeling pressure against her source of magic on her chest. Her panom mark. She couldn't lose her panom mark, her abilities. It was the only thing she had, the only thing that truly mattered.

"Touch her and you will regret it," Jake spat, navy sparks emanating from his hands, his body, his hair.

The Organ Mandor was not smiling anymore. "You don't want to become a problem, boy. Your mind *is* capable. It's just as stubborn as the Fifth itself."

Black arrows made of sparks shot through Lenna's chest before she or Jake could erect another barrier, and she felt the ink on her skin diluting as the black sparks erased her panom mark. The power balance that felt uneven at the effort of Giving to keep the barrier in place—

The magical balance didn't feel uneven anymore because there was no balance. No magic.

Lenna Brachyan was not a panom.

Lenna crumpled into the floor, her mind fogged with fear and frustration and anger and fear. Fear, so much fear. She opened her hand, willing her sparks to appear. Emptiness was all she had left. In her hands, her mind, and her heart.

Lenna didn't know if things happened in her head or in reality when she saw Ayla with tears in her eyes. When Jake placed a hand on her neck, and they moured away, the surroundings spinning almost as much as her own thoughts. As her own life.

42

Hope

Tall trees surrounded the small clearing where Ciaran had moured Hope. She would have stopped to marvel at the red-tinged night sky above her if the corpse of her mother wasn't laying at her feet. She had been staring at it blankly for seconds, minutes, hours.

What had she done?

What had she done, forcing her mother to come here? Who had she thought she was, confronting the Organ Mandor with nothing but her human force and the stupid blood that only could fuel vehicles? Why did she ever think such a being would be compassionate and explain himself?

Hope had believed that somewhere inside her father, he would remember what he had felt for her mother. That the fact that he discarded them instead of killing them somehow meant that Rhei Coralt had indeed loved her mother.

In front of Hope was his love. His redemption.

Dead.

Hope let her tears flow freely, painfully, as she cried on her mother's chest. Aurora's chest was cold as the cruel heart of her killer, and she would never hold Hope's body tight again.

"I'm so sorry," she said, her voice cutting between devastated sobs. It didn't even matter if her words were intelligible; Aurora would not listen to her ever again. "I never meant for this to happen."

A shadow moved in the clearing, and Hope remembered Ciaran was here. He had taken her here. She didn't even know where exactly she was, or if it was safe, or if that man was reliable to be around, or if the night would swallow her whole and take her to the deep pit of pain.

None of that mattered.

This woman she was crying on had been all that had ever mattered. The woman who had been with her every single day since she was born. The woman who had died internally all those years ago but had managed to re-flourish from her damage. The woman who had taught her to be resilient. Who had taught her how to defend herself, how to fight and how to kill. Who had been her sole companion all her life. Who had loved her and helped her grow.

The woman Hope had never given up on, who she had always fought for.

But there was nothing else to fight for.

All that remained were endless tears and pain. So much pain and so many tears. And her mother's dead body.

43

Lenna

L enna's mind kept spinning, even as the floor settled under her feet. She was barely aware of Jake moving her into a black armchair, forcing her stiff body to sit.

"Hey," he said, his voice soft.

The fucking Organ Mandor had taken her powers away. She was not a panom. She would never be anything of worth again. She would never help Raoul or any other innocents in this broken society. Lenna clenched her fists, ignoring the pain as her nails dug into her skin.

"Brachyan," Jake said firmly, putting a cautious hand on her thigh.

Her golden eyes met his silver ones, and she acknowledged her surroundings at last. A luxurious, black and navy bedroom in the shape of a petal that could only be his private chambers.

She was still in the House of the motherfucker who had taken her heirloom and her powers away. The heirloom part she would have felt relief for, were it not for the absolute emptiness and sorrow she felt at losing the biggest part of her identity that had come with it.

"I don't want to be here," Lenna said, swallowing her hatred as if nothing was happening. As if her entire world was not falling apart.

"You want me to take you to your chambers?" Jake asked.

Theon would probably be there, and she didn't want to see him. She didn't want to see or talk to anyone.

"I don't want to be in his fucking House. In his city," Lenna said, even if the entire island of Thyria belonged to this man she hated so much. "I just want to go home," she whispered.

"I can take you to the North House," Jake said, and Lenna nodded, silently putting a hand on top of his.

A hand on her neck. The floor disappeared from under their feet again, and Corentre was gone.

The wooden walls of her room in the North House were warmly familiar, and the wide panel windows opening to her balcony let her breathe in the much-needed fresh air. Her bed, her things, her heart had been here all those years, and even the smell seemed to welcome her back. She silently thanked the epitellia wards for allowing Jake to moure her there because of her identity.

"Don't let this make you miserable, Brachyan," Jake said.

"Said the most powerful panom heir of Thyria to a panomless former heir," Lenna snorted. "Seems like a Cardinals-damned grim joke."

"Your inner fire doesn't depend on your powers," he said, and she turned to look at him. His face was serious, his eyes lined with anger and determination. "You are much more than a panom."

"You don't need to be here anymore. You are no longer my Panom Guidor," Lenna said, turning to look at the gardens in front of her. And before he could say anything else that would make her reconsider, she added, "I want to be alone."

She was home, and yet she had never felt such loneliness and emptiness invading every single part of her being.

44

Hope

The accumulated tiredness of the past few days perhaps had taken its toll at last, or perhaps Hope hadn't fallen asleep properly until the early morning, between sobs and tears and pain and grief. When she opened her swollen eyes, the pale sun was shining brightly above the small clearing.

Her back was sore from laying on her mother's chest for the Fifth knew how many hours. Her mouth and throat felt dry as arid dunes.

Ciaran emerged from the trees with—

"Is that water?" Hope approached him with fast steps and shoved down the whole water pouch Ciaran handed her. Fresh water was underestimated. He sat down on a bunch of rocks, berries and apples in front of him. An offering.

"I thought beings on your island had nicer meals," she said, taking a huge bite of an apple. It had been too long since she had eaten something as tasty.

"We have all sorts of food, yet nothing can beat what the Cardinals provide through nature," Ciaran said. "I'm glad you're eating. I thought you maybe didn't want to."

"I need strength for what I need to do," Hope said. She had a long list of things she needed to do, starting with burying her mother and ending with killing her father.

Hope finished the apple and walked around the clearing, tapping on the ground with her foot until she found the perfect spot. She kneeled and started digging, the wound on her palm reopening under the old bandage.

The agony in her heart and the blood on her hands didn't stop her. She wouldn't stop. Nothing had ever stopped her before, and nothing would stop her now.

The sun above her indicated it was barely past meridiem, and if she dug without stopping, she would finish before the sunset. Ciaran started digging with his bare hands next to her, metallic and biological one.

They stopped and looked at each other. She knew that, as a panom, he surely had many other ways to do this, yet he seemed to understand why she needed to do it by hand. She needed to feel the pain, to do this for *her*.

Another tear flowed down her cheek, and Ciaran's blue eyes followed its path down the soil mixed with the blood from her hand. His lips were tight as he bowed his head slightly and resumed digging.

The grave was deep enough to place Aurora's body when the sky was brushed with reds and oranges. Hope's hand was an utter mess, but that had been part of the point.

Hope cleaned her mother's hair, removed the dirt from her clothes. She took Aurora's blades from their sheaths, placing them on the sides of her body, and helping her inert hand hold her favorite dagger by the hilt. She had been a warrior all her life, and she would be a warrior wherever the Cardinals guided her now.

Hope went into the woods and came back with the most beautiful leaves she could find. Yellow, Cardinal-red, orange, and different shades of brown, all in different shapes that she carefully placed over her mother's body, a nature-made blanket to wish her farewell.

Hope used another water pouch Ciaran had brought to clean her own blood from her clothes, her face, her hands. She let her long black hair go and redid her two braids, just as her mother always preferred them.

"Would you mind bringing Nina here? She knew my mother."

Ciaran nodded and moured away. A few minutes later, he returned with Nina, and he must have filled her in, because Nina already had tears in her eyes as she hugged Hope tightly.

"She was a brave woman," Nina said, her head tight against Hope's chest.

Hope's own tears had dried, as if the pain she had allowed herself to suffer had worked its way in and out. She gently let go of Nina and turned towards the blanket of beautiful leaves.

"I will always remember you, Mother. Whenever I wake, whenever I fall asleep, I will remember you. Whenever I walk in the woods or see trees around me. Whenever I think about giving up, but instead fight with all my might. Whenever I let myself feel sorrow. Whenever I clean my blades, just as you showed me. Whenever I use them to kill an enemy. When I kill the being that destroyed your heart. I promise you, Mother, I will not stop until I kill the Organ Mandor of Thyria. I will not stop until his blood is on my hands and I avenge your death."

Hope clenched her teeth with rage and sorrow and grief. A bird cried somewhere in the woods. "I love you, and I am sorry. May the Cardinals guide you to peace."

Hope looked at Ciaran. She wasn't sure if she had any strength left in her soul to pour the massive amount of soil onto her mother's body. He seemed to read this in her eyes and nodded, opening his hands and letting the soil move carefully on top of Aurora until there was a neat, small mound in the clearing.

Internally, Hope would have to endure living with that hollow emptiness, the raw guilt for the rest of her life.

"Let's go," Hope said, approaching Ciaran next to Nina.

He had promised he would keep the epitellia wards around this area for the rest of his days, protecting her mother's peace and guidance.

With a final look at her mother's grave, Ciaran moured them away.

45

Lenna

Lenna didn't want to be here. Yet she wasn't sure if *here* meant her bedroom, the North House, or her own body. Not that she had any fucking idea of where else she could go.

It had seemed a wise idea to return home.

Now, contemplating leaving her rooms to encounter her beloved mother or father, or the gossipy servants that used to run to Ayla, and realizing that her sister was most surely not in this house because she was in Corentre learning from her Panom Guidor about how to be a fucking panom... Discouraging. The wise idea was utterly discouraging.

But Lenna was not one to hide away. So, she got her panomless shit together and closed her door with a bang, heading to the only person in this House—now that Theon wasn't here—who would most likely not judge her or hate her as much as her own family.

Theon. She didn't feel as if she had abandoned him, since he was a full-ass grown man who could do whatever the fuck he wanted. Nevertheless, she had asked him to go to Corentre for her, and here she was, back in the North House, *without* him.

That Lenna didn't bump into any other person until his office in the library was a Cardinals-damned miracle she should be grateful for—not that she cared about the Cardinals much anymore.

Swift steps and a familiar face followed the knocks on the office door.

"Hi, Leo," Lenna said before she hugged the extremely stiff man and sat on his desk. "Long time no see."

"I need more information before deciding whether to be happy or sad about your presence," Leo Pharlin said, frowning. The wrinkles hadn't changed during the past few months, and neither had the gray hair or the kindness behind his green eyes.

"Long story short, Ayla is now the heir of the North House and the Organ Mandor punished me for having a *female twisted mind*, so I'm not a panom anymore."

"Can he do that?" Leo asked.

"He definitely can. It's done," she said. "So, here I am, looking for a safe place called home but not feeling safe or at home at all. I feel so done with life. Saying *done* because *feeling lost* is closer to admitting I'm a fucking loser, even though that would definitely be more accurate."

Leo exhaled deeply, putting his hands on his hips. "Do your parents know you're here?"

Lenna chuckled. "Not yet. I haven't had the pleasure of seeing their smug faces when they discover Ayla is the heir."

"What are you going to do now?"

Lenna lifted her eyebrows. "Other than hate the fucking Organ Mandor with my whole heart for the rest of my life? That's an excellent question."

"Not a very productive plan, is it?" he asked, his lips twisting to the side as they always did when he asked her an academic question.

"I don't want to let this man rule as if there are no consequences, but stopping him seems impossible. He wants to kill a friend of mine, so I guess my first plan needs to be figuring out how to avoid that."

"Use that brain of yours, Lenna. I know you've been looking forward to being a panom since you were little, but you only received your full powers a few months ago," Leo said. "Your brilliant brain and rebellious heart have always been there, and they still are. You just need to give them some credit. Not all of us have magic, but all of us can make a difference."

"I'll see what I do. In case I don't see you again, thank you for your patience all these years." She smiled at the man who had taught her so many more important things than textbooks and history and languages.

Leo smiled back, a proud glimmer in his eyes. "Magic or no magic, it's people like you who don't accept *no* as an answer, who don't accept the rules without challenging them, who change the world. Even if you don't consider this house your home anymore, you will always find a friend here."

Something was missing in this place. Lenna wasn't sure if it was her sister, who had always been around the North House ready to be to be a rightful pain in the ass; Theon, who she had always been looking forward to seeing in their next training or hanging out during the past couple of years living here, or something else.

The skin on her forearm tickled under the thin black shirt and she pulled it up to her elbow to see the incoming ink. The elegant writing made her bite her lip to hold her smile in.

Are you going to be in your self-pity cloud for much longer, Brachyan?

The navy ink vanished from her skin, but her smile lingered for a while longer.

From what Lenna had seen, she still had the very basic golden sparks she used to play with before her Fifth Ceremony, which probably meant she also could send ink.

Already missing me, heir of the nation?

She opened the doors of the chambers belonging to the Ruler of the North House and found her parents in a meeting with the Northern Elite, just as a servant had informed her a few minutes ago.

"Not so sorry to interrupt," Lenna said, tilting her head to the side with a smile.

Veronica Brachyan stood, something like relief in her eyes, while Jasper Brachyan just looked at her. The members of the Elite left the room without asking questions, some gathering papers and items spread on the wide table.

The last Elite member closed the door behind him.

"Nothing like some awkwardness in your own home," Lenna said. "Shocked to see I didn't bleed to death after the five Lawful Stabs? Or that I actually care to say hi after none of you bat an eyelid when the fucking Organ Mandor was stabbing me in your fucking faces?"

"Watch that mouth, Lenna Brachyan," her father warned.

"I don't need to watch anything anymore, actually. Luckily for you, I pissed the Organ Mandor off so much, he striped the heirloom from my blood and passed it to dear Ayla. Thyria didn't break in half because, apparently, our blood is similar enough to cope with it. Lucky me, I won't have to play your political bullshit games any longer."

"You never behaved like the heir of this House should," her father said, his lips in a tight line.

"We love you, Lenna," her mother said, and Lenna almost choked with laughter.

"What a funny fucking way to show your love," she said. "I came home to seek some sort of emotional shelter. So naïve of me, I know, but so revealing to realize I have lost nothing here. I won't be around much longer. Don't miss me too much." She blew a kiss in the air and left the room.

She hadn't mentioned that she wasn't a panom anymore, but she didn't need their pity or their shame. It was her own fucking problem.

46

Hope

The view of Corentre across the windows was breathtaking. That the wall covering a whole side of the dark living room Ciaran had moured them to was fully made of glass instead of bricks or wood didn't make it easier to stop staring outside.

The red-tinged moon was visible, but its red reflection on top of the small, white clouds was beautiful. Small, flickering lights illuminated the streets, converging on the very center of the city.

The sight of an extraordinarily large crystal dome crowned the middle of the impressive palace. The stars reflected off its radiant cupola, as if all the light on this planet and above led to the same place. Hope inhaled at the magnificence of the palace and how small and insignificant it made her feel.

Because she knew what that place was. She had already been in the throne room of the Organ House, and it had ended catastrophically.

Nina muttered something about coming back soon and her steps grew distant before a door closed somewhere in the house. Hope didn't need to hear him to know she wasn't alone.

"How do I kill him?" she asked, staring at the white walls of the palace. The hatred tasted bitter in her words.

Ciaran walked towards the window, leaning his back on it. Hope blinked, unable to decide if she would ever rely on a piece of glass to keep her alive with such ease and lack of worry. The look on his face was something between respect and interest, but she doubted it was because of the window.

"No human being will ever be able to kill the Organ Mandor," Ciaran said, looking at her. She couldn't help but notice he had not only a metal ring on his bottom lip, but also a few on top of his ear, barely visible underneath the dark hair. "Can I have your hand?"

Hope hesitated for only half a second before extending her hurt hand to him, her healthier one touching the hilt of a blade with her fingertips. He held the offered hand, not missing the movement of the other one.

"Just because Nina trusts you doesn't mean I do."

"I could have killed you last night if I wanted to. I could have killed you this morning when you were asleep. I could kill you now," Ciaran said, and Hope smiled at how bold he was for believing his magic was faster than her blades. At this short distance, she had the advantage. He seemed to read the *I'd-love-to-see-you-try* in her face, and she could have sworn a hint of amusement glittered on his eyes before he added, "But I don't have a single reason to do so. I'm not your enemy."

"Why do you want my hand?"

"To tell you how to kill him." Ciaran closed his metallic hand, and the bandage on top of hers vanished, revealing the deep cut that had worsened after digging the grave. At least her skin was clean now. He didn't flinch as he said, "I need some drops of your blood."

"My blood is in high demand as of late," Hope sighed. "Help yourself." If he could truly tell her anything of use, she would definitely take it.

Ciaran's metallic hand drew a small line in the air above Hope's hand. She held in a gasp as the scab reopened for the Fifth knew which time.

The index finger of his metallic hand touched the middle of the reopened wound, and a shiver went down her spine, making her close her eyes. Where pain should have been, there was only the cool touch of his finger.

When Hope opened her eyes, Ciaran was staring at her, his eyes slightly glazed as if he too had felt something.

"Are you happy for me to continue?" Ciaran asked.

Hope didn't have a clue about what he was doing, only that she wanted it to be over as soon as possible before her knees buckled. She nodded.

Ciaran didn't look at her hand again, as if he had already memorized the precise location, length, and depth of her wound. His blue eyes seemed to look inside Hope's soul as his metallic index finger traced the exact shape again. Hope was expecting the powerful sensation this time and managed to keep her eyes mostly open, even as her body tensed.

His nostrils flared slightly, and Hope's own sense of smell identified the copper scent of her blood. Ciaran lifted her now bleeding hand to his mouth and licked the length of her open wound, a low sound leaving her mouth before she could control it.

The world seemed to stop, her thoughts paused, on hold, with only a deep need for him to lick her again.

Without removing her hand from his lips, Ciaran closed his now drunk-looking eyes, inhaling through his nose, the warmth of every exhale sending a shudder over Hope's skin.

Fuck, if this wasn't the most intimate thing Hope had ever experienced. Her own irregular breaths were louder, but she couldn't control them.

Ciaran inhaled sharply, opening his blue eyes and separating his warm mouth from her skin, giving Hope her hand back. As if a spell had broken, Hope widened her eyes, wondering what the Fifth had just happened.

Ciaran cleared his throat, and his usually straight, muscular posture somehow seemed affected as well.

Hope didn't dare ask.

With a start, Nina entered the room, smiling calmly as she said, "I told the others, and they are on their way." Then, she looked from Hope to Ciaran and back to Hope, her nostrils flaring. "Am I interrupting something?"

"Ciaran was just about to tell me how to kill the Organ Mandor," Hope said, not taking her eyes from his blue ones.

Nina made a choking sound as Ciaran said, "Your blood is *extremely* powerful."

"How does he know about your b—" Nina started, but Hope gave her a look that screamed *not now*. "She can't be more powerful than the Organ Mandor, though, can she?"

Ciaran hesitated, his fingers playing with his metal ring. "Your father *is* the Organ Mandor. His panom blood is in your veins. You are the first female with Core panom blood in generations. The Cardinals protect you somehow."

"I couldn't believe my eyes when a cardinal appeared in the middle of the vessels and started guiding you," Nina said, shaking her head.

"A cardinal guided me to the chamber underneath the Invisible Grand. I didn't know it existed. Which probably means that not only one Cardinal protects you, but two."

"That bird has been my buddy since I was little. It always visited me in our treehouse in Verdania."

Mentioning her basic treehouse while standing in the middle of this fully furnished, stylish living room with more attention to detail that she had ever seen made her feel minuscule. Yet, the image of the treehouse came with memories of her mother, and a whole wave of very painful feelings.

Ciaran's eyebrows rocketed to the sky. "A fucking cardinal was your *buddy*?"

"It is *a* cardinal, but not *the* Cardinal," she snapped.

Ciaran chuckled, and he must have decided it was not worth an argument, because he said, "If you want any real chance at killing your father, you need a Fifth Ceremony to become a full panom and access the worlds of magic waiting for you. If that is not enough, we will have to consider desperate measures."

A door opened on the other side of the living room, and Nina turned to the door. The knowing look on her face reminded Hope that Nina had probably slept here while she had been in the clearing last night, and she probably knew whoever these people were.

Hope recognized Brendon, giving him a small nod of acknowledgement.

"Fucking Cardinals above," a beautiful woman with long, dark curls said, her mouth wide open, eyeing Hope from top to bottom and back to top. "How many weapons can a single person carry?"

Hope said nothing, her body tense. Her eyes slightly narrowed and her jaw clenched. She didn't miss noticing the similar traits between this woman and the other tall man behind her. Same dark hair, same skin tone, same curious, beautiful eyes. Was everyone in this island gorgeous?

Another woman was shorter, with a shoulder-long black bob and a perfectly straight fringe, her lips painted with a cardinal red. She was looking at Hope with a mix of interest and awe.

"Okay, fifteen weapons that I can see. I absolutely adore your killing style," the woman with dark curls said, laughing out loud. Hope never considered the black leathers of the courtrades to have anything to do with *style*.

The woman looked at Ciaran with a grin. "You should be proud of yourself for keeping your balls intact after a night with this absolute boss."

"No one said his balls were intact," Hope said, dead serious.

"You two can discuss my balls later." There was definitely a hint of amusement in Ciaran's eyes. "Meet Sasha, Carson, and Indianna." He inclined his head towards them as he named them, Sasha owning the curls and Indianna owning the bob. "You already know Brendon. Everyone, meet Hope."

"You already know Mister Stiff-as-the-Fifth," Carson said, pointing to Ciaran, and Hope couldn't help but think he had been anything but stiff a few minutes before. "So don't worry about being socially awkward."

Hope raised her eyebrows, turning to Nina, who crunched her face in an apology.

Nina took Hope's hand as she inhaled deeply and said, "The Organ Mandor found out about Raoul and brought him to a healing center in Corentre. Indianna is a professionally trained healer and works there."

Hope's eyes snapped at Ciaran. Rhei Coralt mentioning Ciaran's passion for aiding discarded beings now clicked.

"How can we get him out of there?" Hope asked Indianna.

"It's quite complex. The Beftac Center is heavily guarded right now because of him."

"It doesn't matter." Ciaran was looking at Nina, no trace of doubt or hesitation in his words. The others looked at him with the type of deference that was well-earned. "We will take Raoul to a safe place where we can keep him safe and out of the Organ Mandor's hands until we figure out how to wake him."

Tears of relief and gratitude lined Nina's eyes, and Hope squeezed her hand tighter.

Ciaran was now staring right into Hope's eyes. "But first, Hope must become a panom, and it will be us running her Fifth Ceremony."

47

Lenna

Even if the North House hadn't felt welcoming, Borealia was as busy and full of life as always. Lenna had decided to visit a less...Elite nightclub.

The Broken Spine was too dark for their souls. Circular black leather couches lined the walls of private spaces separated by red curtains, round tables sitting in the centers.

Lenna had been drinking myster for the Fifth knew how many hours, and it was already ante meridiem, if the flickering stars out the dark window were any indication. Her only company was the loud beat of the music thundering against the growing haziness of her mind as each glass disappeared.

She sent ink to Theon, unsure whether it would reach him, but was anything really sure in her life anymore?

You'd never believe where I am. A lot has happened. We need a proper catch up. I hope to see you soon. Don't cause too much trouble and leave the poor House alone.

She sighed. Her life was a fucking mess.

She had long realized that her parents didn't care about her, at least not in any way that mattered. She didn't even think they knew her or really cared enough to try.

As for knowing them, the beings behind the titles, Lenna had given up many years ago. There had been too many useless attempts at having any sort of connection with them, always followed by a dismissal or a fucking excuse.

None of this was new, but it was still hurtful to realize how the two people meant to love her most didn't give a fucking shit about her.

Lenna chugged another half glass of myster down, the burn of the liquid down her throat almost pleasant as she drowned out her feelings.

The lack of her powers was a fucking source of pain too. One she would have to learn to live with.

She had royally fucked up. Yet she didn't regret it. She would never regret not bending in front of someone like the Organ Mandor. She would never regret standing up for her beliefs and her truth. If these were the Cardinals-damned consequences, so be it.

The Organ Mandor was a fucking idiot if he truly believed she was inferior for being female. He wanted to obliterate the fact that the five female damned Cardinals had created his nation, that the damn Cardinal Queen had been precisely that: a *queen*.

Even with her thoughts blurred between the myster and the anger, she had her next steps clear.

Lenna would return to Corentre, to check in with Ciaran after his punishment, to see if Indianna had any other information about Raoul. Their brilliant minds could surely work out a plan to remove Raoul from the claws of the Organ Mandor. She was looking forward to seeing Sasha as well, to exchange smut books and stupid jokes. And most importantly, she was looking forward to other unfinished business. So, she willed her golden ink into the ether, without giving it a second thought.

I need a ride.

48

Lenna

The red curtain of her private compartment moved swiftly, a sudden breeze pushing it to the side.

"What type of ride, sweet fire?" Jake was leaning against the arch, pure mischief in his eyes that tightened every fiber of Lenna's body.

"One that takes me where I need to be," Lenna answered, biting her lip and wondering if she could walk the three steps to him in a straight line without falling. Her black heels wouldn't make it any easier.

Her eyelids were heavy, and yet it was impossible to take her eyes from him—from his now dark grey eyes to those Cardinals-damned full lips, his dark hair falling on the top of his handsome face, his muscled body and those hands that surely could work wonders.

Jake's eyes glowed with delight, as if he knew exactly what she wanted, what she needed with her whole body.

"There is only one place *I* need to be tonight," Jake said, tilting his head back slightly. He paced towards the table she was sitting on. Lenna didn't move an inch as he pushed between her thighs. She felt his growing hardness, and he looked at her as if she was myster and he was there to drink her. "And that's inside you."

Lenna chuckled, drinking the rest of her glass as her other hand grabbed the vast size of him and stroked him firmly through his black pants. "Then what the fuck are you waiting for?"

Jake grabbed her waist and pulled her towards the edge of the table. The high slits on both sides of her bronze dress made it so easy to open her legs, to push her core against his length. He grabbed her hair in a fist as their mouths collided.

An explosion of tongues and teeth and lips followed. This man tasted like pure silver and ginger, and she couldn't get enough of him. She wanted to taste *all* of him. The empty glass of myster rolled to the floor as her hands broke open the buttons of his shirt, finally able to delight at every single muscle of his arms, his shoulders, his back, that thick, long shape pressed into the apex of her legs, driving her fucking crazy.

Jake pulled the silk lace from behind her neck, undoing the bow that kept her dress together at her waist, leaving her exposed.

"You're fucking beautiful," he said, his voice gravel as he took a step back to admire her. Lenna saw the desire in his eyes and thought she would melt.

Jake put his hands under her knees and pulled her forwards, her hips hanging off the table, and Lenna couldn't help but recline her back onto the black stone of the table. He kneeled in front of her, his hands grabbing each side of her exposed ass thanks to her lace thong before he hooked her knees over his shoulders.

One of his hands left her cheek, and she almost whine at the loss, but then she felt a flick of his hand, and suddenly, her underwear was gone. His hand was back in place as his tongue went straight to her core, twisting and licking and sucking as only a fucking expert could.

Jake moved his skilled tongue to her clit, playing with it as two fingers entered her, pumping into her in tandem.

She moaned loudly, her back arching against the cold black stone, and he gripped her ass with his spare hand harder.

Lenna grabbed his hair, looking down at those dark grey eyes as he devoured her.

"You taste even better than I ever dreamed, Brachyan," he groaned into her. "Molten honey. Pure, sweet fire."

Lenna was barely aware of the surrounding nightclub, and that no one had interrupted them yet made a small part of her wonder if he had shut the noise out of this compartment, or if Jake had willed the other beings away when he moured here.

Because there was no undoing this. He wanted her and she wanted him. If not being the heir of the North House meant she could fuck this man as much as she wanted, as often as she wanted, she would send a thank you note to the Organ Mandor.

She pulled his head towards her face, his tongue moving away while his blessed fingers didn't let go. Lenna's body tensed as he twisted those fingers inside her, and she let go of a small scream of pleasure.

"My turn," Lenna panted as he came up to kiss her, her tongue dragging across his lips.

"Not tonight, sweet fire." The corner of his lips twisted upwards in mischief, and he turned her body softly but firmly, her breasts pressed against the cold stone of the table. "Tonight, you're all mine."

She bent over at the waist, leaving her bare ass exposed. She was at his mercy. He grabbed her round ass tightly, massaging it in rough circles as he groaned, "So fucking perfect."

She moaned as his thick, velvet length settled between her cheeks, sliding up and down as he pushed her cheeks tightly together with his hands.

Lenna slipped a hand down to her core, pumping her fingers in and out. She was going to die from pleasure at Jake's cock rubbing against her ass, the sound of him, the touch of his hands on her body.

Jake stopped, removing away from her body. Lenna looked back at him over her shoulder, wide eyed. The sight of his hardened length, his muscled body, the deep desire in his handsome face... It was magnificent.

"Don't you fucking stop now," she said, biting her lip and pushing her body against his.

His eyes were full of dark promises as he held his length in his hand and opened her legs with the other. Lenna held his stare, her breath coming out in pants as she reined in her absolute desperation.

He touched the tip of his length to her core, and she moaned. She needed more, and she needed it now.

"What do you want, sweet fire?" The tip of his hard cock stilled, and she struggled to keep her eyes from closing in bliss.

"I want all of you right fucking now, Jake," she gasped, her back arching as she opened her legs for him.

"You want me to what?" he asked. His breathing was ragged as he tapped his cock against her core, teasing her.

"Fuck me. Please," she gasped, her body shaking with need. She was going to fucking explode if he made her wait any longer.

But he didn't. He didn't warn her either, not as his whole, extraordinarily hard length sank inside her, as deep as it could go, and she fucking screamed.

Navy and golden sparks flickered around them as Jake struck deep thrusts inside her, over and over, each one sending her into a spiral of fucking pleasure she had never experienced before. Then, Jake pulled out, and Lenna stood before he could boss her around again, even if she had thoroughly enjoyed it. She pushed his muscled chest to the circular couch, forcing him to sit.

Lenna kneeled in front of him, grabbing his cock as she slid her mouth over his crown. She opened her mouth wide to fit as much of his length as she could. Jake grabbed her red hair with both fists, his eyes following every movement of her mouth as her golden eyes stared back at him. He was fucking delicious, and his moans were otherworldly.

Jake tilted his head back. "Fucking Cardinals, Lenna."

She savored the velvet of his hard flesh, the warmth emanating from him, until Jake grabbed her breasts and pulled her up, sitting her on top of him.

"What is it you want, Jake?" She removed her hand from her entrance, the tip of his length barely touching the wetness of her core.

"I want to see you come for me," he gasped, licking her neck.

She grabbed his cock with one hand, placing it precisely at the right spot so he could strike home, but not impaling herself. Not yet.

"*You want me to what?*" Lenna said, tilting her head backwards as his tongue played with the soft spot behind her ear.

"Let me fuck you until you come for me, Lenna. *Please.*"

The raw need in Jake's voice was her undoing—not that she could wait a second longer to have him inside her again anyway.

So, Lenna sheathed him completely inside her, and damn every single Cardinal one by one if his length didn't go as deep as it had ever been. She lifted up slowly and sat back on him in a fast movement. Out slowly, in quickly.

His ragged breath was a melody with her own, his half-opened mouth against her neck as he grabbed her ass with both hands, helping pull her body up and down, down and up.

Lenna tilted her head backwards, her back arching as she moaned hoarsely, her pleasure uniting with his deepest growl as he moved his hips skilfully against her until they both stilled, climaxing in unison, melted together in lust and heat.

She was him, and he was her, and they were one.

49

Hope

Apparently, Ciaran's friends had a petal of the panom mark, just a petal each. It didn't make any sort of sense in Hope's mind, but since she hadn't even know panom marks existed until recently, she would not start questioning other people's marks, half-marks, quarter-marks, or whatever the Fifth these beings had.

Ciaran insisted that all that was needed for a successful Fifth Ceremony was the individual in question to convert to full panom with five sources of panom blood, regardless of these being birth blood, acquired blood or recipient blood.

"The panom society and most Rulers of the Houses love to make a big fuss of any Fifth Ceremony, aligning it with the birth date and all. It's all pretense and political bullshit," Ciaran said, a half-bored look on his face.

Maybe it was the ink covering his biological arm, the metal ring on his bottom lip or the ones on his ears, or that he didn't seem to care about his long dark hair being attractively messy, but Hope believed this man couldn't care less about societal expectations or political games.

"I don't understand what you get from this." Hope was looking at Indianna, Sasha, and Ciaran. Nina was taking a shower, and Carson and Brendon were working at whatever jobs they had.

That right there was what had kept her awake for many hours the previous night, despite the extremely comfortable and wide bed in the guest room.

"Who gets what from what?" Sasha asked, cocking an eyebrow.

"I don't know any of you. Why would you want to waste your time doing this Fifth Ceremony thing to help me?"

Sasha and Indianna crossed a confused look. Ciaran didn't take his blue eyes from her. "You have panom blood by birth, but your father will never allow you to have a Fifth Ceremony if it means you might access powers greater than his. His whole rule could end by you becoming a panom." Hope very much doubted that was the case, but she only swallowed before he continued. "I saw that motherfucker kill your mother with my own eyes. I would love to see someone hand him his ass."

"And also, why wouldn't we help you?" Indianna said. "It's your birthright. It's only fair that you can use what your blood already owns."

Before Hope had a chance to reply, Ciaran tensed, his hands at the ready on both sides. He stood up, walking towards the main entrance of his house before someone knocked decisively.

"Not like you to knock before entering, Lenna," Hope heard him say, and Hope didn't let go of the blades she just gripped from her belt, because he added, "What the fuck is *he* doing here?"

"Nice to see you alive too, Ciaran. He is with me," a female voice said matter-of-factly. "We need to talk."

Hope didn't need to see Ciaran to know he was looking at said *he* with deadly eyes. "You do half a move wrong, and I fucking kill you. I won't give a shit about repercussions. Are we clear?"

"So bossy, Ciaran," the man teased.

"Oh, for Cardinals' sake. Will you two shut the fuck up and leave your dick length competitions for another day?" The sound of high heels storming into the apartment followed the voice of this woman. "Where is everyone?"

Fire-red waves of hair covered the woman's head, and the effect when she walked was hypnotizing. Her golden eyes were analytical and clever and landed straight on Hope the instant she crossed the doorway to the living room. She wasn't very tall, but her posture was straight, as if she was the Ruler of the Cardinals-damned world.

She stopped dead, and a gorgeous man entered a few steps behind. His black clothes matched his black hair, yet his eyes were silver and intense, like someone full of secrets. His expression, with a raised eyebrow and full lips tight in a semi smirk, was that of someone who ruled the world. The shape of his jaw was unusually familiar.

"Who are you?" Hope did not let go of the blades. Not yet.

The man stared at Hope from top to bottom, his silver eyes narrowing. Hope was totally on board with Ciaran's plan. If he so much as blinked with anything that looked like bad intentions, she would stick a dagger in his eyelid. Her expression must have reflected that, because his chin lifted upwards.

The woman didn't seem to care about his attitude or her daggers. "Lenna Brachyan, proud ex-heir of the North House. And Jake Coralt, not-so-proud heir of the Organ House." She blinked before adding, "And you are?"

"I'm Hope, daughter of Rhei Coralt." She smiled grimly. Her daggers left her hands, aimed at Jake's thighs until she could assess if he was a danger like his father. "Nice to meet you, brother."

Jake grabbed the blades with his bare hands, smiling despite the red drops falling from his palms.

"I can't make half a move wrong, but your people can throw blades at me? And beings complain about the unfairness of the system." He did a movement with his hand, and the daggers flew away, landing at a side table far from Hope. "And by the way, I have no sisters. Sorry to disappoint."

Lenna raised her eyebrows with a mix of shock and absolute enjoyment. "Not like you to not hurt someone daring to attack you."

"It's not gentleman-like to kill a pretty woman at first sight." He shrugged.

Lenna laughed out loud. "Since when are you anything remotely close to a gentleman? Do gentlemen flirt with their sisters? Fucking gross."

"I'm not flirting, and she's not my sister. There are no living females in my bloodline other than my mother."

"Because your sadistic father exterminated them all. But she's right. I have... proved it," Ciaran said, as if he didn't want to explain that proving meant tasting her blood. "Hers is pure Core panom blood."

Lenna walked towards Sasha, giving her a tight hug and grinning as she said, "And to think, we would have missed this if I hadn't dragged Jake here because of the whole Raoul situation."

Nina's silver hair peaked through the archway. "You know my brother?"

Lenna's golden eyes widened as she brought a hand to her wide-opened mouth.

50

Lenna

"**N**o fucking way," Lenna repeated, wide eyed and unable to close her mouth.

This woman was a replica of Raoul; same snow-white hair, same light blue eyes, same pale skin, same devastating beauty. After months of wanting to see him, to find him and take him somewhere safe, the sight of this woman seemed to ease some of the tightness in Lenna's chest, even if she wasn't him.

"You must be one of the Brachyan sisters," Raoul's sister said, looking at her red hair. "Raoul was always talking about you." She smiled, the sweetest thing Lenna had seen in a long while.

As if her own sister had somehow felt summoned, Lenna felt a tickle on her forearm and read Ayla's silver ink:

I'm so sorry about what happened.
I never wanted it to be like that.
If you need anything, please let me know.

The ink vanished from her skin as quick as Lenna dismissed her sister's words, the memory of her lost heirloom, and her current powerlessness. Enough was going on already to be worrying about her own sister.

"Did you just appear out of nowhere? How the Cardinals' fuck did I not know you existed?" Lenna frowned. Swearing in front of her sweet smile made her almost feel bad. Almost.

"Your mother always kept me busy with laundry and kitchen duties at the North House."

Of course, her mother did.

"As for just appearing out of nowhere... It's a long story, but that's a pretty accurate description."

"What's your name?"

"Nina," Raoul's sister smiled. "If you were going to say something about my brother's situation, please go ahead."

Lenna turned to Ciaran and Indianna and asked, "How are we getting him out?"

"We have a plan," Ciaran said, turning to look at Jake. "We need to take a brief trip to the Cardinals' Temple as soon as possible. If you want to make yourself useful, ensure your father stays the fuck away from there when it's time."

Jake cocked his eyebrow. "It's one thing not agreeing with my father's methods; it's another entirely to help in rebellious or unlawful activities behind his back."

"Don't you keep saying you like to push limits and boundaries? Prove it," Lenna spat.

"It would be my pleasure." The word *pleasure* with the now dark grey of his eyes did funny things to the rhythm of her heart, and the shiver down her spine seemed to agree.

Lenna's lips tightened in a thin line. She faced the dark-haired woman with two long braids, Hope, and said, "Nobody has lost anything in that Temple. I'm guessing you will have your Fifth Ceremony there as Ciaran is convinced you have pure Core blood. All I will say is, enjoy the powers while your father lets you, because he took mine away."

Ciaran tensed, his voice low and somber as he asked, "Is that what he did?"

"After I called him a piece of shit with powers and refused to apologize for telling him to fuck off." Lenna smiled sarcastically.

"So, what do you have now, mark-wise?"

"A whole sweet nothing," she said. "Other than my *very* useful ink and *very* pretty golden sparks. Basically, what I had before my Fifth."

Ciaran walked towards her. "May I see?"

Lenna opened the zip at the front of her top, revealing the skin underneath. She felt Jake tensing at her side, surely noting her lack of bra. "Nothing. I told you."

Ciaran touched the skin where her mark used to be, and Lenna felt a small prickle. "No one can remove the original core of the owner's mark without killing them."

Lenna zipped her top up and said to Jake, "How generous of your father to not kill me."

Jake's fists tensed, his chin lifting upwards, as if he was considering what he would have done if that had been the case. "You wouldn't have been the only dead one."

She wasn't sure if he meant he would have killed his father or that he would have died trying. Considering how untouchable the fucking Organ Mandor seemed to be, probably the latter.

"You could be a full panom again if you get the four petals donated," Ciaran said. "I have one petal for you."

Even though the donations to Brendon, Carson, Indianna, and Sasha were single petals, how the Fifth did Ciaran ever have enough for all those donations? She doubted he would be willing to share that information in a room with so many open fronts, especially as Jake's eyes were glimmering with profound interest.

"Do I want to be a panom again?" Lenna said, a slight hesitation lacing her words.

"Fuck yes you do, Brachyan," Jake snapped.

"When I had finally assumed I wouldn't be a panom, that I was not an absolute damned loser because of that..." she swallowed. "If that means becoming the heir again... Cardinals guide me, I don't want *that*."

She didn't take her amber eyes from Jake's silver ones. What sort of being did it make her that she cared more about being with Jake than representing the House that had raised her? The House could get royally fucked. Her priorities had definitely shifted over the past few weeks, days, hours.

"In an ideal world, the Organ Mandor does not find out you have become a panom again. Otherwise I don't see any scenario in which he doesn't kill you," Ciaran said. "Death and the Organ Mandor are the only ways to transfer heirlooms so you won't become the heir of the North House again."

Lenna grinned. "What a shame."

Jake looked at her with a side smile that seemed to say *Free reign to fulfil our mutual desires, sweet fire*, and her core heated at the thought.

Ciaran looked at Jake and Lenna. "You two shouldn't have a problem with panomquakes even if Lenna was the heir. Because Hope has pure Core panom *female* blood, which means—"

"That she is the true Cardinals-blessed heir of the Organ House," Jake finished, his voice cutting, his eyes narrowing as the fact sank in.

"Cardinals above, I don't think I can take any more big revelations. I'm going to fucking collapse," said Sasha, sitting down on the couch. She put her hands at the sides of her face, curls going in all directions.

"But we caused a panomquake when... Well, the other day. That big panomquake, it was Jake and I doing... *things*." Lenna put her hands on her waist, a frown on her face.

"The about-to-fuck type of things," Jake unnecessarily clarified.

"Inconveniently similar timing," Ciaran said. "Because I saw Hope stepping into Thyria for the first time in her life, and the panomquake was definitely caused by her presence."

"And you have known this since *when* exactly, Ciaran?" Hope spat, anger lining her voice.

"I've had suspicions since I saw you, but you were busy throwing blades at me. Then, the Organ Mandor intercepted us, and then we were in the woods... I didn't know for sure until I checked your blood."

Something Lenna couldn't identify passed through Hope's eyes as he mentioned the last bit, but it was gone quickly, replaced by cold irritation.

Lenna turned to Jake, doubting how he would take not being the lawful heir of the Organ House, the successor to his father, the future Organ Mandor, but Jake didn't seem to care.

Instead, his expression had no trace of doubt as he looked right back at her.

"I will donate two petals to you," Jake said, and the glimmer in his eyes read more than physical heat. It heated another part of her being, a part she didn't want to hand over so easily.

"You have two to give?" Ciaran asked him.

"I would be stupid to offer what I can't give."

Ciaran nodded, looking at Jake with all seriousness and consideration. Lenna had no words; she swallowed the emotion threatening to make her throw herself into Jake's arms and kiss the fuck out of him. This was dangerous territory.

"We need one more petal and we are good to go," Ciaran said. "Two Fifth Ceremonies in one. The Cardinals won't know what hit them. Any idea who could donate you a petal?"

Lenna hesitated, an idea forming in her mind.

The chances of pure offering coming from Ayla's guilt were slim, but Lenna had bits of information she could use to blackmail her into donating a petal, information that Ayla wouldn't want her parents to know, like some illegal magical devices she owned, the network of spies she had formed in the North House, and some of her escapades.

She lifted a hand and sent her very useful golden ink with a wicked smile on her face.

Dear sister: I need something.

51

Hope

"I'm not leaving my daggers here," Hope said pointedly. "I don't care how sacred the Cardinals' Temple is."

In the wide, dark living room, Sasha let out an exasperated sigh.

"I took a blade to my first Fifth Ceremony and nothing happened," Lenna said without lifting her gaze from the book Sasha had given her. The red-haired woman was dressed in an impressively tight dress fully made of transparent beads like the one Hope was meant to wear after the daggers' debate was settled.

"You what?" Jake asked. "I examined every single part of your body that day, and I didn't see anything."

Lenna's eyes jumped from the page on her book and winked at Jake, smirking. "Every single part of my body, huh?"

Jake's eyes darkened as he looked at Lenna lazily from head to toe. The Fifth only knew what these two were playing at.

"The Cardinals didn't mind Lenna's dagger. They won't mind about a few of mine," Hope concluded, heading to the guest room where, a few minutes earlier, Ciaran had made her dress appear.

Putting this dress on was somewhere very high amidst the most awkward things Hope had ever done.

This dress was everything she would never be. It was luxurious, seductive, ostentatious, and unavoidably provocative. Unavoidably, because no matter how many times Hope tried to readjust it to cover some parts of her skin better, the beaded tissue only readapted its shape to her body. She might feel less exposed if she was truly naked instead.

"Are you sure *this* is the only way to fully channel my inner powers?" Hope asked Ciaran as she walked into the living room after braiding her long hair in a crown.

Ciaran's gaze didn't move from Hope's eyes despite her reference to the very exposing dress, and she was grateful for that. She had never missed the protection of her leathers more, even the pitch-black clothes from the courtrades.

"Do you really need to take all these weapons?" Ciaran asked, nodding at the daggers she held, and the metal ring on his bottom lip bobbed as if he was trying to contain a smile.

"You never know when they might come in handy."

Ciaran moved his hands, and the skirt of Hope's dress split in two legs, wrapping around her skin.

She smiled with pure relief and joy at the fact that if she had to use her weapons, this would allow free movement when fighting. She wrapped a belt in each thigh, adjusting them to get a perfect fit. She put a strap under her chest, circling it around her back, then lifting side straps atop her shoulders that connected the strap under her breasts. The daggers were securely sheathed immediately after.

Much, much better. Still feeling naked, but well-armed.

"I think the Cardinals would absolutely be onboard with this total badass vibe, you know." Sasha nodded with approval.

"If she is truly the heir of the Organ House, the Cardinals might already be onboard with it," Lenna replied, as if Hope wasn't there. "Because they must have kept a close eye on her all her life, I mean." She lifted her eyes from the page she was reading and grabbed her cup of tea before she asked Jake, "Are you sure your father will be distracted enough?"

Jake scoffed. "Sure as the Fifth. Nothing like a national alert that criminal organizations have attacked the four Cardinal Houses simultaneously and are holding their members hostage in unknown locations."

Lenna made a weird sound, lifting her eyebrows. "You almost made me choke."

Jake smirked as he said, "You are not the first woman to say that to me."

Lenna seemed to hesitate for a moment, as if she was internally debating rolling her eyes, but then she snorted and said, "I earned that one. But have you actually let criminal organizations inside the Houses?"

"No. I held a few members of each House hostage myself and left them in random places within their cities. Before you ask, no one is irreversibly hurt, just temporarily unconscious. Hopefully, it will take a few hours of every roixer and panom attention to find every being and, more importantly, the *criminals*," Jake chuckled.

Hope couldn't stop staring at him, trying to see all the details of his features and expressions.

If what these people were saying was true, Jake could consider Hope a usurper of his heirloom, a future usurper of the throne made of bones and black feathers. Yet, he didn't seem too bothered by it. Either that, or he was planning something big to destroy her when she least expected it. Regardless, Hope knew she should never trust him. She couldn't read his true intentions between all the smirks and teasing and without knowing someone's true motive, he could be a liability to her own survival.

"Sometimes I don't know if I should fear you or admire you," Lenna seemed to whisper to herself, tilting her head to the side.

52

Lenna

The panoms, meaning Jake and Ciaran, had decided it was better to do both Fifth Ceremonies separately, since both had quite unusual circumstances and neither of them were sure about how the additional sources of magic, especially Hope's, would impact the land.

Hence why Lenna's ceremony was going to be the first.

Ayla had surprisingly agreed to donate a petal without asking further questions. Lenna didn't fully believe her unusually generous ink messages until her twin sister was moured into the antechamber of the Cardinals' Temple by Jake.

It was damn lucky that Jake had somehow been up to take part in this, since the epitellia wards of the Organ House would have proved impossible to cross otherwise.

Jake, Ayla, and Ciaran circled Lenna in an empty triangle under the Temple's dome.

Lenna couldn't truly make out why Ayla had decided to donate the South Petal to her, but she was not going to dig in too deep if that made her sister reconsider that as the current heir of the North House she was better off with a full petal mark. Maybe recent events had made Ayla realize that the political system she had always been so in love with was royally, masterfully fucked up.

"Ready to start?" Ciaran asked.

"I don't think this is going to work, but whatever," Ayla said, staring at Lenna. "If this lets you be a panom and it doesn't stop me from being one, it's worth a try."

"Of course you will still be a panom," Jake said.

"Does it matter which petal I donate?" Ayla asked, lifting her chin in a movement that Lenna had seen hundreds of times.

"Whichever petals the recipient receives, her blood will readjust until it's a fully-formed panom mark," Ciaran explained. Something like relief eased at the confirmation that she would not have a mark made of four South Petals or four East Petals. "In your case, since you don't have spare petals yet and you'll be donating from your original panom mark, you won't be able to use the magic of the petal you donate. The balance between your magics will feel uneven and on edge for a while."

"Can *for a while* be more precise?" Ayla said.

"For five years. Until the next petal grows and replaces the empty space," Jake said. Lenna didn't miss Ciaran's eyes narrowing.

Lenna's eyes widened. Petals fucking *grew*? And most importantly, both *had* spare petals to donate? And Ciaran had already donated four before. That she knew of. Cardinals knew how many more they had in the past and what had they done with them.

"Wait, how old are you two?" she asked.

"That's a conversation for another time," Ciaran said.

Lenna turned to face Jake, her eyes wide with urgency. The urgency appeared to be more related to the fact that she wanted to know how old the man she'd been fucking and thinking about all these weeks was, rather than the fact that the Organ Mandor would not be kept busy in the Cardinal Houses searching for inexistent criminals for the rest of his damned life.

"You enjoyed my expertise," Jake said, the side of his delicious mouth curling upwards. His eyes slipped over her lips, as if he was fucking her all over again, the instant need heating her already-needing-but-pissed-off core.

"You and your expertise can fuck off if all you do is lie." Lenna crossed her arms in front of her chest.

"I never lie, sweet fire. Not to you."

"*Sweet fire*?" Ayla's top lip curled, exposing her teeth with disgust. "Dearest Cardinals guide me. Can we start the Ceremony before I pass out?"

Ciaran cleared his throat, extending both hands in front of him, and Lenna felt the familiar warmth flowing through her body as he recited, "May the light enfold your strength."

From the corner of her eyes, she saw something floating towards her. Her body wanted to sing, enjoying the familiar sensation of some power in her veins, so she let herself go as Jake said, also opening his palms towards her, "May the darkness accept your weakness."

Ayla followed suit. "May the world cherish your mind."

Those were petals definitely floating *into* her, right in between her breasts, where her panom mark had been. A silver petal came from Ayla, Ciaran's petal dark green, Jake's navy.

The colors of their souls, their inks and sparks, the colors of their own marks, came to join Lenna's own golden core.

"May the Cardinals guide your soul," Ciaran said.

"May the Fifth unleash your magic," Jake said, another navy petal floating towards her body, warming her soul and heart. The emotion in his eyes met her own, and she couldn't stop looking at him. She wasn't sure she could ever stop looking at him again.

This man had no reason to help her. Yet, here he was, helping her in all the manners that mattered—by apologizing for his fuck up with her book of Cause, teaching her to use the four Cardinal powers, being stabbed himself trying to protect her, Healing her in the cell, standing up to his own father to advocate for her, making her experience pleasure as intense as it had ever existed, and now, allowing her to be what she had always treasured most: a panom.

Maybe, and only maybe, what she treasured most had changed. Maybe, and only maybe, the emotion in her golden eyes wasn't caused only by her original and recipient magic meeting and cherishing each other in her newly formed panom mark. Maybe, she realized, what she felt for this man had a name.

"May the light enfold your strength. May the darkness accept your weakness. May the world cherish your mind. May the Cardinals guide your soul. May the Fifth unleash your magic," the three of them said as a cardinal flew across the crystal dome and started circling her, lifting her into the air in that familiar-and-yet-not way. It was impossible to get used to a true cardinal doing dizzying circles around oneself, not when her blood was welcoming back the powers the Organ Mandor had stolen from her, golden light radiating from every bead of her dress into the Cardinals' Temple.

She didn't need to look in her chest to know the donated petals had readjusted, for there was her golden, full panom mark.

Lenna Brachyan was a panom again.

53

Hope

The door connecting the antechamber and the dome room of the Cardinals' Temple opened, and Jake and Lenna entered, their shoulders touching—or maybe they were holding hands—followed by Ciaran and another fire-haired woman who resembled Lenna, but...

There. Her eyes weren't the purified liquid gold of Lenna's, but green like the purest spring fields of Verdania, and her hair, while equally intense in color, was longer and sleek, a curtain of fire.

The woman started when she saw Nina, as if she had been struck by lightning. If this woman dared hurt her friend, Hope would make sure the red-head ended up worse.

"Hurt her and I will end you," Hope said, her voice low and calm. The woman looked at her, green eyes widening as she left both hands in a stance that usually meant someone was innocent. Except Hope was so done taking the word, or the actions, of theoretically innocent strangers—even if she was about to let five of them help her.

It didn't sit well with her, but she didn't seem to have any other option if she wanted to achieve her plan.

The muscled man pacing at the other side of the room was smirking.

"The brunette one can give you a run for your money, Lenna."

Thane, or something starting with T, if she remembered correctly from the rushed introductions. A friend of Lenna, Ciaran had explained with no trace of joy. The way he moved, though... That man was a fighter, hence why Hope hadn't taken her eyes off him since Jake had moured them here.

Nina and whatever-his-name were the only ones not taking part in either of the Fifth Ceremonies; they were here for what would happen after.

"Your turn." Ciaran tilted his head towards Hope, opening the door for her.

Hope's steps didn't falter. They never faltered. And yet, overwhelming feelings raced inside her.

It was happening. The revelation of her panom mark by the compassom back in Verdania had ended with Hope about to become a full panom. She was about to be given access to whatever powers her blood silently held since she was born.

The blood that had caused the Organ Mandor to discard her. The blood that would make her the heir of the Organ House. The blood she was determined to use to kill her father.

The transparent beads on her chest expanded slightly as she inhaled deeply.

She walked until she was right under the gigantic crystal dome, and Ciaran, Sasha, Indianna, Carson, and Brendon formed a circle around her.

This was happening, and it was happening now.

Hope's eyes met Ciaran's blue ones, and she nodded, trying to relax her body but not daring to close her eyes.

Brendon extended his arms in front of her, and Hope had a dagger in her hand before his reached the line of his shoulders.

His gorgeous face paled, and he swallowed before saying, "I'm just doing what Ciaran told us to do. Just my hands. Empty, weapon-less, pretty much magicless hands. Promise."

Hope exhaled deeply, sheathing her dagger. Her shoulders were so damn tense. "Sorry," she muttered. Her reflexes would need to hold for a few minutes until this was over.

"No matter what happens, once the Fifth Ceremony is started, we must carry on until its end. No matter what happens." Ciaran's voice was grave.

Brendon seemed extremely relieved about not having a sharp blade pointing at his body again. He looked at his hands, palms facing Hope, and said, "May the light enfold your strength."

An invisible but boiling wave hit Hope's chest, and she did her best to not take a step backwards.

"May the darkness accept your weakness," Sasha said. The wave this time was stronger, spreading from her chest into her brain, her fingertips, her toes. It was hot, vibrant, and powerful.

"May the world cherish your mind." That was Carson's voice.

"May the Cardinals guide your soul," Indianna said.

Hope's body was trembling so much, she could barely stand. Or was the *world* trembling with her?

"May the Fifth unleash your magic," Ciaran said, and Hope roared as the power filling her veins threatened to burst through her body.

The light emanating from her through every transparent bead of her outfit was red. Arterial red, Nina had said in another life.

The five beings around her said in unison, "May the light enfold your strength. May the darkness accept your weakness. May the world cherish your mind. May the Cardinals guide your soul."

Her blood, body, soul, and mind were red. The world was red. The crystal dome was red. And that was a very familiar red bird flying towards her. Arterial red, Cardinal red. Hope would have grinned at the sight if she hadn't been busy trying to stay alive with the unending power threatening to burn her alive.

"May the Fifth unleash your magic," their united voices said.

Time seemed to stop as the cardinal circled her body in impossibly fast rings, her feet letting go of the trembling ground. The cardinal spiralled around Hope until her body was horizontal in the air under the dome. Her blood burned so hot, it was hard to keep her eyes open.

The cardinal flew to the top of the Temple, and just when Hope thought it was going to disappear through the crystal dome, it faced her. The eyes of the cardinal were not the eyes of a bird. They were the eyes of a creature made by magic, the eyes of a wise and determined female. The eyes of a goddess.

A goddess trapped in the body of a cardinal diving towards Hope. Towards her chest. A goddess who flew *through* her chest.

Hope's back arched mid-air, and she felt two limbs extending from her back. No, not limbs. *Wings.* Two huge, splayed wings, beautifully and perfectly feathered in the same color the world had turned into, the color still emanating from her.

The Cardinal was gone, and Hope's wings had gone with it.

Then, her body was falling before Ciaran's powerful hands were on her back and under her knees, catching her in time to avoid catastrophe.

That was the Cardinals' Temple, not red anymore. That was the dome, its broken crystals raining down on them.

That was a panomquake breaking their world.

54

Lenna

The panomquake started like any other: the ground slightly shaking, things trembling, a background hum coming from underneath. That was, until the floor moved like a wave in the sea, and Lenna heard the crystal dome on the other side of the antechamber door fucking explode. She heard ripping noises coming from outside the Organ House, as if the actual land was breaking in half.

"If anyone had any doubt about that woman being the heir of the Organ House, that was a hell of a Fifth Ceremony."

"Cardinals. We need to get the fuck out of here before my father gets here," Jake said. He was the only one who could moure them out, and there were too many of them in there. "Ladies." He offered both hands to Ayla and Lenna so he could moure, and he winked. He fucking *winked*, even though the island had probably split in half and the Organ Mandor could kill them all.

His firm hand touched the back of Lenna's neck softly, a shiver going down her spine. His thumb stroked her skin for the few seconds the mouring lasted before he left them in a barely illuminated alley and disappeared.

Ciaran and Hope were moured in shortly after, and Jake was gone again before Lenna had time to gasp, Ciaran carrying a limp Hope in his arms. The moment he set foot in the alley, he bent his knee to the ground and Gave the floor a cushioned mat, where he carefully placed Hope.

"Fuck, is she alive?"

"She better be, or I will kill that fucking Cardinal myself," Ciaran said through his teeth, holding his breath.

His index and middle fingers were on Hope's throat, checking for her pulse, and he must have found it, because he inhaled sharply, closing his eyes for half a second. He proceeded to do circling Healing movements over her heart with his biological hand, the metallic one Healing the small cuts on her face, hands, and feet. Some of the transparent beads of her outfit were broken too, but they had kept the skin underneath safe. Ciaran himself was full of cuts, but he didn't seem to care one bit.

Lenna kneeled on the other side of Hope and started Healing her skin as well. Ciaran was now circling over Hope's heart with both hands, his blue eyes not leaving Hope's closed ones.

Damn if it didn't feel good to use her powers again. Damn if she hadn't been born to do this, even if she'd tried to convince herself otherwise. Lenna fully focused on the Healing, barely noticing that Jake kept mouring people in at lightning speed. Nina kneeled next to Hope's head, stroking her black hair.

"Hope! Hope, wake up!" Tears lined Nina's blue eyes. "What happened to her?"

"What the land felt, her body must have suffered many times worse." Ciaran's circles became faster and more intense, dark green sparks jumping from his fingers to Hope's chest as it rose and fell with slow and shallow breaths. A couple of red sparks joined Ciaran's ones, and they seemed to dance with each other before the red ones vanished.

Indianna and Sasha were moured in next before Indianna checked her pulse. "Her heart rate is too slow. We need someone Healing her brain immediately, or we risk it not receiving enough oxygen and having catastrophic consequences." Jake was gone again before he could even listen to what Indianna had ordered. Fuck, when had they thought that bringing so many people was a good fucking idea?

Ayla kneeled between Nina and Ciaran. Her Northern Majesty had finally cared to help the woman perishing in front of her. She took over the constant circling Healing motions over Hope's head, and Lenna felt a long-standing hateful knot in her chest easing.

Jake moured in the group's last, Carson and Brendon, and kneeled between Lenna and Nina.

"Three fucking panoms Healing you and you don't wake the fuck up?" Anger lined Jake's voice. "I don't give a Cardinals-damned shit about who you are. We haven't risked our necks for nothing, so *wake the fuck up*."

"You don't talk to her like that," Ciaran said, baring his teeth. "All of you, get the fuck out of here. This is clearly not working."

"Out as in *out, out*?" Lenna said. The cuts on Hope's skin were mostly healed now, the skin sewn back together by magic.

"Just give me some space. Please." Ciaran's voice was tense, and the last word was definitely not in his usual vocabulary.

They all stood, walking down the alley, giving him exactly what he asked for.

55

Hope

She was dead, yet she was alive. She was conscious, but she wasn't.

She was in the middle of nowhere, surrounded by red sparks and red feathers. She didn't feel her heart beating. She didn't feel her daggers. Did she have any daggers? She had a body, and yet she didn't, so it was pointless to look down.

She felt something far, far away, as if coming from another world or another life.

A female flew towards her from the undefined whiteness above, landing next to her. Her wings were red, massive, the pale skin of her unnaturally perfect face dissolving with the dress made of red feathers that marked her body. Her hair was long and red, waving around her as if wild strands of crackling fire.

"My dearest. We can talk at last." The voice of the winged female was ancient and young, grave and friendly.

Hope blinked. "Who are you? Am I dead? Dying?" her voice was soft. She didn't feel the air coming down her throat. Maybe they were speaking mind to mind. Maybe she was imagining it all.

"You are neither dead nor dying. We have met many times before, but never in this form. I am the Core Cardinal." Her smile was gentle, caring.

"What is this place?" Hope looked around, but the complete whiteness surrounding her was blinding. She would rather fix her stare on the red Cardinal in front of her.

"It's nowhere and it's everywhere. The world is waiting for you when you are ready. You will do many great things, Hope Nevada. Your life is barely starting now. I hope you enjoy your magic as much as my sisters and I did."

"The other Cardinals were your sisters?" she asked, blinking again.

"The North, West, South, and East Cardinals *are* my sisters."

Hope smiled. It would be nice not to be completely alone, to have someone else to rely upon.

She felt something touch her head, but when she lifted a hand, there was nothing but her hair. She felt a familiar voice wanting to enter the whiteness, but somehow, the message didn't reach her.

The whiteness had a few dancing sparks floating around, and Hope followed them with her eyes. They were beautiful.

She lifted a hand in front of her and wished for sparks to appear. A shoot of red floated through the whiteness, whirling around and interacting with the dark green sparks. Hope grinned. Beautiful indeed.

"I came to greet you now that you can use their four magics. I came to warn you too." Her voice was so peaceful, even if the Cardinal's face was grave.

Hope tilted her head. She couldn't think about anything that could worry such a being.

The Core Cardinal continued, "She who remains in the deep sleep is awakening. She who should be contained for many more years might rise before it's time."

"You are worried," Hope said, blinking.

"You should be too, my dearest. She was strong enough to try to possess the snow child, to take him to the last place he belonged."

"Is the child harmed?" Hope said, frowning. She didn't wish harm to any infant.

"The child lives because she couldn't invade him. When she wakes, she will find you."

"Who is she?" Hope asked.

"The Cardinal Queen."

Hope nodded silently. She wasn't sure if she was ever going to wake up, but if she did, and she remembered this conversation, then maybe she would worry about said queen.

"You were born for this, Hope Nevada. We have been waiting for you for a long, long time." The Core Cardinal smiled, emotion filling her red eyes as she swallowed proudly. "There is no such thing as limits. Everything you wish, you can accomplish."

Another voice, an angry one, seemed to bounce against the whiteness, but she wasn't worried. She was safe here, protected by the Core Cardinal herself.

The Core Cardinal who was nowhere to be seen.

Another voice seemed to come from afar, but this time, she heard it. It sounded like home, like the pine woods.

"You made your mother a promise, Hope. *Vitam tradere*. Please, open your eyes. You must come back."

She felt something on her lips, even if there was nothing in front of her.

Vitam tradere. A life for a life. She remembered now.

Her mother had traded her life, and her father would have to pay with his.

Hope walked towards the path of dark green sparks and opened her eyes.

56

Lenna

"What a disappointment if she dies before even getting started," Jake said, his voice almost bored, despite Lenna noticing the small bit of tension in his biceps.

"Wanted to share Daddy with little sis?" Theon said next to him, smirking.

Lenna didn't have time to tell him that today was not the day to push it, because Jake's hand was already on Theon's neck.

"Who the *fuck* do you think you are?" Jake's voice was lethally calm. The hatred in his eyes made Lenna wonder if this was not only about Theon's question, but about how Jake had found them in her chambers.

"Someone pointing a blade at your royal balls, mate." Theon smiled, his voice barely audible as Jake tightened the grip on his throat.

"*I don't share,*" Jake growled. Yes, definitely about the finger-licking situation from a few weeks ago.

Jake's spare hand was moving, and Theon's blade was Taken. The mouth Lenna had been savoring was now grinning, even though his eyes were pure cutting, lethal silver. This man was fucking scary. That somehow made him hotter, if that was even possible. Another flicker of a hand, and Theon's pants were gone, his face getting bluer by the second as his air was cut off. Another flicker, and ten sharp blades were approaching Theon's balls.

"Fucking Cardinals. That's enough, Jake. He's my friend," Lenna snapped.

"Your *friend* better learn how to speak respectfully and how to keep his hands to him-fucking-self." Jake glanced at her but relaxed his grip on Theon's throat. He inhaled desperately while trying to not move his feet or legs to avoid being stabbed in the testicle. Lenna Took the blades away and Gave some pants to Theon without looking at his exposed legs.

As if Jake knew a damned thing about speaking respectfully or keeping his hands to himself, for Cardinals' sake. She'd have a conversation later with him about there being absolutely no need to act like a territorial prick, even if it had heated her blood. But she had to pick her battles tonight, especially since, at the other end of the alley, Hope's body in Ciaran's arms wasn't limp anymore.

Jake also looked that way and muttered, "About time."

Lenna started walking towards Ciaran and Hope, somehow feeling as if she was interrupting something. Ciaran's arms were around Hope's chest and back, her face close to his, and all they seemed to do was stare at each other. Perhaps the Fifth Ceremony had given the woman some sort of concussion, or she had lost half her mind with all the new power in her veins.

The approaching steps seemed to take Hope and Ciaran out of their trance, and both looked up. Hope stood with unnerving speed, already in her usual fighting-and-ready-to-kill stance, looking at Lenna and the person immediately behind her. She didn't need to check to know it was Jake.

"Have we lost much time? How long was I...?"

"We've lost so much precious time, yes," Jake cut her off.

"What matters is that you are okay, Hope, because...are you?" Nina walked towards Hope, putting her pale hands on both sides of her face.

"I'm... different, but okay," she looked at Ciaran, as if he somehow had or was the answer to a question she hadn't asked. Fuck, if these two weren't awkward.

"Do I need to get in the middle of whatever the Fifth this is?" Ayla asked, a deep frown on her usually smooth and controlled face. Oh, true. She had only signed up to help Lenna with her Fifth, nothing else.

"We're rescuing Raoul," Lenna said.

Ayla swallowed, glanced at Nina, and said, "I'm in." Then, she stared at Lenna, her twin sister's green eyes reading *how-dare-you-keep-this-from-me*.

"We must rush. That panomquake was the worst in centuries, and it surely caused total chaos worldwide. We need to use the commotion and every distraction to extract Raoul now."

Ciaran was right. They had to rush before the roixers, the Roix Reigner, the Organ Mandor and Cardinals knew who else caught and exterminated them one by one.

"Raoul is in the Southern wing, fifth floor, second and last security vault," Indianna said, and Ciaran Gave a map of the Beftac Center on the wall in front of them, tracing the place Indianna pointed to be their ultimate goal—childhood-discarded-and-somehow-returned-friend and Nina's semi-identical-lost-brother.

"Every single door needs a staff badge," Indianna continued. "We have mine, and Brendon issued two more at the Invisible Grand, so we stick in three groups. Before any of you panoms think about breaking the security doors: don't. Lethal gases will release on top of the roixers being alerted immediately, and you won't live to see another ante meridiem."

"Funny that the Beftac Center for Injured Beings is the one injuring beings," Theon said.

"We take the safety of our patients seriously," Indianna said matter-of-factly. "I think it's better if each group has a panom, a skilled fighter, and someone with common sense. Unless anyone else has a better idea?"

"Common sense is a myth," Lenna scoffed.

"I'm not sure what we'll find inside. Many patients have probably collapsed with the panomquake, even if our machines are secured to them to prevent any unexpected disconnections, but this was an extraordinary one," Indianna explained. "Two roixers are always stationed at the entrance to each security vault, so there will be four there. Inside the vault, there is always one roixer and three healers. Please don't kill the healers unless *absolutely* necessary. I know every single one of them, and we—*they*—are not the enemy here. We work our asses off to fix the damage my mother and her roixers cause left, right, and center."

Right. Because Indianna's mother was—

"Your mother is the Roix Reigner?" Hope asked.

"I wish it wasn't the case, but it is." Indianna's lips tightened into a thin line.

"My mother was the Roix Reigner before her."

To live knowing your mother was ordering such atrocities, every single day… Lenna's gaze unavoidably went to Hope and Jake. Talk about parents constantly committing atrocities.

Ciaran was looking at Hope and Lenna. "You two need to change into normal clothes. No chance we won't be noticed with you two half-naked in shiny beads walking down the corridors."

Lenna allowed Jake a last top-to-bottom assessment of her indeed very exposed body, and the lust in his dark grey eyes made her want to melt. She then Took the dress and Gave herself clothes appropriate for fighting: a zipped, long-sleeved, full-body black jumpsuit tight to every single curve of her body, especially—

"Fucking perfect ass, Brachyan." Jake's voice was guttural behind her, low so that only Lenna could hear it. His muscular hands gripped her ass, and for a moment, Lenna wished the whole rescue was over so she could focus on those hands and everything she needed them to do.

For the sake of not fucking him in the alley in front of so many people, she only arched her back and pressed her ass against—there, his already hardening cock. She closed her eyes, all her concentration aimed at not squeezing his delicious length or rubbing her ass against it. Cardinals guide her to the Beftac Center right fucking now.

By the time Lenna had gathered as much composure as she could find, which wasn't much, and had taken a step away from Jake, Hope was dressed in the black leathers she always seemed most comfortable in, multiple weapons on her, as usual.

After five minutes of briefing how each group would approach the security vault, they split.

Indianna, Nina, Ciaran, and Hope would go first, Lenna, Jake, Sasha, and Theon as the next group. Jake had given Theon a deathly look that would have killed some people on the spot from a heart attack, but Theon had only shrugged with a smirk. Lenna had asked them to keep their male-ego issues aside during the extraction.

Brendon, Carson, and Ayla formed the last group. The latter didn't seem very convinced about risking her life next to two guys she had never met before, but since they needed a panom and no one was interested in splitting up, the debate was settled.

Indianna put her badge on the wall of the dark alley and traced a four-petal panom mark with it, the metallic piece scratching against the bricks. When she finished the last petal, the circle of the panom opened a tunnel through the wall, and she put a hand inside, presumably to keep it open. Lenna could see the bright lights of the corridors on the other side of the tunnel.

"After you." Indianna nodded to Hope.

Hope jumped in, crawling towards the lights, followed by Ciaran, Nina, and finally Indianna. Her black bob bounced over her shoulders as she crawled, the last thing they saw before the wall closed as if nothing had ever happened.

Lenna smiled at Jake, Sasha, and Theon, waving the badge Brendon had given her. "Let's become official saviors." She winked and turned to the wall to draw the same mark she bore on her chest.

57

Hope

The Beftac Center for Injured Beings was absolute chaos.

Indianna was guiding Nina, Ciaran, and Hope through side corridors that were mostly empty, save for a couple of beings crushed under what appeared to be shelves full of machinery.

Hope had caused this. *Her* panomquake had killed them. Even if she had countless deaths on her hands, these deaths left a tight knot in her chest, similar to the one her mother's death had caused. A growing knot of Cardinals-damned guilt.

Luckily, they had encountered no roixers yet. Had the distraction in the Houses focused them elsewhere? Or perhaps roixers were never around the Beftac Center except in the security vaults of the fifth floor on the Southern wing.

Every single door in the building had to be opened with the badge, which was both ridiculous and extreme in equal parts. The doors were extra layers of security, but they were not soundproof.

The screams, cries, and desperate sobs had been filling Hope's ears since she had entered the building through the tunnelled wall. The worst part was that not all of them were adult voices. No. Even running across one of many maintenance rooms, it was obvious. There definitely were infants and children suffering too.

Suffering because of *her*. Because of her newly-released magic that had almost killed her, because of her direct connection to the Cardinals. She would have stopped to reflect if there was anything she could have done differently, anything to avoid such a panomquake with disastrous consequences. Except she was using those disastrous consequences as a distraction to rescue her friend's brother.

Cardinals guide her, but right now, Indianna was the one guiding her, through maintenance rooms full of broken equipment and a couple small fires Ciaran had extinguished, laundry rooms flooded because of destroyed pipes, and multiple laboratories littered with parts of microscopes and shards of glass from vials and flasks.

The areas where patients lived were close enough to still hear the despair and pain of the beings and the multiple beeping monitors and alarms but distant enough to not see them.

"Southern wing, everyone," Indianna said, placing the metal badge against the crystal door that opened an instant later, revealing a circular room with a ceiling towering five-stories high, leading to multiple corridors on each level. Hope had underestimated how big a healing center could be.

Indianna turned towards the second on the left, running in silence as the other three followed her. Hope saw Indianna's steps faltering, her pace slowing down, as if she was going to enter the rooms and help the patients. Deep down, Hope wished Indianna would do exactly that—these people didn't deserve to die—but Indianna didn't enter those rooms. Instead, she started sprinting, as if trying to resist the urge to go in a completely different direction.

Steps, door, badge, more doors, more badge-touching, change of corridors, more steps. Hope's sense of orientation was refined, and yet she doubted if she would be able to walk all the way back.

On the next turn of a corner, they faced a wide-eyed healer with dried blood on his forehead, holding onto a pole. He swallowed, his eyebrows lifting as he looked at Ciaran and Hope. "Weapons are forbidden in the Beftac Center."

"They're with me, John," Indianna said, a reassuring smile on her beautiful face.

The ginger-haired man's face frowned, as if he was trying to make sense of what his colleague had just said, and then he glanced at the daggers Hope was now gripping in each hand. He shook his head vigorously, taking a step towards the wall where a big, triangular red button sat.

"Don't—" Indianna started.

But the man was too close, his index finger mere inches of the button that no doubt would alert the whole damned Beftac Center if not also the Organ House. Over Hope's dead body was this mission going to be risked by someone not listening.

The dagger hit John's skull right between his eyes, and his body hit the floor a heartbeat later, his finger safely away from the red button.

Hope would have said sorry if it had made a difference, but it didn't.

Stepping over his dead corpse, they continued their way to the fifth floor. If she hadn't lost count—and she knew she hadn't—they were one floor away. Indianna's badge let them into another corridor of stairs, and they rushed up.

Compared to the rest of the Beftac Center, the fifth floor of the Southern wing was too damn quiet.

Indianna put a finger to her lips, and Hope felt a tickle on her skin as a violet message appeared on her forearm.

The corridor on the right leads straight into the corridor with both security vaults. Four roixers are always there. Two towards our end and two towards the other end.

The message was gone, and Hope nodded. *The other end*, where the second group, the one formed by Lenna, Jake, Sasha, and Theon, would arrive shortly if everything had gone well and by some Cardinals-blessed miracle they hadn't gotten lost in the labyrinth this place was.

Ciaran moved his hand, and Hope knew it had not only tickled her skin but also every other member of the three groups.

In position.
This corridor is too fucking quiet.

Dark green ink.
Dark. Green. Ink. And that handwriting...

Hope gasped, looking at Ciaran, unable to read the blue eyes staring back at her.

It couldn't be. It certainly couldn't be.

Another prickle on her forearm, and the message was golden this time.

> Ready to roll, bitches.
> Waiting for the slow ones.

That must be Lenna and her group, which meant Brendon, Carson, and Ayla would hopefully arrive soon. Less than a minute had passed when the tickling sensation was followed by a silver, handwritten sentence:

> The slow ones were the fastest
> considering we entered last.
> On your mark, Ciaran.

This was it. Hope grabbed her favorite daggers firmly, the side of her mouth curling upwards at the familiar adrenaline rushing through her veins. Whatever deaths happened from now onwards, she would have no remorse or guilt.

Her back was against the edge of the wall, straddling both corridors. Ciaran was next to her, his biceps straining against her own. She didn't wait to read Ciaran's message. She didn't need to.

As soon as she felt the prickling sensation on her skin, she stepped forward, using the first part of a heartbeat to locate the closest two targets in their Cardinal-red uniforms and the second part to send her blades flying. They simultaneously struck home, the first roixer down with a blade crossing his neck from side to side and the second with a blade across his still-open mouth.

On the other end of the corridor, Lenna and Jake stood over a couple of other roixers choking on the floor, grabbing their throats and kicking desperately in silence.

"So cruel, Jake," Lenna whispered, something like a frown on her face, "to make them suffer like that."

Lenna closed her hand and exhaled dramatically as Jake looked at her. "What did you try to do?" His voice was also low, presumably to avoid alerting the other roixers that they were about to be attacked.

"Take their hearts," Lenna said, both hands on her generous hips. "But it didn't work."

"Feral, Brachyan." Jake's voice was low and graver, and was he...? Yes, that was definitely a proud grin. "Organs can't be Taken, but they can be Harmed."

Next to Hope, Ciaran moved his arm, and the roixers stopped moving. "This is not the fucking time or place for one of your lessons." His voice didn't leave room for argument.

Ayla, Brendon, and Carson entered through a door in front of the vaults.

"Did we miss all the fun?" Brendon asked, disappointment in his eyes.

Someone was trembling next to Hope, and she didn't need to look to know it was Nina. She couldn't even imagine what she felt being so close to her brother after having risked her own life so many times to keep him safe. She would have held Nina's shaky hand, but Hope was cleaning her bloody blades on the red uniforms of her recent kills.

Sasha chuckled. "These panoms are too desperate to kill."

Indianna walked towards the door of the security vault closest to the end. As the rest gathered around her, she whispered, "One roixer and three healers inside each vault."

Two more roixers to kill. These four had gone down like flies, nice and easy.

Jake and Lenna went towards the door of the other vault in case the roixer inside came out to see what was happening.

She felt Ciaran right next to her, and Hope nodded to Indianna, who touched the badge against the door of the security vault and moved to the side as the crystal door opened wide.

Hope's daggers left her hands as soon as she located the target.

Except there wasn't one roixer in there—there were at least two dozens, all looking at them, as if they had been waiting patiently for their arrival.

Behind them, immobile in a bed, a white-haired man lay unconscious.

58

Lenna

There were roixers fucking everywhere.

One second, Lenna and Jake were in front of the security vault, ready in case the beings inside noticed the killing next door and wrongly decided to be curious. The next second, the door had opened, and she couldn't count how many roixers were there.

Multiple pairs of boots hit the floor, and a quick glimpse verified her greatest fears. There were roixers jumping from the damn ventilation panels in the ceiling. The corridor of the fifth floor was flooded with red uniforms.

Five different roixers held Sasha, Brendon, Carson, Indianna, and Nina firmly, their bodies locked in particular positions, a variety of swords at their necks.

Ayla somehow managed to keep the roixers hands off her, or maybe they hadn't attempted to restrain a panom, which perhaps explained why they hadn't touched Jake or Lenna either.

On the other side of the corridor, in front of the security vault where Raoul was meant to be, stood Hope, blades in her hands that she hadn't yet thrown. Lenna followed Hope's line of sight to find it wholly focused on the blood dripping from Nina's neck, the sword of the roixer pressing harder against her pale skin.

Lenna couldn't see Ciaran or Theon, but considering how capable they both were, she had little doubt they could hold their own.

"Stop that blade, or I'll stop your heart," Hope said, her dark eyes locked with the blond roixer holding Nina. He seemed massive next to the trembling, white-haired woman.

Jake moved next to Lenna and gently brushed his fingers over her waist.

"Talking about heartbeats... I would love to see how many of you I can Harm in one go," Jake said, the corner of his lip curling upwards. "But I guess if so many of you are here, the Roix Reigner can't be very far. Unless she's hiding?"

"The Roix Reigner has never hidden before, so why the bloody hell would she hide now?" a female voice from the side of the corridor called, the mass of roixers parting to let her through.

"I knew you wouldn't leave so many dogs off your leash," Jake continued. "Their dependent, fried brains would have to work. They wouldn't even know where to start."

"Don't worry about them, Jake. You should worry about what your father will do when he hears about this."

The woman in front of them was so similar to Indianna, a shiver went down Lenna's spine. The hatred in her green eyes was different, and so was her perfectly straight fringe and tight bun with a generous dose of grey hairs. The red uniform was full of thin, dark leathered lines that distinguished her from the rest, but the pink lips, the straight nose, even the high cheeks... Indianna and her mother were almost identical.

"What exactly do you think *this* is?" Jake asked the Roix Reigner. Lenna doubted Jake was about to go down the route of lying and saying they were casually visiting a friend.

"An attempt at rescuing the discarded being unlawfully and mysteriously repatriated." Her expression was a mockery of a smile, mixed with a curling lip most would define as repulsion. "What a friendly crowd of rebel fools." The Roix Reigner looked around at them, stopping when she reached Indianna. "Why does it not surprise me that you are one of them, daughter?"

There was no chance the Roix Reigner could have known this, not when they had improvised the timing of their Fifth Ceremonies and had come here straight after Hope's panomquake. Did the Roix Reigner have any clue *who* was standing in front of the other security vault and had caused such a panomquake?

Lenna saw the realization of her own conclusion in Hope's almost-black, lethally cold eyes.

Someone had betrayed them.

It couldn't be. She trusted these people with her entire heart, save for Hope and Nina, who she barely knew. Lenna's neck almost snapped, twisting to face Ayla.

Ayla shook her head slowly, something like physical pain in her green eyes as she frowned. Had her twin sister agreed so easily to donate a fucking petal to her so she could then sell Lenna to the Roix? Had Lenna been so damn stupid to believe for half a second that there was something remotely like kindness in her sister's heart? That her apologies, her will to help, her sadness after Lenna had been tortured, had been *genuine*?

"You bitch," Lenna muttered.

"It wasn't me. I swear on the Fifth," Ayla said, tears lining her green eyes. She had always been so good at theatrics—

"Was it the panom or the fighter?" Hope asked the Roix Reigner, her lips in a thin line.

What the Cardinals' fuck was she going on about? The heir of the Organ House must have hit her head harder than they realized.

"The panom," Lenna spat, pointing at Ayla. "*This* fucking panom."

"I swore on the Fifth, Lenna!" Ayla said, her voice breaking. Master of spinning lies indeed.

"I didn't mean that one," Hope said. "*Who* was it, Roix Reigner?"

"I guess there's no pride in not owning the truth," a voice Lenna knew as well as her own said from behind the roixers.

This couldn't be happening. This had to be a big fucking misunderstanding, or maybe a big fucking nightmare she was about to wake up from.

The roixers made space for a man Lenna knew all too well. At least, she had *thought* she knew him all too well. He was a man who had been at her side for the past two years, who she had cherished as her best friend and confidant, who had taught her how to defend herself, how to fight.

"Did you forget whose payroll I'm on?" Theon asked Lenna, and she wanted to punch his grin off his face. Other than the immediate need to be aggressive, her brain had seemed to stop, unable to form any reasonable thoughts or say any words. She noticed Jake tensing next to her, navy sparks jumping from his fingertips.

"How?" Lenna asked incredulously.

"How did I let your father know, or how did *he* inform the Roix Reigner? Or how the fuck have I waited this long pretending I was your puppet friend who would move to another city just to be closer to you? Because I wonder that every single day too," Theon said.

"How long have you had a petal?" Lenna asked, bile surging up her throat.

"Egocentric but not stupid—that's what I like about you." Theon winked. "Your father gave me one the day he asked me to train you. That way, we could communicate through ink, and he could keep a close eye on you. He almost revealed it when I told him you had confided in me about your sneaky visit to the West House, but he decided it was more useful to continue monitoring you through our pretend friendship. Why do you think he let me come to Corentre? You can't genuinely think your father gives a shit about how well you fight."

Each word was a direct hit to Lenna's chest.

"The good thing is that I can finally go back to my normal life. Though I haven't missed the red uniform much, to be honest. Never been a fan." He smiled, looking at the Roix Reigner.

"You're lucky your father is busy with a simultaneous attack on all the Houses," the Roix Reigner said. "Otherwise, he would kill you himself." Lenna wasn't sure if she was talking to her, Ayla, or Jake, but she was pretty sure that in all cases, her statement would be true and applicable.

Jake scoffed. "He has always been extremely selective with the inks he receives."

"A simultaneous attack, Reigner?" a roixer with a white band over his uniform asked.

"A bunch of organized criminals and the fucking courtrades causing trouble again. Nothing we can't manage."

The fucking *what* causing trouble? Lenna could have sworn she saw a hint of a smile on Hope's lips, but she was too busy refusing to believe Theon was a traitor to figure out why, golden sparks on her fingertips.

"Can I kill him?" Jake asked Lenna with all the deathly calm in the world, not taking his silver eyes off Theon.

A movement on Lenna's right made her look. Carson had gotten free of the roixer's grip and hit him with an elbow into the nose. Theon was in front of him in no time, twisting his neck and leaving him dead on the floor.

Sasha gasped, a raw scream leaving her throat. "You fucking traitor!"

Theon had just killed Sasha's brother in front of her and hadn't even bothered to avoid his lifeless hand as he returned to the Roix Reigner's side.

From the corner of her eye, Lenna thought the shadows around Hope seemed to emanate anger, but she couldn't get her eyes off Theon to understand how.

"I'd rather kill him myself," Lenna said.

59

Hope

"I'd rather kill him myself," Lenna said.

Too many people had been involved in this rescue. Too many strangers. Too many risks. If anything, this betrayal had proven again that people couldn't be trusted. Ever.

The expression on Lenna's face was a combination of rage, devastation, and deep confusion. Yet, in the middle of this now-troublesome rescue, Hope couldn't help but feel relieved that the traitor had been the damn fighter and not the panom who had vanished the moment he had killed two of the roixers in the security vault.

Hope shouldn't care too much about his intentions or his alliances, but deep down, she knew it would have affected her if the man had been a traitor. Ciaran's body had disappeared, and she couldn't exactly tell how she knew, but it was not as when someone moured away. It was...different, as if his presence and his pine-and-night scent still lingered around her, but she couldn't see him. She could have sworn she had even felt Ciaran's raw anger when Carson's body dropped to the floor.

Hope's eyes locked with Nina's panicked ones. She would not let the life of her first friend end at the hands of anyone, let alone a military force governed by the Organ Mandor.

She saw it in the eyes of the others too. There were genuine feelings between them. Jake was standing next to Lenna, his body protecting her, presumably from the roixers inside the other security vault. Lenna couldn't take the eyes off Theon for long, but when she did, her jaw clenched angrily at how the roixers were holding Sasha, Brendon, and Indianna, the weapons trained on their bodies. Sasha was biting her bottom lip as tears ran down her cheeks, unable to take her eyes off her dead brother. Indianna's lips were curled, looking at her mother with the maximum hate one being could muster. Ayla's tearful eyes moved from Lenna to Nina, her hands clenched into fists with jumping silver sparks.

Nina was looking at Hope with fear, but also expectation and something else. Raoul was a few feet away from her, and Hope nodded, looking at Nina, trying to reassure her.

Raoul was here. Because the roixers hadn't had time to move him with the short notice of the fighter's ink or because they were stupid enough to think the Roix stood a chance against all of them, Hope didn't know. Not that it mattered.

"I wondered when we were going to start killing." Ciaran materialized next to Hope, shadows curling at his feet.

"Bloody courtrade," the Roix Reigner spat. "The Organ Mandor should have killed you when he found out."

The smile on Ciaran's lips was both utterly terrifying and the most beautiful thing Hope had ever seen. "Only an arrogant shithead like him could believe that amputating the arm with my Llunal mark would be *enough to clean me* of my courtrade blood."

Hope tried to resist the urge to open her eyes wide and lift her eyebrows, but her peripheral vision noted that Lenna didn't seem to care one bit about her expression being an open book as her jaw dropped. Hope couldn't take her dark eyes from Ciaran, even if focusing on him in a corridor so full of armed enemies was a risky move.

Ciaran was a panom *and* a courtrade. There would be time for questions and explanations later, if they survived. Right now, he looked at Hope with that side smile she wanted to caress.

Ciaran leaned into her and whispered, so softly that only she could hear, "Do your worst, Hope."

She was so ready for this, to exterminate every single one of these roixers and the Roix Reigner herself. The adrenaline was building up again in her veins, rushing as if she couldn't keep it in, and maybe she couldn't, because arterial-red sparks were swirling around the blades she held tight.

She whispered back, "Do your worst, Ciaran."

Hope recognized the shadows coming from his fingertips—she had seen them in action during those long weeks in the vessels—except Ciaran's shadows were dancing, adorned with dark green sparks.

Ciaran unleashed his shadows, and Hope unleashed her daggers.

60

Lenna

Lenna had never seen someone kill like Hope. She was death incarnate, dressed in black and blood. Her daggers flew without faltering, with unnervingly perfect aim, strength, and will.

A couple of roixers confronted her in hand-to-hand combat, and Hope fucking smiled at them. She kicked up, making contact with a roixer's balls, and as soon as he bent over, her dagger was waiting under his now-bleeding chin. Cardinals, she was fast.

The other roixer grabbed her other arm, aiming to twist it as he moved the blade of his short sword to her neck, but it never made it. She slid blade against blade masterfully, removing the roixer's ability to push it against her body until her dagger was in his abdomen, and his blood leaked into his red uniform.

Around Hope's non-stop kills, continuous swirls of shadows snapped from Ciaran's fingers, wrapping around roixers' throats at impossible speed. Wherever the shadows went, snapping bones followed, and bodies on the floor appeared.

Alone, Ciaran and Hope were devastatingly efficient. Together, they were absolutely lethal and utterly terrifying.

Lenna had no clue what the shadow business was about, but if it helped Ciaran not end up unbalanced inside from Harming, to kill roixers without wasting time to Heal anybody, she was on board with it.

Jake had taken Hope and Ciaran's opening as his cue, and Cardinals damn him if he didn't look like he was enjoying Harming roixers in creative ways.

He hadn't stepped away from Lenna, and his warmth on her back was reassuring in the middle of the bloodshed. Whichever roixer he set those silver eyes on, whichever roixer screamed in agony. Unless he removed the air from their lungs instead, made their eyes roll backwards into their brains, or made their necks twist, in which cases they could not scream or beg for mercy.

As if the man that Lenna wanted in her life knew what mercy was.

If Jake was feeling any pain as his inner magical balance became uneven with so much Harming, he didn't show any signs. But hadn't this man submitted to pain so many times that it was as natural to him as breathing?

There was only one being in the corridor that Lenna wanted to focus on: the being she had considered a friend.

The man fighting next to the Roix Reigner with all the skill in the world.

How stupid had Lenna been to never give two damned fucks about where had Theon learned to fight? On this island or any other, someone as skilled as Theon had to have been trained by the best and only Thyrian military force. It was so obvious now. And it was also obvious that Sasha, Brendon, and Indianna were nowhere as able to fight the Roix.

Lenna risked another quick glance to the corridor to find... There, a sleek mass of red hair surrounded by silver sparks. Ayla was keeping up against the roixers side-by-side a white-haired woman fighting with all her might, despite the blood falling from a deep cut in her neck. Ayla and Nina were *still* alive.

Fuck, Lenna knew she had to kill Theon, and she had to do it now, before he killed anyone else. She also knew that if she asked Jake, he would do it without batting an eye.

The sharp feeling in her gut from his betrayal was more painful than any physical hit she would receive tonight. She doubted that the pain would go away anytime soon. Yet she would not stay still for a second longer.

It was cardinally poetic that Lenna's first ever Harming was against the traitor who had handed them to the Roix.

She made a mental note to thank Jake for explaining the theory of Harming in that cell, and for providing multiple examples in the past couple of minutes, even if some of them were sophisticatedly complicated. Bodies in red kept falling down.

It must have been the bloodbath doing funny things to her mind, because if she looked at Jake's side grin, at his silver eyes focusing on his next targets... If she focused solely on him, on the precise movements of his panom hands in front of him, on how he hadn't left her side and how his navy sparks seemed to caress her skin... She couldn't wait for this fucked up rescue to be done.

Lenna raised her hands in front of her, golden sparks tickling the skin on her palms as if encouraging her.

"You shit-eating cunt!" Lenna shouted, and Theon turned to face her, earning a hit on his cheek from Brendon's elbow. "I hope your miserable life was as mediocre and worthless as your friendship. I hope the Fifth makes your existence as wretched as you deserve."

Theon opened his mouth as if he was going to say something.

Pity that Lenna had already heard him say enough bullshits for the rest of her life. Pity that her hands were already tracing a vertical cut in the air as she visualized pulling the East petal from her mark and cutting Theon's heart in half. There was no point in making him suffer for longer, not when Lenna didn't want to waste another second with this being.

Theon's body dropped to the floor, and Lenna bit her lips to resist the urge to cry in anger and despair.

Jake lifted her chin and kissed her deeply, as if they weren't surrounded by living roixers and the damn Roix Reigner herself. He took his time, savoring her lips and allowing her to get lost in his. Lenna didn't care if he had Given some sort of panom barrier around them or if he believed the roixers wouldn't dare interrupting them. Lenna didn't care, because all that mattered in the world was him and the feelings that the warm contact of their tongues made clearer than ever.

Jake gently pulled his lips away. "I'm so fucking proud of you, sweet fire."

Lenna would have loved to reply if she hadn't felt so dizzy from his kiss. Not his kiss—from the Harming. That was her inner panom balance totally tilted, and she didn't know if she could focus enough to Heal anyone in time before she fell to the—

Jake's powerful arms grabbed her waist in time to avoid a pathetic fall to the floor. Cardinals, the world was spinning so badly around her. Lenna pressed her shut eyes against his very comfortable chest to avoid seeing the dead roixers above her instead of underneath her. She inhaled his leather and ginger scent deeply, as if it could somehow help. Thank the Fifth, it made her feel safe, even if her uneven scale was still very much present. Jake walked somewhere, bracing her against him.

Lenna opened her eyes enough to see they were inside the security vault. A moving bed with a white head bouncing from side to side was likely a good indicator that Raoul was indeed inside.

How were they going to get out of the Beftac Center? Even if they killed every single roixer and the Roix Reigner herself, there was no way they could walk through the maze back to the alley, especially with Lenna unable to stand and Raoul unconscious.

The epitellia wards made it impossible to moure in or out of any part of this building, and yet—

"The windows," Lenna whispered.

Jake either caught her idea or had already formed it himself, because he said, "Everyone better be good at jumping in turns."

61

Hope

The security vault was a mess of dismembered, strangled, or impaled bodies.

Jake was barely a few steps from the door, Lenna snug against him, frowning. His hands moved, and the bodies not-so-neatly piled in a corner of the vault. A *high* pile. From Ciaran's hands, a swift of air passed through the room, drying the blood on the floor.

"What the fuck are they waiting for?" Ciaran spat, looking at the door to the corridor.

As if on cue, Nina and Ayla ran in, Nina dodging a knife. Ayla was bleeding but was good enough to be gaping at Raoul's body. Nina continued running until she was holding her brother's hand in hers, crying, stroking his equally white hair.

Hope took the few steps that separated her from the doorway and threw a blade at the heart of the roixer who had attempted to kill Nina. The corridor was another mess of bodies, but at least a dozen of roixers and the Roix Reigner were still standing, putting up a fight.

"Can you do the body-moving thing with Carson?" Hope asked Jake in a rush.

Jake was helping Lenna sit at the end of Raoul's bed, but Ciaran's blue eyes flickered as he nodded. "I'll do it." A few seconds later, Carson's cold body was laying by the glass window of the security vault, ready for launch.

Jake, Ciaran, and Hope were by the door, waiting for the others, who had their hands busy trying to stay alive. It was impressive enough that they were still breathing.

Jake cut the legs of the roixer fighting Sasha, his fall allowing her to run to the vault. Ciaran's shadows were on the loose again, blinding and strangling one of Indianna's opponents. Hope's blades found purchase in the eyes of the other roixer fighting against her.

"What about me, fuckers?" Brendon shouted.

"Move your ass!" Ciaran shouted back, moving from the door to let Sasha and Indianna inside.

The Roix Reigner was running after them, shouting, "Over my dead body!"

Jake lifted his hands with a macabre smile. "Over your dead body it is."

Indianna gripped his forearm and placed her body in front of Jake's. "Don't kill my mother. Please," she begged, her voice trembling.

Jake looked at her, hesitation lining his silver eyes. After a few seconds that felt like a lifetime, he nodded. "I won't kill her *this time*. Consider it a personal favor."

His hand was moving, and the Roix Reigner's body slammed against the corridor wall, leaving her unconscious on the floor but still breathing.

Indianna's eyes widened, but she said, "Thank you."

Brendon sprinted inside the security vault, and Jake finally crossed the doorway again, doing something with his hands that kept the other roixers outside. The doorway was translucent, blurry yet clear enough to see the roixers trying to make their way through.

Jake walked towards Lenna, moving his hands towards the window covering an entire wall of the security vault. And then, the window was gone.

"The plan is simple. We jump in turns, and we moure while in the air," Jake said.

Hope felt Ciaran beside her before seeing him. She couldn't avoid looking at him, and she found him staring back, those blue eyes analyzing and assessing.

"I moure Lenna," Jake continued. Lenna nodded, still sitting at the end of Raoul's bed, a hand covering her eyes.

"I can moure Sasha and Indianna. Ayla, you will have to moure Brendon and Carson's body," Ciaran said.

"I have *never* moured before, let alone with two other beings—one of them *dead*—while jumping." Ayla frowned.

"But you are a brilliant and capable woman, are you not?" Ciaran's eyes narrowed, and the look he gave Ayla, Hope wouldn't have wanted for herself. "Brendon can hold Carson's body. All you have to do is touch both of them before jumping and do not let go of their skins under *any* circumstances. And then you take a mental step thinking about the Crystal Clear Safehouse by Sweetgum Beech."

Ayla snorted. "Whatever. I'll try. I can't promise we won't end up smashed on the Cardinals-damned street. In fact, it is very likely that will happen, so please, if we don't get to the crystal-whatever-house soon, can someone come back and moure our three dead bodies there? Thank you in advance." Her smile was forced, and Hope could have sworn she had seen Lenna make the same expression before. Lenna didn't appear to be anywhere near smiling right now, though.

Ciaran turned to Hope, talking to her as if they were alone and not in a room full of people. "You have to moure Nina and Raoul out," Ciaran told her, his voice calm but firm.

Hope swallowed. She had done the maths as soon as Jake shared the plan. There were five panoms in the room, but Lenna was incapacitated. Whether she was feeling sick or weak, Hope couldn't tell, but she could not stand independently, so mouring was not even an option. Jake, Ciaran, Ayla, and Hope were the only ways to get out of here.

She didn't need to say she had only been a panom for less than a few hours or that she had no clue what the powerful magic flowing in her veins could do, or that she had never heard of the safe house or Sweetgum Beech. She didn't need to say any of that, because Ciaran already knew. And it changed nothing.

"Mouring Raoul might be more difficult. I can moure him and Nina if you want, and you moure Sasha and Indianna," Ciaran offered.

Hope hesitated. That Ciaran had offered to moure Sasha and Indianna and leave Nina and Raoul for her was not a challenge, but a recognition of the two most valuable beings in Hope's eyes. Yet, having the responsibility of ensuring Nina and Raoul arrived safely was enormous, and the chances of something going wrong were too great. To trust anyone with that responsibility, to put their lives in his hands in such a dangerous time...

Ciaran wasn't *anyone*, though.

When she had fallen unconscious after her Fifth Ceremony, hadn't she awoken in his arms unharmed? Hadn't he been there when she jumped out of the vessels and helped the courtrades, Nina, her mother, and her to moure away? Hadn't he moured her mother's body to a secure space in the woods and helped Hope dig her grave with his own hands? Hadn't he moured Nina to be with her while she said farewell to her mother? Hadn't he ensured she became a panom against all the odds and despite the catastrophic consequences?

"I will be very grateful if you can moure Nina and Raoul, Ciaran," Hope said. Ciaran bowed his head slightly, not taking his eyes from hers. "I will do my best to moure Sasha and Indianna."

Ciaran smiled. "To the Crystal Clear Safehouse by Sweetgum Beech."

"There." Hope smiled back.

Jake held Lenna against his chest and helped her stand, a firm hand under her shoulders as he walked towards the opening where the window used to be. Lenna kept her eyes shut tight, looking like she was going to vomit.

"This is goodbye, then." Jake moved two fingers to his head as if taking off a non-existent hat. Without further ado, he jumped from the edge into the dark night, holding Lenna tightly against him.

"If I wait any longer, I will reconsider how unwise this plan is and opt out," Ayla said, walking towards the edge. Brendon picked up the body of his friend with all the gentleness in the world as Ayla placed her sweaty and trembling hands on their necks.

"Absolutely, totally unwise." She inhaled and exhaled twice. "On three. One, two, three!"

They jumped into the night, and while her grip on their necks was strong, they didn't vanish, their bodies falling.

"Fuck, fuck, fuck!" Sasha shouted, peeking down at the five-story drop to the street. "Okay, they are gone. I think they moured before falling all the way." She looked at Indianna and Ciaran, frowning. "Fuck, that was so scary."

Hope walked towards the precipice, Indianna walking with her until they met Sasha, who lifted her curly mass of hair so Hope could touch her skin. Indianna's nape was much easier to reach thanks to her bob.

She didn't want to peek underneath. It didn't matter if the drop was five or fifteen-stories high—even the highest trees in Verdania were nowhere near this.

"See you on the other side," Ciaran said.

"See you on the other side," Hope returned, giving one last glance towards Raoul and Nina, Ciaran and his blue eyes.

Gripping the necks of the women so hard, it was a miracle their blood didn't stop flowing, they jumped into the night.

62

Lenna

The sunlight through the window was brighter and warmer than ever, as if the sun wasn't a mere light bulb like in the North Petal, but a source of heat too, and damn if Lenna didn't appreciate that warmth. As for the seaside sounds that had lulled her to sleep the past few times... Lenna was wondering if this place was paradise.

It wasn't the first time Lenna was awake in the beach house in the South Petal since Jake had moured them, but it was the first time she felt like the actual owner of her body. No sick feelings, no blurry sight, no upside-down stomach... Everything felt exactly where it should be.

Recovering the uneven inner balance after Harming Theon to kill him had been definitely worse than she had expected. She would have to get better at it if she wanted to be of any use in future fights. Because there would be more fights, especially since the whole Roix was looking for them. Jake was a master of coping with uneven scales and skilled at Harming, maybe *excessively*, but she could use some direction.

Lenna's loud stretch would have made cats jealous. Thinking about cats... Her hands let off golden sparks that immediately took form until a furry golden face was rubbing against her hand.

"Morning, cutie." Lenna grinned.

After a long round of strokes and not-gentle-at-all cuddles, she let the lynx cub wander around the beach house, though only after insisting she would make her go away if she didn't behave. Those golden eyes had seemed both extremely pissed and extremely hurt, and Lenna felt almost guilty.

Lenna Gave herself a white-lace dress that matched the very white walls of the luxurious house and the very white sand of the beach outside. Her red hair seemed almost out of place, but she smiled, thinking about how much someone liked her fire hair. Where the fuck was said someone?

She crossed the archway leading to the seashore, passing through a pool as blue as the cloudless sky. When the waves lapped against her bare feet, she took a few breaths in to admire the view.

The immense Radel Sea expanded in all directions. Somewhere on the horizon, she could see different dark masses that one would have thought were other islands.

It was nice to think properly, but now, thoughts were rushing in at an overwhelming speed.

She needed to thank Ayla for not being the awful bitch Lenna had always believed she was—or not being the awful bitch *anymore*, because she had definitely been precisely that in the past. The option of Ayla not being well hurt too much to even consider. She needed to talk to her properly, and sending a mere ink was not enough.

She needed to check if Ciaran and Raoul were fine, if Sasha, Indianna and Brendon were safe, if there was going to be a burial of some sort for Carson, if Raoul was still unconscious or in a deep sleep or Cardinals knew what, and if there was any way to wake him without killing him by accident.

She needed to figure out what to do with the soul-ripping anger Theon's betrayal had left behind. Images of him over the past years flew through her mind, moments she had enjoyed with her friend that were too damn painful to even remember right now. She had killed him and his betrayal, and he could be fucked all the way to the Fifth for all she cared. But the anger, the pain... They could not be killed so easily.

Then there was the matter of the man who Harmed as easily as breathing. The man who had pushed Lenna to her limits, who had given her space but hadn't let her dwell on her sadness for too long, who had given her the maximum help to become a panom again, while also giving her the most pleasure. The man who had awoken what she had been keeping safe all her life. The man who had awoken her heart.

If she only found the Cardinals-damned man somewhere in this idyllic and secluded area of the world.

From the first few times Lenna had woken, she only remembered a couple of conversations. The first time, she had opened her eyes to find Jake asleep in the chair next to her bed, and she had seen the stupidly big room with the open night sky through the open windows. That time, she had said little other than "fuck", "Cardinals-sake", and "rich-ass". But she remembered what his laugh had done to her chest, him explaining something about this being a hideout space in Thyria that he had built in secret, protected by strong epitellia wards, that he had never shared with anyone else.

The second time, she had sat in bed and tried to drink the water on the side table when he entered with a bowl full of fresh fish. She had asked him if he could do normal things such as fishing, and he smirked before saying that surely Taking fresh fish from the sea counted as fishing.

Now, the sun was not just warm—it was fucking *boiling*. After minutes standing on the white-sanded beach, her skin was already sweaty despite the more-than-welcome salty breeze. Somewhere from inside the house came a loud noise of ceramic breaking, followed by an angry but very cute roar and a low growl that made Lenna smile.

Since mister-nowhere-to-be-found hadn't yet made an appearance and she was melting under the sun, she walked towards the welcoming pool. She couldn't be bothered to Give herself a swimming suit, so she just removed her white dress and the white-laced underwear and jumped head-first into the water.

Damn all the Cardinals if this wasn't as refreshing as the actual Fifth. When she emerged and combed her now-sleek hair back with her hands, she saw the golden cub peeking through the windows of the top floor. Nosy cat. Lenna had to find a name for her, another minor task to her ever-growing to-do list.

"I take the fact that you haven't drowned as proof you have recovered." Jake's voice from the other side of the terrace made Lenna jump.

"Never felt better." Lenna grinned. "This place is insane. Were you here all this time?"

"I just moured back. I went to see the others at the Crystal Clear House. Ciaran must have granted me access, because I felt the epitellia wards, but they let me through."

"How are they? I need specifics, details, all the information you can give me," Lenna urged him.

Jake must not have gotten the urgent part, because he simply removed his shirt. He closed his silver eyes to the sun, as if to allow every single part of his skin to absorb the much-needed vitamins.

"The enjoyment of your eyelids is less important than you updating me about the survival of my friends and my damned sister, Jake Coralt." Lenna crossed her bare arms under the water, despite it covering her neck.

He opened his eyes slowly. Even from the distance, Lenna could have sworn he was looking straight at her naked body. "My enjoyment is never secondary, Brachyan."

He jumped into the water face-first, exactly as she had done a few minutes before. Lenna could have sworn he did something with his hand while he was in the air.

He emerged in front of her, grabbing her thighs from underneath, clutching her in his robust arms. Damn if this man wasn't hot and distracting as fuck. She reminded herself to ask him again how her friends and twin were doing, but his bare and very muscular chest touching her now-peaked nipples made it extremely difficult to focus.

"Have you missed me, sweet fire?" His voice was gravel against the skin of her neck. Lenna arched her back at the tone, and the muscles in his arms tensed further, his hands grabbing her bare ass so tightly that she had to suppress a moan.

Fuck, yes, she had.

"You're not getting *any* of this until you fucking give me information about your visit to the Crystal Clear House," she insisted, more trying to convince herself than him.

Her feet floated in the water moved backwards to grab onto his legs, and... The movement of his hand mid-jump must have been to Take away all his clothes, because her feet curled against his muscled legs, and as he adjusted his grip on her ass and moved her slightly lower, she felt his extremely hard, delicious length exposed.

Jake groaned and pulled back to stare into her golden eyes. "You don't want any of this, do you?" He bit his bottom lip, his eyes glittering with amusement and silver fire as he moved his hips to make the tip of his cock press against her core.

She wanted to kiss him, fuck him and love him so badly that it took all her restraint not to do it there and then.

But not yet. She grabbed his cock with her hand, pumping it, and damn if it didn't heat her even more to see him tilting his head backwards under the sun, enjoying every single movement of her grip. She put the tip of his perfect length right at her opening, not letting go of his hard shape, and moved her hips to welcome just the tip.

Just the fucking tip, because he would not win this one. Lenna saw the smug satisfaction in his dark silver eyes a moment before she went to kiss him, but she stopped right in front of his lips. At that precise moment, she stopped his cock from going any deeper as her hips halted.

"The information," Lenna demanded. She had no clue about how long she could hold his length from driving inside her, but she doubted it was going to be much.

"No fucking way. You can't stop there," Jake gasped and went to bite her bottom lip, but Lenna moved her face back an inch, quick enough that he barely grazed her. Damn if she didn't want all of it.

"The information, or I'm getting out of the fucking pool," Lenna insisted. There was no way she could do that.

"Such a beautiful liar, sweet fire," he said, gripping her ass tighter and pressing his chest against hers. "Carson is dead, Raoul is in a coma, the rest alive and well or healing. Now stop caring so much about them and fuck me, Lenna."

She smiled. Maybe it was her name on his lips, that he had obliged or that she had controlled herself long enough to put aside that massive worry so she could enjoy the pleasure all that much more.

Whatever it was, she would take it as she took that hot, desperate kiss on her lips, and that beautiful, hard-as-fuck cock in her core.

63

Hope

The red moonlight penetrated the crystal walls and ceiling of the apartment facing Sweetgum Beech. Hope hadn't asked if it was a panom thing or pure science that the crystal ceilings darkened during the day, protecting the inhabitants from the direct sunlight, but became clear at nighttime, allowing that exquisite Terrhan tinge of redness through.

That the whole attic could only be seen by those Ciaran allowed was definitely magic. So was the fact that entrance was limited to mouring, and only for who he permitted to.

If the Organ Mandor, the Roix Reigner or any roixer only knew they were here, in the very center of Corentre, "hiding away"...

The musical show at Sweetgum Beech had been going on for hours, and Hope enjoyed the loud music and the bright and colorful water fountains for the last few minutes. On the wide balcony, Brendon, Sasha, and Indianna had been dancing and laughing since the very start, emptying bottles of myster as the hours passed.

Maybe one day, Hope would get used to the loudness, the busyness, the brightness of such things. Maybe not. Maybe she would always prefer the peace and quiet nature provided. Maybe she would find a balance.

For now, she welcomed the quiet that followed when she closed the glass door to the balcony.

She walked to the room that had been occupied since they had arrived, the room where Raoul was kept comfortable, attended to every single hour of the day and night. Next to his bed, Nina was reading a book.

"Do you need anything, Nina?" Hope asked.

Nina smiled, looking at her brother with such love and expectation that it was painful to see. Hope had heard Nina talking to him countless times, explaining what had happened since Verdania, talking about the weather, the flowers on the patio, the books she was reading.

"No, thank you. Ayla is kindly cooking me something."

Hope nodded, grateful once again that the heir of the North Petal had saved Nina's back during the fights at the Beftac Center.

In the past few days in the Crystal Clear House, any time Hope offered Nina a drink, she kindly accepted, but Hope hadn't failed to note there was always a just-finished or about-to-finish cup of nice-smelling teas next to her. She also knew Nina barely left her brother's side, and it wasn't her doing.

Twice, Raoul had muttered something like "crannodez" that none of them had deciphered. Nina was convinced he knew she was there, paying attention and listening to him, that he was trying to tell her something, so she didn't risk more time away from him than absolutely necessary, even if Indianna had insisted it was important that Nina looked after herself in order to look after others.

After a whole day of crying, Sasha had decided Carson *wouldn't want her to be a crybaby for the rest of her life* and that she should do *something more useful than make her very pretty eyes red as fuck.*

So, the two dancers in the rooftop were the ones leading the efforts to wake Raoul. Indianna, as a healer, and Sasha, as a scientist, had come up with a couple of different drugs they had tested on a reluctant Brendon. They had come up with a modified version of one that was *safe to ingest and definitely worth a shot* and had given it to Raoul earlier that morning. Yet, it was now almost ante meridiem, and nothing had happened.

Tomorrow was another day, and hopefully, they would have other ideas worth trying. Ciaran had already tried Healing him with no success. Ayla had once offered to Heal Raoul simultaneously, as they had apparently done when Hope had been unconscious after her Fifth Ceremony. Raoul hadn't even moved a finger.

These days, Brendon was mainly focusing on misleading roixers with false tips and intercepting any vital pieces of information on their network as he apparently used to do while working at the Invisible Grand.

Carson's body was kept cold in a special room until they were safe to moure somewhere without being caught or risking their lives to bury him as he rightly deserved.

Life as a fugitive was not a new thing for Hope, but this was something new and very different.

Hope felt safe. Ciaran had explained to her how epitellia wards worked and, even if she hadn't tried to create any yet, she believed they worked. She felt safe amongst these people who, save for Nina, she had not known for more than a few days or weeks.

Hope knew exactly where every single one of her daggers was in her allocated bedroom, that it would take her precisely eight seconds and a half to get to them sprinting from the furthest spot of the Crystal Clear House. She could also Give them to herself, as Ciaran had taught her, but she felt safe enough to not have them with her all the time.

The panom bits—or the powers, as she less preferred to refer to her own—had been much easier to understand and use than she thought, as if her body already knew what to do and how to do it.

As if she had truly been born for this.

She was convinced that the Core Cardinal had said something similar when she dreamed about her. She had to figure out all she could remember from that conversation soon, but tonight, there was another conversation outstanding.

Hope went to the patio on the opposite side of the house, immediately hit with the powerful scent of jasmine. That and... there, night and pine. She followed his scent right to the bench where Ciaran was sitting, contemplating the small, trickling fountain surrounded by pretty bushes and fruit trees. This had been Hope's favorite part of the Crystal Clear House since the first day.

Ciaran looked at her and moved to the side, making space for her to sit next to him.

"Thank you," Hope said. "It's a beautiful night."

"Nights are always beautiful," Ciaran said, more to himself than to her. Did he know his scent was like night? Perhaps it was the shadows in him.

"The note my mother received at the Trading Table. It was you," Hope said. It wasn't a question. She had known since she had seen his dark green ink on her skin at the Beftac Center. The same handwriting.

"It was me."

"And the map of Raoul's location for Nina." She knew that too. "But the compassom?"

"It was me," Ciaran said, looking at her, his blue eyes glittering under the stars.

"How did you know?"

"I have always known. Part of it, not all of it."

Hope frowned. The others said he usually wasn't very clear or talkative, but he wasn't as ambiguous with her.

Ciaran chuckled at her expression. He added, "Imagine having five paths around you and being absolutely sure which one you're meant to take."

"Intuition, I call that."

"It is intuition, and it is something else, something magical. Something words can't explain." Ciaran smiled, and Hope cracked one as well. "But I knew I was meant to do that. The Cardinals or Llunal were moving their strings for me."

"Are they Cardinals, or is it Llunal you believe in?" She didn't care if she was too inquisitive or asking too personal of questions.

"Can't it be both?" he said, and she felt the breeze—or was it a shadow?—caress her cheek.

"Have you always been panom and courtrade?"

"My father is panom, and my mother was courtrade, even if she never joined their society. That's why Rhei Coralt killed her. I have been dual-powered since birth."

Hope looked at him. His mother had died at the hands of the same wicked being, even if it had been a long time ago.

"The other day, you said nothing can compete with the Fifth Power. I want it. I don't want even the remote possibility of my father walking out alive when I see him," Hope said.

"I fear you are not the only one who wants it. It will not come cheap."

"You want it too?" She wouldn't be surprised at all.

"I do, but I was thinking about Lenna. She sent me an ink a few hours ago, something along the lines of *you better get your asses healed quickly so we can get the Fifth Power or die trying. Time to take those motherfuckers for a ride.* Your brother must have convinced her."

Hope grinned. That woman. "She is not a woman who needs convincing."

Ciaran laughed. "That's so true."

The door to the patio opened with a bang, a wide-eyed Sasha shouting, "Raoul is awake!" before disappearing back inside.

They were on their feet, running.

Hope entered the room first. Raoul's ocean-eyes were open on his pale face, Nina crying and smiling as she kissed his hand and white hair.

Raoul didn't smile.

He grabbed Nina by the neck as he stared at Hope and said, "The Crown of Death is rising again."

END OF BOOK 1

The story continues in *Petals for Deadly Power*.

The Panom Saga

Petals for Vicious Secrets

Petals for Deadly Power

Petals for Broken Wings

Author's note

Thank you so much for reading Petals for Vicious Secrets! I hope you enjoyed my debut novel as much as I enjoyed bringing Hope, Ciaran, Lenna, Jake, Nina, Ayla, and their stories to life. Their journey continues in the second book in the Panom Saga: *Petals for Deadly Power*.

If you enjoyed this book, I would be extremely grateful if you would consider leaving a review on Amazon or Goodreads. Reviews are extremely important for authors, and they do make a difference!

I would love to keep in touch! If you'd like to be the first to know about new releases, exclusive content, and magical bits, you can find me on Instagram, Tiktok and Facebook. You can also join my newsletter at marthamonteval.com.

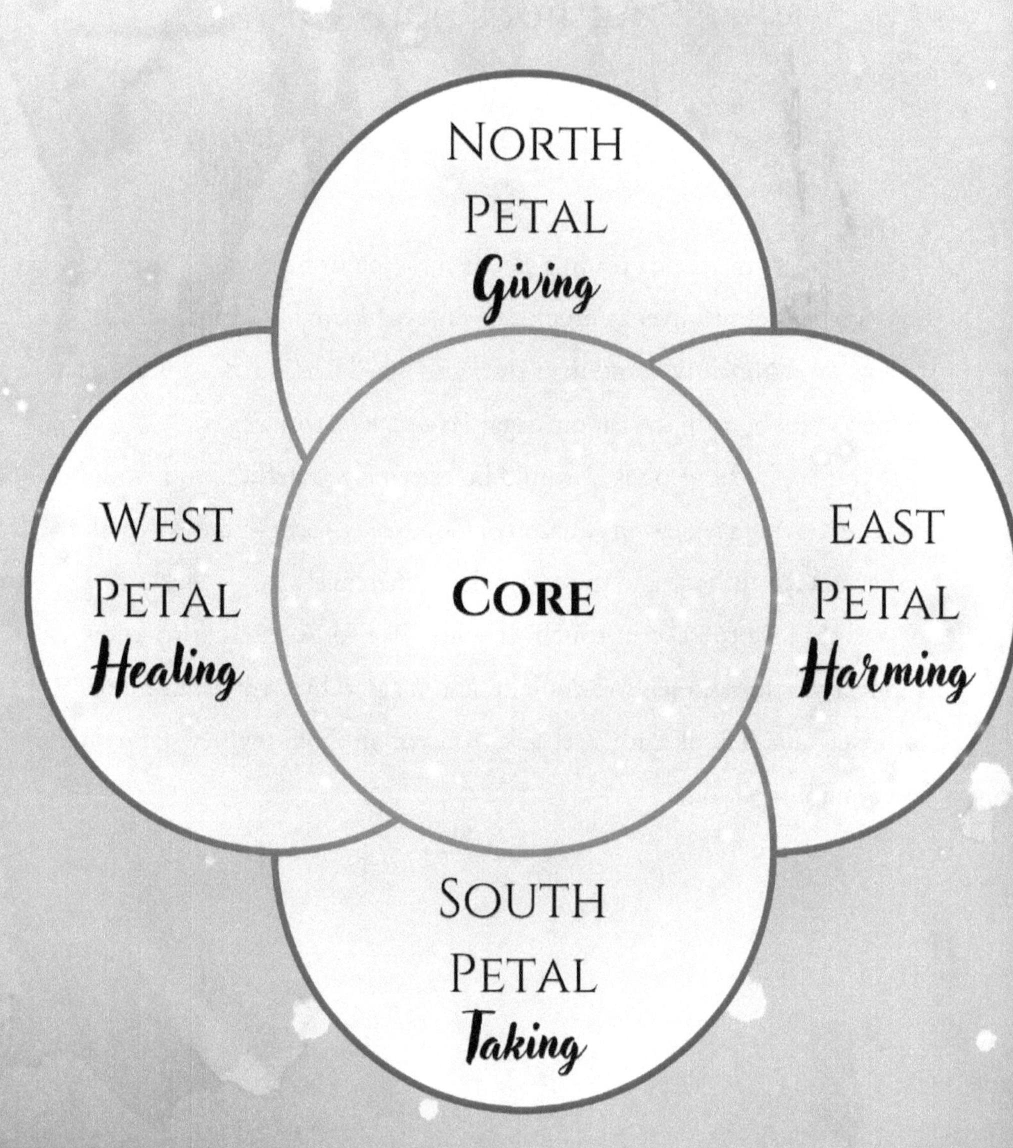

NORTH
PETAL
Giving

WEST
PETAL
Healing

CORE

EAST
PETAL
Harming

SOUTH
PETAL
Taking

Lenna Brachyan

Ayla Brachyan

Ciaran Castel

Indianna Halia

Rhei Coralt

Jake Coralt

Glossary

Ante meridiem – Time since the death of night until the sun is at its highest point in the sky.

Beftac Center for Injured Beings – Biggest healing center in Corentre.

Being - Any individual in Terrha, such as a human, a panom, a courtrade, or other.

Black Lawful Stab – A legendary blade made of black crystal, with lethal powers to kill irreversibly. The Black Lawful Stab only obeys the Organ Mandor of Thyria. Blood of the Cardinal Queen was used to create it.

Borealia – Capital of the North Petal in the North of Thyria.

Cardinal Houses – A term to refer to the North House, South House, East House and West House of Thyria.

Cardinal Queen – Queen of Cardinals.

Cardinals – Five goddesses of panom magic, creators of the Petals and builders of Thyria. The North Cardinal, East Cardinal, South Cardinal, West Cardinal and Core Cardinal are sisters.

Cardinals' Temple – Sacred temple in the Organ House in the very center of Thyria, where Fifth Ceremonies take place.

Compassom – A rare device that allows invisible panom marks to be seen on the skin of a panom-to-be or potential panom.

Core Cardinal – Goddess of the Organ Core, inner circle of the panom mark, and the Organ House, responsible for keeping harmony between the opposite magics so the land doesn't collapse.

CoreCode – A game played with dies and cards.

Corentre – Capital of Thyria, in the Organ Core, home to the Organ House.

Corolla - Petal-shaped snack, sold in the cities of Thyria.

Courtrade – Being blessed by Llunal and gifted with the god's powers: shadow-wielding and whispers of night.

Crois – A courtrade metallic weapon with the shape of a semicircle.

Crystal Clear Safehouse - Safehouse in Corentre owned by Ciaran Castel, protected from unwanted visitors, invisible to the eye of any being he hasn't allowed access.

Deliseen – An interactive panel found in exclusive Elite manors and some Houses.

Discarded being – An individual exiled to the cruel island of Verdania, usually as punishment. Discarding is a responsibility of the panoms belonging to the Organ House.

Dual-powered - Being who is both a panom and a courtrade.

East Cardinal – Goddess of the East Petal and the East House, creator of the Harming power.

East House – One of the five political houses of Thyria, in the East Petal and governed by the East House Ruler.

East Petal – Physical location on the East of Thyria, home to the East House. The East Petal of the panom mark is the one responsible for the Harming power, and must be balanced with its opposite power on the West Petal, responsible for Healing.

Elite – A selected group of humans who hold a significant amount of power, wealth, or influence. Humans can gain entry to the Elite by donating generous amounts to the five Houses of Thyria, or by earning their value because of unique abilities, knowledge or skills.

Epitellia – Invisible barriers that protect a place and restrict the entrance from unwanted beings.

Fifth Ceremony – A sacred ceremony that allows a panom access to their unleashed magical powers and gets the four-petal mark magically inked on their skin.

Fifth Crusade - A five-trial journey to prove to the five Cardinals the worth of five panoms who aim to earn the Fifth Power. The Fifth crusade consists of five ordeals, undertaken by five strivers. Each ordeal belongs to a Cardinal, and requires dominance of their pertinent power in order to succeed. The North Cardinal's ordeal needs a striver who has full control of the Giving power. The South Cardinal's ordeal demands the striver masters Taking. The striver for the West Cardinal's ordeal has to dominate Healing, and the one for the East Cardinal's ordeal must be an adept at Harming.

Fifth Power – An ancient power which is extremely dangerous and difficult to get.

Giving – One of the four panom powers, originally from the North Cardinal, which requires the panom to use the North Petal of their panom mark. Its opposite power is Taking.

Groll – The lowest-value coin in Thyria. There are twenty-five grolls in one valer.

Harming – One of the four panom powers, originally from the East Cardinal, which requires the panom to use the East Petal of their panom mark. Its opposite power is Healing. This power is more complex to dominate than Giving and Taking.

Healing – One of the four panom powers, originally from the West Cardinal, which requires the panom to use the West Petal of their panom mark. Its opposite power is Harming. This power is more complex to dominate than Giving and Taking.

Ink – A message sent from a panom to another being, which appears on the skin of the recipient with the color of the sender's magic and with the sender's handwriting. The message disappears once the recipient has read it.

Inner balance / Inner harmony / Inner scale – Essential scale individual to each panom that must be balanced when using opposite magics (Giving and Taking are opposite magics, and Healing and Harming as well). When the inner harmony is uneven because one power has been used more than its opposite, the panom suffers certain signs and symptoms that can incapacitate and be fatal.

Interpetal Bullef – Communication center that ensures respectful harmony between the Houses and its Rulers.

Invisible Grand – The most secretive organization of Thyria.

Jofryo River – River that surrounds the inner circle of Thyria.

Llunal – God of shadows and darkness.

Mouring – The ability to transport from one place to another using panom magic. A panom can moure independently or moure two other beings at the same time by touching the back of their necks.

Myster – A drink with alcoholic properties.

Navia - Crescent-moon shaped vehicle that stays afloat in the seas, owned by courtrades, fueled by the power and magic of Llunal.

Necroseer - Being who can see, listen and speak with the dead.

North Cardinal – Goddess of the North Petal and the North House, creator of the Giving power.

North House – One of the five political houses of Thyria, in the North Petal and governed by the North House Ruler.

North Petal – Physical location on the North of Thyria, home to the North House. The North Petal of the panom mark is the one responsible for the Giving power, and must be balanced with its opposite power on the South Petal, responsible for Taking.

Ordeal - A challenge or trial where a panom proves their worth to one of the Cardinal goddesses, in order to obtain a red-crystal feather required to earn the Fifth Power. Also see: Fifth crusade.

Organ Core – Circular shape in the middle of the four petals of Thyria and the panom mark.

Organ Mandor – True Ruler of Thyria and Ruler of the Organ House. Every human and panom being must answer to the Organ Mandor, including the four Rulers of the Cardinal Houses.

Orster – Scientific center of research and investigation with the laboratories better guarded by the Organ House.

Panom – Being with magical abilities, blessed by the Cardinals and gifted with their magic. A panom gets access to their powers after the Fifth Ceremony.

- **Acquired panom / Converted panom** – Being who gets their panom mark by marriage.

- **Blood panom** – Being who gets their panom mark at birth.

- **Potential panom / Panom-to-be** – Being with an invisible panom mark on their skin who will only become panom after a Fifth Ceremony takes place.

- **Recipient panom** – Being who gets their panom mark by donation.

Panom Guidor – Experienced panom assigned to guide and teach a new panom how to control the four powers after their Fifth Ceremony.

Panom mark – Four-petal-shaped mark with a circular inner part, with the same shape as Thyria. This mark is permanently inked on the skin of panom beings and allows them to perform magic. Before the Fifth Ceremony, this mark can only be seen on a panom-to-be by using a compassom. The panom mark of each panom has a unique color, the same color as their ink and sparks.

Panomquake – A sudden violent shaking of the ground, typically causing great destruction, because of instability amongst the balance between the five Houses of Thyria.

Past meridiem – Time since the sun is at its highest point in the sky until the death of night.

Red Lawful Stab – A legendary blade made of red crystal, infused with powers for centuries. Blood of the five Cardinals was used to create it. It affects females worse than males.

Roix – An organized military organization equipped for fighting and establishing order.

Roix Reigner – Highest authority in the Roix, to whom all roixers must obey.

Roixer – A military member of the Roix armed and trained to fight, who obeys orders from the Roix Reigner and the Organ Mandor.

South Cardinal – Goddess of the South Petal and the South House, creator of the Taking power.

South House – One of the five political houses of Thyria, in the South Petal and governed by the South House Ruler.

South Petal – Physical location on the South of Thyria, home to the South House. The South Petal of the panom mark is the one responsible for the Taking power, and must be balanced with its opposite power on the North Petal, responsible for Giving.

Striver - An aspirant taking part in the Fifth crusade. Also see: Fifth crusade.

Sweetgum Beech – The biggest square of Corentre.

Taking – One of the four panom powers, originally from the South Cardinal, which requires the panom to use the South Petal of their panom mark. Its opposite power is Giving.

Terrha – World inhabited by beings.

Thyria – A four-petal-shaped island in the middle of the Radel Sea, with five political Houses.

Trading Day – A day every week when the Rulers provide supplies and resources on the Trading Table for the discarded beings living in Verdania.

The inhabitants of Verdania can suit themselves to the whatever the Trading Table provides.

Valer – The highest-value coin. One valer is worth twenty-five grolls.

Verdania – An island in the Radel Sea where discarded beings are sent to.

Vessels – Underwater net of tunnels connecting different islands in the Radel Sea. Vessels are circular-shaped empty tunnels, with blue-tinged membranes separating them from the water of the Radel Sea. A vessel always connects to another vessel, creating a net to ensure the flow of the magic above them.

Vitam tradere – A blood bound effort between two beings to start killing to keep living.

Waholt – A vehicle made of metallic wagons that travels on land, floating above ground.

West Cardinal – Goddess of the West Petal and the West House, creator of the Healing power.

West House – One of the five political houses of Thyria, in the West Petal and governed by the West House Ruler.

West Petal – Physical location on the West of Thyria, home to the West House. The West Petal of the panom mark is the one responsible for the

Healing power, and must be balanced with its opposite power on the East Petal, responsible for Harming.

Acknowledgements

My debut wouldn't have been half as fun and exciting without you, Hannah. Our simultaneous reads and debriefs of our never-ending TBR lists make everything way more enjoyable. Thanks for being an amazing alpha reader, a supportive and encouraging friend, and an excellent colleague. I treasure your friendship with so much love!

Thank you, Neil, for the marshmallow clouds and for your choking line. You nailed it. I'm so glad we convinced you to read romantasy! Sorry, not sorry for ruining the rest of your reading life.

The Bears have been pivotal in making this writing journey not a lonely one. I feel so lucky to be surrounded by people who celebrate my small steps so much. The meeting opening with a "she finished it!!!" is one I will never forget. Thank you, thank you, thank you to every single one of you.

Big thank you to Bianca for the stunning cover. I cried when I saw it. What a talented artist you are!

To Alexa, thank you for helping Petals shine brighter!

Mabel and Laura, thank you for existing.

Emma, thank you for helping me digest and untangle my thoughts and feelings so they are easier to understand and less painful to write.

To all my book boyfriends and girlfriends: thank you for the inspirations.

To the little girl who dreamed to be a writer when she grew up: I see you. Thanks for not giving up.

To you, the reader. Thank you for reading my first novel!